More

D0008853

The Forgotten Garden

"Like Frances Hodgson Burnett's beloved classic *The Secret Garden,* Kate Morton's *The Forgotten Garden* takes root in your imagination and grows into something enchanting." —Amazon.com

"A satisfying read. . . . Just the thing for readers who like multigenerational sagas with a touch of mystery." —*Booklist*

"A beautifully written and satisfying novel." —*Daily Express* (UK)

"In haunting tones reminiscent of Ian McEwan's *Atonement* as well as Carlos Ruiz Zafón's *The Shadow of the Wind,* Morton weaves a tale of unknown parentage, family intrigue and generational secrets that keeps the reader turning pages into the wee hours of the night."
—*Winnipeg Free Press* (Manitoba, Can.)

The House at Riverton

"[A] stunning debut." —*People*

"Morton triumphs with a riveting plot, a touching but tense love story and a haunting ending." —*Publishers Weekly* (starred review)

"This novel will challenge your definitions of friendship, family and, most of all, trust." —*Hallmark Magazine*

"An extraordinary debut . . . written with a lovely turn of phrase. [Morton] knows how to eke out tantalizing secrets and drama."
—*The Sunday Telegraph* (UK)

Also by Kate Morton

The House at Riverton

The Distant Hours

THE FORGOTTEN GARDEN

A Novel

KATE MORTON

W

WASHINGTON SQUARE PRESS
New York London Toronto Sydney

W

WASHINGTON SQUARE PRESS
A Division of Simon & Schuster, Inc.
1230 Avenue of the Americas
New York, NY 10020

First Washington Square Press trade paperback edition February 2010

WASHINGTON SQUARE PRESS and colophon are registered
trademarks of Simon & Schuster, Inc.

For information about special discounts for bulk purchases,
please contact Simon & Schuster Special Sales at
1-866-506-1949 or business@simonandschuster.com.

The Simon & Schuster Speakers Bureau can bring authors to your live event.
For more information or to book an event, contact the Simon & Schuster Speakers
Bureau at 1-866-248-3049 or visit our website at www.simonspeakers.com.

Designed by Davina Mock-Maniscalco
Map by Ian Faulkner

Manufactured in the United States of America

25   27   29   30   28   26   24

The Library of Congress has cataloged the hardcover edition as follows:

Morton, Kate, date.
The forgotten garden : a novel / Kate Morton.
p. cm.
1. Abandoned children—Australia—Fiction. 2. English—Australia—Fiction.
3. Country homes—England—Cornwall (County)—Fiction. 4. Grandmothers—
Fiction. 5. Inheritance and succession—Fiction. 6. Domestic fiction. I. Title.
PR9619.4.M74F67 2009
823'.92—dc22
2009003071

ISBN 978-1-4165-5054-9
ISBN 978-1-4165-5055-6 (pbk)
ISBN 978-1-4165-7206-0 (ebook)

For Oliver and Louis
More precious than all the spun gold in Fairyland

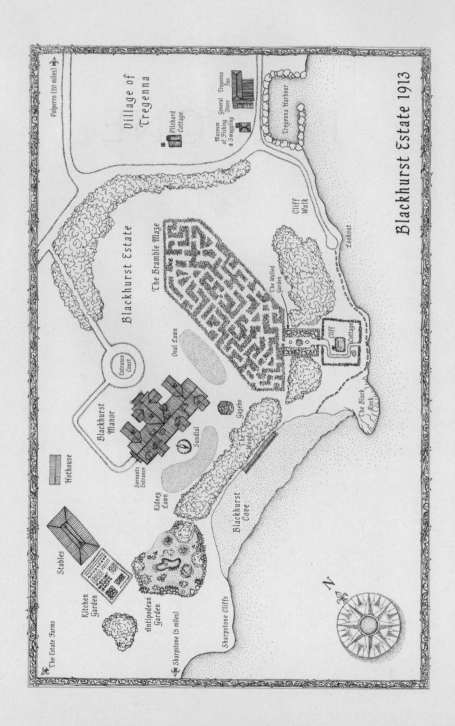

Blackhurst Estate 1913

PART ONE

ONE

I T was dark where she was crouched but the little girl did as she'd been told. The lady had said to wait, it wasn't safe yet, they had to be as quiet as larder mice. It was a game, just like hide-and-seek.

From behind the wooden barrels the little girl listened. Made a picture in her mind the way Papa had taught her. Men, near and far, sailors she supposed, shouted to one another. Rough, loud voices, full of the sea and its salt. In the distance: bloated ships' horns, tin whistles, splashing oars and, far above, grey gulls cawing, wings flattened to absorb the ripening sunlight.

The lady would be back, she'd said so, but the little girl hoped it would be soon. She'd been waiting a long time, so long that the sun had drifted across the sky and was now warming her knees through her new dress. She listened for the lady's skirts, swishing against the wooden deck. Her heels clipping, hurrying, always hurrying, in a way the little girl's own mamma never did. The little girl wondered, in the vague, unconcerned manner of much-loved children, where Mamma was. When she would be coming. And she wondered about the lady. She knew who she was, she'd heard Grandmamma talking about her. The lady was called the Authoress and she lived in the little cottage on the far side of the estate, beyond the maze. The little girl wasn't supposed to know. She had been forbidden to play in the bramble maze. Mamma and Grandmamma had told her it was dangerous to go near the cliff. But sometimes, when no one was looking, she liked to do forbidden things.

3

Dust motes, hundreds of them, danced in the sliver of sunlight that had appeared between two barrels. The little girl smiled and the lady, the cliff, the maze, Mamma left her thoughts. She held out a finger, tried to catch a speck upon it. Laughed at the way the motes came so close before skirting away.

The noises beyond her hiding spot were changing now. The little girl could hear the hubbub of movement, voices laced with excitement. She leaned into the veil of light and pressed her face against the cool wood of the barrels. With one eye she looked upon the decks.

Legs and shoes and petticoat hems. The tails of colored paper streamers flicking this way and that. Wily gulls hunting the decks for crumbs.

A lurch and the huge boat groaned, long and low from deep within its belly. Vibrations passed through the deck boards and into the little girl's fingertips. A moment of suspension and she found herself holding her breath, palms flat beside her, then the boat heaved and pushed itself away from the dock. The horn bellowed and there was a wave of cheering, cries of "Bon voyage!" They were on their way. To America, a place called New York, where Papa had been born. She'd heard them whispering about it for some time, Mamma telling Papa they should go as soon as possible, that they could afford to wait no longer.

The little girl laughed again; the boat was gliding through the water like a giant whale, like Moby Dick in the story her father often read to her. Mamma didn't like it when he read such stories. She said they were too frightening and would put ideas in her head that couldn't be got out. Papa always gave Mamma a kiss on the forehead when she said that sort of thing, told her she was right and that he'd be more careful in the future. But he still told the little girl stories of the great whale. And others—the ones that were the little girl's favorite, from the fairy-tale book, about eyeless crones, and orphaned maidens, and long journeys across the sea. He just made sure that Mamma didn't know, that it remained their secret.

The little girl understood they had to have secrets from Mamma. Mamma wasn't well, had been sickly since before the little girl was born. Grandmamma was always bidding her be good, warning her that if Mamma were to get upset something terrible might happen and it would be all her fault. The little girl loved her mother and didn't want to make her sad, didn't want something terrible to happen, so she kept things secret. Like the fairy stories, and playing near the maze, and the times Papa had taken her to visit the Authoress in the cottage on the far side of the estate.

"Aha!" A voice by her ear. "Found you!" The barrel was heaved aside and the little girl squinted up into the sun. Blinked until the owner of the voice moved to block the light. It was a big boy, eight or nine, she guessed. "You're not Sally," he said.

The little girl shook her head.

"Who are you?"

She wasn't meant to tell anybody her name. It was a game they were playing, she and the lady.

"Well?"

"It's a secret."

His nose wrinkled, freckles drew together. "What for?"

She shrugged. She wasn't supposed to speak of the lady, Papa was always telling her so.

"Where's Sally, then?" The boy was growing impatient. He looked left and right. "She ran this way, I'm sure of it."

A whoop of laughter from further down the deck and the scramble of fleeing footsteps. The boy's face lit up. "Quick!" he said as he started to run. "She's getting away."

The little girl leaned her head around the barrel and watched him weaving in and out of the crowd in keen pursuit of a flurry of white petticoats.

Her toes itched to join them.

But the lady had said to wait.

The boy was getting further away. Ducking around a portly man with a waxed moustache, causing him to scowl so that his features scurried towards the center of his face like a family of startled crabs.

The little girl laughed.

Maybe it was all part of the same game. The lady reminded her more of a child than of the other grown-ups she knew. Perhaps she was playing, too.

The little girl slid from behind the barrel and stood slowly. Her left foot had gone to sleep and now had pins and needles. She waited a moment for feeling to return, watched as the boy turned the corner and disappeared.

Then, without another thought, she set off after him. Feet pounding, heart singing in her chest.

Two

❦

In the end they held Nell's birthday party in the Foresters' building, up on Latrobe Terrace. Hugh had suggested the new dance hall in town, but Nell, echoing her mother, had said it was silly to go to unnecessary expense, especially with times as tough as they were. Hugh conceded, but contented himself by insisting she send away to Sydney for the special lace he knew she wanted for her dress. Lil had put the idea in his head before she passed away. She'd leaned over and taken his hand, then shown him the newspaper advertisement, with its Pitt Street address, and told him how fine the lace was, how much it would mean to Nellie, that it might seem extravagant but it could be reworked into the wedding gown when the time came. Then she'd smiled at him, and she was sixteen years old again and he was smitten.

Lil and Nell had been working on the birthday dress for a couple of weeks by then. In the evenings, when Nell was home from the newspaper shop and tea was finished, and the younger girls were bickering lethargically on the verandas, and the mosquitoes were so thick in the muggy night air you thought you'd go mad from the drone, Nell would take down her sewing basket and pull up a seat beside her mother's sickbed. He would hear them sometimes, laughing about something that had happened in the newspaper shop: an argument Max Fitzsimmons had had with this customer or that, Mrs. Blackwell's latest medical complaint, the antics of Nancy Brown's twins. He would linger by the door, filling his pipe with tobacco and listening as Nell lowered her voice, flushed with pleasure as she recounted something Danny had

7

said. Some promise he'd made about the house he was going to buy her when they were wed, the car he had his eye on that his father thought he could get for a song, the latest Mixmaster from McWhirter's department store.

Hugh liked Danny; he couldn't wish more for Nell, which was just as well seeing as the pair had been inseparable since they'd met. Watching them together reminded Hugh of his early years with Lil. Happy as larks they'd been, back when the future still stretched, unmarked, before them. And it had been a good marriage. They'd had their testing times, early on before they'd had the girls, but one way or another things had always worked out . . .

His pipe full, his excuse to loiter ended, Hugh would move on. He'd find a place for himself at the quiet end of the front veranda, a dark place where he could sit in peace, or as near to peace as was possible in a house full of rowdy daughters, each more excitable than the last. Just him and his flyswatter on the window ledge should the mosquitoes get too close. And then he'd follow his thoughts as they turned invariably towards the secret he'd been keeping all these years.

For the time was almost upon him, he could feel that. The pressure, long kept at bay, had recently begun to build. She was nearly twenty-one, a grown woman ready to embark on her own life, engaged to be married no less. She had a right to know the truth.

He knew what Lil would say to that, which was why he didn't tell her. The last thing he wanted was for Lil to worry, to spend her final days trying to talk him out of it, as she'd done so often in the past.

Sometimes, as he wondered about the words he'd find to make his confession, Hugh caught himself wishing it on one of the other girls instead. He cursed himself then for acknowledging he had a favorite, even to himself.

But Nellie had always been special, so unlike the others. Spirited, more imaginative. More like Lil, he often thought, though of course that made no sense.

THEY'D STRUNG ribbons along the rafters—white to match her dress and red to match her hair. The old wooden hall might not have had the spit and polish of the newer brick buildings about town, but it scrubbed up all right. At the back, near the stage, Nell's four younger sisters had arranged a table for birthday gifts and a decent pile had begun to take shape. Some of the ladies from church had got together to make the supper, and Ethel Mortimer was giving the piano a workout, romantic dance tunes from the war.

Young men and women clustered at first in nervous knots around the walls, but as the music and the more outgoing lads warmed up, they began to split into pairs and take to the floor. The little sisters looked on longingly until sequestered to help carry trays of sandwiches from the kitchen to the supper table.

When the time came for the speeches, cheeks were glowing and shoes were scuffed from dancing. Marcie McDonald, the minister's wife, tapped on her glass and everybody turned to Hugh, who was unfolding a small piece of paper from his breast pocket. He cleared his throat and ran a hand over his comb-striped hair. Public speaking had never been his caper. He was the sort of man who kept himself to himself, minded his own opinions and happily let the more vocal fellows do the talking. Still, a daughter came of age but once and it was his duty to announce her. He'd always been a stickler for duty, a rule follower. For the most part anyway.

He smiled as one of his mates from the wharf shouted a heckle, then he cupped the paper in his palm and took a deep breath. One by one, he read off the points on his list, scribbled in tiny black handwriting: how proud of Nell he and her mother had always been; how blessed they'd felt when she arrived; how fond they were of Danny. Lil had been especially happy, he said, to learn of the engagement before she passed away.

At this mention of his wife's recent death, Hugh's eyes began to smart and he fell silent. He paused for a while and allowed his gaze to roam the faces of his friends and his daughters, to fix a moment on Nell, who was smiling as Danny whispered something in her ear. As a cloud seemed to cross his brow, folk wondered if some important announcement was coming, but the moment passed. His expression lightened and he returned the piece of paper to his pocket. It was about time he had another man in the family, he said with a smile, it'd even things up a bit.

The ladies in the kitchen swept into action then, administering sandwiches and cups of tea to the guests, but Hugh loitered a while, letting people brush past him, accepting the pats on the shoulder, the calls of "Well done, mate," a cup and saucer thrust into his hand by one of the ladies. The speech had gone well, yet he couldn't relax. His heart had stepped up its beat and he was sweating though it wasn't hot.

He knew why, of course. The night's duties were not yet over. When he noticed Nell slip alone through the side door, on to the little landing, he saw his opportunity. He cleared his throat and set his teacup in a space on the gift table, then he disappeared from the warm hum of the room into the cool night air.

Nell was standing by the silver-green trunk of a lone eucalypt. Once, Hugh thought, the whole ridge would've been covered by them, and the gullies on either side. Must've been a sight, that crowd of ghostly trunks on nights when the moon was full.

There. He was putting things off. Even now he was trying to shirk his responsibility, was being weak.

A pair of black bats coasted silently across the night sky and he made his way down the rickety wooden steps, across the dew-damp grass.

Nell must have heard him coming—sensed him perhaps—for she turned and smiled as he drew close.

She was thinking about Ma, she said as he reached her side, wondering which of the stars she was watching from.

Hugh could've wept when she said it. Damned if she didn't have to bring Lil into it right now. Make him aware that she was observing, angry with him for what he was about to do. He could hear Lil's voice, all the old arguments . . .

But it was his decision to make and he'd made it. It was he, after all, who'd started the whole thing. Unwitting though he might have been, he'd taken the step that set them on this path and he was responsible for putting things right. Secrets had a way of making themselves known and it was better, surely, that she learned the truth from him.

He took Nell's hands in his and placed a kiss on the top of each. Squeezed them tight, her soft smooth fingers against his work-hardened palms.

His daughter. His first.

She smiled at him, radiant in her delicate lace-trimmed dress.

He smiled back.

Then he led her to sit by him on a fallen gum trunk, smooth and white, and he leaned to whisper in her ear. Transferred the secret he and her mother had kept for seventeen years. Waited for the flicker of recognition, the minute shift in expression as she registered what he was telling her. Watched as the bottom fell out of her world and the person she had been vanished in an instant.

THREE

CASSANDRA hadn't left the hospital in days, though the doctor held out little hope her grandmother would regain lucidity. It wasn't likely, he said, not at her age, not with that amount of morphine in her system.

The night nurse was there again, so Cassandra knew it was no longer day. The precise time she couldn't guess. It was hard to tell in here: the foyer lights were constantly on, a television could always be heard though never seen, carts tracked up and down the halls no matter what the hour. An irony that a place relying so heavily on routine should operate so resolutely outside time's usual rhythms.

Nonetheless, Cassandra waited. Watching, comforting, as Nell drowned in a sea of memories, came up for air again and again in earlier times of life. She couldn't bear to think her grandmother might defy the odds and find her way back to the present, only to discover herself floating on the outer edge of life, alone.

The nurse swapped the IV's empty bag for a fat bladder, turned a dial on the machine behind the bed, then set about straightening the bedclothes.

"She hasn't had anything to drink," Cassandra said, her voice sounding strange to her own ears. "Not all day."

The nurse looked up, surprised at being spoken to. She peered over her glasses at the chair where Cassandra sat, a crumpled blue-green hospital blanket on her lap. "Gave me a fright," she said. "You been here all day, have you? Probably for the best. Won't be long now."

Cassandra ignored the implication of this statement. "Should we give her something to drink? She must be thirsty."

The nurse folded the sheets over and tucked them matter-of-factly beneath Nell's thin arms. "She'll be all right. The drip here takes care of that." She checked something on Nell's chart, spoke without looking up. "There's tea-making facilities down the hall if you need them."

The nurse left and Cassandra saw that Nell's eyes were less open, staring. "Who are you?" came the frail voice.

"It's me, Cassandra."

Confusion. "Do I know you?"

The doctor had predicted this but it still stung. "Yes, Nell."

Nell looked at her, eyes watery grey. She blinked uncertainly. "I can't remember . . ."

"Shhh . . . It's all right."

"Who am I?"

"Your name is Nell Andrews," Cassandra said, taking her hand. "You're ninety-five years old. You live in an old house in Paddington."

Nell's lips were trembling—she was concentrating, trying to make sense of the words.

Cassandra plucked a tissue from the bedside table and reached to gently wipe the line of saliva on Nell's chin. "You have a stall at the antique center on Latrobe Terrace," she continued softly. "You and I share it. We sell old things."

"I do know you," said Nell faintly. "You're Lesley's girl."

Cassandra blinked, surprised. They rarely spoke of her mother, not in all the time Cassandra was growing up and not in the ten years she'd been back, living in the flat beneath Nell's house. It was an unspoken agreement between them not to revisit a past they each, for different reasons, preferred to forget.

Nell started. Her panicked eyes scanned Cassandra's face. "Where's the boy? Not here, I hope. Is he here? I don't want him touching my things. Ruining them."

Cassandra's head grew faint.

"My things are precious. Don't let him near them."

Some words appeared, Cassandra tripped over them. "No . . . No, I won't. Don't worry, Nell. He's not here."

LATER, WHEN her grandmother had slipped into unconsciousness again, Cassandra wondered at the mind's cruel ability to toss up flecks of the past. Why, as she neared her life's end, her grandmother's head should ring with the voices of people long since gone. Was it always this way? Did those with passage booked on death's silent ship always scan the dock for faces of the long-departed?

Cassandra must have slept then, because the next thing she knew the hospital's mood had changed again. They'd been drawn further into the tunnel of night. The hall lights were dimmed and the sounds of sleep were everywhere around her. She was slumped in the chair, her neck stiff and her ankle cold where it had escaped the flimsy blanket. It was late, she knew, and she was tired. What had woken her?

Nell. Her breathing was loud. She was awake. Cassandra moved quickly to the bed, perched again on its side. In the half-light Nell's eyes were glassy, pale and smudged like paint-stained water. Her voice, a fine thread, was almost frayed through. At first Cassandra couldn't hear her, thought only that her lips were moving around lost words uttered long ago. Then she realized Nell was speaking.

"The lady," she was saying. "The lady said to wait . . ."

Cassandra stroked Nell's warm forehead, brushed back soft strands of hair that had once gleamed like spun silver. The lady again. "She won't mind," she said. "The lady won't mind if you go."

Nell's lips tightened, then quivered. "I'm not supposed to move. She said to wait, here on the boat." Her voice was a whisper. "The lady . . . the Authoress . . . Don't tell anyone."

"Shhh," said Cassandra. "I won't tell anyone, Nell. I won't tell the lady. You can go."

"She said she'd come for me, but I moved. I didn't stay where I was told."

Her grandmother's breathing was labored now, she was succumbing to panic.

"Please don't worry, Nell, please. Everything's okay. I promise."

Nell's head dropped to the side. "I can't go . . . I wasn't supposed to . . . The lady . . ."

Cassandra pressed the button to call for help but no light came on above the bed. She hesitated, listened for hurried footsteps in the hall. Nell's eyelids were fluttering, she was slipping away.

"I'll get a nurse—"

"No!" Nell reached out blindly, tried to grasp hold of Cassandra. "Don't leave me!" She was crying. Silent tears, damp and glistening on her paling skin.

Cassandra's own eyes glazed. "It's all right, Grandma. I'm getting help. I'll be back soon, I promise."

Four

❦

THE house seemed to know its mistress was gone, and if it didn't exactly grieve for her, it settled into an obstinate silence. Nell had never been one for people or for parties (and the kitchen mice were louder than the granddaughter), so the house had grown accustomed to a quiet existence with neither fuss nor noise. It was a rude shock, then, when the people arrived without word or warning, began milling about the house and garden, slopping tea and dropping crumbs. Hunched into the hillside behind the huge antique center on the ridge, the house suffered stoically this latest indignity.

The aunts had organized it all, of course. Cassandra would've been just as happy to have gone without, to have honored her grandmother privately, but the aunts would hear none of it. Certainly Nell should have a wake, they said. The family would want to pay their respects, as would Nell's friends. And besides, it was only proper.

Cassandra was no match for such ingenuous certitude. Once upon a time she would have put up an argument, but not now. Besides, the aunts were an unstoppable force, each had an energy that belied her great age (even the youngest, Aunt Hettie, wasn't a day under eighty). So Cassandra had let her misgivings fall away, resisted the urge to point out Nell's resolute lack of friends, and set about performing the tasks she'd been allotted: arranging teacups and saucers, finding cake forks, clearing some of Nell's bric-a-brac so that the cousins might have somewhere to sit. Letting the aunts bustle around her with all due pomp and self-importance.

16

They weren't really Cassandra's aunts, of course. They were Nell's younger sisters, Cassandra's mother's aunts. But Lesley had never had much use for them, and the aunts had promptly taken Cassandra under their wing in her stead.

Cassandra had half thought her mother might attend the funeral, might arrive at the crematorium just as proceedings got under way, looking thirty years younger than she really was, inviting admiring glances as she always had. Beautiful and young and impossibly insouciant.

But she hadn't. There would be a card, Cassandra supposed, with a picture on the front only vaguely suited to its purpose. Large swirling handwriting that drew attention to itself and, at the bottom, copious kisses. The sort that were easily dispensed, one pen line scarred by another.

Cassandra dunked her hands into the sink and moved the contents about some more.

"Well, I think that went splendidly," said Phyllis, the eldest after Nell and the bossiest by far. "Nell would've liked it."

Cassandra glanced sideways.

"That is," Phyllis continued, pausing a moment as she dried, "she would've once she'd finished insisting she hadn't wanted one in the first place." Her mood turned suddenly maternal. "And how about you? How've you been keeping?"

"I'm all right."

"You look thin. Are you eating?"

"Three times a day."

"You could do with some fattening up. You'll come for tea tomorrow night, I'll invite the family, make my cottage pie."

Cassandra didn't argue.

Phyllis glanced warily about the old kitchen, took in the sagging range hood. "You're not frightened here by yourself?"

"No, not frightened—"

"Lonely, though," said Phyllis, nose wrinkling with extravagant sympathy. "Course you are. Only natural, you and Nell were good company for each other, weren't you?" She didn't wait for confirmation, rather laid a sunspotted hand on Cassandra's forearm and pressed on with the pep talk. "You're going to be all right, though, and I'll tell you why. It's always sad to lose someone you care for, but it's never so bad when it's an oldie. It's as it should be. Much worse when it's a young—" She stopped midsentence, her shoulders tensed and her cheeks reddened.

"Yes," said Cassandra quickly, "of course it is." She stopped washing cups and leaned to look through the kitchen window into the backyard. Suds slipped down her fingers, over the gold band she still wore. "I should get out and do some weeding. The nasturtium'll be across the path if I'm not careful."

Phyllis clutched gratefully the new string of purpose. "I'll send Trevor round to help." Her gnarled fingers tightened their grip on Cassandra's arm. "Next Saturday all right?"

Aunt Dot appeared then, shuffling in from the lounge with another tray of dirty teacups. She rattled them on to the counter and pressed the back of a plump hand to her forehead.

"Finally," she said, blinking at Cassandra and Phyllis through impossibly thick glasses. "That's the last of them." She waddled into the kitchen proper and peered inside a circular cake container. "I've worked up quite a hunger."

"Oh, Dot," said Phyllis, relishing the opportunity to channel discomfort into admonition, "you've just eaten."

"An hour ago."

"With your gallbladder? I thought you'd be watching your weight."

"I am," said Dot, straightening and cinching her sizeable waist with both hands. "I've lost seven pounds since Christmas." She refastened the plastic lid and met Phyllis's dubious gaze. "I *have*."

Cassandra suppressed a smile as she continued to wash the cups.

Phyllis and Dot were each as round as the other, all the aunts were. They got it from their mum, and she from her mum before. Nell was the only one who'd escaped the family curse, who took after her lanky Irish dad. They'd always been a sight together, tall, thin Nell with her round, dumpling sisters.

Phyllis and Dot were still bickering and Cassandra knew from experience that if she didn't provide a distraction the argument would escalate until one (or both) tossed down a tea towel and stormed off home in high dudgeon. She'd seen it happen before yet had never quite grown accustomed to the way certain phrases, eye contact that lasted a mite too long, could relaunch a disagreement started many years before. As an only child, Cassandra found the well-worn paths of sibling interaction fascinating and horrifying in equal parts. It was fortunate the other aunts had already been shepherded away by respective family members and weren't able to add their two cents' worth.

Cassandra cleared her throat. "You know, there's something I've been meaning to ask." She lifted her volume a little, she'd almost gotten their attention. "About Nell. Something she said in the hospital."

Phyllis and Dot both turned, cheeks similarly flushed. The mention of their sister seemed to settle them. Remind them why they were gathered here, drying teacups. "Something about Nell?" said Phyllis.

Cassandra nodded. "In the hospital, towards the end, she spoke about a woman. The lady, she called her, the Authoress. She seemed to think they were on some kind of boat?"

Phyllis's lips tightened. "Her mind was wandering, she didn't know what she was saying. Probably a character from some television show she'd been watching. Wasn't there some series she used to like, set on a boat?"

"Oh, Phyll," said Dot, shaking her head.

"I'm sure I remember her talking about it . . ."

"Come on, Phyll," said Dot. "Nellie's gone. There's no need for all of this."

Phyllis folded her arms across her chest and huffed uncertainly.

"We should tell her," said Dot gently. "It won't do any harm. Not now."

"Tell me what?" Cassandra looked between them. Her question had been asked to preempt another family row; she hadn't expected to uncover this strange hint of secrecy. The aunts were so focused on one another, they seemed to have forgotten she was there. "Tell me what?" she pressed.

Dot raised her eyebrows at Phyllis. "Better to have it come from us than for her to find out some other way."

Phyllis nodded almost imperceptibly, met Dot's gaze and smiled grimly. Their shared knowledge made them allies again.

"All right, Cass. You'd better come and sit down," she said finally. "Put the kettle on, will you, Dotty love? Make us all a nice cuppa?"

Cassandra followed Phyllis into the sitting room and took a seat on Nell's sofa. Phyllis eased her wide rear onto the other side and worried a thread loose. "Hard to know where to start. Been so long since I thought about it all."

Cassandra was perplexed. All of what?

"What I'm about to tell you is our family's big secret. Every family's got one, you can be sure of that. Some are just bigger than others." She frowned in the direction of the kitchen. "Now, what's taking Dot so long? Slow as a wet week, she is."

"What is it, Phyll?"

She sighed. "Promised myself I'd never tell anyone else. The whole thing has caused so much division in our family already. Would that Dad had kept it to himself. Thought he was doing the right thing, though, poor bugger."

"What did he do?"

If Phyllis heard, she made no acknowledgment. This was her story and she was going to tell it her way and in her own sweet time. "We were a happy family. We hadn't much of anything but we were happy enough. Ma and Pa and we girls. Nellie was the eldest, as you know, then a gap of a decade or so on account of the Great War, then the rest of us." She smiled. "You wouldn't credit it, but Nellie was the life and soul of the family back then. We all adored her—thought of her as a mother of sorts, we younger ones did, especially after Ma got sick. Nell looked after Ma so carefully."

Cassandra could imagine Nell doing that, but as for her prickly grandmother being the life and soul of the family . . .

"What happened?"

"For a long time none of us ever knew. That's the way Nell wanted it. Everything changed in our family and none of us knew why. Our big sister turned into somebody else, seemed to stop loving us. Not overnight, it wasn't as dramatic as all that. She just withdrew, bit by bit, extricated herself from the lot of us. Such a mystery, it was, so hurtful, and Pa wouldn't be drawn on the subject, no matter how we needled him.

"It was my husband, God rest him, who finally put us on the right path. Not intentionally, mind—it wasn't like he set out to discover Nell's secret. Fancied himself a bit of a history buff, that's all. Decided to put together a family tree once our Trevor was born. Same year as your mum, 1947 that was." She paused and eyed Cassandra shrewdly, as if waiting to see whether she had somehow intuited what was coming. She had not.

"One day he came into my kitchen, I remember it clear as day, and said he couldn't find any mention of Nellie's birth in the registry. 'Well, of course not,' I said. 'Nellie was born up in Maryborough, before the family pulled up sticks and moved to Brisbane.' Doug nodded then and said that's what he'd thought, but when he'd sent away for details from Maryborough they told him none existed." Phyllis looked meaningfully at Cassandra. "That is, Nell didn't exist. At least not officially."

Cassandra looked up as Dot came in from the kitchen and handed her a teacup. "I don't understand."

"Of course you don't, pet," said Dot, sitting herself in the armchair beside Phyllis. "And for a long time, neither did we." She shook her head and sighed. "Not until we spoke to June. At Trevor's wedding, that was, wasn't it, Phylly?"

Phyllis nodded. "Yes, 1975. I was that mad at Nell. We'd only recently lost Pa and here was my eldest boy getting married, Nellie's nephew, and she didn't even bother to show. Took herself off on holiday instead. That's what got me talking that way with June. I don't mind saying I was having a good old whinge about Nell."

Cassandra was confused. She'd never been great at keeping track of the aunts' extensive web of friends and family. "Who's June?"

"One of our cousins," said Dot, "on Ma's side. You'd have met her at some point, surely? She was a year or so older than Nell and the two of them thick as thieves when they were girls."

"Must've been close," said Phyllis, with a sniff. "June was the only one Nell told when it happened."

"When what happened?" said Cassandra.

Dot leaned forward. "Pa told Nell—"

"Pa told Nell something he never should've," said Phyllis quickly. "Thought he was doing the right thing, poor man. Regretted it the rest of his life, things were never the same between them."

"And he was always partial to Nell."

"He loved us all," snapped Phyllis.

"Oh, Phyll," said Dot, rolling her eyes. "Can't admit it even now. Nell was his favorite, pure and simple. Ironic, as it turns out."

Phyllis didn't respond, so Dot, pleased to take the reins, continued. "It happened on the night of her twenty-first birthday," she said. "After her party—"

"It wasn't after the party," said Phyllis, "it was during." She turned towards Cassandra. "I expect he thought it was the perfect time to tell her, beginning of her new life and all that. She was engaged to be married, you know. Not your grandpa, another fellow."

"Really?" Cassandra was surprised. "She never said anything."

"Love of her life, you ask me. Local boy, not like Al."

Phyllis spoke the name with a lick of distaste. That the aunts had disapproved of Nell's American husband was no secret. It wasn't personal, rather the shared disdain of a citizenry resenting the influx of GIs who'd arrived in World War II Brisbane with more money and smarter uniforms, only to abscond with a fair share of the city's womenfolk.

"So what happened? Why didn't she marry him?"

"She called it off a few months after the party," said Phyllis. "Such an upset. We were all of us so fond of Danny, and it broke his heart, poor fellow. He married someone else eventually, just before the second war. Not that it brought him much happiness. He never came back from fighting the Japs."

"Did her father tell Nell not to marry him?" said Cassandra. "Is that what he told her that night? Not to marry Danny?"

"Hardly," Dot scoffed. "Pa thought the sun shone out of Danny. None of our husbands ever matched up."

"Then why did she break it off?"

"She wouldn't say, wouldn't even tell him. Nearly drove us round the bend trying to figure it out," said Phyllis. "All we knew was that Nell wouldn't talk to Pa, and she wouldn't talk to Danny."

"All we knew until Phylly spoke to June," said Dot.

"Near on forty-five years later."

"What did June say?" said Cassandra. "What happened at the party?"

Phyllis took a sip of tea and raised her eyebrows at Cassandra. "Pa told Nell she wasn't his and Ma's."

"She was adopted?"

The aunts exchanged a glance. "Not exactly," said Phyllis.

"More like she was found," said Dot.

"Taken."

"Kept."

Cassandra frowned. "Found where?"

"On the Maryborough wharf," said Dot. "Where the big ships

used to come in from Europe. They don't now, of course, there's much bigger ports, and most people fly these days—"

"Pa found her," Phyllis interjected. "When she was just a wee thing. It was right before the Great War started. Folks were leaving Europe in droves and we were only too happy to take them here in Australia. Pa was the port master at the time, it was his job to see to it that those that were travelling were all who they said they were, had arrived where they meant to. Some of them had no English to speak of.

"As I understand it, one afternoon there was something of a kerfuffle. A ship came into port after a shocking journey from England. Typhoid infections, sunstroke, they'd had the lot, and when the ship arrived there were extra bags and persons unaccounted for. It was all a mighty headache. Pa managed to get it sorted, of course—he was always good at keeping things in order—but he waited around longer than usual to be sure and let the night watchman know all that had happened, explain why there were extra bags in the office. It was while he was waiting that he noticed there was still someone left on the docks. A little girl, barely four years old, sitting on top of a child's suitcase."

"No one else for miles," said Dot, shaking her head. "She was all alone."

"Pa tried to find out who she was, of course, but she wouldn't tell him. Said she didn't know, she couldn't remember. And there was no name tag attached to the suitcase, nothing inside that would help, either, not as far as he could tell. It was late, though, and getting dark, and the weather was turning bad. Pa knew she must be hungry, so eventually he decided there was nothing for it but to take her home with him. What else could he do? Couldn't just leave her there on the rainy docks all night, could he?"

Cassandra shook her head, trying to reconcile the tired and lonely little girl of Phyllis's story with the Nell she knew.

"As June tells it, next day he went back to work expecting frantic relatives, police, an investigation—"

"But there was nothing," said Dot. "Day after day there was nothing. No one said anything."

"It was as if she'd left no trace. They tried to find out who she was, of course, but with so many people arriving each day . . . There was so much paperwork. So easy for something to slip through the cracks."

"Or someone."

Phyllis sighed. "So they kept her."

"What else could they do?"

"And they let her think she was one of theirs."

"One of us."

"Until she turned twenty-one," said Phyllis. "And Pa decided she should know the truth. That she was a foundling with nothing more to identify her than a child's suitcase."

Cassandra sat silently, trying to absorb this information. She wrapped her fingers around her warm teacup. "She must have felt so alone."

"Too right," said Dot. "All that way by herself. Weeks and weeks on that big ship, winding up on an empty dock."

"And all the time after."

"What do you mean?" Dot said, frowning.

Cassandra pressed her lips together. What *did* she mean? It had come to her in a wave. The certainty of her grandmother's loneliness. As if in that moment she had glimpsed an important aspect of Nell that she'd never known before. Or rather, she suddenly understood an aspect of Nell she'd known very well. Her isolation, her independence, her prickliness. "She must have felt so alone when she realized she wasn't who she'd thought she was."

"Yes," said Phyllis, surprised. "Must admit, I didn't see that at first. When June told me, I couldn't see that it changed things all that much. I couldn't for the life of me understand why Nell had let it affect her so badly. Ma and Pa loved her well and we younger ones worshipped our big sister; she couldn't have hoped for a better family."

She leaned against the sofa's arm, head on hand, and rubbed her left temple wearily. "As time's gone on, though, I've come to realize—that happens, doesn't it?—I've come to see that the things we take for granted are important. You know, family, blood, the past . . . They're the things that make us who we are and Pa took them from Nell. He didn't mean to, but he did."

"Nell must've been relieved that you finally knew, though," said Cassandra. "It must've made it easier in some way."

Phyllis and Dot exchanged a glance.

"You did tell her you'd found out?"

Phyllis frowned. "I almost did a number of times, but when it came down to it I just couldn't find the words. I couldn't do it to Nell. She'd gone so long without breathing a word of it to any of us, she'd rebuilt her entire life around the secret, worked so hard at keeping it to herself. It seemed . . . I don't know . . . almost cruel to tear down those walls. Like pulling the rug out from under her a second time." She shook her head. "Then again, perhaps that's all claptrap. Nell could be fierce when she wanted to, perhaps I just didn't have the courage for it."

"It's nothing to do with courage or its lack," said Dot firmly. "We all agreed it was for the best, Phylly. Nell wanted it that way."

"I suppose you're right," said Phyllis. "All the same, it's not like there weren't opportunities, the day Doug took the suitcase back, for one."

"Just before Pa died," Dot explained to Cassandra, "he had Phylly's husband drop the suitcase over to Nell. Not a word as to what it was, mind. That was Pa, as bad as Nell for keeping secrets. He'd had it hidden away all those years, you see. Everything still inside, just as when he found her."

"Funny," said Phyllis. "As soon as I saw the suitcase that day I thought of June's story. I knew it must be the one Pa had found with Nell on the wharf all those years ago, yet in all the time it had been at the back of Pa's storeroom I'd never given it a thought. Didn't connect it with Nell and her origins. If I ever considered it at all, it was to wonder what Ma and Pa had ever wanted with such a funny-looking case. White leather with silver buckles. Tiny it was, child-size . . ."

And although Phylly continued to describe the suitcase, she needn't have bothered, for Cassandra knew exactly how it looked.

What was more, she knew what it contained.

FIVE

CASSANDRA knew where they were going as soon as her mother wound down the window and told the petrol station attendant to "Fill her up." The man said something and her mother laughed girlishly. He winked at Cassandra before letting his gaze fall to her mother's long brown legs in their cutoff denim shorts. Cassandra was used to men staring at her mother and thought little of it. Rather, she turned to look out her own window and thought about Nell, her grandmother. For that's where they were going. The only reason her mother ever put more than five dollars of petrol in the car was to make the hour-long trip up the South East Freeway to Brisbane.

Cassandra had always been in awe of Nell. She'd only met her five times before (as far as she could remember), but Nell wasn't the kind of person one easily forgot. For a start, she was the oldest person Cassandra had ever seen in real life. And she didn't smile like other people did, which made her seem rather grand and more than a little frightening. Lesley didn't speak much of Nell, but once, when Cassandra was lying in bed and her mother was fighting with the boyfriend before Len, she'd heard Nell referred to as a witch, and though Cassandra had stopped believing in magic by then, the image wouldn't leave her.

Nell *was* like a witch. Her long silvery hair rolled into a bun on the back of her head, the narrow wooden house on the hillside in Paddington, with its peeling lemon-yellow paint and overgrown garden, the neighborhood cats that followed her everywhere. The way she had

28

of fixing her eyes straight on you, as if she might be about to cast a spell.

They sped along Logan Road with the windows down and Lesley singing along to the radio—the new ABBA song that was always on *Countdown*. After crossing the Brisbane River they bypassed the center of town and drove through the cottage-clad hills of Paddington. Off Latrobe Terrace, down a steep slope and midway along a narrow street was Nell's place.

Lesley jerked the car to a halt and shut off the ignition. Cassandra sat for a moment, hot sun shining through the windscreen onto her legs, skin under her knees glued to the vinyl seat. She hopped out of the car when her mum did and stood beside her on the pavement, gazing upwards, involuntarily, at the tall, weatherboard house.

A thin, cracked concrete path ran up one side. There was a front door, way up top, but someone years ago had enclosed the stairway so that the entrance was obscured, and Lesley said that no one ever used it. Nell liked it that way, she added: it stopped people from dropping in unexpectedly, thinking they were welcome. The gutters were old and wonky, with large rust-rimmed holes that must've let through buckets of water when it stormed. No sign of rain today, though, Cassandra thought, as a warm breeze set the wind chimes to jangling.

"Christ, Brisbane's a stink-hole," said Lesley, peering over the top of her large bronze sunglasses and shaking her head. "Thank God I got out."

A noise then from the top of the path. A sleek caramel cat fixed the new arrivals with a look, distinctly unwelcoming. Squeaky hinges on a gate, then footsteps. A tall, silver-haired figure appeared by the cat. Cassandra drew breath. Nell. It was like coming face-to-face with a figment of her imagination.

They all stood, observing one another. Nobody spoke. Cassandra had the strange sensation of being witness to a mysterious ritual of adulthood that she couldn't quite understand. She was wondering why they continued to stand, who would make the next move, when Nell broke the silence. "I thought you agreed to call first in the future."

"Good to see you, too, Mum."

"I'm in the middle of sorting boxes for auction. I've things everywhere, there's no room to sit."

"We'll manage." Lesley flicked her fingers in Cassandra's direction. "Your granddaughter's thirsty, it's bloody hot out here."

Cassandra shifted uncomfortably and looked at the ground. There was something odd about her mother's behavior, a nervousness she wasn't accustomed to and couldn't articulate. She heard her grandmother exhale slowly.

"All right, then," said Nell, "you'd better come inside."

NELL HADN'T been exaggerating about the mess. The floor was covered in scrunched newspaper, great crinkly mounds. On the table, an island amid the sea of newsprint, were countless pieces of china and glass and crystal. Bric-a-brac, Cassandra thought, pleasing herself by remembering the term.

"I'll put the kettle on," said Lesley, gliding to the other side of the kitchen.

Nell and Cassandra were left alone then and the older woman fixed her eyes on Cassandra in that uncanny way she had.

"You've grown taller," she said eventually. "But you're still too thin."

It was true. The kids at school were always telling her so.

"I was thin like you," said Nell. "You know what my father used to call me?"

Cassandra shrugged.

"Lucky Legs. Lucky they don't snap in half." Nell started pulling teacups off hooks attached to an old-fashioned cabinet. "Tea or coffee?"

Cassandra shook her head, scandalized. For though she had

turned ten in May, she was still a little girl and not accustomed to grown-ups offering her grown-up drinks.

"I don't have squash or fizzy drinks," warned Nell, "or any of those sorts of things."

She found her tongue. "I like milk."

Nell blinked at her. "It's in the fridge. I keep plenty for the cats. The bottle will be slippery, so don't drop it on my floor."

When the tea was poured, Cassandra's mum told her to scoot. The day was too bright and sunny for a little girl to be cooped up inside. Grandma Nell added that she could play under the house but she wasn't to disturb anything. And she most certainly was not to enter the downstairs flat.

IT WAS one of those desperate antipodean spells where the days seem strung together with no gaps between. Fans do little else but move the hot air around, cicadas threaten to deafen, to breathe is to exert, and there is nothing for it but to lie on one's back and wait for January and February to pass, the March storms to come, and then finally the first April gusts.

But Cassandra didn't know that. She was a child and had a child's stamina for difficult climates. She let the screen door slap closed behind her and followed the path into the back garden. Frangipani flowers had dropped and were baking in the sun, black and dry and shrunken. She smudged them with her shoe as she walked. Drew some pleasure from watching the smears scar the blond concrete.

She sat on the little iron garden seat in the clearing at the top and looked down at the strange garden of her mysterious grandmother, the patched-up house beyond. She wondered what her mother and grandmother were speaking of, why had they come to visit today, but no matter how she twisted the questions in her mind, she could divine no answers.

After a time, the distraction of the garden proved too great. Her questions dropped away, and she began to harvest pregnant Busy Lizzie pods while a black cat watched from a distance, pretending disinterest. When she had a nice collection, Cassandra climbed up onto the lowest bough of the mango tree in the back corner of the yard, pods cupped gently in her hand, and began to pop them, one by one. Enjoying the cold, gooey seeds that sprayed across her fingers, the pussycat's surprise when a pod shell dropped between her paws, her zeal as she mistook it for a grasshopper.

When they were all discharged, Cassandra brushed her hands on her shorts and let her gaze wander. On the other side of the wire fence was a huge white rectangular building. It was the Paddington Theatre, Cassandra knew, though it was closed now. Somewhere nearby her grandmother had a secondhand shop. Cassandra had been there once before on another of Lesley's impromptu visits to Brisbane. She'd been left with Nell while her mother went off to meet someone or other.

Nell had let her polish a silver tea set. Cassandra had enjoyed that, the smell of the Silvo, watching as the cloth turned black and the teapot shiny. Nell even explained some of the markings—lion for sterling, leopard's head for London, a letter for the year it was made. It was like a secret code. Cassandra had hunted at home later that week, hoping to find silver that she could polish and decode for Lesley. But she hadn't found any. She had forgotten until now how much she'd enjoyed the task.

As the day wore on and the mango leaves began to sag with heat and the magpies' songs got stuck in their throats, Cassandra made her way back down the garden path. Mum and Nell were still in the kitchen—she could see their shadowy silhouettes through the gauze of the screen—so she continued around the side of the house. There was a huge wooden sliding door on runners and when she pulled the handle it opened to reveal the cool, dim area beneath the house.

The dark formed such a contrast to the bright outdoors that it was like crossing the threshold into another world. Cassandra felt a jolt of excitement as she went inside and walked around the room's rim. It was a large space but Nell had done her best to fill it. Boxes of varying shapes and sizes were stacked from floor to ceiling around three sides, and along the fourth leaned odd windows and doors, some with broken glass panes. The only space left uncovered was a doorway, halfway along the furthest wall, which led into the room Nell called "the flat." Peering inside, Cassandra could see it was about the size of a bedroom. Makeshift shelves, heavy with old books, spanned two walls, and there was a fold-out bed in the corner, a red, white and blue patchwork quilt draped across it. A small window let in the room's only light, but someone had nailed wooden palings across it in places. To keep burglars out, Cassandra supposed. Though what they would want with such a room she couldn't imagine.

She had a strong urge to lie on the bed, to feel the cool of the quilt beneath her warm skin, but Nell had been clear—she could play downstairs but she wasn't allowed inside the flat—and Cassandra had a habit of obedience. Rather than enter the flat and collapse onto the bed, she turned away. Went back to the spot where some child, long ago, had painted hopscotch squares on the cement floor. She nosed about the edges of the room for a suitable stone, discarded a few before settling on one that was even in shape, with no jagged angles to send it off course.

Cassandra rolled it—a perfect landing in the middle of the first square—and began to hop. She was up to number seven when her grandmother's voice, sharp as broken glass, cut through the floor from upstairs. "What kind of a mother are you?"

"No worse than you were."

Cassandra remained still, balancing on one leg in the middle of a square as she listened. There was silence, or at least there was silence as far as Cassandra could tell. More likely they had just lowered their voices again, remembered that the neighbors were only a few yards away on either side. Len was always reminding Lesley when they argued that it wouldn't do to have strangers knowing their business. They didn't seem to mind that Cassandra heard every word.

She began to wobble, lost her balance and lowered her foot. It was only for a split second, then she had it raised again. Even Tracy Waters, who had a reputation among the Grade Five girls for being the strictest of hopscotch judges, would have allowed it, would have let her continue the round, but Cassandra had lost her enthusiasm for playing. Her mother's tone of voice had left her unsettled. Her tummy had started to ache.

She tossed her stone aside and stepped away from the squares.

It was too hot to go back outside. What she really felt like doing was reading. Escaping into the Enchanted Wood, up the Faraway Tree, or with the Famous Five into Smuggler's Top. She could picture her book, lying on her bed where she'd left it that morning, right near the pillow. Stupid of her not to bring it; she heard Len's voice, as she always did when she'd done something dumb.

She thought then of Nell's shelves, the old books lining the flat. Surely Nell wouldn't mind if she chose one and sat down to read? She'd be careful to do no harm, to leave things just as she'd found them.

The smell of dust and time was thick inside. Cassandra let her gaze run along the rows of book spines, red and green and yellow, and waited for a title to arrest her. A tabby cat was stretched across the third shelf, balanced in front of the books in a strip of sunlight. Cassandra hadn't noticed it before and wondered where it had come from, how it had entered the flat without her seeing. The cat, seeming to sense that she was under scrutiny, pushed up on her front legs and fixed Cassandra with a look of majesty. Then she leaped in a single fluid motion to the floor and disappeared beneath the bed.

Cassandra watched her go, wondering what it would be like to move so effortlessly, to vanish so completely. She blinked. Perhaps not so completely after all. Where the cat had brushed under the quilt, something was now exposed. It was small and white. Rectangular.

Cassandra knelt on the floor and lifted the quilt edge. Peered beneath. It was a tiny suitcase, an old suitcase. Its lid sat askew and Cassandra could see some of the way inside. Papers, white fabric, a blue ribbon.

The certainty came over her suddenly, the feeling that she must know exactly what it held, even if it meant breaking Nell's rules further. Heart flickering, she slid the suitcase out and leaned the lid against the bed. Began to look over the things inside.

A silver hairbrush, old and surely precious, with a little leopard's head for London stamped near the bristles. A white dress, small and pretty, the sort of old-fashioned dress Cassandra had never seen, let alone owned—the girls at school would laugh if she wore such a thing. A bundle of papers tied together with a pale blue ribbon. Cassandra let the bow slip loose between her fingertips and brushed the ends aside to see what lay beneath.

A picture, a black-and-white sketch. The most beautiful woman Cassandra had ever seen, standing beneath a garden arch. No, not an arch, a leafy doorway, the entrance to a tunnel of trees. A maze, she thought suddenly. The strange word came into her mind fully formed.

Scores of little black lines combined like magic to form the picture, and Cassandra wondered what it would feel like to create such a thing. The image was oddly familiar and at first she couldn't think how that could be. Then she realized—the woman looked like someone from a children's book. Like an illustration from an olden-days fairy tale, the maiden who turns into a princess when the handsome prince sees beyond her ratty clothing.

She set the sketch on the ground beside her and turned her attention to the rest of the bundle. There were some envelopes with letters inside, and a notebook full of lined pages that someone had covered with long, curly handwriting. It might have been a different language for all that Cassandra knew, she certainly couldn't read it. Brochures and torn-out pages of magazines had been tucked in the back with an old photograph of a man and a woman and a little girl with long plaits. Cassandra recognized none of them.

Beneath the notebook she found the book of fairy tales. The cover was green cardboard, the writing gold: *Magical Tales for Girls and Boys,* by Eliza Makepeace. Cassandra repeated the author's name, enjoying the mysterious rustle against her lips. She opened it up and inside the front cover was a picture of a fairy sitting in a bird's woven nest: long flowing hair, a wreath of stars around her head, and large, translucent wings. When she looked more closely, Cassandra realized that the fairy's face was the same as that in the sketch. A line of spidery writing curled around the base of the nest, proclaiming her "Your storyteller, Miss Makepeace." With a delicious shiver, she turned to the first fairy tale, sending startled silverfish scrambling in all directions. Time had colored the pages yellow, worked and worried at the edges. The paper felt powdery, and when she rubbed a dog-eared corner it seemed to disintegrate a little, fall to dust.

Cassandra couldn't help herself. She curled up on her side in the center of the camp bed. It was the perfect place for reading, cool and quiet and secret. Cassandra always hid when she read, though she never quite knew why. It was as if she couldn't shake the guilty suspicion that she was being lazy, that surrendering herself so completely to something so enjoyable must surely be wrong.

But surrender she did. Let herself drop through the rabbit hole and into a tale of magic and mystery, about a princess who lived with a blind crone in a cottage on the edge of a dark wood. A brave princess, far braver than Cassandra would ever be.

She was two pages from the end when footsteps on the floor-boards above caught her attention.

They were coming.

She sat up quickly and swung her legs over the side of the bed, feet onto the floor. She wanted desperately to finish, to find out what would happen to the princess. But there was nothing for it. She straightened the papers, tossed everything back into the suitcase and slid it under the bed. Removed all evidence of her disobedience.

She slipped from the flat, picked up a stone and headed for the hopscotch squares again.

By the time her mum and Nell appeared at the sliding door, Cassandra could make a pretty convincing case that she'd been playing hopscotch all afternoon.

"Come here, kiddo," said Lesley.

Cassandra dusted off her shorts and went to her mother's side, wondered as Lesley wrapped an arm around her shoulders.

"Having fun?"

"Yes," said Cassandra cautiously. Had she been found out?

But her mother wasn't cross. Quite the opposite; she seemed almost triumphant. She looked at Nell. "Told you, didn't I? Takes care of herself, this one."

Nell didn't answer and Cassandra's mum continued: "You're going to stop here with Grandma Nell for a bit, Cassie. Have an adventure."

This was a surprise; her mum must have more business in Brisbane. "Will I have lunch here?"

"Every day, I reckon, until I get back to collect you."

Cassandra was aware suddenly of the sharp edges of the stone she was holding. The way the corners pushed into her fingertips. She looked from her mother to her grandmother. Was it a game? Was her mother making a joke? She waited to see whether Lesley would burst out laughing.

She didn't. Merely gazed at Cassandra, blue eyes wide.

Cassandra could think of nothing to say. "I didn't bring my pajamas," was what she managed in the end.

Her mother smiled then, quickly, broadly, with relief, and Cassandra glimpsed somehow that the point of refusal had been passed. "Don't worry about that, you duffer. I've packed you a bag in the car. You didn't think I'd drop you off without a bag, did you?"

Through all this Nell was silent, stiff. Watching Lesley with what

Cassandra recognized as disapproval. She supposed her grandmother didn't want her to stay. Little girls had a habit of getting in the way, Len was always saying so.

Lesley skipped to the car and leaned through the open window at the back to pull out an overnight bag. Cassandra wondered when she'd packed it, why she hadn't let Cassandra pack it herself.

"Here you are, kiddo," said Lesley, tossing the bag to Cassandra. "There's a surprise in there for you, a new dress. Len helped me choose it."

She straightened and said to Nell, "Just a week or two, I promise. Just while Len and me get ourselves sorted." Lesley ruffled Cassandra's hair. "Your Grandma Nell's looking forward to having you stay. It'll be a real, proper summer holiday in the big smoke. Something to tell the other kids when school starts again."

Cassandra's grandmother smiled then, only it wasn't a happy smile. Cassandra thought she knew how it felt to smile like that. She often did so herself when her mother promised her something she really wanted but knew might not happen.

Lesley brushed a kiss on her cheek, gave her hand a squeeze and then, somehow, she was gone. Before Cassandra could give her a hug, could tell her to drive safely, could ask her when exactly she'd be back.

LATER, NELL made dinner—fat pork sausages, mashed potatoes, and mushy peas from a can—and they ate in the narrow room by the kitchen. Nell's house didn't have fly screens on the windows like Len's unit on Burleigh Beach; instead Nell kept a plastic swatter on the window ledge beside her. When flies or mosquitoes threatened, she was a quick draw. So swift, so practiced were these attacks that the cat, asleep on Nell's lap, barely flinched.

The stumpy pedestal fan on top of the fridge beat thick, moist air back and forth while they ate; Cassandra answered her grandmother's occasional questions as politely as she could, and eventually the ordeal of dinner ended. Cassandra helped to dry the dishes, then Nell took her to the bathroom and started running lukewarm water into the tub.

"Only thing worse than a cold bath in winter," Nell said matter-of-factly, "is a hot bath in summer." She pulled a brown towel from the cupboard and balanced it on the toilet tank. "You can shut the water off when it reaches this line." She pointed out a crack in the green porcelain, then stood, straightening her dress. "You'll be all right, then?"

Cassandra nodded and smiled. She hoped she'd answered correctly; adults could be tricky sometimes. For the most part, she knew, they didn't like it when children made their feelings known, not their bad feelings anyway. Len was often reminding Cassandra that good children should smile and learn to keep their black thoughts to themselves. Nell was different, though. Cassandra wasn't sure how she knew it, but she sensed Nell's rules were different. All the same, it was best to play things safe.

That was why she hadn't mentioned the toothbrush, or lack of toothbrush. Lesley was always forgetting such things when they spent time away from home, but Cassandra knew a week or two without it wouldn't kill her. She looped her hair up into a bun and tied it on top of her head with an elastic band. At home she wore her mother's shower cap, but she wasn't sure if Nell had one and didn't want to ask. She climbed into the bath and sat in the tepid water, gathered her knees up close and shut her eyes. Listened to the water lapping the sides of the tub, the buzz of the lightbulb, a mosquito somewhere above.

She stayed like that for some time, climbing out only reluctantly when she realized that if she put it off any longer, Nell might come looking for her. She dried herself, hung the towel carefully over the shower rail, lining up the edges, then got into her pajamas.

She found Nell in the sunroom, making up the daybed with sheets and a blanket.

"It's not usually for sleeping on," said Nell, patting a pillow into place. "The mattress isn't much to speak of and the springs are a bit hard, but you're only a waif of a girl. You'll be comfy enough."

Cassandra nodded gravely. "It won't be for long. Just a week or two, just while Mum and Len get things sorted."

Nell smiled grimly. She looked about the room, then back to Cassandra. "Anything else you need? A glass of water? A lamp?"

Cassandra half wondered whether Nell had a spare toothbrush but couldn't formulate the words required to ask. She shook her head.

"In you hop, then," said Nell, lifting a corner of the blanket.

Cassandra slid obediently into place and Nell pulled up the sheets. They were surprisingly soft, pleasantly worn with an unfamiliar yet clean smell.

Nell hesitated. "Well, good night."

"Good night."

Then the light was off and Cassandra alone.

In the dark, strange noises were amplified. Traffic on a distant ridge, a television in one of the neighboring houses, Nell's footsteps on the floorboards of another room. Outside the window, the wind chimes were clattering, and Cassandra realized that the air had become charged with the smell of eucalypt and road tar. A storm was coming.

She curled up tight beneath the covers. Cassandra didn't like storms; they were unpredictable. Hopefully it would blow over before it really got going. She made a little deal with herself: if she could count to ten before the next car droned over the nearby hill, everything would be okay. The storm would pass quickly and Mum would come back for her within the week.

One. Two. Three . . . She didn't cheat, didn't rush . . . Four. Five

. . . Nothing so far, halfway there . . . Six. Seven . . . Breathing quickly, still no cars, almost safe . . . Eight—

Suddenly, she sat bolt upright. There were pockets inside the bag. Her mum hadn't forgotten, she'd just tucked the toothbrush in there for safekeeping.

Cassandra slipped out of bed as a violent gust tossed the chimes against the windowpane. She crept across the room, bare feet cooled by a draft of wind that sneaked between the floorboards.

The sky above the house grumbled ominously, then turned spectacularly to light. It felt dangerous, reminded Cassandra of the storm in the fairy tale she'd read that afternoon, the angry storm that had followed the little princess to the crone's cottage.

Cassandra knelt on the floor, rummaging in one pocket after another, willing the toothbrush's familiar shape to meet her fingertips.

Big fat raindrops started falling, loud on the corrugated-iron roof. Sporadic at first, then increasing until Cassandra could hear no gaps between.

It wouldn't hurt to recheck the main part of the bag while she was at it: a toothbrush was only small, maybe it was tucked so far down she'd missed it? She pushed her hands in deep and pulled everything out from inside. The toothbrush was not there.

Cassandra blocked her ears as another clap of thunder shook the house. She picked herself up and folded her arms across her chest, aware vaguely of her own thinness, her inconsequence, as she hurried back to bed and climbed under the sheet.

Rain poured over the eaves, ran down the windows in rivulets, spilled from the sagging gutters that had been caught unawares.

Beneath the sheet, Cassandra lay very still, hugging her own body. Despite the warm muggy air there were goose bumps on her upper arms. She knew she should try to sleep. She'd be tired in the morning if she didn't and no one liked to spend time with a grump.

Try as she might, though, sleep wouldn't come. She counted sheep, sang silent songs about yellow submarines, and oranges and lemons, and gardens beneath the sea, told herself fairy tales. But the night threatened to stretch on endlessly.

As lightning flashed, rain poured and thunder tore open the sky, Cassandra began to weep. Tears that had waited a long time for escape were finally released under the dark veil of rain.

How much time passed before she became aware of the shadowy figure standing in the doorway? One minute? Ten?

Cassandra caught a sob in her throat, held it there although it burned.

A whisper, Nell's voice. "I came to check the window was closed."

In the dark Cassandra held her breath, wiped at her eyes with the corner of the sheet.

Nell was close now; Cassandra could sense the strange electricity generated when another human stands near without touching.

"What is it?"

Cassandra's throat, still frozen, refused to let words pass.

"Is it the storm? Are you frightened?"

Cassandra shook her head.

Nell sat stiffly on the edge of the daybed, tightened her dressing gown around her middle. Another flash of lightning and Cassandra saw her grandmother's face, recognized her mother's eyes with their slightly downturned corners.

The sob was finally dislodged. "My toothbrush," she said, through tears. "I don't have my toothbrush."

Nell looked at her a moment, startled, then gathered Cassandra in her arms. The little girl flinched at first, surprised by the suddenness, the unexpectedness of the gesture, but then she felt herself surrender. She collapsed forward, head resting against Nell's soft, lavender-scented body, shoulders shaking as she wept warm tears into Nell's nightie.

"There, now," Nell whispered, hand smoothing Cassandra's hair. "Don't you worry. We'll find you another one." She turned her head to look at the rain sluicing against the window and rested her cheek on the top of Cassandra's head. "You're a survivor, you hear? You're going to be all right. Everything's going to be all right."

And although Cassandra couldn't believe that things would ever be all right, she was comforted a little by Nell's words. Something in her grandmother's voice suggested that Nell understood. That she knew just how frightening it was to spend a stormy night alone in an unfamiliar place.

Six

❧

THOUGH he was late home from port, the broth was still warm. That was Lil, bless her, she wasn't the sort to serve up cold soup to her fellow. Hugh spooned the last of it into his mouth and leaned back against his chair, gave his neck a rub. Outside, distant thunder rolled along the river and into town. An invisible draft set the lamplight to flickering, coaxed the room's shadows from hiding. He let his tired gaze follow them across the table, around the base of the walls, along the front door. Dancing dark on the skin of the shiny white suitcase.

Lost suitcases he'd had plenty of times. But a little girl? How the hell did someone's child wind up sitting on his wharf, alone as you please? She was a nice little thing, too, as far as he could tell. Pretty to look at, strawberry blond hair like spun gold and real deep blue eyes. A way of looking at you that told you she was listening, that she understood all you were saying, and all you weren't.

The door to the veranda opened and Lil's soft, familiar shape materialized. She pulled the door gently behind her and started down the hall. Brushed a bothersome curl behind her ear, the same unruly curl that'd been jumping out of place all the time he'd known her. "She's asleep now," Lil said as she reached the kitchen. "Frightened of the thunder, but she couldn't fight it for long. Poor little lamb was as tired as the day."

Hugh took his bowl to the counter and dunked it in tepid water. "Little wonder, I'm tired myself."

"You look it. Leave the washing up to me."

"I'm all right, Lil love. You go in, I won't be long."

But Lil didn't leave. He could sense her behind him, could tell, the way a man learns to, that she'd something more to say. Her next words sat pregnant between them and Hugh felt his neck tense. Felt the tide of previous conversations draw back, suspend a moment, preparing to crash once more upon them.

Lil's voice, when it came, was low. "You needn't pussyfoot around me, Hughie."

He sighed. "I know that."

"I'll come through. Have before."

"Course you will."

"Last thing I need is for you to treat me like an invalid."

"I don't mean to, Lil." He turned to face her. Saw that she was standing on the far side of the table, hands resting on the back of a chair. The stance, he knew, was supposed to convince him of her stability, to say "all is as it was," but Hugh knew her too well for that. He knew that she was hurting. Knew also there was nothing he could bloody well do to set things right. As Dr. Huntley was so fond of telling them, some things just weren't meant to be. It didn't make it any easier, though, not on Lil and not on him.

She was by his side then, bumping him gently with her hip. He could smell the sweet, sad milkiness of her skin. "Go on. Get yourself to bed," she said. "I'll be in soon." The carefully rendered cheerfulness made his blood chill, but he did as she said.

She was true to her word, wasn't far behind him, and he watched as she cleaned the day from her skin, pulled her nightdress over her head. Though her back was turned, he could see how gently she eased the clothing over her breasts, her stomach that was still swollen.

She glanced up then and caught him looking. Defensiveness chased vulnerability from her face. "What?"

"Nothing." He concentrated on his hands, the calluses and rope

45

burns earned by his years on the wharves. "I was just wondering about the little one out there," he said. "Wondering who she is. Didn't give up her name, I s'pose?"

"Says she doesn't know. Doesn't matter how many times I ask, she just looks back at me, serious as can be, and says she can't remember."

"You don't think she's fooling, do you? Some of them stowaways do a darn good line in fooling."

"Hughie," scolded Lil. "She's no stowaway, she's little more than a baby."

"Easy, Lil love. I was just asking." He shook his head. "Only it's hard to believe she could've clean forgot like that."

"I've heard of it before, amnesia it's called. Ruth Halfpenny's father got it, after his fall down the shaft. That's what causes it, falls and the like."

"You think she might've had a fall?"

"Couldn't see any bruises on her, but it's possible, ain't it?"

"Ah, well," said Hugh, as a flash of lightning lit the room's corners, "I'll look into it tomorrow." He shifted position, lay on his back and stared at the ceiling. "She must belong somewhere," he said quietly.

"Yes." Lil extinguished the lamp, casting them into darkness. "Someone must be missing her like the dickens." She rolled over as she did each night, turning her back on Hugh and shutting him out of her grief. Her voice was muffled by the sheet. "I tell you, they don't deserve her, though. Bloody careless. What kind of person could lose a child?"

LIL WATCHED out the back window where the two little girls were running back and forth below the clothesline, laughing as the cool damp sheets brushed their faces. They were singing again, another of Nell's songs. That was one thing that hadn't slipped her memory, the songs; she knew such a lot of them.

Nell. That's what they were calling her now, after Lil's mum, Eleanor. Well, they had to call her something, didn't they? The funny little thing still couldn't tell them her name. Whenever Lil quizzed her, she widened those big blue eyes and said she didn't remember.

After the first few weeks, Lil stopped asking. Truth be told, she was just as happy not to know. Didn't want to imagine Nell with any name other than the one they'd given her. Nell. It suited her so well; no one could say it didn't. Almost as if she'd been born to it.

They'd done their best to find out who she was, where she belonged. That's all anyone could ask of them. And although initially she'd told herself that they were just minding Nell for a time, keeping her safe until her people came for her, with every day that passed Lil became more certain that there were no such people.

They'd fallen into an easy routine, the three of them. Breakfast together in the morning, then Hughie would leave for work and she and Nell would get started on the house. Lil found she liked having a second shadow, enjoyed showing Nell things, explaining how they worked, and why. Nell was a big one for asking why—why did the sun hide at night, why didn't the fire flames leap out of the grate, why didn't the river get bored and run the other way?—and Lil loved supplying answers, watching as understanding dawned on Nell's little face. For the first time in her life Lil felt useful, needed, whole.

Things were better with Hughie, too. The sheet of tension that the past few years had strung between them was beginning to slip away. They'd stopped being so damned polite, tripping over their carefully chosen words like two strangers drafted into close quarters. They'd even started to laugh again sometimes, easy laughter that came unforced like it had before.

As for Nell, she took to life with Hughie and Lil like a duck, to the Mary River. It didn't take long for the neighborhood kids to discover there was someone new in their midst, and Nell perked up something tremendous at the prospect of other children to play with. Young Beth Reeves was over the fence at some point every day now. Lil loved the sound of the two girls running about together. She'd been waiting so long, had so looked forward to a time when little voices might squeal and laugh in her own backyard.

And Nell was a most imaginative child. Lil often heard her describing long and involved games of make-believe. The flat, open yard became a magical forest in Nell's imagination, with brambles and mazes, even a cottage on the edge of a cliff. Lil recognized the places Nell described from the book of children's fairy tales they'd found in the white suitcase. Lil and Hughie had been taking it in turns to read the stories to Nell at night. Lil had thought them too frightening at first, but Hughie had convinced her otherwise. Nell, for her part, didn't seem bothered a whit.

From where she stood, watching at the kitchen window, Lil could tell that's what they were playing today. Beth was listening, wide-eyed, as Nell led her through an imaginary maze, flitting about in her white dress, sun rays turning her long red plaits to gold.

Nell would miss Beth when they moved to Brisbane, but she'd be sure to make new friends. Children did. And the move was important. There was only so long Lil and Hughie could tell people that Nell was a niece from up north. Sooner or later the neighbors were going to start wondering why she hadn't gone home. How much longer she'd be staying.

No, it was clear to Lil. The three of them needed to make a fresh start somewhere they weren't already known. A big city where people wouldn't ask questions.

SEVEN

❧

BRISBANE, 2005

IT was a morning in early spring and Nell had been dead just over a week. A brisk wind wove through the bushes, twirling the leaves so that their pale undersides fluttered towards the sun. Like children thrust suddenly into the spotlight, flitting between nerves and self-importance.

Cassandra's mug of tea had long grown cold. She'd set it on the cement ledge after her last sip and forgotten it was there. A brigade of busy ants whose way had been thwarted was now forced to take evasive action, up the mug's edge and through the handle to the other side.

Cassandra didn't notice them, though. Sitting on a rickety chair in the backyard, beside the old laundry, her attention was on the rear wall of the house. It needed a coat of paint. Hard to believe five years had passed already. The experts recommended that a weatherboard house should be repainted every seven, but Nell hadn't held with such convention. In all the time Cassandra had lived with her grandmother, the house had never received a full coat. Nell was fond of saying that she wasn't in the business of spending good money to give the neighbors a fresh view.

The back wall, however, was a different matter—as Nell said, it was the only one they ever spent any time looking at. So while the sides and front peeled beneath the fierce Queensland sun, the back was a thing of beauty. Every five years the paint charts would come out and a great deal of time and energy would be spent debating the merits

49

of a new color. In the years Cassandra had been around it had been turquoise, lilac, vermilion, teal. Once it had even hosted a mural of sorts, unsanctioned though it might have been . . .

Cassandra had been nineteen and life was sweet. She was in the middle of her second year at the College of Art, her bedroom had morphed into a studio so that she had to climb across her drawing board to reach her bed each night and she was dreaming of a move to Melbourne to study art history.

Nell was not so keen on the plan. "You can study art history at Queensland Uni," she said whenever the subject was raised. "No need to drag yourself down south."

"I can't stay living at home forever, Nell."

"Who said anything about forever? Just wait a little while, find your feet here first."

Cassandra pointed to her Doc-clad feet. "Found 'em."

Nell didn't smile. "Melbourne's an expensive city to live in and I can't afford to pay your rent down there."

"I'm not picking up glasses at the Paddo Tav for fun, you know."

"Pah, with what they pay, you can put off applying to Melbourne for another decade."

"You're right."

Nell cocked her chin and raised a dubious eyebrow, wondering where such sudden capitulation was leading.

"I'll never save enough money myself." Cassandra bit her bottom lip, arresting a hopeful smile. "If only there were someone willing to spot me a loan, a loving person who wanted to help me follow my dreams . . ."

Nell picked up the box of china she was taking to the antique center. "I'm not going to stand around here and let you paint me into a corner, my girl."

Cassandra sensed a hopeful fissure in the once-solid refusal. "We'll talk about it later?"

Nell rolled her eyes skywards. "I fear we will. And then again and again and again." She huffed a sigh, signaling that the subject was, for now at least, closed. "Have you got everything you need to do the back wall?"

"Check."

"You won't forget to use the new brush on the boards? I don't want to stare at loose bristles for the next five years."

"Yes, Nell. And just to get things straight, I dip the brush into the paint tin before putting it on the boards, right?"

"Cheeky girl."

When Nell arrived home from the antique center that afternoon, she rounded the corner of the house and stopped still, appraising the wall in its shiny new coat.

Cassandra stepped back and pressed her lips together to stop from laughing. Waited.

The vermilion was striking, but it was the black detailing she'd added over in the far corner that her grandmother was staring at. The likeness was uncanny: Nell sitting on her favorite chair, holding aloft a cup of steaming tea.

"I seem to have painted you into a corner, Nell. Didn't mean to, I just got carried away."

Nell's expression was unreadable.

"I'm going to do me next, sitting right beside you. That way, even when I'm in Melbourne, you'll remember that we're still a pair."

Nell's lips had trembled a little then. She'd shaken her head and set down the box she'd brought back from the stall. Heaved a sigh. "You're a cheeky girl, there's no doubt about that," she'd said. And then she'd smiled despite herself and cupped Cassandra's face in her hands. "But you're my cheeky girl and I wouldn't have you any other way . . ."

A noise, and the past was chased away, dispersed into the shadows like smoke by the brighter, louder present. Cassandra blinked and wiped her eyes. Far above her a plane droned, a white speck in a sea of bright blue. Impossible to imagine there were people inside, talking and laughing and eating. Some of them looking down just as she was looking up.

Another noise, nearer now. Shuffling footsteps.

"Hello there, young Cassandra." A familiar figure appeared at the side of the house, stood for a moment catching his breath. Ben had once been tall, but time had a way of molding people into shapes they themselves no longer recognized, and his was now the body of a garden gnome. His hair was white, his beard wiry and his ears inexplicably red.

Cassandra smiled, genuinely pleased to see him. Nell was not one for friends and had never hidden her distaste for most other humans, their neurotic compulsion for the acquisition of allies. But she and Ben had seen eye to eye. He was a fellow trader at the antique center, a one-time lawyer who'd turned his hobby into a job when his wife died, his firm suggested gently it might be time to retire and his purchase of secondhand furniture threatened to squeeze him out of home.

When Cassandra was growing up he'd been a father figure of sorts, offering wisdom she'd appreciated and disdained in equal measure, but since she'd been back living with Nell, he'd become her friend, too.

Ben pulled a faded deck chair from beside the concrete laundry tub and sat down carefully. His knees had been damaged as a young man in the Second War and gave him grief aplenty, especially when the weather was turning.

He winked over the rim of his round glasses. "You've got the right idea. Beaut spot, this, nice and sheltered."

"It was Nell's spot." Her voice sounded strange to her ears and she wondered vaguely how long it had been since she'd spoken aloud to anyone. Not since dinner at Phyllis's place a week before, she realized.

"That'd be right. Count on her to know just where to sit."

Cassandra smiled. "Would you like a cuppa?"

"Love one."

She went through the back door into the kitchen and set the kettle on the stove. The water was still warm from when she'd boiled it earlier.

"So, how've you been keeping?"

She shrugged. "I've been all right." Came back to sit on the concrete step near his chair.

Ben pressed pale lips together, smiled slightly so that his moustache tangled with his beard. "Has your mum been in touch?"

"She sent a card."

"Well, then . . ."

"Said she would've liked to make it down but she and Len were busy. Caleb and Marie—"

"Of course. Keep you busy, teenagers."

"Not teenagers anymore. Marie just turned twenty-one."

Ben whistled. "Time flies."

The kettle began shrilling.

Cassandra went back inside and drowned the teabag, watched as it bled the water brown. An irony that Lesley had turned out to be such a conscientious mother second time around. So much in life came down to timing.

She dribbled in some milk, wondering vaguely whether it was still okay, when she'd purchased it. Before Nell died, surely? The label was stamped 14 September. Had that date passed? She wasn't sure. It didn't smell sour. She carried the mug out and handed it to Ben.

"I'm sorry . . . the milk . . ."

He took a sip. "Best tea I've had all day."

He eyed her a moment as she sat down, seemed about to say something but thought better of it. He cleared his throat. "Cass, I've come on official business, as well as social."

That death should be followed by official business was no surprise and yet she felt dizzy, caught off guard.

"Nell had me make out her will. You know how she was, said she didn't like the idea of divulging her personal affairs to a stranger."

Cassandra nodded. That was Nell.

Ben pulled an envelope from the pocket inside his blazer. Age had blunted its edges and turned white to cream.

"She made it some time ago." He squinted at the envelope. "In 1981, to be exact." He paused, as if waiting for her to fill the silence. When she didn't, he continued: "Pretty straightforward for the most part." He withdrew the contents but didn't look at them, leaned forward so his forearms rested on his knees. Nell's will dangled from his right hand. "Your grandmother left you everything, Cass."

Cassandra was not surprised. Touched, perhaps, and suddenly, perversely, lonely, but not surprised. For who else was there? Not Lesley, certainly. Though Cassandra had stopped blaming her mother long ago, Nell had never been able to forgive. To abandon a child, she had once said to someone, when she thought Cassandra couldn't hear, was an act so cold, so careless, it refused forgiveness.

"There's the house, of course, and some money in her savings account. All of her antiques." He hesitated, eyed Cassandra, as if gauging her preparedness for something yet to come. "And there's one thing more." He glanced at the papers. "Last year, after your grandmother was diagnosed, she asked me to come for tea one morning."

Cassandra remembered. Nell had told her when she brought in breakfast that Ben was visiting and that she needed to see him in private. She'd asked Cassandra to catalogue some books for her, up at the antique center though it had been years since Nell had taken an active role in the stall.

"She gave me something that day," he said. "A sealed envelope. Told me I was to put it with her will and open it only if . . . when . . . well, you know."

Cassandra shivered lightly as a sudden cool breeze brushed across her arms.

Ben waved his hand. The papers fluttered but he didn't speak.

"What is it?" she said, a familiar kernel of anxiety heavy in her stomach. "You can tell me, Ben. I'll be okay."

Ben looked up, surprised by her tone. Confounded her by laughing. "No need to look so worried, Cass, it's nothing bad. Quite the opposite really." He considered for a moment. "More a mystery than a calamity."

Cassandra exhaled; his talk of mysteries did little to relieve her nervousness.

"I did as she said. Put the envelope aside and didn't open it till yesterday. Could've knocked me down with a feather when I saw." He smiled. "Inside were the deeds to another house."

"Whose house?"

"Nell's house."

"Nell doesn't have another house."

"It would appear she does, or did. And now it's yours."

Cassandra didn't like surprises, their suddenness, their randomness. Where once she'd known how to surrender herself to the unexpected, now the very suggestion heralded a surge of instant fear, her body's learned response to change. She picked up a dry leaf lying by her shoe, folded it in half and in half again as she thought.

Nell hadn't mentioned another house, not in all the time they'd lived together, while Cassandra was growing up and since she'd been back. Why not? Why would she have kept such a thing secret? And what could she have wanted with it? An investment? Cassandra had heard people in the coffee shops on Latrobe Terrace talking about rising property prices, investment portfolios, but Nell? Nell had always poked fun at the inner-city yuppies who shelled out small fortunes for the tiny wooden workers' cottages of Paddington.

Besides, Nell'd reached retirement age long ago. If this house were an investment, why hadn't she sold it? Used the money to live on? Dealing in antiques had its rewards, but financial remuneration was not chief among them, not these days. Nell and Cassandra made enough to live on but not much besides. There'd been times when an investment would've come in pretty handy, yet Nell had never breathed a word.

"This house," Cassandra said finally, "where is it? Is it nearby?"

Ben shook his head, smiled bemusedly. "That's where this whole thing gets *really* mysterious. The other house is in England."

"England?"

"The UK, Europe, other side of the world."

"I know where England is."

"Cornwall, to be precise, a village called Tregenna. I've only got the deeds to go by, but it's listed as 'Cliff Cottage.' From the address, I'd guess it was part of a larger country estate originally. I could find out if you like."

"But why would she . . . ? How could she . . . ? " Cassandra exhaled. "When did she buy it?"

"The deeds are stamped 6 December 1975."

She folded her arms across her chest. "Nell hasn't even been to England."

It was Ben's turn to look surprised. "Yes, she has. She went on a trip to the UK, back in the mid-1970s. She never mentioned it?"

Cassandra shook her head slowly.

"I remember when she went. I hadn't known her long, it was a few months before you came on the scene, when she still had the little shop near Stafford Street. I'd bought a few pieces from her and we were acquaintances, if not yet friends. She was gone just over a month. I remember because I'd put a cedar writing desk on layaway right before she left, a birthday gift for my wife—least it was s'posed to be, didn't turn out that way in the end. Every time I went to collect it, the shop was closed.

"Don't have to tell you, I was fuming. It was Janice's fiftieth and the desk was perfect. When I paid the deposit Nell didn't mention that she was going on holiday. In fact, she made a point of outlining her layaway terms, made it clear she was expecting weekly payments and that I'd need to collect the desk within a month. She wasn't a storage facility, she said, she'd have more stock coming in and needed the room."

Cassandra smiled; it sounded just like Nell.

"She was absolutely insistent, that's what made it so odd when she wasn't there all that time. After I got over the initial irritation I became quite worried. Even thought about calling the police." He waved his hand. "Didn't have to, as it turned out. On my fourth or fifth visit I bumped into the lady next door, who was collecting Nell's mail. She told me Nell was in the UK but became quite indignant when I started asking questions about why she'd left so suddenly and when she'd be back. The neighbor said she was just doing as she'd been asked and knew no more than that. So I kept on checking, my wife's birthday came and went, then one day the shop was open, Nell was home."

"And she'd bought a house while she was away."

"Evidently."

Cassandra pulled her cardigan closer around her shoulders. It made no sense. Why would Nell go on holiday like that, out of the blue, buy a house, then never go back? "She didn't tell you anything about it? Not ever?"

Ben raised his eyebrows. "We're talking about Nell. She wasn't one for volunteering confidences."

"But you and she were close. Surely at some point she must have mentioned it?" Ben was shaking his head. Cassandra persisted: "But when she got back. When you finally collected the writing desk. Didn't you ask her why she'd left so suddenly?"

"Course I did, a number of times over the years. I knew it must've been important. She was different, you see, when she got back."

"How?"

"More distracted, mysterious. I'm sure it's not just hindsight that makes me say so. A couple of months later was the closest I came to finding out. I was visiting her in her shop and a letter arrived, postmarked Truro. I arrived at the same time as the postman, so I took the mail in for her. She tried to act casually but I was getting to know her better by then; she was excited to receive that letter. Made an excuse to leave me as soon as she could."

"What was it? Who was it from?"

"Must admit, curiosity got the better of me. I didn't go as far as to look at the letter itself, but I flipped the envelope over later, when I saw it on her desk, just to see who'd sent it. I memorized the address on the back and had an old colleague in the UK look it up for me. The address was for an investigator."

"You mean like a detective?"

He nodded.

"They really exist?"

"Sure."

"But what would Nell have wanted with an English detective?"

Ben shrugged. "I don't know. I guess she had some mystery she was trying to get to the bottom of. I dropped hints for a while, tried to draw her out, but all to no avail. I let it go after that, I figured everyone's entitled to their secrets and Nell'd tell me if she wanted to. Truth be told, I still felt guilty for the bit of snooping I'd already done." He shook his head. "Got to admit, I'd love to know. It's played on my mind a long time, and this"—he waved the deed—this just caps it off. Even now your grandmother has the strangest ability to confound me."

Cassandra nodded absently. Her mind was elsewhere, making connections. It was Ben's talk of mysteries that had done it, his suggestion that Nell must've been trying to solve one. All the secrets that had materialized in her grandmother's wake were beginning to knit together: Nell's unknown parentage, her arrival as a child at an ocean port, the suitcase, the mysterious trip to England, this secret house . . .

"Ah, well." Ben tossed the dregs of his tea into a pot of Nell's red geraniums. "I'd better head off. I've a man coming to see me about a mahogany sideboard in fifteen minutes. It's been a bugger of a sale to make; I'll be glad to see the end of it. Anything you'd like me to do when I'm up at the center?"

Cassandra shook her head. "I'll come up myself on Monday."

"No rush, Cass. I told you the other day, I'm happy to keep an eye on your space as long as you need. I'll bring you any money they're holding when I'm finished this afternoon."

"Thanks, Ben," she said. "For everything."

He stood and tucked the squatter's chair back where it had come from, left the deed beneath his teacup. He was about to disappear around the corner and down the side of the house when he hesitated and turned back. "You look after yourself, now, you hear? That wind gets much stronger you'll blow away."

Kindly concern lined his forehead and Cassandra found it hard to meet his gaze. It offered too clear a window to his thoughts and she couldn't bear to see him remembering the way she used to be.

"Cass?"

"Yep, will do." She waved as he left, listened as his car engine faded down the street. His sympathy, though well intentioned, always seemed to carry with it an indictment. Disappointment, however faint, that she'd been unable—or unwilling—to recover her old self. It didn't occur to him that she might have chosen to remain this way. That where he saw reserve and loneliness, Cassandra saw self-preservation and the knowledge that it was safer when one had less to lose.

She scuffed the toe of her sneaker against the cement path and shook away sad old thoughts. Then she picked up the deed. Noticed, for the first time, the little note stapled to its front. Nell's aged scrawl, near impossible to read. She held it close, then further away, slowly picked out the words. *For Cassandra,* it said, *who will understand why.*

Eight

Nell ran quickly through the documents again—passport, ticket, traveler's checks—then zipped up her travel wallet and gave herself a stern talking-to. Really, it was becoming compulsive. People flew every day, or so she was led to believe. Strapped themselves into seats within gigantic tin cans and consented to being catapulted into the sky. She took a deep breath. Everything would be fine. She was a survivor, wasn't she?

She made her way through the house, checking the window locks as she went. Scanned the kitchen, made sure she hadn't left the gas leaking, the freezer ice melting, power outlets switched on. Finally, she carried her two suitcases through the back door and locked up. She knew why she was nervous, of course, and it wasn't only a fear of forgetting something, or even a fear of the plane dropping from the sky. She was nervous because she was going home. After all this time, a lifetime, she was finally going home.

It had happened so suddenly in the end. Her father, Hugh, had only been dead a couple of months and here she was opening the door to her past. He must've known she would do so. When he pointed out the suitcase to Phyllis, told her to deliver it to Nell when he was gone, he must've guessed.

As she waited by the road for the taxi, Nell glanced up at her pale yellow house. So tall from this angle, unlike any house she'd seen before, with its funny little backwards staircase closed in years before, stripy awnings painted pink, blue and white, the two dormer windows at the top. Too narrow, too boxy ever to be considered elegant, and yet she loved it. Its awkwardness, its patched-up quality, its lack of clear provenance. Victim of time and a succession of owners, each intent on placing their stamp on its enduring facade.

She'd bought it in 1961, after Al died and she and Lesley returned from America. The house had been neglected, but its position on the Paddington slopes behind the old Plaza Theatre had felt about as close to home as Nell could get. And the house had rewarded her faith, had even provided her with a new income. She'd stumbled upon the room of broken furniture locked up in the dark underneath and spied a table that took her fancy—barley-twist legs and a drop leaf. It was in pretty bad nick but Nell hadn't thought twice, she'd bought some sandpaper and shellac, and set about bringing it back to life.

It had been Hugh who'd taught her how to restore furniture. When he came back from the war, and the baby sisters had started being born, Nell had taken to following him around on weekends. She'd become his helper, learned her dovetail joints from her box combing, her shellac from her varnish, the joy of taking a broken object and putting it back together. It had been a long time since she'd done so, though, and she'd forgotten, until she saw that table, that she knew how to perform such surgery, forgotten that she loved it so much. She could've wept as she massaged the shellac into the barley-twist legs, breathed the familiar fumes, only she hadn't been the weeping kind.

A wilting gardenia near her suitcase caught Nell's attention and she remembered that she'd neglected to arrange for someone to water her garden. The girl who lived behind had agreed to put out milk for the visiting cats, and she'd found a woman to collect mail at the shop, but the plants had slipped her mind. Just went to show where her head was at, to forget her pride and joy like that. She would have to ask one of her sisters, phone from the airport, or even the other side of the world. Give them a real shock, the sort they'd come to expect from their big sister Nell.

Hard to believe they'd all been so close once. Of the many things her father's confession had stolen from her, their loss had left the deepest wound. She'd already been eleven when the first of them came along but the instant bond had almost knocked her over. She'd known, even before Ma told her, that it was her responsibility to look after these little sisters, to make sure they were safe. Her reward was their devotion, their insistence that Nell cradle them when they were hurt, their firm little bodies pressing against hers after they'd suffered a nightmare and crept into bed beside her to pass the long night.

But Pa's secret had changed everything. His words had tossed the book that was her life into the air and the pages had been blown into disarray, could never be put back together to tell the same story. She found she couldn't look at her little sisters without seeing her own foreignness, and yet she couldn't tell them the truth. To have done so would've destroyed something in which they believed implicitly. Nell had figured it was better they thought her strange than knew her to be a stranger.

A Black and White taxi turned into the street and she held out her arm to wave it over. The driver loaded her suitcase while she climbed into the backseat.

"Where to, love?" he said, slamming his door closed.

"The airport."

He nodded and they set off, weaving through the maze of Paddington streets.

Her father had told her when she turned twenty-one, the whispered confession that robbed her of her self.

"But who am I?" she'd said.

"You're you. Same as always. You're Nell, my Nellie."

She could hear how much he wanted it to be so, but she'd known better than that. Reality had shifted by a few degrees and left her out of sync with everyone else. This person she was, or thought she was, did not really exist. There was no Nell O'Connor.

"Who am I really?" she'd said again, days later. "Please tell me, Pa."

He'd shaken his head. "I don't know that, Nellie. Your mum and me, we never knew that. And it never mattered to us."

She'd tried not to let it matter to her, either, but the truth was it did. Things had changed, and she could no longer meet her father's eyes. It wasn't that she loved him any less, only that the easiness had disappeared. The affection she had for him, invisible, unquestioned in the past, had gained a weight, a voice. It whispered when she looked at him, "You're not really his." She couldn't believe, no matter how vehemently he insisted, that he loved her as he said, as much as he loved her sisters.

"Course I do," he'd said when she asked him. His eyes revealed his astonishment, his hurt. He took out his handkerchief and wiped it across his mouth. "I knew you first, Nellie, I've loved you longest."

But it wasn't enough. She was a lie, had been living a lie, and she refused to do so any longer.

Over the course of a few months, a life that had been twenty-one years in the making was systematically dismantled. She left her job at Mr. Fitzsimmons's news agency and found a new one as an usherette at the Plaza Theatre. She packed her clothes into two small cases and arranged to share a flat with the girlfriend of a girlfriend. And she broke off her engagement to Danny. Not right away; she'd lacked the courage then to make a clean break. She'd let it fall apart for months, refused to see him much of the time, behaved unpleasantly when she did consent to meet. Her cowardice had made her hate herself more, a reassuring self-hatred that confirmed her suspicion that she deserved all that was happening.

It took a long time to get over, splitting up with Danny. His knockabout face, the honest eyes and easy smile. He'd wanted to know why, of course, but she couldn't bring herself to say. There were no words to tell him that the woman he loved, whom he hoped to marry, no longer existed. How could she expect him to value her, still to want her, once he realized she was someone disposable? That her own true family had discarded her?

The taxi turned into Albion and sped east towards the airport. "Where you headed, then?" the driver asked, eyes meeting Nell's in the rearview mirror.

"London."

"Family there?"

Nell looked out of the smeary car window. "Yes," she said. Hopefully.

She hadn't told Lesley she was going, either. She'd thought about it, imagined herself picking up the telephone and dialing her daughter's number—the most recent in a line that snaked down her index file and curled into the margin—but each time she'd dismissed the idea. In all likelihood she'd be home before Lesley even realized she was gone.

Nell didn't need to wonder where the problems with Lesley had started, she knew well enough. They'd got off on the wrong foot and never found the right one. The birth had been a shock, the violent arrival of the screaming, bawling parcel of life, all limbs and gums and panicked fingers.

Night after night Nell had lain awake in the American hospital, waiting to feel the connection people spoke of. To know that she was powerfully and absolutely tied to this little person she'd grown inside her. But the feeling had never come. No matter how hard she tried, how much she willed it, Nell remained isolated from the fierce little wildcat who sucked and tore and scratched at her breasts, always wanting more than she could give.

Al, on the other hand, had been smitten. Smote. He hadn't seemed to notice that the baby was a holy terror. Unlike most men of his generation, he was delighted to hold his daughter, to nestle her in the crook of his arm and take her walking with him down the wide Chicago streets. Sometimes Nell would watch, bland smile plastered on her face, as he gazed, love-stung, at his baby girl. He'd look up and, in his misted eyes, Nell would see reflected her own emptiness.

Lesley had been born with a vein of wildness running through her, but Al's death in 1961 ruptured it. Even as Nell broke the news, she'd seen the film of jaded dissolution settle in her daughter's eyes. Over the next few months, Lesley, always something of a mystery to Nell, withdrew further into her cocoon of adolescent certainty that she despised her mother and wanted nothing more to do with her.

Understandable, of course, if not acceptable—she was fourteen, an impressionable age, and her father had been the apple of her eye. The move back to Australia hadn't helped, but that was retrospect talking. Nell knew better than to allow exhibits of hindsight into the court of self-blame. She'd done what seemed best at the time: she wasn't an American, Al's ma had died a few years earlier and for all intents and purposes they were alone. Strangers in a strange land.

When Lesley left home at seventeen, hitched her way over Australia's east hip and down its thigh to Sydney, Nell'd been happy enough to let her go. With Lesley out of the house, she figured she might finally get rid of the black dog that'd sat on her back for the past seventeen years, whispering that of course she was a terrible mother, of course her daughter couldn't stand her, it was in the blood, she hadn't deserved children in the first place. No matter how warm Lil had been, Nell came from a tradition of bad mothers, the sort who could abandon their children with ease.

And it hadn't turned out so badly. Twelve years later and Lesley was closer to home now, living on the Gold Coast with her latest fellow and her own daughter, Cassandra. Nell'd only met the girl a couple of times. Lord knew who the father was; Nell refrained from asking. Whatever the case, he must've had some sense about him, for the granddaughter showed little of the mother's wildness. Quite the opposite. Cassandra was a child whose soul seemed aged before her time. Quiet, patient, thoughtful, loyal to Lesley—a beautiful child, really. There was an underlying seriousness, somber blue eyes whose edges turned down and a pretty mouth that Nell suspected might be glorious if she ever smiled with unwary joy.

The Black and White taxi came to a halt outside the Qantas doors, and as Nell handed the driver his fare she pushed all thought of Lesley and Cassandra aside.

She'd spent enough of her life waylaid by regret, drowning in untruths and uncertainty. Now was the time for answers, to find out who she was. She hopped out and glanced skywards as a rumbling plane flew low overhead.

"Have a good trip, love," said the taxi driver, carrying Nell's suitcase to a waiting cart.

"Yes, I will."

And she would; answers were finally within reach. After a lifetime of being a shadow, she was to become flesh and blood.

THE LITTLE white suitcase had been the key, or rather its contents had. The book of fairy tales published in London in 1913, the picture on its frontispiece. Nell had recognized the storyteller's face immediately. Some deep and ancient part of her brain provided the names before her conscious mind caught up, names she had thought belonged only to a childhood game. The lady. The Authoress. Not only did she now know the lady was real, she also knew her name. Eliza Makepeace.

Her first thought, naturally enough, was that this Eliza Makepeace was her mother. When she'd made inquiries at the library, she had clenched her fists as she waited, hoping the librarian would discover that Eliza Makepeace had lost a child, spent her life searching for a missing daughter. But it was, of course, too simple an explanation. The librarian had found very little on Eliza, but enough to know the writer going by that name had been childless.

The passenger lists had offered little more elucidation. Nell had checked every ship that left London for Maryborough in late 1913 but the name Eliza Makepeace appeared on none of them. There was a chance Eliza had written under a nom de plume, of course, and had booked passage under her real name, or even an invented one, but

Hugh hadn't told Nell which ship she'd arrived on, and without that knowledge there was no way of narrowing the list of possibilities.

Nonetheless, Nell was undeterred. Eliza Makepeace was important, had played some role in her past. She *remembered* Eliza. Not clearly, they were old memories and long repressed, but they were real. Being on a boat. Waiting. Hiding. Playing. And she was beginning to recall other things, too. It was as if remembering the Authoress had lifted some sort of lid. Jagged memories began to appear: a maze, an old woman who frightened her, a long journey across the water. Through Eliza, she knew, she would find herself, and to find Eliza she needed to go to London.

Thank God she'd had the money to afford the flight. Thank her father, really, for he'd had more to do with it than God. Inside the white suitcase, alongside the book of fairy tales, the hairbrush, the little girl's dress, Nell had found a letter from Hugh, tied up with a photograph and a check. Not a fortune—he hadn't been a wealthy man—but enough to make a difference. In his letter he'd said he wanted her to have a little something extra, hadn't wanted the other girls to know. He'd helped them out financially during his life but Nell had always refused assistance. This way, he figured, she couldn't say no.

Then he'd apologized, written that he hoped someday she might forgive him, even if he'd never been able to forgive himself. It might please her to know he'd never got over his guilt, that it had crippled him. He'd spent his life wishing he'd never told her and if he'd been a braver man he'd have wished he hadn't kept her. To wish that would be to wish Nell out of his life, though, and he preferred to keep his guilt than give her up.

The photograph was one she'd seen before, though not for a long time. It was black-and-white—more rightly brown and white—taken decades ago. Hugh, Lil and Nell, before the sisters came along and stretched their family with laughter and loud voices and girlish shrieks. It was one of those studio shots where the frame's inhabitants look a

little startled. Like they've been plucked from real life, made miniature, then repositioned inside a doll's house full of unfamiliar props.
Looking at it, Nell had the surest feeling that she could remember it
being taken. She couldn't recall much from her childhood, but she sure
as hell remembered the instant dislike she'd taken to that studio, the
chemical smell of the developing fluids. She'd put the photo aside then
and picked up her father's letter again.

No matter how many times she read it, she found herself wondering at his choice of words: "his guilt." She supposed he meant he
was guilty for having thrown her life into disarray with his confession,
and yet the word sat uneasily. Sorry, perhaps, regretful, but guilty? It
seemed an odd choice. For no matter how much Nell wished it hadn't
happened, no matter that she'd found it impossible to continue on in a
life she knew was false, she had never thought her parents culpable.
After all, they'd only done what they thought best, what *was* best.
They'd given her a home and love when she'd been without. That her
father had thought himself guilty, had imagined that *she* might think
him so, was disquieting. And yet it was too late now to ask him what
he meant.

NINE

NELL had been with them six months when the letter arrived at the port office. A man in London was looking for a little girl, four years of age. Hair: red. Eyes: blue. She'd been missing near on eight months and the fellow—Henry Mansell, said the letter—had reason to believe she'd been boarded on a ship, possibly a transport headed for Australia. He was seeking her on behalf of his clients, the child's family.

Standing by his desk, Hugh felt his knees buckle, his muscles liquefy. The moment he'd been dreading—had surely always known was coming—was upon him. For despite what Lil believed, children, especially children like Nell, didn't go missing without someone raising the alarm. He sat in his chair, concentrated on breathing, looked quickly at the windows. He felt suddenly conspicuous, as if he were being watched by an unseen foe.

He ran a hand over his face, then rested it across his neck. What the hell was he going to do? It was only a matter of time before the other fellows arrived on the job and saw the letter. And although it was true he was the only one who'd seen Nell waiting alone on the wharf, that wouldn't keep them safe for long. Word would get out in the town—it always did—and someone would put two and two together. Would realize that the little girl staying with the O'Connors on Queen Street, the one with the unusual way of speaking, sounded an awful lot like the little English girl who was missing.

No, he couldn't risk anyone reading the contents. Hugh observed himself, his hand shaking a little. He folded the letter neatly in half, then in half again, and put it inside his coat pocket. That'd take care of it for now.

He sat down. There, he felt better already. He just needed time and space to think, to work out how he was going to convince Lil that the time had come to give Nell back. Plans for the move to Brisbane were already well under way. Lil had given word to the landlord that they'd be vacating, she'd started packing their possessions, such as they were, had put word around town that there were opportunities for Hugh in Brisbane that they'd be fools to pass up.

But plans could be canceled, would have to be canceled. For now that they knew there was someone looking for Nell, well, that changed things, didn't it?

He knew what Lil would say to that: they didn't deserve Nell, these people, this man, Henry Mansell, who had lost her. She'd beg him, plead with him, insist they couldn't possibly hand Nell over to someone who could be so careless. But Hugh would make her see that it wasn't a question of choice, that Nell wasn't theirs, had never been theirs, that she belonged to someone else. She wasn't even Nell anymore, her own name was looking for her.

When he climbed the front stairs that afternoon, Hugh stood for a moment, collecting his thoughts. As he breathed the acrid smoke drifting from the chimney, pleasant for having come from the fire that warmed his hearth, some unseen force seemed to lock him into place. He had the vague sense of standing on a threshold, the crossing of which would change everything.

He breathed deeply, pushed open the door and his two girls turned to face him. They were sitting by the fire, Nell on Lil's lap, her long red hair hanging in wet strands as Lil combed it.

"Pa!" said Nell, excitement animating a face already pink with warmth.

Lil smiled at him over the top of the little one's head. The smile that had always been his undoing. Ever since he'd first set eyes on her, coiling the ropes down at her father's boatshed. When was the last time he'd seen that smile? It was before the babies, he knew. The babies of theirs that refused to be born right.

Hugh met Lil's smile, then set down his bag, reached inside his pocket where the letter was burning its hole, felt its smoothness beneath his fingertips. He turned towards the range where the biggest pot was steaming. "Dinner smells good." Blasted frog in his throat.

"My ma's morgy broth," said Lil, picking at the tangles in Nell's hair. "You coming down with something?"

"What's that?"

"I'll make you up some lemon and barley."

"Only a tickle," said Hugh. "No need for bother."

"No bother. Not for you." She smiled at him again and patted Nell's shoulders. "There, now, little one, Ma's got to jump up now and check on the tea. You sit here until your hair dries. Don't want you catching a chill like your pa here." She glanced at Hugh as she spoke, eyes loaded with a contentment that poked at his heart so that he had to turn away.

ALL THROUGH dinner the letter sat heavy in Hugh's pocket, refusing to be forgotten. Like metal to a magnet, his hand was drawn. He couldn't put his knife down to rest without his fingers slipping into his coat, rubbing against the smooth paper, death sentence to their happiness. The letter from a man who knew Nell's family. Well, at least that's what he said—

Hugh straightened suddenly, wondering at the way he'd immediately accepted this stranger's claims. He thought again of the letter's contents, pulled the lines from his memory and scanned them through for evidence. The flood of cool relief was instant. There was nothing, nothing in the letter that suggested for certain it was truth. There were any number of queer people out there engaged in all kinds of complicated schemes. There was a market for little girls in some countries, he knew that, white slavers were always on the lookout for little girls to sell—

But it was ridiculous. Even as he clutched desperately at such possibilities he knew how unlikely they were.

"Hughie?"

He looked up quickly. Lil was watching him in a funny way.

"You were away with the fairies." She laid a warm palm against his forehead. "Hope you're not coming down with a fever."

"I'm fine." Sharper than he intended. "I'm fine, Lil love."

She pressed her lips together. "I was just saying. I'm going to take this little lady in to bed. She's had a big day, all tuckered out."

As if on cue, Nell surrendered to a huge yawn.

"Good night, Pa," she said contentedly when the yawn was done with. Before he knew it she was in his lap, curled into him like a warm kitten, arms snaked around his neck. He was aware as never before of the roughness of his skin, the whiskers on his cheeks. He folded his arms around her birdlike back and closed his eyes.

"Good night, Nellie love," he whispered into her hair.

He watched them disappear then, into the other room. His family. For in some way that he couldn't explain, even to himself, this child, their Nell, with her two long plaits, lent a solidity to him and Lil. They were a family now, an unbreakable unit of three, not just two souls who'd decided to put their lot in together.

And here he was, considering breaking it apart—

A sound in the hall and he looked up. Lil, framed beneath the wooden fretwork, watching him. Some trick of the light drew red from her dark hair and planted a glow deep within her eyes, black moons beneath their long lashes. A thread of feeling tugged at the corner where her lips met, pulling her mouth into the sort of smile that described an emotion too powerful to be expressed verbally.

Hugh smiled back tentatively and his fingers slipped once more into his pocket, ran silently across the surface of the letter. His lips parted with a soft click, tingled with the words he didn't want to speak but wasn't sure he could stop.

Lil was by his side then. Her fingers on his wrist sent hot shocks to his neck, her warm hand on his cheek. "Come to bed."

Ah, were there ever words as sweet as those? Her voice contained a promise and—like that—his mind was made up.

He slipped his hand into hers, held it firm and followed as she led.

As he passed the fireplace he tossed the paper on top. It sizzled as it caught, burned a brief reproach on his peripheral vision. But he didn't stop, he just kept walking and never looked back.

TEN

❧

LONG before it was an antique center, it had been a theatre. The Plaza Theatre, a grand experiment in the 1930s. Plain from the outside, a huge white box cut into the Paddington hillside, its interior was another story. The vaulted ceiling, midnight blue with cutout clouds, had been backlit originally to create the illusion of moonlight, while hundreds of tiny lights twinkled like stars. It had done a roaring trade for decades, back in the days when trams had rattled along the terrace and Chinese gardens had flourished in the valleys, but though it had prevailed against such fierce adversaries as fire and flood, it had fallen victim softly and swiftly to television in the 1960s.

Nell and Cassandra's stall was directly below the proscenium arch, stage left. A rabbit warren of shelves obscured by countless pieces of bric-a-brac, odds and ends, old books and an eclectic assortment of memorabilia. Long ago the other dealers had started calling it Aladdin's as a joke and the name had stuck. A small wooden sign with gold lettering now proclaimed the area *Aladdin's Den*.

Sitting on a three-legged stool, deep within the maze of shelves, Cassandra was finding it difficult to concentrate. It was the first time she'd been inside the center since Nell's death and it felt strange to sit among the treasures they'd assembled together. Odd that the stock should still be here when Nell was gone. Disloyal of it, somehow. Spoons that Nell had polished, price tickets with her indecipherable spider's-web scrawl across them, books and more books. They'd been Nell's weakness, every dealer had one. In particular, she loved books

74

written at the end of the nineteenth century. Late Victorian with glorious printed texts and black-and-white illustrations. If a book bore a message from giver to recipient, so much the better. A record of its past, a hint as to the hands it had passed through in order to make its way to her.

"Morning."

Cassandra looked up to see Ben holding out a takeout coffee.

"Sorting stock?" he said.

She brushed a few fine strands of hair from her eyes and took the proffered drink. "Moving things from here to there. Back again most times."

Ben took a sip of his own coffee, eyed her over his cup. "I've got something for you." He reached beneath his knitted vest to withdraw a folded piece of paper from his shirt pocket.

Cassandra opened the page and flattened out its creases. Printer paper, white, a patchy black-and-white picture of a house at the center. A cottage, really, stone from what she could make out, with blotches—creepers perhaps?—across the walls. The roof was tiled, a stone chimney visible behind the peak. Two pots balanced precariously at its top.

She knew what this house was, of course, didn't need to ask.

"Been having a bit of a dig," said Ben. "Couldn't help myself. My daughter in London managed to make contact with someone in Cornwall and sent me this photo over the e-mail."

So this was what it looked like, Nell's big secret. The house she'd bought on a whim and kept to herself all this time. Strange, the picture's effect on her. Cassandra had left the deed on the kitchen table all weekend, had looked at it each time she walked past, thought of little else, but seeing this picture was the first time it had felt real. Everything came into sharp focus: Nell, who went to her grave not knowing who she really was, had bought a house in England and left it to Cassandra, had thought she'd understand why.

"Ruby's always had a knack for finding things out, so I set her to chasing up information about past owners. I thought if we knew who your grandma bought the house from, it might shed a little light on why." Ben pulled a small spiral notebook from his breast pocket and angled his glasses to best observe the page. "Do the names Richard and Julia Bennett mean anything to you?"

Cassandra shook her head, still looking at the picture.

"According to Ruby, Nell bought the property from Mr. and Mrs. Bennett, who themselves bought it in 1971. They bought the nearby manor house, too; turned it into a hotel. The Blackhurst Hotel." He looked at Cassandra hopefully.

Again she shook her head.

"You sure?"

"Never heard of it."

"Ah," said Ben, shoulders seeming to deflate. "Ah, well, then." He flicked the notebook shut and leaned his arm on the nearest bookcase. "I'm afraid that's the extent of my sleuthing. Long shot, I suppose." He scratched his beard. "Typical of Nell to leave a mystery like this. It's the darnedest thing, isn't it, a secret house in England?"

Cassandra smiled. "Thanks for the picture, and thank your daughter for me."

"You can thank her yourself when you're over on that side of the pond." He shook his takeout cup, then eyed the sipping hole to check that it was empty. "When do you think you'll go?"

Cassandra's eyes widened. "You mean to England?"

"A picture's all well and good, but it's not the same as really seeing a place, is it?"

"You think I should go to England?"

"Why not? Twenty-first century, you could be there and back inside a week, and you'll have a much better idea of what you want to do with the cottage."

Despite the deed lying plain on her table, Cassandra had been so preoccupied with the theoretical fact of Nell's cottage, she'd completely failed to consider it in practical terms: there was a cottage in England waiting for her. She scuffed at the dull wooden floor, then peered through her fringe at Ben. "I guess I should sell it."

"Big decision to make without setting foot inside." Ben tossed his cup into the overflowing trash bin by the cedar desk. "Wouldn't hurt to take a look, eh? It obviously meant a lot to Nell, to have kept it all this time."

Cassandra considered this. Fly to England, by herself, out of the blue. "But the stall . . ."

"Pah! Center staff'll take care of your sales, and I'll be here." He indicated the laden shelves. "You've got enough stock to last through the next decade." His voice softened. "Why not go, Cass? It wouldn't hurt to get away for a bit. Ruby's living in a shoebox in South Kensington, working at the V&A. She'll show you around, look after you."

Look after her: people were always offering to look after Cassandra. Once, a lifetime ago, she'd been a grown-up with her own responsibilities, had looked after others.

"And what have you got to lose?"

Nothing, she had nothing to lose, no one to lose. Cassandra was suddenly weary of the topic. She hoisted a slight, yielding smile and added an "I'll think about it" for good measure.

"There's a girl." He patted her shoulder and made to leave. "Oh, almost forgot, I did turn up another interesting little titbit. Sheds no light on Nell and her house, but it's a funny coincidence all the same, what with your art background, all those drawings you used to do."

To hear years of one's life, one's passion, described so casually, relegated so absolutely to the past, was breathtaking. Cassandra managed to keep a weak smile afloat.

"The estate that Nell's house is on used to be owned by the Mountrachet family."

The name meant nothing and Cassandra shook her head.

He raised an eyebrow. "The daughter, Rose, married a certain Nathaniel Walker."

Cassandra frowned. "An artist . . . An American?"

"That's the one, portraits mostly, you know the sort of thing. Lady So-and-So and her six favorite poodles. According to my daughter, he even did one of King Edward in 1910, just before he died. Pinnacle of Walker's career, I'd say, though Ruby seemed unimpressed. She said his portraits weren't his best work, that they were a bit lifeless."

"It's been a while since I . . ."

"She preferred his sketches. That's Ruby, though, always happiest when she's swimming against the current of popular opinion."

"Sketches?"

"Illustrations, magazine pictures, black-and-white."

Cassandra inhaled sharply. "The Maze and Fox drawings."

Ben lifted his shoulders and shook his head.

"Oh, Ben, they were incredible, *are* incredible, amazingly detailed." It had been so long since she'd thought about art history; it surprised her, this surge of ownership.

"Nathaniel Walker came up briefly in a class I took on Aubrey Beardsley and his contemporaries," she said. "He was controversial, but I can't recall why."

"That's what Ruby said. You're going to get on well with her. When I mentioned him she was very excited. She said they have a few of his illustrations in the new exhibition at the V&A. Evidently they're very rare."

"He didn't do many," said Cassandra, remembering now. "I suppose he was too busy with the portraits, the illustrations were more of a hobby. All the same, those he did were very well regarded." She started. "I think we might have one of them here, in one of Nell's books." She climbed onto an upturned milk crate and ran her index finger along the top shelf, stopped when she reached a burgundy spine with faded gold lettering.

She opened it, still standing on the crate, and flicked carefully through the color plates in the front. "Here it is." Without taking her eyes from the page, she stepped down. *The Fox's Lament.*

Ben came to stand by her, adjusted his glasses away from the light. "Intricate, isn't it? Not my cup of tea, but that's art for you. I can see what you admire about it."

"It's beautiful and somehow sad."

He leaned closer. "Sad?"

"Full of melancholy, yearning. I can't explain better than that, something in the fox's face, some sort of absence." She shook her head. "I can't explain."

Ben gave her arm a squeeze, murmured something about bringing her a sandwich at lunchtime and then he was gone. Shuffling in the direction of his stall, more particularly the customer at his stall who was juggling the pieces of a Waterford chandelier.

Cassandra continued to study the picture, wondering how it was she felt so sure about the fox's sorrow. That was the artist's skill, of course, the ability through precise positioning of thin black lines to evoke so clearly such complex emotions . . .

Her lips tightened. The sketch reminded her of the day she'd found the book of fairy tales, when she'd been filling time beneath Nell's house as upstairs her mother prepared to leave her. Looking back, Cassandra realized she could trace her love of art to that book. She'd opened the front cover and fallen inside the wonderful, frightening, magical illustrations. She'd wondered what it must feel like to escape the rigid boundaries of words and speak instead with such a fluid language.

And for a time, as she grew older, she had known: the alchemical pull of the pen, the blissful sensation of time losing meaning as she conjured at her drawing board. Her love of art had led her to study in Melbourne, had led her to marry Nicholas, and to everything else that had followed. Strange to think that life might have been completely different had she never seen the suitcase, had she not felt the curious compulsion to open it and look inside—

Cassandra gasped. Why hadn't she thought of it before? Suddenly she knew exactly what she had to do, where she had to look. The one place where she might uncover the necessary clues to Nell's mysterious origins.

THAT NELL might have rid herself of the suitcase occurred to Cassandra, but she pushed the notion aside with some certainty. For one thing, her grandmother was an antiques dealer, a collector, a bowerbird of the human species. It would have been completely out of character for her to destroy or discard something old and rare.

More importantly, if what the aunts had said was true, the suitcase wasn't a mere historical artefact: it was an anchor. It was all Nell had that linked her to her past. Cassandra understood the importance of anchors, knew all too well what happened to a person when the rope that tied them to their life was cut. She had lost her own anchor twice. The first time as a ten-year-old when Lesley had left her, the second as a young woman (was it really a decade ago?) when, in a split second, life as she knew it had changed and she'd been cast adrift once more.

Later, when she looked back upon events, Cassandra knew it was the suitcase that found her, just as it had done the first time.

After a night spent combing through Nell's cluttered spare rooms, becoming distracted, despite her best intentions, by this memento or that, she'd grown incredibly weary. Not just bone tired, but brain tired. The weekend had taken its toll. It came over her quickly and profoundly, the weariness of fairy tales, a magical desire to surrender herself to sleep.

Rather than go downstairs to her own room, she curled up beneath Nell's bedspread, still in her clothes, and let her head sink into the downy pillow. The smell was breathtakingly familiar—lavender talcum powder, silver polish, Palmolive laundry flakes—and she felt as if she were resting her head on Nell's chest.

She slept like the dead, dark and dreamless. And the next morning, when she woke, she had the sense of having been asleep far longer than one night.

The sun was streaming into the room, through the gap between the curtains—like the light from a lighthouse—and she watched, as she lay there, the pieces of dust, hovering. She could have reached out and caught them on her fingertips, but she didn't. Instead, she allowed her gaze to follow the beam, turning her head towards the spot at which it pointed. The spot high up on the wardrobe, where the doors had come apart in the night, to reveal, on the top shelf, beneath a clump of plastic bags full of clothes for St. Vinnie's, an old white suitcase.

ELEVEN

THE INDIAN OCEAN, NINE HUNDRED MILES
BEYOND THE CAPE OF GOOD HOPE, 1913

IT took a long time to get to America. In the tales Papa had told her, he'd said it was further than Arabia, and the little girl knew it took a hundred days and nights to get there. The little girl had lost count of the days, but it had been quite some time since she'd boarded the boat. So long, in fact, that she'd grown used to the sensation of never ceasing to move. Getting sea legs, it was called; she had learned all about it in tales of Moby Dick.

Thinking of Moby Dick made the little girl very sad. It reminded her of Papa, the stories he read to her of the great whale, the pictures he let her look at in his studio, pictures he'd drawn of dark oceans and great ships. They were called illustrations, the little girl knew, enjoying the length of the word as she said it in her mind, and one day they might be put in a book, a real book that other children would read. For that's what her papa did, he put pictures into storybooks. Or he had on one occasion. He drew paintings of people, too, but the little girl didn't like those, the eyes that followed a person across the room.

The little girl's bottom lip began to tremble the way it sometimes did when she thought of Papa and Mamma, and she bit down on it. In the beginning she had cried a lot. She hadn't been able to help it; she'd missed her parents. But she didn't cry much anymore, and never in front of the other children. They might think she was too little to play with them and then where would she be? Besides, Mamma and Papa would be with her soon. They would be waiting for her, she knew, when the boat arrived in America. Would the Authoress be there, too?

The little girl frowned. In all the time it had taken to find her sea legs, the Authoress had not returned. This puzzled the little girl, for the Authoress had given many stern instructions as to how they were to stay together always, avoid separation no matter what. Perhaps she was hiding. Perhaps it was all part of the game.

The little girl wasn't sure. She was just thankful that she'd met Will and Sally on the deck that first morning, otherwise she wasn't sure she'd have known where to sleep, how to get food. Will and Sally and their brothers and sisters—they had so many, the little girl had a hard time keeping count—knew all about finding food. They'd shown her all kinds of places on the boat where an extra serving of salt beef might be found. (She didn't much like the taste, but the little boy only laughed and said it might not be what she was used to but it did for a dog's life.) They were kind to her, for the most part. The only time they became cross was when she refused to tell them her name. But the little girl knew how to play games, how to follow the rules, and the Authoress had told her that was the most important rule of all.

Will's family had a set of bunks down on the lower decks, with lots of other men, women and children, more people than the little girl had ever seen gathered together in one place. They had a mother traveling with them, too, though they called her "Ma." She wasn't at all like the little girl's own mother; she didn't have Mamma's pretty face and lovely dark hair set up on the top of her head by Poppy each morning. "Ma" was more like the women the little girl had sometimes seen when the carriage passed through the village, with tattered skirts and boots that needed mending, and lined hands like the pair of old gloves Davies wore in the garden.

When Will had first taken the little girl downstairs, Ma had been sitting on the bottom bunk, nursing one baby while another lay crying beside her.

"Who's this, then?" she'd said.

"She won't say 'er name. Says she's waiting for someone, that she's meant to be hiding."

"Hiding, eh?" The woman beckoned the little girl closer. "What you hiding from, then, child?"

But the little girl wouldn't say, just shook her head.

"Where are her folks?"

"I don't think she's got none," said Will. "Not so as I can figure. She was hiding when I found her."

"That right, child? You alone?"

The little girl considered this question and decided it was better to agree than to speak of the Authoress. She nodded.

"Well, well, then. Little thing like you, all alone on the seas." Ma shook her head and jostled the crying baby. "That your case? Bring it here, then, and let Ma take a little look-see."

The little girl watched as Ma unhooked the latches and lifted the top. Pushed aside the book of fairy tales and the second new dress to reveal the envelope below. Ma slid her finger beneath the seal and opened it. Plucked a small pile of paper from within.

Will's eyes widened. "Banknotes." He glanced towards the little girl. "What should we do with her, Ma? Tell the porter?"

Ma stuffed the banknotes back inside the envelope, folded it into thirds, and tucked it down the front of her dress. "Not much point telling anyone on board," she said finally, "not that I can see. She'll stay with us till we get to the other side of the world, then we'll find out who's waiting for her. See how they'd like to thank us for our troubles." She'd smiled then, and dark spaces had appeared between her teeth.

The little girl didn't have much to do with Ma, and for that she was glad. Ma was kept busy with the babies, one of whom seemed always to be attached to her front. They were suckling, or so Will said, though the little girl had never heard of such a thing. Not in people, anyway; she'd seen the baby animals suckling on the estate farms. Those babies were like a pair of little piglets, doing little else but squealing and drinking and fattening. And while the babies kept their ma busy, the others looked out for themselves. They were used to it, Will told her, for they had to do so at home. They came from a place called Bolton and when there were no babies to tend their mother worked in a cotton factory, all the day long. That's why she coughed so much. The little girl understood: her mother was also unwell, though she didn't cough the way Ma did.

In the evenings there was a spot where the little girl and the others would sit, listening to the music coming from above and the sound of feet sliding across shiny floors. That's what they were doing now, sitting in a darkened nook listening. In the beginning, the little girl had wanted to go and see, but the other children had only laughed and said the upper decks weren't for the likes of them. That this space at the bottom of the crew ladder was as close as they were likely to get to the toffs' deck.

The little girl had been silent; she'd never come across rules like those before. At home, with one exception, she was allowed to go where she pleased. The only place she was forbidden was the maze that led to the Authoress's cottage. But this wasn't the same and she'd found it difficult to understand what the boy meant. The likes of them? Children? Perhaps the upper deck was a place where children were not allowed.

Not that she wanted to go up there tonight. She felt tired, had felt that way for days. The sort of weariness that made her legs seem as heavy as forest logs and doubled the height of the stairs. She was dizzy, too, and her breath was hot when it passed her lips.

"Come on," said Will, tiring of the music. "Let's go look for land."

A scramble and they were all on their feet. The little girl pulled herself up and tried to catch her balance. Will and Sally and the others were talking, laughing, their voices swirling around her. She tried to make sense of what they were saying, felt her legs shivering, her ears ringing.

Will's face was suddenly close to hers, his voice loud. "What's the matter? Are you all right?"

She opened her mouth to answer, and as she did so her knees buckled and she began to fall. The last thing she saw before her head hit the wooden step was the bright, full moon, shimmering in the sky above.

THE LITTLE girl opened her eyes. A man was standing above her, serious-looking, with bumpy cheeks and gray eyes. His expression remained unchanged as he moved closer and plucked a small flat paddle from his shirt pocket. "Open."

Before she knew what was happening, the paddle was on her tongue and he was inspecting her mouth.

"Yes," he said. "Fine." He withdrew the paddle and straightened his waistcoat. "Breathe."

She did so and he nodded. "She's fine," he said again. He signaled to a younger man with straw-colored hair whom the little girl recognized from when she'd woken earlier. "There's a live one here. For God's sake get her out of the sickbay before that changes."

"But, sir," said the other man, puffing, "this is the one what hit her head when she fainted. Surely she should rest a bit—"

"We don't have sufficient beds for resting, she can rest when she's back in her cabin."

"I'm not sure where she belongs."

The doctor rolled his eyes. "Then ask her, man."

The straw-haired fellow lowered his voice. "Sir, she's the one I was telling you about. Seems to have lost her memory. Must've happened when she fell."

The doctor peered down at the little girl. "What's your name?"

The little girl thought about this. She heard his words, understood what he was asking of her, but found she couldn't answer.

"Well?" said the man.

The little girl shook her head. "I don't know."

The doctor sighed, exasperated. "I don't have the time or the bed space for this. Her fever's gone. By the smell of her she's from steerage."

"Aye, sir."

"Well? There must be someone there who'll claim her."

"Aye, sir, there's a lad outside, the one what brought her in the other day. Come to check on her just this minute, a brother, I should say."

The doctor peered around the door to look down at the boy. "Where are the parents?"

"The lad says his father's in Australia, sir."

"And the mother?"

The other man cleared his throat, leaned closer to the doctor. "Giving the fishes a feed somewhere near the Cape of Good Hope, most likely, sir. Lost her leaving port three days ago."

"Fever?"

"Aye."

The doctor furrowed his brow and sighed shortly. "Well, bring him in, then."

A young boy, skinny as a sapling, eyes as black as coal, was hoisted before him. "This girl belongs to you?" said the doctor.

"Yes, sir," said the boy. "That is, she—"

"Enough, I don't need life stories. Her fever's gone and the bump on her head's healed. She's not saying much at this point but no doubt she'll pipe up soon enough. It's most likely attention-seeking, knowing what happened to your mother. That's how it is sometimes, especially with children."

"But, sir—"

"That's enough. Take her away." He turned to the crewman. "Give the bed to someone else."

THE LITTLE girl was sitting by the rails, watching the water. White-tipped peaks of blue, rippling beneath the wind's touch. The way was choppier than usual and she surrendered her body to the rolling motion. She felt odd, not ill exactly, just strange. As if a fine white mist had filled her head and settled, refusing to drift away.

It had been that way since she'd woken up in the sickbay, since the strange men had looked her over and sent her off with the boy. He'd taken her downstairs to a dark place full of bunks and mattresses and more people than she'd ever seen before.

" 'Ere." A voice at her shoulder. It was the boy. "Don't forget your case, then."

"My case?" The little girl glanced at the proffered piece of white leather luggage.

"Cor!" said the boy, looking at her strangely. "You really have gone bonkers, I thought you was just pretending for that doctor fellow's sake. Don't tell me you don't even remember your own case? You've been guarding it with your life the whole trip, just about tore us apart if any of us so much as looked at it. Didn't want to upset your precious Authoress."

The strange word rustled between them and the little girl felt an odd prickling beneath her skin. "Authoress?" she said.

But the boy didn't answer. "Land!" he called out, running to lean against the rails that ran around the deck. "There's land! Can you see it?"

The little girl came to stand by him, still clutching the handle of the small white suitcase. She glanced warily at his freckled nose, then turned to look in the direction of his pointed finger. Far in the distance she saw a strip of land, trees of palest green all the way along it.

"That's Australia," said the boy, eyes trained on the distant shore. "My pa's there waiting for us."

Australia, the little girl thought. Another word she didn't recognize.

"We're going to have a new life there, with our own house and everything, even a bit of land. That's what my pa says in his letters. He says we're going to work the land, build a new life for ourselves. And we will, too, even if Ma ain't with us no more." The last he said in a quieter voice. He fell silent for a moment before turning to the little girl and cocking his head towards the shore. "Is that where your pa is?"

The little girl thought about this. "My pa?"

The boy rolled his eyes. "Your dad," he said. "Fellow what belongs with your ma. You know, your pa."

"My pa," the little girl echoed, but the boy was no longer listening. He'd caught sight of one of his sisters and was running off, shouting about land being sighted.

The little girl nodded as he left, though she still wasn't sure what he meant. "My pa," she said uncertainly. "That's where my pa is."

The cry of "Land!" went around the deck and as people became busy all about her the little girl took the white suitcase to a spot by a pile of barrels, a nook to which she was unaccountably drawn. She sat down and opened the case, hoping to find some food. There was none, so she settled instead for the book of fairy tales lying on top of the other contents.

As the boat drew nearer to shore, and tiny dots in the distance became seagulls, she opened the book across her lap and gazed at the beautiful black-and-white sketch of a woman and a deer side by side in the clearing of a thorny forest. And somehow, though she could not read the words, the little girl realized that she knew this picture's tale. Of a young princess who traveled a great distance across the sea to find a precious, hidden item belonging to someone she dearly loved.

TWELVE

CASSANDRA leaned against the cold, rough plastic of the cabin and looked through the window, down to the vast blue ocean that covered the globe for as far as the eye could see. The very same ocean little Nell had traversed all those years before.

It was the first time Cassandra had been overseas. That is, she'd been to New Zealand once, and had visited Nick's family in Tasmania before they were married, but never further afield. She and Nick had talked about taking off to the UK for a few years: Nick would write music for British TV and there had to be plenty of work for art historians in Europe. But they hadn't made it and she'd buried the dream long ago, beneath the pile of others.

And now here she was, aboard a plane, by herself, flying to Europe. After she'd spoken with Ben at the antique center, after he'd given her the picture of the house, after she'd found the suitcase, it turned out there was room for little else in her mind. The mystery seemed to attach itself to her and she couldn't shake it off, even if she tried. To tell the truth, she didn't want to; she liked the constancy of preoccupation. She enjoyed wondering about Nell, this other Nell, the little girl whom she hadn't known.

It was true that even after she'd found the suitcase she hadn't intended to travel directly to the UK. It had seemed far more sensible to wait, to see how she felt in a month's time, maybe plan a trip for later. She couldn't just be jetting off to Cornwall on a whim. But then she'd had the dream, same as she'd been having on and off for a decade. She was standing in the middle of a field with nothing on the horizon in any direction. The dream had no sense of malevolence, just unendingness. Ordinary vegetation, nothing that excited the imagination, pale reedy grass, long enough to brush the ends of her fingers, and a light and constant breeze that kept it rustling.

In the beginning, years ago when the dream was new, she'd known she was looking for someone, that if she were only to walk in the right direction she would find them. But no matter how many times she'd dreamed the scene, she'd never seemed to manage it. One undulating hill would be replaced by another; she'd look away at the wrong moment; she'd suddenly wake up.

Gradually, over time, the dream had changed. So subtly, so slowly, she didn't notice it happening. It wasn't that the setting changed: physically all remained as ever. It was the feeling of the dream. The certainty that she would find what it was she sought just slipped away, until one night she knew there was nothing, no one waiting for her. That no matter how far she walked, how carefully she searched, how much she wanted to find the person she was looking for, she was alone . . .

Next morning the desolation had lingered, but Cassandra was used to its dull hangover and went about her life as usual. There was no sign that the day was to be anything other than ordinary, until she went to the nearby shopping center to buy bread for lunch and wound up pausing by the travel agency. Funny, she'd never really noticed it was there. Without quite knowing how or why, she found herself pushing open the door, standing on the sea-grass matting, a wall of consultants waiting for her to speak.

Cassandra remembered later feeling dull surprise at that point. It seemed she was a real person after all, a solid human being, moving in and out of the orbits of others. No matter that she so often felt herself to be living half a life, to be a half-light.

At home afterwards, she'd stood for a moment, replaying the morning's events, trying to isolate the instant in which her decision had been made. How she'd gone to the shops for bread and come back with an airline ticket. And then she went into Nell's room, pulled the suitcase back down from its hiding spot and took everything from inside. The book of fairy tales, the sketch with *Eliza Makepeace* written on its back, the lined exercise book with Nell's handwriting scrawled across each page.

She made herself a milky coffee and sat up in Nell's bed, doing her best to decipher the god-awful handwriting, transcribing it onto a clean pad of paper. Cassandra was reasonably good at unraveling handwritten notes from previous centuries—it went with the territory for a secondhand dealer—but old-fashioned writing was one thing, it had a pattern to it. Nell's hand was just messy. Purposely, perversely messy. To make matters worse, the notebook had suffered water damage at some point in its history. Pages were stuck together, wrinkled blotches were laced with mold, and to rush was to risk tearing the pages and forever obscuring the entries.

It was slow going, but Cassandra didn't need to go far to realize that Nell had been trying to solve the mystery of her identity.

August 1975. Today they brought me the white suitcase. As soon as I saw it, I knew what it was.

I pretended casualness. Doug and Phyllis don't know the truth and I didn't want them to see that I was shaking. I wanted them to think only that it was an old suitcase of Dad's that he'd wanted me to have. After they'd gone, I sat looking at it for a time, willing myself to remember: who I am, where I am from. It was no use, of course, and so, at length, I opened it.

There was a note from Dad, an apology of sorts, and beneath it other things. A child's dress—mine I suppose—a silver hairbrush and a book of fairy tales. I recognized it immediately. I turned the cover and then I saw her, the Authoress. The words came fully formed. She is the key to my past, I'm sure of it. If I find her, I will finally find myself. For that is what I intend to do. In this notebook I will chart my progress, and by its end, I will know my name and why I lost it.

CASSANDRA TURNED carefully through the moldy pages, filled with suspense. Had Nell done what she set out to do? Found out who she was? Is that why she'd bought the house? The final entry was dated November 1975 and Nell had just arrived home to Brisbane:

I'm going back as soon as I've tied things up here. I'll be sorry to leave my house in Brisbane, and my shop, but what does it compare with finally finding my truth? And I'm so close. I know it. Now that the cottage is mine, I know the final answers will follow. It is my past, my self, and I have nearly found it.

Nell had been planning to leave Australia for good. Why hadn't she? What had happened? Why hadn't she written another entry?

Another look at the date, November 1975, and Cassandra's skin prickled. It was two months before she, Cassandra, had been deposited at Nell's place. Lesley's promised week or two had stretched on indefinitely until it turned into forever.

Cassandra set the notebook aside as realization hardened. Nell had taken up the parental reins without skipping a beat, had stepped in and given Cassandra a home and a family. A mother. And never for an instant had she let Cassandra know of the plans her arrival had interrupted.

CASSANDRA TURNED from the aircraft window and pulled the book of fairy tales from her carry-on, laid it across her lap. She didn't know what had made her so certain that she wanted to bring the book on board with her. It was the bond with Nell, she supposed, for this was the book from the suitcase, the link with Nell's past, one of the few possessions that had accompanied the little girl across the seas to Australia. And it was something about the book itself. It exercised the same compulsion over Cassandra that it had when she was ten years old and had first discovered it downstairs in Nell's flat. The title, the illustrations, even the author's name. Eliza Makepeace. Whispering it now, Cassandra felt the strangest shiver tiptoe along her spine.

As the ocean continued to stretch below, Cassandra turned to the first story and began to read, a story called "The Crone's Eyes," which she recognized from the hot summer's day long ago.

The Crone's Eyes

by Eliza Makepeace

Once in a land that lay far across the shining sea there lived a Princess who didn't know she was a Princess, for when she was but a small child her kingdom had been ransacked and her royal family slain. It so happened that the young Princess had been playing that day outside the castle walls and knew nothing of the attack until night began its fall towards earth and she set aside her game to find her home in ruins. The little Princess wandered alone for a time, until finally she came to a cottage on the edge of a dark wood. As she knocked upon the door, the sky, angered by the destruction it had witnessed, broke apart in rage and spat fierce rain across the land.

Inside the cottage there lived a blind crone, who took pity on the girl and determined to give her shelter and raise her as her own. There was much work to be done in the crone's cottage, but the Princess was never heard to complain, for she was a true Princess with a pure heart. The happiest folk are those that are busy, for their minds are starved of time to seek out woe. Thus did the Princess grow up contented. She came to love the changing seasons and learned the satisfaction of sowing seeds and tending crops. And although she was becoming beautiful, the Princess did not know it, for the crone had neither looking glass nor vanity and thus the Princess had not learned the ways of either.

One night, in the Princess's sixteenth year, she and the crone sat in the kitchen eating their supper. "What happened to your eyes, dear crone?" asked the Princess, who had wondered for a long time.

The crone turned towards the Princess, skin wrinkled where her eyes should be. "My sight was taken from me."

"By whom?"

"When I was but a maiden, my father loved me so much that he removed my eyes so I need never witness death and destruction in the world."

"But, dearest crone, you can no longer witness beauty, either," said the Princess, thinking of the pleasure she gained from watching her garden blossom.

"No," said the crone. "And I would very much like to see you, my Beauty, grow."

"Could we not seek your eyes somewhere?"

The crone smiled sadly. "My eyes were to be returned by a messenger when I attained my sixtieth year, but on the night ordained, my Beauty arrived with a great lashing storm on her heels, and I was unable to meet him."

"Might we find him now?"

The crone shook her head. "The messenger could not wait, and my eyes were taken instead to the deep well in the land of lost things."

"Could we not journey there?"

"Alas," said the crone, "the way is far, and the road paved with danger and deprivation."

By and by, the seasons changed, and the crone became weaker and paler. One day, when the Princess was on her way to pick apples for the winter store, she came upon the crone, sitting in the fork of the apple tree, lamenting. The Princess stopped, startled, for she had never seen the crone upset. As she listened, she realized that the crone was speaking to a solemn grey and white bird with a striped tail. "My eyes, my eyes," she said. "My end approaches and my sight will never be restored. Tell me, wise bird, how will I know my way in the next world if I cannot see myself?"

Quickly and quietly, the Princess returned to the cottage, for she knew what she must do. The crone had sacrificed her eyes to provide the Princess with shelter and now must this kindness be repaid. Although she had never traveled beyond the forest rim, the Princess did not hesitate. Her love for the crone was so fathomless that if all the grains of sand in the ocean should be stacked up end to end, they would not run so deep.

The Princess woke with the first dawn of morning and wandered forth into the forest, stopping not until she reached the shore. There she set sail, crossing the vast sea to the land of lost things.

The way was long and hard, and the Princess was bewildered, for the forest in the land of lost things looked vastly different from that to which she was accustomed. The trees were cruel and jagged, the beasts ghastly, even the birds' songs made the Princess tremble. The more frightened she became, the faster she ran, until finally she stopped, her heart thundering in her chest. The Princess was lost and knew not where to turn. She was about to despair, when the solemn grey and white bird appeared before her. "I am sent by the crone," said the bird, "to lead you safely to the well of lost things, where you will find your fate."

The Princess was much relieved and set off after the bird, her stomach grumbling, for she had been unable to find food in this strange land. By and by, she came upon an old woman sitting on a fallen log. "How fare you, Beauty?" said the old woman.

"I am so hungry," said the Princess, "yet I know not where to seek food."

The old woman pointed to the forest and suddenly the Princess saw that there were berries hanging from the trees, and nuts growing in clusters on the ends of branches.

"Oh, thank you, kind woman," said the Princess.

"I did nothing," said the old woman, "except to open your eyes and show you what you knew was there."

The Princess continued after the bird, more satisfied now, but as they went the weather began to change and the winds grew cold.

By and by, the Princess came upon a second old woman sitting on a tree stump. "How fare you, Beauty?"

"I am so cold, yet I know not where to seek warm clothes."

The old woman pointed to the forest, and suddenly the Princess saw brambles of wild roses with the softest, most delicate petals. She coated herself with them and was much warmer.

"Oh, thank you, kind woman," said the Princess.

"I did nothing," said the old woman, "except to open your eyes and show you what you knew was there."

The Princess continued after the grey and white bird, more satisfied now, and warmer than before, but her feet began to ache, for she had walked so far.

By and by, the Princess came upon a third old woman sitting on a tree stump. "How fare you, Beauty?"

"I am so tired, yet I know not where to seek carriage."

The old woman pointed to the forest, and suddenly, in a clearing, the Princess saw a shiny brown fawn with a gold ring around his neck. The fawn blinked at the Princess, a dark, thoughtful eye, and the Princess, who was kind of heart, held out her hand. The fawn came to her and bowed his head so she might ride upon his back.

"Oh, thank you, kind woman," said the Princess.

"I did nothing," said the woman, "except to open your eyes and show you what you knew was there."

The Princess and the fawn followed the grey and white bird further and further into the dark forest, and as days passed the Princess came to understand the fawn's soft and gentle language. As they spoke, night after night, the Princess learned that the fawn was in hiding from a treacherous hunter sent to kill him by a wicked witch. So grateful was the Princess for the fawn's kindness that she undertook to keep him safe from his tormentors.

Good intentions pave the way to ruin, however, and early next morning the Princess woke to find the fawn absent from his usual place by the fire. In the tree above, the grey and white bird twittered in agitation, and the Princess jumped quickly to her feet, following where the bird led. As she drew deeper into the nearby brambles, she heard the fawn weeping. The Princess hurried to his side and saw there an arrow in his flank.

"The witch hath found me," spoke the fawn. "As I collected nuts for our journey she ordered her archers to shoot me. I ran as far and as fast as I could, but when I reached this spot I could go no further."

The Princess knelt by the fawn and so great was her distress at witnessing his pain that she began to weep over his body, and the truth and light from her tears caused his wound to heal.

Over the next days the Princess tended the fawn, and once his health was restored they continued their journey to the edge of the vast woods. When they broke finally through the rim of trees, the coastline lay before them and the glistening sea beyond.

"Not much further north," said the bird, "stands the well of lost things."

Day had ended and dusk thickened into night, but the shingles of the beach shone like pieces of silver in the moonlight, marking their way. They walked north until finally, at the top of a craggy black rock, could be seen the well of lost things. The grey and white bird bid them farewell and flew away, her duty discharged.

When the Princess and the fawn reached the well, the Princess turned to stroke her noble companion's neck. "You cannot come with me down the well, dear fawn," she said, "for this must I do alone." And summoning up the bravery she had discovered on her journey, the Princess jumped into the opening, and fell and fell towards the bottom.

The Princess tumbled in and out of sleep and dreams until she found herself walking in a field where the sun made the grass glimmer and the trees sing.

Suddenly, as if from nowhere, a beautiful fairy appeared, with long, swirling hair that glistened like spun gold and a radiant smile upon her face. The Princess felt instantly at peace.

"You have come a long way, weary traveler," said the fairy.

"I have come that I might return to a dear friend her eyes. Have you seen the globes of which I speak, bright fairy?"

Without a word, the fairy opened her hand and in it were two eyes, the beautiful eyes of a maiden who had seen no ill in the world.

"You may take them," said the fairy, "but your crone will never use them."

And before the Princess could ask what the fairy meant, she woke to discover she was lying by her dear fawn at the top of the well. In her hands was a small wrapped parcel in which lay the crone's eyes.

For three months, the travelers journeyed back across the land of lost things, and over the deep blue sea, to arrive once more in the Princess's homeland. When they drew near to the crone's cottage, on the edge of the dark, familiar wood, a huntsman stopped them and confirmed the fairy's prediction. While the Princess had been traveling in the land of lost things, the crone had passed peacefully to the next world.

At this news, the Princess began to weep, for her long journey had been in vain, but the fawn, who was as wise as he was good, told his Beauty to stop crying. "It matters not, for she did not need her eyes to tell her who she was. She knew it by your love for her."

And the Princess was so grateful for the fawn's kindness that she reached out and stroked his warm cheek. Just then, the fawn was changed into a handsome prince, and his golden ring became a crown, and he told the Princess how a wicked witch had put a spell on him, trapping him in the body of a fawn until a fair maiden might love him enough to weep over his fate.

He and the Princess were betrothed and lived together happily and busily evermore in the crone's little cottage, her eyes watching over them eternally from a jar atop the fireplace.

Thirteen

HE was a scribble of a man. Frail and fine and stooped from a knot in the center of his knobbled back. Beige slacks with grease spots clung to the marbles of his knees, twiglike ankles rose stoically from oversized shoes, and tufts of white floss sprouted from various fertile spots on an otherwise smooth scalp. He looked like a character from a children's story. A fairy story.

Nell pulled herself away from the window and studied again the address in her notebook. There it was, printed in her own unsightly hand: *Mr. Snelgrove's Antiquarian Bookshop, No. 4 Cecil Court, off Charing Cross Road—London's foremost expert on fairy-tale writers and old books in general. Might know about Eliza?*

The librarians at the Central Reference Library had given her his name and address the day before. They'd been unable to rummage up any information on Eliza Makepeace that Nell hadn't already found, but had told her that if there was anyone who could help her further with her search, it was Mr. Snelgrove. Not the most sociable of fellows, that much was certain, but he knew more about old books than anyone else in London. He was as old as time itself, one of the younger librarians joked, and had probably read the book of fairy tales when it was hot off the press.

A cool breeze brushed against her bare neck and Nell gathered her coat tight about her shoulders. With a deep, clear breath of purpose, she pushed open the door.

A brass bell tinkled in the doorjamb and the old man turned to look at her. Thick spectacle lenses caught the light, shone like two round mirrors, and impossibly large ears balanced on the sides of his head, white hair colonizing them from within.

He tilted his head and Nell's first thought was that he was bowing—some vestige of manners from an earlier time. When pale, glassy eyes appeared over the rim of his glasses she realized he was merely improving his view of her.

"Mr. Snelgrove?"

"Yes." Tone of a tetchy headmaster. "Yes, indeed. Well, come in, do. You're letting the wretched air through."

Nell stepped forward, aware of the door closing behind her. A little current sucking out, leaving the warm, stale air to resettle.

"Name," said the man.

"Nell. Nell Andrews."

He blinked at her. "Name," he said again, enunciating crisply, "of the book for which you are searching."

"Of course." Nell glanced again at her notebook. "Though it's not so much a case of searching for a book."

Mr. Snelgrove blinked again slowly, a parody of patience.

He was weary of her already, Nell realized. This caught her off guard; she was used to playing the wearied herself. Surprise brought with it a pesky stammer. "Th-that is . . ." She paused, trying to compose herself. "I already have the book in question."

Mr. Snelgrove sniffed sharply and large nostrils clamped shut. "Might I suggest, madam," he said, "that if you already have the book in question, you have little need for my humble services." A nod. "Good day."

And with that he shuffled away, returned his attention to the towering bookshelf by the stairs.

She had been dismissed. Nell opened her mouth. Closed it again. Turned to leave. Stopped.

No. She had come a long way to unravel a mystery, her mystery, and this man was her best chance of shedding some light on Eliza

Makepeace, why she might have been escorting Nell to Australia in 1913.

Pulling herself to her full height, Nell crossed the floorboards to stand by Mr. Snelgrove. She cleared her throat, rather pointedly, and waited.

He didn't turn his head, merely continued shelving his books. "You are still here." A statement.

"Yes," said Nell firmly. "I have come to show you something and I don't intend to leave until I've done so."

"I fear, madam," he said through a sigh, "that you have wasted your time just as you are now wasting mine. I don't sell items on commission."

Anger prickled Nell's throat. "And I don't wish to sell my book. I ask only that you take a look at it so that I might gain an expert opinion." Her cheeks were warm, an unfamiliar sensation. She was not a blusher.

Mr. Snelgrove turned to appraise her, that pale, cool, weary gaze. A thread of emotion (which one, she could not tell) plucked neatly at his lip. Wordlessly, and with the slightest of movements, he indicated a little office behind his shop counter.

Nell hurried through the doorway. His agreement was the sort of tiny kindness that had a habit of poking holes in one's resolve. A tear of relief threatened to break through her defenses and she dug inside her bag, hoping to find an old tissue so she might stop the traitor in its tracks. What on earth was happening to her? She wasn't an emotional person, she knew how to keep control. At least, she always had. Until recently, until Doug had delivered that suitcase and she'd found the storybook inside, the picture as its frontispiece. Started remembering things and people, like the Authoress; fragments of her past, glimpsed through tiny holes in the fabric of her memory.

Mr. Snelgrove closed the glass door behind him and shuffled across a Persian carpet dulled by its coat of long-settled dust. He navigated his way between motley mounds of books that were arranged, mazelike, on the floor, then dropped into the leather chair on the far side of the desk. Fumbled a cigarette from a battered packet and lit it.

"Well"—the word floated out on a stream of smoke—"come on, then. Let me cast my gaze across this book of yours."

Nell had wrapped the book in a tea towel when she left Brisbane. A sensible idea—the book was old and precious, it needed protection—yet here, in the dim light of Mr. Snelgrove's trove, the domesticity implied by its shroud embarrassed her.

She untied the string and slipped off the red-and-white-checked cloth, restrained herself from pushing it deep within her bag. Then she handed the book across the table into Mr. Snelgrove's waiting fingers.

Silence descended, punctured only by the ticking of a concealed clock. Nell waited anxiously while he turned the pages, one by one.

Still he said nothing.

Perhaps he required further explanation. "What I was hoping—"

"Silence." A pale hand was lifted; the cigarette wedged between two fingers threatened to relinquish its ash tip.

Nell's words stuck in her throat. He was without doubt the rudest man she had ever had the misfortune to deal with, and given the character of some of her secondhand-dealing associates, that was saying something. Nonetheless, he was her best chance of finding the information she needed. She had little choice but to sit, chastised, watching and waiting as the cigarette's white body morphed into an improbably long cylinder of ash.

Finally, the ash detached itself and dropped, lightly, to the ground. Joined the other dusty corpses that had died similar silent deaths. Nell, by no means a keen housekeeper, shuddered.

Mr. Snelgrove took one last, hungry drag and squashed the spent cigarette filter into a heaving ashtray. After what seemed an eternity, he spoke through a cough. "Where did you come by this?"

Was she imagining the tremor of interest in his voice? "I was given it."

"By whom?"

How to answer that one. "By the author herself, I think. I don't really remember. I was given it as a child."

He was watching her keenly now. His lips tightened, trembled a little. "I've heard of it, of course, but in all my days I confess I've never seen a copy."

The book lay upon the table now and Mr. Snelgrove ran his hand lightly over its cover. He let his eyelids flutter closed and uttered a sigh of deep well-being, that of the desert walker finally delivered to water.

Surprised by this shift in demeanor, Nell cleared her throat and clutched at words. "It's rare, then?"

"Oh yes," he said softly, opening his eyes once more, "yes. Exceptionally rare. Only one edition, you see. And the illustrations, Nathaniel Walker. This would be one of the only books he ever did." He opened the cover and gazed at the frontispiece. "It's a rare specimen, indeed."

"And what about the author? Do you know anything about Eliza Makepeace?" Nell caught her breath as he wrinkled his gnarled old nose. Dared to hope. "She's proved rather elusive. I've only managed to turn up the most spare of details."

Mr. Snelgrove pushed himself to standing and glanced longingly at the book before turning to a wooden box on the shelf behind. Its drawers were small and, when he pulled one open, Nell saw it was filled to the brim with rectangular cards. He riffled through, muttering to himself, until finally he withdrew one.

"Here we are, then." His lips moved as he scanned the card and in time the volume raised. "Eliza Makepeace . . . stories appeared in various periodicals . . . Only one published collection," he tapped a finger on Nell's book, "which we have right here . . . very little scholarly work on her . . . except . . . Ah yes."

Nell sat straighter. "What is it? What have you found?"

"An article, a book that mentions your Eliza. It contains a little biography if I remember." He shuffled to a bookcase that ran floor to ceiling. "Relatively recent, only nine years old. According to my note, it should be filed somewhere . . ." He ran a finger along the fourth shelf, hesitated, continued, stopped. "Here." He grunted as he pulled down a book and blew dust from its top. Then he turned it over and squinted at the spine. *"Fairy Tales and Fiction Weavers of the Late Nineteenth and Early Twentieth Centuries* by Dr. Roger McNab." He licked his fingertip and turned to the index, traced down the list. "Here we are, Eliza Makepeace, page forty-seven."

He pushed the open book across the table to Nell.

Her heart was racing, pulse flickering beneath her skin. She was warm, very warm. She fumbled the pages to forty-seven, read Eliza's name at the top.

Finally, finally, she was making progress, a biography that promised to flesh out the one person to whom she knew she was somehow linked. "Thank you," she said, the words catching in her throat. "Thank you."

Mr. Snelgrove nodded, embarrassed by her gratitude. He tilted his head in the direction of Eliza's book. "I don't suppose you're seeking a good home for this one?"

Nell smiled slightly and shook her head. "I'm afraid I couldn't part with it. It's a family heirloom."

The bell tinkled. A young man stood on the other side of the glass office door, staring uncertainly at the towers of sagging shelves.

Mr. Snelgrove nodded curtly. "Well, if you change your mind, you know where to find me." Peering over his glasses at the new customer, he huffed shortly. "Why do they always hold the door open?" He began his shuffle back towards the shop. *"Fairy Tales and Fiction Weavers* is three pounds," he said as he passed Nell's chair. "You may sit here and avail yourself of the facilities for a brief time, just be sure and leave the money on my counter when you leave."

Nell nodded her agreement and, as the door closed behind him, heart pounding, she began to read.

A writer of the first decade of the twentieth century, Eliza Makepeace is best remembered for her fairy tales, which appeared regularly in various periodicals over the years spanning 1907 to 1913. She is generally credited with having authored thirty-five stories, however this listing is incomplete and the true extent of her output may never be known. An illustrated collection of Eliza Makepeace's fairy tales was published by the London press Hobbins and Co. in August 1913. The volume sold well and received favorable reviews. The Times *described the stories as "a strange delight that evoked in this reviewer the enchanting and sometimes frightening sensations of childhood." The illustrations by Nathaniel Walker were praised especially and are thought by some to rank among his best work.* They were a departure from the oil portraits for which he is now better remembered.*

Eliza's own story began on 1 September 1888, when she was born in London. The birth records for that year indicate that she was born a twin, and the first twelve years of her life were spent in a tenement house at 35 Battersea Church Road. Eliza's pedigree is rather more complex than her humble origins might suggest. Her mother, Georgiana, was the daughter of an aristocratic family, inhabitants of Blackhurst Manor in Cornwall. Georgiana Mountrachet caused a society scandal when, at the age of seventeen, she ran away from the family estate with a young man far beneath her own social class.

Eliza's father, Jonathan Makepeace, was born in London in 1866 to a penniless Thames bargeman and his wife. He was the fifth of nine children and grew up in the slums behind the

---

* See Thomas R. Collins, *Sketching the Past* (Hamilton Hudson, 1959) and Reginald Coyte, *Famous Illustrators* (Wycliffe Press, 1964).

London docks. Although his death in 1888 occurred before Eliza was born, Eliza's published tales seem to reinterpret events that were likely experienced by a young Jonathan Make-peace during his childhood on the river. For instance, in "The River's Curse," the dead men hanging from the fairy gallows are almost certainly based on scenes Jonathan would have wit-nessed as a boy at Execution Dock. We must presume that these stories were passed to Eliza through her mother, Georgiana, embellished perhaps, and stored in Eliza's memory until she be-gan to write herself.

How the son of a poor London bargeman came to meet and fall in love with the high-born Georgiana Mountrachet remains a mystery. In line with the secretive nature of her elopement, Georgiana left no information about events leading to her de-parture. Attempts to learn the truth are further thwarted by her family's diligent efforts to smother the story. There was very little coverage in the newspapers and one must search further afield, in contemporary letters and diaries, to find mention of what must surely have been a great scandal at the time. The oc-cupation listed on Jonathan's death certificate is "Sailor," how-ever the precise nature of his employment is unclear. It is speculation only that leads this writer to suggest that perhaps Jonathan's life on the seas brought him briefly to the rocky shores of Cornwall. That perhaps, on the cove of her family's estate, Lord Mountrachet's daughter, famed throughout the county for her flame-haired beauty, chanced to meet the young Jonathan Makepeace.

Whatever the circumstances of their meeting, that they were in love cannot be doubted. Alas, the young couple were not to be granted years of happiness. Jonathan's sudden and somewhat inexplicable death less than ten months after their elopement must have dealt a devastating blow to Georgiana Mountrachet, who was left alone in London, unwed, pregnant, and with neither family nor financial security. Georgiana was not one to flounder, however: she had abandoned the strictures of her social class and, after the birth of her babies, abandoned, too, the name Mountrachet. She performed copy work for the legal firm of H. J. Blackwater and Associates of Lincoln's Inn, Holborn.

There is some evidence that Georgiana's fine penmanship was a gift for which she found ample expression in her youth. The Mountrachet family journals, donated in 1950 to the holdings at the British Museum, contain a number of playbills composed with careful lettering and accomplished illustrations. In the corner of each playbill, the "artist" has written her name in tiny print. Amateur theatricals were, of course, popular in many of the great houses, however the playbills for those at Blackhurst in the 1880s occur with greater regularity and seriousness than was perhaps usual.

Little is known of Eliza's childhood in London, other than the house in which she was born and spent her early years. One can posit, however, that her life was governed by the dictates of poverty and the difficult business of survival. In all probability, the tuberculosis that would be Georgiana's ultimate killer was already stalking her in the mid-1890s. If her condition followed the common path, by the latter years of the decade, breathlessness and general weakness would have precluded regular work. Certainly, the accounts for H. J. Blackwater support this timetable of decline.

There is no evidence that Georgiana sought medical attention for her illness, but fear of medical intervention was common in the period. During the 1880s, TB was made a notifiable disease in Britain and medical practitioners were bound by law to report instances of the illness to government authorities. Members of the urban poor, frightened of being sent to sanatoriums (which more usually resembled prisons), were loath to seek help. Her mother's illness must have had a great effect on Eliza, both practically and creatively. It is almost certain that she would have been required to contribute financially to the household. Girls in Victorian London were employed in all manner of menial positions—domestic servants, fruit sellers, flower girls—and Eliza's depiction of mangles and hot tubs in some of her fairy tales suggests that she was intimately acquainted with the task of laundering. The vampirelike beings in "The Fairy Hunt" may also reflect the early nineteenth-century belief that sufferers of consumption were vampire-afflicted: sensitivity to bright light, swollen red eyes, very pale skin and the characteristic bloody cough were all symptoms that fed this belief.

Whether Georgiana made any attempt to contact her family after Jonathan's death, and as her own health deteriorated, is unknown. However, in this writer's opinion, it seems unlikely. Certainly, a letter from Linus Mountrachet to an associate, dated December 1900, suggests that he had only recently learned of Eliza, his little London niece, and was shocked to think that she had passed a decade in such terrible conditions. Perhaps Georgiana feared that the Mountrachet family might be unwilling to forgive her original desertion. If her brother's letter is anything to go by, such fear was unfounded.

"After so many long years spent searching abroad, trawling the seas and scouring the lands, to think my beloved sister was so near all along. And allowing herself to suffer such privations! You will see that I spoke truth when I told you of her nature. How little she seemed to care that we loved her so and longed only for her safe homecoming . . ."

* * *

Though Georgiana never made such a homecoming, Eliza was destined to return to the bosom of her maternal family. Georgiana Mountrachet died in June 1900, when Eliza was eleven. The death certificate names her killer as consumption and her age as thirty. After her mother's death, Eliza was sent to live with her mother's family on the Cornish coast. It is unclear how this family reunion was effected, but one can safely assume that, despite the unfortunate circumstances precipitating it, for the young Eliza this change of location was a most fortunate occurrence. Relocation to Blackhurst Manor, with its grand estate and gardens, must have been a welcome relief, offering safety after the dangers of the London streets. Indeed, the sea became a motif of renewal and possible redemption in Eliza's fairy tales.

Eliza is known to have lived with her maternal uncle's family until the age of twenty-five. However, her whereabouts thereafter remain a mystery. Various theories have been formulated as to her life after 1913, though all are yet to be proved. Some historians suggest that she most likely fell victim to the spread of scarlet fever that enveloped the Cornish coast in 1913. Others, perplexed by the late-1936 publication of her final fairy tale, "The Cuckoo's Flight," in the journal Literary Lives, suggest that she spent her time traveling, seeking the life of adventure championed by her fairy tales. This tantalizing idea has yet to receive any serious academic attention and, despite such theories, the fate of Eliza Makepeace, along with the date of her death, remains one of literature's mysteries.

There exists a charcoal sketch of Eliza Makepeace, drawn by the well-known Edwardian portrait artist Nathaniel Walker. Found after his death among his unfinished works, the sketch, entitled The Authoress, currently hangs in the Tate Gallery in London. Although Eliza Makepeace published only one complete collection of fairy tales, her work is rich in metaphorical and sociological texture and would reward scholarship. Where earlier tales like "The Changeling" show a strong influence from the European fairy-tale tradition, later tales like "The Crone's Eyes" suggest a more original and, one would venture, autobiographical approach. However, like many female writers of the first decade of this century, Eliza Makepeace fell victim to the cultural shift that occurred after the momentous world events of the early century (the First World War and women's suffrage to name but two) and slipped from readers' attention. Many of her stories were lost during the Second World War, when the British Museum was robbed of entire runs of its more obscure periodicals. As a consequence, Eliza and her fairy tales are relatively unknown today. Her work, along with the author herself, seems to have disappeared from the face of the earth, lost to us like so many other ghosts of the early decades of the century.

Fourteen

HIGH above Mr. and Mrs. Swindell's rag and bottle shop, in their narrow house by the Thames, there was a tiny room. Little more than a closet, really. It was dark and damp, with a fusty smell (the natural consequence of poor drainage and nonexistent ventilation), discolored walls that cracked in summer and seeped through winter, and a fireplace whose chimney had been blocked so long it seemed churlish to suggest it should be otherwise. Yet despite its meanness, the room above the Swindells' shop was the only home Eliza Makepeace and her twin brother, Sammy, had ever known, a modicum of safety and security in lives otherwise devoid of both. They had been born in the autumn of London's fear, and the older Eliza grew the more certain she became that this fact, above any other, made her what she was. The Ripper was the first adversary in a life that would be filled with them.

The thing Eliza liked best about the room upstairs, indeed, the only thing she liked beyond its bare status as shelter, was the crack between two bricks, high above the old pine shelf. She was eternally grateful that the slapdashery of a long-ago builder, combined with the tenacity of the local rats, had begot a nice fat gap in the mortar. If Eliza lay flat on her stomach, stretched herself right along the shelf with her eye pressed close against the bricks and her head cocked just so, she could glimpse the nearby bend of the river. From such a secret vantage point she was able to watch unobserved as the tide of busy daily life ebbed and flowed. Thus were Eliza's twin ideals achieved: she was able to see, yet not be seen. For though her own curiosity knew no bounds, Eliza didn't like to be watched. She understood that to be noticed was dangerous, that certain scrutiny was akin to thieving. Eliza knew this because it was what she most liked to do, store images in her mind to be replayed, revoiced, recolored as she pleased. To weave them into wicked stories, flights of fancy that would have horrified the people who'd provided unwitting inspiration.

And there were so many people to choose from. Life on Eliza's bend of the Thames never stopped. The river was London's lifeblood, swelling and thinning with the ceaseless tides, transmitting the beneficent and the brutal alike, in and out of the city. Although Eliza liked it when the coal boats came in at high water, the watermen rowing people back and forth, the lighters bringing in cargo from the colliers, it was low tide when the river really came to life. When the levels dropped sufficiently for Mr. Hackman and his son to start dragging for bodies whose pockets needed clearing; when the mudlarks took up position, scouring the stinking mud for rope and bones and copper nails, anything they could find that might be swapped for coin. Mr. Swindell had his own team of mudlarks and his own patch of mud, a putrid square he kept guarded as if it contained the Queen's own gold. Those who dared cross his boundary line were likely as not to find their waterlogged pockets being fleeced by Mr. Hackman next time the tide dropped.

Mr. Swindell was always hounding Sammy to join the mudlarks. He said it was the boy's duty to repay his landlord's charity wherever he could. For though Sammy and Eliza managed to scrape together enough to cover the rent, Mr. Swindell never let them forget that their freedom rested on his willingness not to advise the authorities of their recent change in circumstances. "Them do-gooders what come sniffing round would be very interested to learn that two young orphans, likes of yourselves, has been left to fend alone in the big old world. Very interested, indeed," was his common refrain. "By rights I should of given you up soon as your ma breathed her last."

"Yes, Mr. Swindell," Eliza would say. "Thank you, Mr. Swindell. Very kind of you it is, too."

"Harrumph. Don't you go forgetting it, neither. By the goodness of me and my missus's hearts you're still here." Then he would look down his quivering nose and, by sole virtue of his mean-spiritedness, set his pupils to narrowing. "Now, if that lad, with his knack for finding things, would find his way into my mud patch, I might be convinced you was worth keeping. Never did meet a lad with a better nose."

It was true. Sammy had a talent for turning up treasures. Ever since he was a tiny boy, pretty things had seemingly gone out of their way to lie at his feet. Mrs. Swindell said it was the idiot's charm, that the Lord looked after fools and madmen, but Eliza knew that wasn't true. Sammy wasn't an idiot, he just saw better than most because he didn't waste his time in talking. Not a word, ever. Not once in all his twelve years. He didn't need to, not with Eliza. She always knew what he was thinking and feeling, always had. He was her twin after all, two halves of the one whole.

That was how she knew he was frightened of the river mud, and although she didn't share his fear, Eliza understood it. The air was different when you got near the water's edge. Something in the mud fumes, the swooping of the birds, the strange sounds that bounced between the ancient banks of the river . . .

Eliza knew also that it was her responsibility to look after Sammy, and not just because Mother had always told her so. (It was Mother's inexplicable theory that a bad man—she never said who—was lurking, intent upon finding them.) Even when they were very small Eliza had known that Sammy needed her more than she needed him, even before he caught the fever and was nearly lost to them. Something in his manner left him vulnerable. Other children had known it when they were small, grown-ups knew it now. They sensed somehow that he was not really one of them.

And he wasn't, he was a changeling. Eliza knew all about changelings. She'd read about them in the book of fairy tales that had sat for a time in the rag and bottle shop. There'd been pictures, too. Fairies and sprites who looked just like Sammy, with his fine strawberry hair, long ribbony limbs and round blue eyes. The way Mother told it, something had set Sammy apart from other children ever since he was a babe: an innocence, a stillness. She used to say that while Eliza had screwed up her little red face and howled for a feeding, Sammy had never cried. He used to lie in his drawer, listening, as if to beautiful music floating on the breeze that no one but he could hear.

Eliza had managed to convince her landlords that Sammy shouldn't join the mudlarks, that he was better off cleaning chimneys for Mr. Suttborn. There weren't many boys Sammy's age still engaged in sweeping, she reminded them, not since the laws against child sweeps were passed, and there was no one who could clean the narrower chimneys over Kensington Way quite like a skinny lad with pointy elbows made just for climbing dark and dusty chutes. Thanks to Sammy, Mr. Suttborn was always fully booked, and there was much to be said, surely, for regular coins? Even when weighed against the hope that Sammy might pluck something valuable from the mud.

Thus far the Swindells had been made to see reason—they liked Sammy's coins, just as they'd happily taken Mother's when she was alive and doing the copy work for Mr. Blackwater—but Eliza wasn't sure how long she could keep them at bay. Mrs. Swindell in particular had difficulty seeing beyond her greed, and was fond of making veiled threats, muttering about the do-gooders who'd been sniffing about, looking for muck to sweep from the streets to the workhouse.

Mrs. Swindell had always been afraid of Sammy. She was the sort of person for whom fear was the natural response to anything beyond explanation. Eliza had once heard her whispering to Mrs. Barker, the coal-whipper's wife, saying she'd heard it from Mrs. Tether, the midwife who delivered the two of them, that Sammy had been born with the cord around his neck. Should never've made it through the first night, would've breathed his last when he took his first but for the work of mischief. 'Twas the Devil's work, she said; the boy's mother made a deal with Him downstairs. You only had to look at him to know it—the way his eyes gazed deep within a person, the stillness in his body, so unlike the other lads his age—oh yes, indeed, there was something very wrong with Sammy Makepeace.

Such tall tales made Eliza even more fiercely protective of her twin. At night sometimes, when she lay in bed listening to the Swindells arguing, their little daughter, Hatty, bawling over the top, she liked to imagine dreadful things happening to Mrs. Swindell. That she might fall, by accident, into the fire when she was washing, or slip beneath the mangle and be squeezed to death, or drown in a vat of boiling lard, headfirst, skinny legs the only part of her that remained to evidence her gruesome end . . .

Speak of the Devil and she shall appear. Round the corner into Battersea Church Road, shoulder bag fat with spoils, came Mrs. Swindell. Home after another profitable day spent hunting little girls with pretty dresses. Eliza pulled herself away from the crack and shimmied along the shelf, used the edge of the chimney to ease herself down.

It was Eliza's job to launder the dresses Mrs. Swindell brought home. Sometimes when she was boiling the dresses over the fire, minding not to tear the spider-web lace, Eliza wondered what those little girls thought when they saw Mrs. Swindell waving her confectionery bag at them, the confectionery bag full of shiny bits of colored glass. Not that the little girls ever got near the bag to know the trick that had been played. No fear. Once she had them alone in the alley, Mrs. Swindell got their pretty dresses off them so fast they didn't have time to scream. They probably had nightmares afterwards, Eliza thought, like the nightmares she had about Sammy stuck up the chimney. She felt sorry for them—Mrs. Swindell on the hunt was a fearful thing indeed—but it was their own fault. They shouldn't be so greedy, always wanting more than they already had. It never ceased to amaze Eliza that little girls born to grand houses and fancy perambulators and lacy frocks should fall victim to Mrs. Swindell for such a small price as a bag of boiled sweets. They were lucky all they lost was a dress and some peace of mind. There were worse losses to be had in the dark alleyways of London.

Downstairs, the front door slammed.

"Where are you, then, girl?" The voice came rolling up the stairs, a hot ball of venom. Eliza's heart sank as it hit her: the hunt had not gone well, a fact which boded ill for the inhabitants of 35 Battersea Church Road. "Get downstairs and ready the supper or you'll book yourself a hiding."

Eliza hurried down the stairs and into the rag and bottle shop. Her gaze passed quickly over the dim shapes, a collection of bottles and boxes reduced by darkness to geometric oddities. By the counter, one such shape was moving. Mrs. Swindell was bent over like a mud crab rummaging in her bag, sifting through various lace-trimmed dresses. "Well, don't just stand there gawking like that idjit brother of yours. Get the lantern lit, stupid girl."

"The stew's on the stove, Mrs. Swindell," said Eliza, hurrying to light the gas. "And the dresses are almost dry."

"Should think so, too. Day after day I go out, trying to earn the coin, and all's you have to do is get the dresses laundered. Sometimes I think I'd be better off doing it myself. Shove you and your brother out on your ears." She puffed a nasty sigh and sat in her chair. "Well, come over here, then, and get my shoes off."

While Eliza was knelt on the ground, massaging the narrow boots loose, the door opened again. It was Sammy, black and dusty. Wordlessly, Mrs. Swindell held out her bony hand and beckoned slightly with her fingers.

Sammy dug into the pocket at the front of his overalls, pulled out two copper coins and laid them where they were due. Mrs. Swindell eyed them suspiciously before kicking Eliza aside with her sweaty stockinged foot and hobbling to the moneybox. With a slant-eyed glance over her shoulder, she pulled the key from the front of her blouse and turned it in the lock. Stacked the new coins atop the others, smacking her lips wetly as she calculated their total.

Sammy came to the stove and Eliza fetched a pair of bowls. They never ate with the Swindells. It wasn't right, Mrs. Swindell said, for the two of them to be getting ideas about their being part of the family. They was hired help, after all, more like servants than tenants. Eliza began ladling out their stew, pouring it through the sieve as Mrs. Swindell insisted: it didn't do to waste the meat on a pair of ungrateful wretches.

"You're tired," Eliza whispered. "You started so early this morning."

Sammy shook his head, he didn't like her to worry.

Eliza glanced towards Mrs. Swindell, checked her back was still turned before slipping a small piece of hock into Sammy's bowl.

He smiled slightly, warily, his round eyes meeting Eliza's. Seeing him like this, shoulders deflated with the day's heavy labors, face plastered with the soot from rich men's chimneys, grateful for the morsel of leathery meat, made her want to wrap her arms around his small frame and never let him go.

"Well, well. What a pretty picture," Mrs. Swindell said, clapping the moneybox lid shut. "Poor Mr. Swindell, out in the mud digging for the treasures what put food in your ungrateful mouths"—she waggled a knobbly finger in Sammy's direction—"while a young lad the likes of you is making free in his house. It ain't right, I tells you, it ain't right at all. When those do-gooders come back, I've a good mind to tell them so."

"Does Mr. Suttborn have more work for you tomorrow, Sammy?" Eliza spoke quickly.

Sammy nodded.

"And the day after that?"

Another nod.

"That's two more coins this week, Mrs. Swindell."

Oh, how meek she managed to make her voice!

And how little it mattered.

"Insolence! How dare you backchat. If it weren't for Mr. Swindell and me, you two sniveling worms'd be out on your ears, scrubbing floors in the workhouse."

Eliza drew breath. One of the last things Mother had done was to obtain an undertaking from Mrs. Swindell that Sammy and Eliza should be allowed to stay on as tenants for as long as they continued to meet the rent and contribute to the household.

"But, Mrs. Swindell," Eliza said cautiously, "Mother said you undertook—"

"Undertook? Undertook?" Angry bubbles of saliva burst in the corners of her mouth. "I'll give you undertook. I undertook to tan your hide till you can't sit down no longer." She rose suddenly and reached for a leather strap hanging by the door.

Eliza stood firm, though her heart was thumping.

Mrs. Swindell stepped forward, then stopped, a cruel tic trembling her lips. Without a word she turned towards Sammy. "You," she said. "Come over here."

"No," Eliza said quickly, gaze darting to Sammy's face. "No, I'm sorry, Mrs. Swindell. It was insolent of me, you're right. I . . . I'll make it up to you. Tomorrow I'll dust the shop, I'll scrub the front step, I'll . . . I'll . . ."

"Muck out the water closet shed and rid the attic of rats."

"Yes." Eliza was nodding. "All of it."

Mrs. Swindell stretched the strap out straight before her, a horizon of leather. She glanced beneath her eyelashes, from Eliza to Sammy and back. Finally, she released one side of the strap and hooked it again into place by the door.

A shower of dizzy relief. "Thank you, Mrs. Swindell."

Hand shaking a little, Eliza passed the bowl of stew to Sammy and picked up the ladle to serve her own.

"Stop right there," said Mrs. Swindell.

Eliza looked up.

"You," said Mrs. Swindell, pointing at Sammy. "Clean the new bottles and get them set up on the shelf. There'll be no stew till it's done." She turned to Eliza. "And you, girl, get upstairs and out of my sight." Her thin lips quivered. "You'll go without tonight. I've no intention of feeding a rebellion."

WHEN SHE was younger, Eliza had liked to imagine that her father would one day appear and rescue them. After Mother and the Ripper, Father the Brave was Eliza's best story. Sometimes, when her eye was sore from being pressed against the bricks, she would lie back on the top shelf and imagine her gallant father. She would tell herself that Mother's account was wrong, that he hadn't really drowned at sea but had been sent away on an important journey and would someday return to save them from the Swindells.

Though she knew it to be fantasy, no more likely to happen than for fairies and goblins to appear from between the fireplace bricks, it didn't dim the pleasure she took from imagining his return. He would arrive outside the Swindells' house—on a horse, she always thought. Riding the horse, not in a carriage pulled behind, a black horse with a glistening mane and long, muscular legs. And everyone in the street would stop what they were doing and stare at this man, her father, handsome in his black riding costume. Mrs. Swindell, with her miserable pinched face, would peer over the top of her washing line, over the top of the pretty dresses snatched that morning, and she'd call to Mrs. Barker to come and see all that was happening. And they would know who this was, that it was Eliza and Sammy's father come to rescue them. And he would ride them to the river, where his ship would be waiting, and they'd sail off across the ocean to faraway places with names she'd never heard of.

Sometimes, on the rare occasions when Eliza had been able to convince her to join in telling tales, Mother had spoken of the ocean.

For she had seen it with her own eyes, and was thus able to furnish her stories with sounds and smells that were magical to Eliza—crashing waves and salty air, and fine grains of sand, white rather than the slimy black sediment of the river mud. It wasn't often, though, that Mother joined in at story time. For the most part she disapproved of stories, especially of Father the Brave. "You must learn to know the difference between tales and truth, my Liza," she would say. "Fairy tales have a habit of ending too soon. They never show what happens afterwards, when the prince and princess ride off the page."

"But what do you mean, Mother?" Eliza would ask.

"What happens to them when they need to find their way in the world, to make money and escape the world's ills."

Eliza had never understood. It seemed irrelevant, though she wouldn't say as much to Mother. They were princes and princesses, they didn't need to make their way in the world, only as far as their magical castle.

"You mustn't wait for someone to rescue you," Mother would continue, a faraway look in her eyes. "A girl expecting rescue never learns to save herself. Even with the means, she'll find her courage wanting. Don't be like that, Eliza. You must find your courage, learn to rescue yourself, never rely on anyone else."

Alone in the upstairs room, simmering with loathing for Mrs. Swindell and anger at her own impotence, Eliza crawled inside the disused fireplace. Carefully, slowly, she reached up as high as she could, felt about with an open hand for the loose brick, pulled it clear. In the small cavity beyond, her fingers grazed the familiar top of the small clay mustard pot, its cool surface and rounded edges. Mindful not to send notice of her actions echoing down the chimney and into Mrs. Swindell's waiting ears, Eliza eased it out.

The pot had been Mother's and she'd kept it secret for years. Days before her death, in a rare moment of consciousness, Mother had told Eliza of the hidey-hole. She bade her retrieve its contents and Eliza had done so: brought the clay pot to Mother's bedside, wide-eyed with wonder at the mysterious hidden object.

Suspense tingled in Eliza's fingertips as she waited for Mother to fumble the pot open. Her movements were clumsy in the last days and the pot's lid was held tight by a wax stopper. Finally, it cracked apart from the base.

Eliza gasped in amazement. Inside the pot was a brooch, the likes of which would have had Mrs. Swindell weeping warm tears down her horrid face. It was the size of a penny, gems lining the decorative outer rim, red and green and shiny, shiny white.

Eliza's first thought was that the brooch had been stolen. She couldn't imagine Mother doing such a thing, but how else had she come to possess such glorious treasure? Where could it have come from?

So many questions and yet she couldn't find her tongue to speak. It wouldn't have mattered if she had; Mother wasn't listening. She was gazing at the brooch with an expression Eliza had never seen before.

"This brooch is precious to me," came the tumble of words. "Very precious." Mother thrust the pot into Eliza's hands, almost as if she could no longer bear to touch it.

The pot was glazed, smooth and cool beneath her fingers. Eliza didn't know how to respond. The brooch, Mother's strange expression . . . it was all so sudden.

"Do you know what it is, Eliza?"

"A brooch. I've seen them on the fancy ladies."

Mother smiled weakly and Eliza thought she must have given the wrong answer.

"Or perhaps a pendant? Come loose from its chain?"

"You were right the first time. It is a brooch, a special kind of brooch." She pressed her hands together. "Do you know what it is behind the glass?"

Eliza looked at the pattern of red-gold threads. "A tapestry?"

Mother smiled again. "In a way it is, though not the sort formed of threads."

"But I can see the threads, plaited together to form a rope."

"They are strands of hair, Eliza, taken from the women in my family. My grandmother's, her mother's before, and so on. It's a tradition. This is called a mourning brooch."

"Because it's worn only in the morning?"

Mother reached out and stroked the end of Eliza's plait. "Because it reminds us of those we've lost. Those who came before and made us who we are."

Eliza nodded soberly, aware, though she wasn't sure how, of having received a special confidence.

"The brooch is worth a lot of money, but I have never been able to bring myself to sell it. I have fallen victim, time and again, to my sentimentality, but that should not stop you."

"Mother?"

"I am not well, my child. Soon it will fall to you to look after Sammy and yourself. It may become necessary to sell the brooch."

"Oh, no, Mother—"

"It may become necessary, and it will be your decision to make. Do not let my reluctance guide you, do you hear?"

"Yes, Mother."

"But if you do need to sell it, Eliza, be careful how you do so. It must not be sold officially, there can be no record."

"Why not?"

Mother looked at her and Eliza recognized the look. She herself had given it to Sammy many times when deciding how honest to be. "Because my family would find out." Eliza was silent; Mother's family, along with her past, was rarely spoken of. "They will have reported it stolen—"

Eliza's brows shot up.

"Erroneously, my child, for it is mine. I was given it by my mother on the occasion of my sixteenth birthday. It was in my family long before that."

"But if it's yours, Mother, why can no one know you have it?"

"Such a sale would reveal our whereabouts, and that cannot happen." She took Eliza's hands, eyes wide, face pale and weak from the effort of speaking. "Do you understand?"

Eliza nodded; she understood. That is, she sort of understood. Mother was worried about the Bad Man, the one she'd been warning them about all their lives. Who could be anywhere, lurking behind corners, waiting to catch them. Eliza had always loved the stories, though Mother never went into sufficient detail to assuage her curiosity. It was left to Eliza to embellish Mother's warnings, to give the man a glass eye, and a basket of snakes, and a lip that curled when he sneered.

"Shall I fetch you some medicine, Mother?"

"Good girl, Eliza, you're a good girl."

Eliza placed the clay pot on the bed beside Mother and fetched the little bottle of laudanum. When she returned, Mother reached out to stroke again the strand of long hair that had unraveled from Eliza's plait. "Look after Sammy," she said. "And take care yourself. Always remember, with a strong enough will, even the weak can wield great power. You must be brave when I . . . if anything should happen to me."

"Of course, Mother, but nothing will happen to you." Eliza didn't believe this and neither did Mother. Everybody knew what happened to people who got the consumption.

Mother managed a sip of medicine, then leaned back against her pillow, exhausted by the effort. Her red hair spread out beside her, revealing her pale neck with its single scar, the fine slice that never faded and had first inspired Eliza's tale of Mother's encounter with the Ripper. Another of the tales she never let Mother hear.

With her eyes still closed, Mother spoke softly, in short, fast sentences: "My Eliza, I say this but once. If he finds you and you need to escape, then, and only then, take down the pot. Don't go to Christie's, don't go to any of the big auction houses. They have records. Go around the corner and ask at Mr. Baxter's house. He'll tell you how to find Mr. John Picknick. Mr. Picknick will know what to do." Her eyelids quivered with the strain of so much speech. "Do you understand?"

Eliza nodded.

"Do you understand?"

"Yes, Mother, I understand."

"Until such time, forget that it exists. Do not touch it, do not show it to Sammy, do not tell a soul. And Eliza?"

"Yes, Mother?"

"Always watch for the man of whom I speak."

AND ELIZA had been good to her word. For the most part. She'd taken the pot down only twice and then merely to look. To float her fingers over the top of the brooch, just as Mother had done, to feel its magic, its inestimable power, before sealing the lid quickly and carefully with candle wax, and stowing it back in place.

And though she took it down today, it wasn't to look at Mother's mourning brooch. For Eliza had made her own addition to the clay pot. Inside was her own treasure, her own contingency for the future.

She plucked out the little leather pouch and held it tightly in her palm. Drew strength from its solidity. It was a trinket Sammy had found in the street and given her. Some wealthy child's plaything, dropped and forgotten, found and revived. Eliza had kept it hidden from the beginning. She knew if the Swindells saw it, their eyes would light up and they'd insist on putting it downstairs in the rag and bottle shop. And Eliza wanted the pouch like she'd never wanted anything before. It had been a gift and it was hers. There weren't many things she could say that about.

It was some weeks before she finally found a use for it, as a hiding place for her secret coins, the ones the Swindells knew nothing about, paid to her by Matthew Rodin, the rat catcher. Eliza had a skill for rat catching, though she didn't like to do it. The rats were just trying to stay alive after all, as best they could in a city that favored neither the meek nor the mild. She tried not to think about what Mother would say—she'd always had a soft spot for animals—instead Eliza reminded herself that she didn't have much choice. If she and Sammy were to stand a chance, they needed coin of their own, secret coin that passed beneath the Swindells' notice.

Eliza sat on the edge of the hearth, clay pot on her lap, and dusted her sooty hands on the underside of her dress. It wouldn't do to wipe them where Mrs. Swindell could see. No good would come once her suspicious nose was set to twitching.

When Eliza was satisfied her hands were clean, she opened the pouch, loosened the soft silken ribbon and gently widened the opening. Peeked inside.

Rescue yourself, Mother had said, and look after Sammy. And that was just what Eliza intended to do. Inside the pouch there were four threepenny bits. Two more and she'd have enough to buy fifty oranges. That was all they needed to start out as orange sellers. The coins they made would buy more oranges and then they'd have their own money, their own little business. They'd be free to find a new place to live, where they were safe, without the watchful, vengeful Swindell eyes upon them. The ever-looming threat of being turned over to the do-gooders and sent to the workhouse—

Footsteps on the landing.

Eliza pushed the coins back into the pouch, tightened its neck and poked it inside the pot. Heart thumping, she slotted the pot back inside the chimney; it could be sealed later. Just in time, she jumped clear and perched, a model of innocence, on the end of the rickety bed.

The door opened and Sammy appeared, still black with soot.

Standing in the doorframe, single candle flickering limply in his hand, he looked so thin Eliza thought it a trick of the light. She smiled at him and he came towards her, reached inside his pocket and retrieved a small potato sneaked from Mrs. Swindell's larder.

"Sammy!" Eliza scolded, taking the soft spud. "You know she counts them. She'll figure it was you who took it."

Sammy shrugged, started rinsing his face in the bowl of water by the bed.

"Thank you," she said, stashing the potato in her mending basket when he wasn't watching. She'd return it in the morning.

"It's getting cold," she said, taking her pinafore off so she wore only her underdress. "It's early this year." She climbed into bed, shivered beneath the thin grey blanket.

Down to his undershirt and shorts, Sammy hopped in beside her. His feet were freezing and she tried to warm them with her own.

"Shall I tell you a story?"

She felt his head moving, his hair brushing her cheek as he nodded. And so she launched into her favorite tale: "Once upon a time, when the night was cold and dark and the streets were empty, and her twin babies were pushing and squirming inside her belly, a young princess heard footfalls behind her, knew instantly whose wicked tread they were . . ."

She'd been telling it for years, though not when Mother could hear. Mother would have said Eliza was upsetting Sammy with her tall tales. Mother didn't understand that children aren't frightened by stories; that their lives are full of far more frightening things than those contained in fairy tales.

Her brother's shallow breaths had become regular and Eliza knew that he had fallen asleep. She stopped her story and reached to take his hand in hers. It was so cold, so bony, she felt a flutter of panic in her stomach. She tightened her grasp, listening to him breathe. "Everything will be all right, Sammy," she whispered, thinking of the leather pouch, the money inside. "I'll make sure of it, I promise."

Fifteen

LONDON, 2005

BEN'S daughter Ruby was waiting for Cassandra when she arrived at Heathrow. A plump woman in her late fifties, with a face that glowed and short silver-grey hair that stood to resolute attention. She had an energy that seemed to charge the air around her; the type of person other people noticed. Before Cassandra could express surprise that this stranger was at the airport to greet her, Ruby had seized Cassandra's suitcase, put a fleshy arm around her and steered them both through the glass doors of the airport and into the fume-filled car park.

Her car was a battered old hatchback, its interior suffused with the scent of musk and the chemical approximation of a flower Cassandra couldn't name. When they were both belted in, Ruby plucked a bag of licorice allsorts from her handbag and offered them to Cassandra, who took a striped cube of brown, white and black.

"I'm addicted," said Ruby, popping a pink one into her mouth and tucking it in her cheek. "Seriously addicted. Sometimes I can't finish the one in my mouth fast enough to move on to the next." She chewed fiercely for a moment, then swallowed. "Ah, well. Life's too short for moderation, wouldn't you say?"

Despite the late hour the roads were alive with cars. They sped along the nighttime motorway, bow-necked streetlamps casting an orange glow on the tarmac below. While Ruby drove quickly, making sharp jabs at the brake only when absolutely necessary, gesticulating and shaking her head at other drivers who dared get in her way, Cas-

129

sandra stared out the window, mentally tracing the concentric rings of London's architectural movements. She liked to think of cities that way. A drive from edge to center was like taking a time capsule into the past. The modern airport hotels and wide, smooth arterial roads morphed into 1940s pebble-dashed houses, then mansion blocks and, finally, the dark heart of Victorian terraces.

As they drew closer to the center of London, Cassandra figured she should tell Ruby the name of the hotel she'd booked for the two nights before she left for Cornwall. She fossicked in her bag for the plastic folder in which she was keeping her travel documents. "Ruby," she said, "are we near Holborn?"

"Holborn? No. Other side of town. Why?"

"That's where my hotel is. I can catch a taxi, of course. I don't expect you to drive me all the way."

Ruby looked at her just long enough for Cassandra to worry that no one's eyes were on the road. "Hotel? I don't think so." She changed gear, braked just in time to avoid collision with a blue van in front. "You're staying with me. I won't hear otherwise."

"Oh, no," said Cassandra, the flash of blue metal still loud in her mind. "I couldn't. It's too much trouble." She began to relax her grip on the car door handle. "Besides, it's too late to cancel my booking."

"Never too late. I'll do it for you." Ruby turned to Cassandra again, seat belt squeezing her large breast so that it almost leaped from her shirt. "It's no trouble. I've made up a bed and I'm looking forward to your visit." She grinned. "Dad'd skin me alive if he thought I'd sent you off to a hotel!"

When they reached South Kensington, Ruby reversed the car into a minuscule space and Cassandra held her breath, silenced by admiration of the other woman's lusty confidence.

"Here we are, then." Ruby plucked the keys from the ignition and gestured towards a white terrace on the other side of the road. "Home sweet home."

The flat was tiny. Tucked deep within the Edwardian house, up two flights of stairs and behind a yellow door. It had only one bedroom, a little shower recess and toilet, and a kitchenette attached to the sitting room. Ruby had set up the sofa bed for Cassandra.

"Only three-star, I'm afraid," she said. "I'll make it up to you at breakfast."

Cassandra glanced uncertainly at the tiny kitchenette and Ruby laughed so hard that her lime green blouse shook. She wiped her eyes. "Oh, Lord, no! I don't mean to cook. Why put oneself through the agony when someone else can do it so much better? I'll take you round the corner to a cafe instead." She flicked the switch on the kettle. "Cuppa?"

Cassandra smiled weakly. What she really wanted to do was let her facial muscles relax out of this pleased-to-meet-you smile. It may have been the fact of having been so far above the earth's surface for such a long time, or just her usual mildly antisocial tendencies, but she was using every ounce of energy to keep up a front of function. A cup of tea would mean at least another twenty minutes of smiling and nodding and, God help her, finding answers to Ruby's constant questions. She thought briefly, with guilty longing, of the hotel room on the other side of town. Then she noticed Ruby was already dunking twin tea bags into twin teacups. "Tea'd be great."

"Here you are, then," said Ruby, handing Cassandra a steaming cup. She sat down on the other side of the sofa and beamed as a cloud of musk-scented air arranged itself around her. "Don't be shy," she said, indicating the sugar pot. "And while you're at it, you can tell me all about yourself. What a thrill, this house in Cornwall!"

AFTER RUBY had finally gone to bed, Cassandra tried to sleep. She was tired. Colors, sounds, shapes, all blurred around her, but sleep was elusive. Images and conversations played rapidly across her brain, a never-ending stream of thoughts and feelings tied together by no theme more specific than that they were hers: Nell and Ben, the antiques stall, her mother, the plane trip, the airport, Ruby, Eliza Make-peace and her fairy tales . . .

Finally she gave up on sleep. Pushed back the covers and climbed off the sofa. Her eyes had adjusted to the dark, so she could make her way to the flat's only window. Its wide ledge jutted out above the radia-tor and if Cassandra pushed aside the curtains she could just fit across it, back against one thick plaster wall, feet touching the other. She leaned forward onto her knees and looked outside, across the skinny Victorian gardens with their stone walls devoured by ivy, towards the street beyond. Moonlight hummed quietly on the ground below.

Although it was almost midnight, London wasn't dark. Cities like London never were, she suspected, not anymore. The modern world had killed nighttime. Once it must have been very different, a city at the mercy of nature. A city where nightfall turned the streets to pitch and the air to fog: Jack the Ripper's London.

That was the London of Eliza Makepeace, the London Cassandra had read about in Nell's notebook, of mist-filled streets and looming horses, glowing lamps that materialized, then vanished again into the fog-laden haze.

Looking down onto the narrow cobbled mews behind Ruby's flat, she could imagine them now: ghostly horsemen coaxing their fright-ened beasts along busy lanes. Lantern men perched high atop the car-riages. Street sellers and harlots, policemen and thieves . . .

Cassandra yawned and rubbed eyes that had grown suddenly heavy.

Shivering though she was not cold, she climbed down from the windowsill and back beneath the covers, closed her eyes and drifted into a dream-filled sleep.

Sixteen

The fog was thick and yellow, the color of pease pudding. It had crept in overnight, rolled down the surface of the river and spread heavily across the streets, around the houses, beneath the doorstops. Eliza watched from the crack between the bricks. Beneath its silent cloak, houses, gas lamps, walls were turned to monstrous shadows, lurching back and forth as the sulfurous clouds shifted around them.

Mrs. Swindell had left her with a pile of laundry, but as far as Eliza could see, there was no point washing anything with the fog as it was—what was white would be grey by day's end. It was just as well to hang the clothes out wet but unlaundered, which is what she'd done. It would save the bar of soap, not to mention Eliza's time. For Eliza had much better things to do when the fog was thick, all the better to hide and all the better to sneak.

The Ripper was one of her best games. In the beginning she had played it by herself, but over time she'd taught Sammy the rules and now they took turns enacting the parts of Mother and the Ripper. Eliza could never decide which role she preferred. The Ripper, she sometimes thought, for his sheer power. It made her skin flush with guilty pleasure, creeping up behind Sammy, stifling a giggle as she prepared to catch him . . .

But there was something seductive in playing Mother, too. In walking quickly, cautiously, refusing to look over her shoulder, refusing to break into a run, trying to keep ahead of the footsteps behind her, as her heartbeat grew loud enough to drown them out and leave her without proper warning. The fear was delicious, it made her skin tingle.

Although the Swindells were both out scavenging (the fog was a gift for those river dwellers who scratched a living by unscrupulous means), Eliza nonetheless went quietly down the stairs, careful to avoid the squeak of the fourth tread. Sarah, the girl who looked after the Swindells' daughter, Hatty, was the sort who liked to curry favor with her employers by making sly reports on Eliza's failings.

At the bottom of the stairs Eliza stopped and scanned the shadowy lumps and bumps of the shop. The fingers of fog had found their way between the bricks and flattened out across the room, hovering heavily over the displays, clustering yellow around the flickering gas lamp. Sammy was in the back corner, sitting on a stool cleaning bottles. He was deep in thought: Eliza recognized the mask of daydream on his face.

With a glance to confirm that Sarah wasn't lurking, Eliza crept towards him.

"Sammy!" she whispered as she made her approach.

Nothing, he hadn't heard.

"Sammy!"

His knee stopped jiggling and he leaned so that his head appeared around the shop counter. Straight hair fell to the side.

"There's a fog out."

His blank expression reflected the self-evidence of this statement. He shrugged slightly.

"Thick as the gutter muck, the streetlamps have all but disappeared. Perfect for the Ripper."

That got Sammy's attention. He was still for a moment, considering, then he shook his head. Pointed at Mr. Swindell's chair with its stained cushion, stuck where the bones of his back pressed into it, night after night, when he returned from the tavern.

"He won't even know we're gone. He'll be ages yet and so will she."

He shook his head again, with slightly less vigor this time.

"They'll be busy all afternoon, neither would pass up an opportunity to make some extra coin." Eliza could tell she was getting to him. He was part of her after all, she'd always been able to read his thoughts. "Come on, we won't be long. We'll go as far as the river and then we'll turn back." Nearly, nearly. "You can choose who you want to be."

That did it, as she'd known it would. Sammy's somber eyes met hers.

He lifted his hand, clenched it in a small, pale fist as if he clutched a knife.

WHILE SAMMY stood by the door, waiting out the ten-second head start always accorded to the person playing Mother, Eliza crept away. She ducked beneath Mrs. Swindell's laundry lines, around the ragman's wagon, and started towards the river. Excitement had her heart hammering. It was delicious, this feeling of danger. Waves of thrilling fear crashed beneath her skin as she sneaked along, weaving her way around people, wagons, dogs and perambulators hazy with fog. All the while her ears were pricked for the footsteps behind her, creeping, creeping, catching her up.

Unlike Sammy, Eliza loved the river. It made her feel close to her father. Mother hadn't been one for volunteering information about the past, but she'd told Eliza once that her father had grown up on a different bend of the same river. Had learned his sailor's ropes on a collier before joining another crew and heading for the high seas. Eliza liked to think about all he must have seen on his river bend, round near Execution Dock. Where pirates were hanged, their bodies left to sway from chains until three tides had washed over them. Dancing the hempen jig, the old-timers called it.

Eliza shivered, imagining the lifeless bodies, wondering what it might feel like to have a final breath squeezed from her own neck, then scolded herself for becoming distracted. It was the sort of lapse to which Sammy usually fell victim. And it was all very well for Sammy; Eliza knew she had to be more careful than that.

Now where were Sammy's footsteps? She strained to hear, concentrated her mind. Listened . . . Gulls by the river, mast ropes creaking, hull timber stretching, a trolley trundling by, the flypaper man calling, "Catch 'em alive-oh," the quick steps of a hurried woman, a paper boy singing out the price of his rag . . .

Suddenly, behind her, a crash. A horse whinnying. A man's voice hollering.

Eliza's heart thumped, she nearly turned. Ached to see what had happened. Stopped herself just in time. It wasn't easy. She was curious by nature, Mother had always said so. She'd shaken her head and clicked her tongue, and told Eliza that if she didn't learn to stop her mind racing on ahead of her she'd end up running into a mountain made of her own imaginings. But if Sammy chanced to be near and saw her peeking she would have to forfeit, and she was almost at the river. The smell of Thames mud mixed with the fog's sulfurous odor. She had almost won, she only had to make it a little further.

There was a hullabaloo of voices now, clattering away behind her, and the jangling of a bell drawing near. Silly horse had probably run into the knife grinder's wagon—the horses always went a little mad in the fog. But what a pest! What chance had she of hearing Sammy if he chose to attack her now?

The rock wall at the river's edge appeared, floating faintly in the haze.

Eliza grinned and broke into a run for the last few yards.

Strictly, to run at all was against the rules, but she couldn't help herself. Her hands hit the slimy rocks and she squealed in delight. She'd made it, she'd won, outwitted the Ripper once again.

Eliza hoisted herself onto the wall and perched triumphantly, facing the street from which she'd come. She drummed her heels against the rock and scanned the sheet of fog for Sammy's creeping shape. Poor Sammy. He'd never been as good at games as she was. He took longer to learn the rules, was less able to adopt the role in which he'd been cast. Pretending didn't come naturally to Sammy, as it did to Eliza.

As she sat, the smells and sounds of the street rushed back upon her. With each breath she tasted the oiliness of the fog, and the bell she'd heard was loud now, coming closer. The people around her seemed excited, all rushing in the one direction, the way they did when the ragman's son had one of his epileptic fits, or when the hurdy-gurdy man came to visit.

Of course! The hurdy-gurdy man, that explained where Sammy was.

Eliza jumped from the wall, scraping her boot on a rock that jutted out at its base.

Sammy never could resist music. He was no doubt standing by the hurdy-gurdy man, mouth slightly open as he gazed up at the organ, all thought of the Ripper and the game evaporated.

She followed the people who were massing, kept apace past the tobacconist's shop, the bootmaker, the pawnbroker. But as the crowd thickened, the bell faded, and still no organ music could be heard, Eliza moved faster.

A nameless dread had settled in her stomach, and she used her elbows to force her way past other people—fancy ladies in their walking skirts, gentlemen in morning coats, street boys, washerwomen, clerks—as all the while she scanned for Sammy.

Reports were beginning to ripple back from the center of the gathering and Eliza caught bits and pieces being exchanged in excited whispers above her head: a black horse that had loomed out of nowhere; a small boy who didn't see him coming; the terrible fog . . .

Not Sammy, she told herself, it couldn't be Sammy. He'd been right behind her, she'd been listening for him . . .

She was close now, had nearly reached the clearing. Could almost see through the fog. Holding her breath, she pushed to the front of the band of onlookers and the gruesome scene was before her.

She took it in all at once, understood immediately. The black horse, the frail body of the boy lying by the entrance to the butcher's shop. Strawberry hair matted deep red where it lay upon the cobblestones. Chest opened by a horse's hoof, blue eyes blank.

The butcher had come out and was kneeling by the body. " 'E's gone, all right. No chance, the little fellow."

Eliza looked back at the horse. He was frisky, frightened by the haze, the crowd, the noise. Sighing great huffs of hot breath, visible as they displaced the fog a little.

"Anyone know the name of this here boy?"

The crowd moved about, jostling as a whole while individuals turned to one another, lifted their shoulders, shook their heads.

"I mighta seen him round," came one uncertain voice.

Eliza met the horse's shiny black eye. As the world and all its noises seemed to spin around her, the horse stood still. They regarded each other and in that moment she felt as if he saw inside her. Glimpsed the void that had opened so quickly she would spend the rest of her life trying to fill it.

"Someone must know him," said the butcher.

The crowd was quiet, the atmosphere all the more eerie for it.

Eliza knew she should feel hatred towards the black beast, should despise his strong legs and smooth, hard thighs, but she didn't. Eyes locked with his, she felt almost recognition, as if the horse understood, as no one else could, the emptiness inside her.

"Righto," said the butcher. He whistled and an apprentice appeared. "Fetch the cart and clear the lad away." The apprentice hurried back inside then returned with a wooden cart. While he loaded the boy's broken body, the crossing sweeper started brooming the bloodied road.

"I believe he lives on Battersea Church Road," came a slow, steady voice. It sounded like one of the men at the law firm where Mother had worked, not a toff's voice exactly, but more plummy than those of the other river dwellers.

The butcher looked up to see where the voice had come from.

A tall man with a pince-nez and a neat but worn coat stepped forward, out of the fog. "I saw him there just the other day."

There was a murmur as the crowd digested this information. Looked anew at the small boy's ruined body.

"Any idea which house, gov'nor?"

The tall man shook his head. "I'm afraid I don't know that."

The butcher signaled to his lad. "We'll take him to Battersea Church Road and ask around. Someone ought to know him."

The horse nodded at Eliza, ducked his head three times, then sighed and looked away.

Eliza blinked. "Wait," she said, almost a whisper.

The butcher looked at her. "Eh?"

All eyes turned to take her in, this speck of a girl with a long plait of rose-gold hair. Eliza glanced at the man with the pince-nez. The lenses were shiny and white, so that she couldn't see his eyes.

The ambulance man held up his hand to silence the crowd. "Well, then, child. Do you know the name of this unfortunate lad?"

"His name is Sammy Makepeace," Eliza said. "And he's my brother."

MOTHER HAD set coin aside for her own burial, but no such provision had been made for her children. Naturally enough: what parent ever allowed that such a thing might be necessary?

"He'll have a pauper's funeral out at St. Bride's," said Mrs. Swindell later that same afternoon. She sucked some soup from her spoon, then pointed it at Eliza, who was sitting on the floor. "They'll be opening the pit again Wednesday. Till then, I expect we'll have to keep him here." She chewed the inside of her cheek, bottom lip pouting. "Upstairs, of course. Can't have the stink keeping customers away."

Eliza had heard of the paupers' funerals at St. Bride's. The large pit, reopened every week, the pile of bodies, the clergyman gabbling a quick service so that he might rescue himself from the dreadful neighborhood stench as soon as possible. "No," she said, "not St. Bride's."

Little Hatty stopped chewing her bread. She let the lump rest behind her right cheek while she looked, wide-eyed, from her mother to Eliza.

"No?" Mrs. Swindell's thin fingers tightened on her spoon.

"Please, Mrs. Swindell," Eliza said. "Let him have a proper burial. Like Mother's." She bit her tongue to save from crying. "I want him to be with Mother."

"Oh, you do, now, do you? A horse-drawn hearse, perhaps? Couple of professional mourners? And I s'pose you think Mr. Swindell and me should be paying for your fancy funeral." She sniffed hungrily, enjoying the sour rant. "Contrary to popular belief, missy, we ain't a charity, so unless you've got yourself the coin, that boy's going to spend his after at St. Bride's. Good enough for the likes of him, it is, too."

"No hearse, Mrs. Swindell, no mourners. Just a burial, a grave of his own."

"And just who do you propose to arrange all that?"

Eliza swallowed. "Mrs. Barker's brother is an undertaker, perhaps he could do it. Surely if *you* ask, Mrs. Swindell . . ."

"Waste a favor on you and your idjit brother?"

"He's not an idiot."

"Stupid enough to get himself trod on by a horse."

"It wasn't his fault, it was the fog."

Mrs. Swindell sucked more soup across her bottom lip.

"He didn't even want to go out," said Eliza.

"Course he didn't," said Mrs. Swindell. "It weren't his sort of caper. It were yours."

"Please, Mrs. Swindell, I can pay."

Twin brows shot skyward. "Oh, you can, can you? With promises and moonbeams?"

Eliza thought of the leather pouch, the shilling it now contained. "I . . . I have some coin."

Mrs. Swindell's mouth dropped open and a trickle of soup escaped. "Some coin?"

"Just a little."

"Why, you sneaky little wench." Lips tightened like the top of a coin purse. "How much?"

"A shilling."

Mrs. Swindell screeched with laughter; a horrendous noise so foreign, so raw, that her little girl began to bawl. "A shilling?" she spat. "A shilling won't buy you the nails to drive shut the coffin."

Mother's brooch, she could sell the brooch. It was true Mother had made her promise not to part with it unless the Bad Man threatened, but surely in a situation such as this . . .

Mrs. Swindell was coughing now, choking on her unexpected mirth. She gave her bony chest a slap, then set little Hatty scuttling across the floor. "Stop with your caterwauling. I can't hear myself think."

She sat a moment, then narrowed her eyes in Eliza's direction. Nodded a few times as a scheme took shape. "All your begging's set my mind. I'm going to see to it personally that the boy gets nothing better than he deserves. He'll have a pauper's funeral."

"Please—"

"And I'll have the shilling for me troubles."

"But, Mrs. Swindell—"

"Mrs. Swindell nothing. That'll learn you for being sneaky, keeping coin hidden. Just you wait until Mr. Swindell gets home and hears about this. Then there'll be hell to pay." She handed Eliza her bowl. "Now get me another serving and you can take Hatty up to bed."

NIGHTS WERE the worst. Street noises took on a garish quality, shadows lurched without reason and, alone in the tiny room for the first time in her life, Eliza fell victim to her nightmares. Nightmares far worse than anything she had imagined in her stories.

In the daytime, it was as if the world had been turned inside out, like a garment on the line. All was the same shape, size and color, but utterly wrong nonetheless. And although Eliza's body performed in the same way it had before, her mind roamed the landscape of her terrors. Again and again she found herself imagining Sammy at the bottom of the St. Bride's pit, lying, limbs askew, where he'd been tossed among the bodies of the nameless dead. Trapped beneath the dirt, eyes opening, mouth trying to call out that there'd been a mistake, he wasn't dead at all.

For Mrs. Swindell had got her way and Sammy had received the burial of a pauper. Eliza had taken the brooch from its hiding spot and gone as far as John Picknick's house, but in the end she couldn't bring herself to sell it. She'd stood out front a full half-hour, trying to decide. She knew if she sold the brooch she'd receive enough money to bury Sammy properly. She also knew Mr. and Mrs. Swindell would want to know where the money had come from and would punish her mercilessly for keeping such a treasure secret.

But it was not fear of the Swindells that decided her. It wasn't even Mother's voice, loud within her memory, making her promise to sell the brooch only if the phantom man came threatening.

It was her own fear that the future held worse than the past. That there would be a time, lurking in the foggy years to come, when the brooch was the lone key to her survival.

She turned around without setting foot inside Mr. Picknick's house and hurried back to the rag and bottle shop, brooch burning a guilty hole in her pocket. And she told herself that Sammy would understand, that he had known as well as she did the cost of life on their river bend.

Then she folded his memory as gently as she could, wrapped it in the layers of emotion—joy, love, commitment—for which she no longer had need, and locked the whole deep inside her. Being empty of such memories and emotions felt right somehow. For with Sammy's death Eliza was half a person. Like a room robbed of candlelight, her soul was cold, dark and empty.

WHEN WAS it that the idea first came to her? Later, Eliza could never be sure. There was nothing different about the day in question. She opened her eyes in the dim of the tiny room as she did each morning and lay still, reentering her body after the harrowing stretch of night.

She pulled back her side of the blanket and sat up, placed bare feet on the floor. Her long plait fell over one shoulder. It was cold; autumn had surrendered to winter and morning was as dark as night. Eliza struck a match and held it to her candlewick, then looked up to where her pinafore was hanging on the back of the door.

What made her do it? What made her reach beyond the pinafore to the shirt and breeches that hung behind? Climb inside Sammy's clothing instead?

Eliza never knew, but it felt right, as if it were the only thing to do. The shirt smelled so familiar, like her own clothes and yet not, and when she pulled on the breeches, she savored the curious sensation of bare ankles, cool air on skin accustomed to stockings. She sat on the floor and laced up Sammy's scuffed boots, a perfect fit.

Then she stood in front of the small mirror and looked. Really looked as the candle flickered beside her. A pale face stared back. Long hair, golden red, blue eyes with pale brows. Without letting her gaze slip, Eliza picked up the pair of sewing scissors that sat in the laundry basket and held her plait out to the side. The rope of her hair was thick and she had to hack through. Finally it dropped into her hand. No longer bound, the hair on her head fell loose, shaggy around her face. She continued to cut until it was the same length that Sammy's had been, then she pulled on his cloth cap.

They were twins, it was little surprise that they should look so similar, and yet Eliza drew breath. She smiled, very slightly, and Sammy smiled back at her. She reached out and touched the cold glass of the mirror, no longer alone.

Thump . . . thump . . .

Mrs. Swindell's broom end on the ceiling below, her daily call to start the laundering.

Eliza picked up her long red braid from the floor, unraveling at the top where it had been detached, and tied a piece of twine around its end. Later she would tuck it away with Mother's brooch. She didn't need it now; it was of the past.

Seventeen

Cassandra had known the buses would be red, of course, and double-decked, but to see them trundling by with destinations like Kensington High Street and Piccadilly Circus above their front windows was nonetheless startling. Like being dropped into a storybook from her childhood, or one of the many films she'd watched where black beetle-nosed taxis scurried down cobbled lanes, Edwardian terraces stood to attention on wide streets and the north wind stretched thin clouds across a low sky.

She had been in this London of a thousand film sets, a thousand stories, for almost twenty-four hours now. When she'd finally woken from her jet-lagged slumber, she'd found herself alone in Ruby's tiny flat, the midday sun slanting between the curtains to cast a narrow ray across her face.

On the little stool beside the sofa bed, there was a note from Ruby.

Missed you at breakfast! Didn't want to wake you—help yourself to anything worth scavenging. Banana in the fruit bowl, leftover something in the fridge, though haven't checked lately—may be all too gruesome! Towels in the bathroom cupboard if you'd like to get clean. I'm at the V&A until 6. You <u>must</u> drop by and see the exhibition I'm curating at the moment. Something v. v. <u>exciting</u> to show you! Rx

P.S. Come early afternoon. Wretched meetings all morning.

So it was, at 1 p.m., with her stomach growling, Cassandra found herself standing in the center of Cromwell Road, waiting for the traffic to stop its seemingly perpetual flow through the veins of the city so she could cross to the other side.

The Victoria and Albert Museum stood large and imposing before her, the cloak of afternoon shadow sliding rapidly across its stone front. A giant mausoleum of the past. Inside, she knew, were rooms and rooms, each one full of history. Thousands of items, out of time and place, reverberating quietly with the joys and traumas of forgotten lives.

Cassandra bumped into Ruby directing a group of German tourists to the new V&A coffee shop. "Honestly," Ruby whispered loudly as they herded away, "I'm all for having a cafe in the building—I like a good coffee as much as the next person—but nothing gets my goat like people who breeze past my exhibition in search of the Holy Grail of sugarless muffins and imported soft drinks!"

Cassandra smiled somewhat guiltily, hoping Ruby couldn't hear her own stomach grumbling at the delicious smells emanating from the cafe. She'd actually been heading there herself.

"I mean, how can they pass up the opportunity to stare the past in the face?" Ruby flapped a hand at the rows of treasure-stocked glass cabinets comprising her exhibition. "How can they?"

Cassandra shook her head and suppressed a rumble. "I don't know."

"Ah, well," Ruby sighed dramatically, "you're here now and the Philistines are but a distant memory. How're you feeling? Not too jet-lagged?"

"I'm fine, thanks."

"You slept well?"

"The sofa bed was very comfy."

"No need to lie," Ruby said with a laugh, "though I appreciate the sentiment. At least the lumps and bumps stopped you sleeping the day away. I would've had to ring and wake you up otherwise. No way I was going to let you miss this." She beamed. "I still can't believe Nathaniel Walker once lived on the same estate your cottage is on! He probably saw it, you know, drew inspiration from it. He may even have been inside." With her eyes bright and round, Ruby hooked an arm through Cassandra's and started down one of the aisles. "Come on, you're going to love this!"

With mild trepidation, Cassandra prepared herself to muster up a suitably enthusiastic reaction no matter what it was that Ruby was so keen to show her.

"There you are, then." Ruby pointed triumphantly at a row of sketches in the cabinet. "What do you think of those?"

Cassandra gasped, leaned forward to get a better look. There would be no need to pretend enthusiasm. The pictures on display both shocked and thrilled her. "But where did they . . . ? How did you . . . ?" Cassandra glanced sideways at Ruby, who clapped her hands together in obvious delight. "I had no idea these existed."

"Nobody did," said Ruby gleefully. "Nobody except the owner, and I can assure you she hadn't given them much thought in a very long time."

"How did you get them?"

"Purely by chance, darling. Purely by chance. When I first conceived the idea for the exhibition, I didn't just want to rearrange the same old Victoriana that people have been shuffling past for decades. So I ran a little classified advert in all the specialist mags I could think of. Very simple, it just read:

WANTED ON LOAN—ARTISTIC OBJECTS OF INTEREST FROM THE TURN OF THE NINETEENTH CENTURY. TO BE DISPLAYED WITH LOVING CARE IN LONDON MUSEUM EXHIBITION.

"Lo and behold, I started receiving phone calls the day the first advert appeared. Most of them were false alarms, of course, Great Aunt Mavis's paintings of the sky and the like, but there were pieces of gold among the rubble. You'd be surprised by the number of priceless items that have survived despite the slightest care."

It was the same with antiques, Cassandra thought: the best finds were always those that had been forgotten for decades, escaped the clutches of enthusiastic do-it-yourselfers.

Ruby looked again at the sketches. "These were among my most prized discoveries." She smiled at Cassandra. "Unfinished sketches by Nathaniel Walker, who'd have thought? I mean, we've got a small collection of his portraits upstairs, and there's some at Tate Britain, but as far as I knew, as far as anyone knew, that was all that had survived. The rest were thought to have—"

"Been destroyed. Yes, I know." Cassandra's cheeks were warm. "Nathaniel Walker was notorious for disposing of preparatory sketches, work he wasn't happy with."

"You can imagine, then, how I felt when the woman handed me these. I'd driven all the way out to Cornwall the day before and had been traipsing from one house to another politely declining various items that were entirely unsuitable. Honestly"—she rolled her eyes skywards—"the things people thought might fit the bill would amaze you. Suffice to say, when I arrived at the house I was just about ready to call it quits. It was one of those seaside cottages with the grey-slate roofs, and I was on the verge of giving up when Clara opened the door. She was a funny little thing, like a character out of Beatrix Potter, an ancient hen dressed in a hausfrau's apron. She ushered me into the tiniest, most cluttered sitting room I'd ever seen—made my place look like a mansion—and she insisted on making me a cuppa. I'd have preferred a whisky at that point, the day I'd had, but I sank down into the cushions and waited to see what utterly worthless object she was going to waste my time with."

"And she gave you these."

"I knew what they were immediately. They're not signed, but they've got his embossing stamp on them. See in the upper left-hand corner. I swear, I started to shake when I saw that. Nearly knocked my cup of tea all over them."

"But how did she get them?" Cassandra asked. "Where did she get them?"

"She said they were among her mother's things," said Ruby. "Her mother, Mary, moved in with Clara after she was widowed, and lived there until she died in the mid-1960s. They were both widows and I gather they were good company for one another. Certainly Clara was delighted to have a captive audience to regale with stories about mother dearest. Before I left she insisted on showing me up the most perilous flight of stairs to take a look at Mary's room." Ruby leaned closer to Cassandra. "What a surprise that was. Mary might have been dead for forty years, but that room looked as if she was about to arrive home at any moment. It was creepy, but in the most delicious way: a slim little single bed, still made up perfectly, a newspaper folded on the bedside table with a half-completed crossword on the upper sheet. And over beneath the window was a little locked chest—tantalizing!" She finger-combed her wild grey hair. "I tell you, it took every bit of restraint I could muster to resist tearing across the room and ripping the lock open with my bare hands."

"Did she open it? Did you see what was inside?"

"No such luck. I remained mercifully restrained and was ushered out a few moments later. I had to content myself with the Nathaniel Walker sketches and Clara's assurances that there'd been no more like them among her mother's things."

"Was Mary an artist, too?" said Cassandra.

"Mary? No, she was a domestic. At least she was to begin with. During the First War she'd worked in a munitions factory and I think she must've left service after that. Well, she left service in a manner of speaking. She married a butcher and spent the rest of her days making black puddings and keeping the chopping boards clean. Not sure which I'd have liked least!"

"Either way," Cassandra said, frowning, "how on earth did she get her hands on these? Nathaniel Walker was famously secretive about his artwork and the sketches are so rare. He didn't give them to anyone, never signed contracts with publishers who wanted to retain copyright of the originals, and that was the finished artwork. I can't imagine what would have made him part with unfinished sketches like these."

Ruby shrugged. "Borrowed them? Bought them? Maybe she stole them. I don't know, and I must admit I don't much mind. I'm happy to chalk it up as one of life's beautiful mysteries. I just thank God she *did* get her hands on them, and that she never realized their value, didn't find them worthy of display, and was thus able to preserve them so beautifully for us through the entire twentieth century."

Cassandra leaned closer to the pictures. Though she'd never seen them before, she recognized them. They were unmistakable: early drafts of the illustrations in the fairy-tale book. Drawn more quickly, the lines scratched eagerly in an exploratory fashion, filled with the artist's early enthusiasm for the subject. Cassandra's breaths shortened as she remembered feeling that sensation herself when she began a drawing.

"It's incredible, having the chance to see a work in progress. It says so much more about the artist, I sometimes think, than the finished work ever could."

"Like the Michelangelo sculptures in Florence."

Cassandra looked sideways at her, pleased by Ruby's perspicacity. "I got goose bumps the first time I saw a picture of that knee emerging from the marble. As if the figure had been trapped inside all along, just waiting for someone with enough skill to come and release him."

Ruby beamed. "Hey," she said, alight with a sudden idea, "it's your only night in London, let's go out to eat. I'm supposed to catch up with my friend, Grey, but he'll understand. Or I'll bring him, too, more the merrier, after all—"

"Excuse me, ma'am," came an American accent, "do you work here?"

A tall black-haired man had come to stand between them.

"I do," said Ruby. "How may I help?"

"My wife and I are mighty hungry and one of the guys upstairs said there was a coffee shop down here?"

Ruby rolled her eyes at Cassandra. "There's a new Carluccio's near the station. Seven o'clock. On me." Then she pressed her lips together and forced a thin smile. "Right this way, sir. I'll show you where it is."

WHEN SHE left the V&A, Cassandra went in search of a delayed lunch. She figured the last meal she'd eaten must have been the airplane supper, a handful of Ruby's Licorice Allsorts and a cup of tea: little wonder her stomach was shouting at her. Nell's notebook had a pocket map of central London glued inside the front cover and as far as Cassandra could tell, no matter which direction she took, she was bound to find something to eat and drink. As she peered at the map she noticed a faint cross written in pen, somewhere on the other side of the river, a street in Battersea. Excitement brushed like feathers on her skin. *X* marked the spot, but which spot exactly?

Twenty minutes later, she bought a tuna sandwich and a bottle of water at a cafe on the Kings Road, then continued down Flood Street towards the river. On the other side, the four smokestacks of Battersea Power Station stood tall and bold. Cassandra felt an odd thrill as she traced Nell's footsteps.

The autumnal sun had come out from hiding and was tossing silver flecks along the surface of the river. The Thames. What a lot the river had seen: innumerable lives spent along its banks, countless deaths. And it was from this river that a boat had left, all those years ago, with little Nell on board. Taking her away from the life she'd known, towards an uncertain future. A future that was now past, a life that was over. And yet it still mattered, it had mattered to Nell and it mattered now to Cassandra. This puzzle was her inheritance. More than that, it was her responsibility.

Eighteen

NELL tilted her head to get a better view. She had hoped that by seeing the house in which Eliza had lived she might somehow recognize it, feel instinctively that it was important to her past, but she did not. The house at 35 Battersea Church Road was utterly unfamiliar. It was plain, and for the most part looked like every other house on the street: three stories, sash windows, thin drainpipes snaking up rough brick walls that time and grime were turning black. The only thing that set it apart was an odd addition at the top of the house. From the outside it appeared that part of the roof had been bricked in to create an extra room, though without seeing it from inside it was difficult to know.

The road itself ran parallel with the Thames. This dirty street with rubbish in its gutters and snotty children playing on its pavement certainly didn't seem the type of place to spawn a writer of fairy tales. Silly, romantic notions, of course, but when Nell had imagined Eliza her thoughts had been fleshed out with images of J. M. Barrie's Kensington Gardens, the magical charm of Lewis Carroll's Oxford.

But this was the address listed in the book she'd bought from Mr. Snelgrove. This was the house where Eliza Makepeace had been born. Where she'd spent her early years.

Nell went closer. There didn't seem to be any activity inside the house, so she dared to lean right up against the front window. A tiny room, a brick fireplace and a poky kitchen. A narrow flight of stairs clung to the wall by the door.

Nell stepped back, almost tripping over a dead potted plant.

A face at the window next door made her jump, a pale face framed by a corona of frizzled white hair. Nell blinked, and when she looked back the face was gone. A ghost? She blinked again. She did not believe in ghosts, not the sort that went bump in the night.

Sure enough, the door to 37 Battersea Church Road swung open with mighty force. Standing on the other side was a miniature woman, about four foot tall with pipe-cleaner legs and a walking stick. From a raised mound on the left of her chin came one long silver hair. "Who're you, girlie?" she said in a muddy cockney voice.

It had been forty years at least since anyone had called her girlie. "Nell Andrews," she said, stepping back from the wizened plant. "I'm just visiting. Just looking. Just trying to—" She held out her hand. "I'm Australian."

"Australian?" said the woman, pale lips drawing back at the sides in a gummy smile. "Why didn't you say so? My niece's husband is Australian. They live in Sydney. You might know of 'em, Desmond and Nancy Parker."

"Afraid not," said Nell.

The old woman's countenance began to sour.

"I don't live in Sydney."

"Ah, well," said the woman somewhat skeptically. "P'haps if you ever get there you'll run into them."

"Desmond and Nancy. I'll be sure to remember."

"He don't get in till late most times."

Nell frowned. The niece's husband in Sydney?

"Fellow what lives next door. Quiet for the most part." The woman dropped her voice to a stage whisper. "Might be a darkie, but he works hard." She shook her head. "Fancy that! An African man living here at number 35. Did I ever think I'd see the day? Ma'd roll in her grave if she knew there was blacks living in the old house."

Nell's interest was piqued. "Your mother lived here, too?"

"That she did," said the old woman proudly. "I was born here, that very house what you're so interested in, matter of fact."

"Born here?" Nell raised her eyebrows. There weren't many people who could say they'd lived their entire life in the one street. "What's that, sixty, seventy years ago?"

"Nearly seventy-eight, I'll have you know." The woman jutted her chin so that the silver hair caught the light. "Not a day less."

"Seventy-eight years," said Nell slowly. "And you've been here all that time. Since"—a quick calculation—"since 1897?"

"I 'ave, December 1897. Christmas baby, I was."

"Do you have many memories? From childhood, I mean?"

She cackled. "Sometimes I think they're the only memories I got."

"It must have been a different place back then."

"Oh, yes," said the old woman sagely, "and that's a fact."

"The woman I'm interested in lived on this street, too. Here at this house, apparently. Perhaps you remember her?" Nell unzipped her bag and withdrew the picture she'd had photostated from the frontispiece of the fairy-tale book. Noticed that her fingers were trembling slightly. "She's drawn to look like a fairy-tale illustration, but if you look closely at her face . . ."

The old woman extended a gnarled hand and took the proffered image, squinted so that rows of wrinkles gathered around each eye. Then she started to cackle.

"You know her?" Nell held her breath.

"I know 'er, all right, I'll remember 'er to me dying days. Used to frighten the bejesus out of me when I was a littl'un. Told me all sorts of wicked stories when she knew my ma weren't around to give 'er a pounding and send 'er scuttling." She looked up at Nell, frowning so that her forehead concertinaed. "Elizabeth? Ellen?"

"Eliza," Nell said quickly. "Eliza Makepeace. She became a writer."

"I wouldn't know about that, not much of a reader, m'self. Can't see the point of all them pages. All's I know is that the girl there in your picture told stories to make your hair stand on end. Kept most of us local kids frightened of the dark, though we was always coming back for more. Don't know where she learned the likes of 'em, herself."

Nell looked again at the house, tried to get a sense of this young Eliza. An inveterate storyteller, scaring the younger children with her tales of terror.

"We missed her when she were taken." The old woman was shaking her head sadly.

"I'd have thought you'd be pleased not to be frightened anymore."

"Not likely," said the old woman, lips moving as though she were chewing her own gums. "There ain't a child alive what don't enjoy a good scare now and then." She dug her walking stick into a spot on the stairs where the cement was crumbling. Squinted up at Nell. "That girl herself got the worst sort of scare, though, far worse than any of her tall tales. Lost her brother, you know, one day in the fog. Nothing she could tell us was as ghastly as what happened to him. It was a big black horse, trod right through his heart." She shook her head. "The girl, she were never the same after that. Went a bit batty, you ask me, cut off all her hair and started wearing breeches if I remembers properly!"

Nell felt a rush of excitement. This was new.

The old woman cleared her throat, withdrew a tissue and spat into it. Continued as if nothing had happened. "There was a rumor going around she were taken to the workhouse."

"She wasn't," said Nell. "She was sent to live with family in Cornwall."

"Cornwall." A kettle began to whistle from inside. "That's nice, then, isn't it?"

"I imagine it was."

"Well then," the old woman said with a nod towards the kitchen, "that's teatime." The pronouncement was so matter-of-fact that for a brief, hopeful moment Nell thought she might be being invited inside, offered tea and countless other anecdotes about Eliza Makepeace. But when the door began to close, the old lady on one side and Nell on the other, the fond fancy passed.

"Wait," she said, pushing her hand out to hold off the closing door.

The old woman held the door ajar as the kettle continued to shrill.

Nell pulled a piece of paper from her handbag and began to scribble on it. "If I write down the address and phone number of the hotel I'm staying at, will you contact me if you remember anything else about Eliza? Anything at all?"

The old woman cocked a silvery eyebrow. She paused briefly, as if sizing Nell up, then took the piece of paper. Her voice when she spoke was slightly changed. "If I think of anything, I'll let you know."

"Thank you, Mrs. . . ."

"Swindell," said the old woman. "*Miss* Harriet Swindell. Never met a man I'd let make me his own."

Nell lifted a hand to wave farewell, but old Miss Swindell's door was already closed. As the kettle finally stopped shouting inside, Nell glanced at her watch. If she hurried, there was still enough time to get to the Tate Gallery. There she could see Nathaniel Walker's portrait of Eliza, the one he'd called *The Authoress.* She pulled the little tourist map of London from her bag and ran her finger up the river until she found Millbank. With a final glance down Battersea Church Road, as a red London bus shuddered past the banks of Victorian houses that had played host to Eliza's childhood, Nell set off.

AND THERE she was, *The Authoress,* hanging on the gallery wall. Just as Nell remembered her. Thick braid slung over one shoulder, frilly white collar buttoned to her chin so that her fine neck was encased, hat on her head. Quite different from the sorts of hats usually worn by Edwardian ladies. Its lines were more masculine, its pitch more jaunty, its wearer irreverent somehow, though Nell wasn't sure how she knew that. She closed her eyes. If she tried hard enough she could almost remember a voice. It came to mind at times, a silvery voice, full of magic and mystery and secrets. But it always slipped away before she could clasp the memory to her, make it her own to command and recall.

People were moving behind her and Nell opened her eyes again. *The Authoress* came once more into frame and Nell walked closer. The portrait was unusual: for one thing, it was a charcoal sketch, more a study than a portrait. The framing was interesting, too. The subject wasn't facing the artist but had been drawn as if walking away, as if she'd turned back her gaze only at the last minute and been frozen in that moment. There was something engaging in her wide eyes, her lips parted as if to speak; and something uncomfortable, too. It was the absence of even the hint of a smile, as if she'd been surprised. Observed. Caught.

If only you could speak, Nell thought. Then perhaps you could tell me who I am, what I was doing with you. Why we boarded that boat together and why you didn't come back for me.

Nell felt set upon by the dull weight of disappointment, though what revelations she'd imagined might be gleaned from Eliza's portrait, she didn't know. Not imagined, she corrected herself, hoped. Her entire quest was based on hope. The world was an awfully large place and it wasn't easy to find a person who'd gone missing sixty years earlier, even if that person was oneself.

The room with the Walkers was beginning to empty and Nell found herself surrounded on all four sides by the silent gazes of the long-dead. All observing her in that strange, heavy way the portrait subject has: eyes, eternally watchful, following the viewer around the room. She shivered and slipped on her coat.

The other portrait caught her eye when she was almost at the door. As her gaze fell upon the painting of the dark-haired woman with pale skin and plump red lips, Nell knew exactly who she was. A thousand snatches of long-forgotten memories combined in an instant, certainty flooded every cell. It wasn't that she recognized the name printed beneath the portrait, *Rose Elizabeth Mountrachet*—the words themselves meant very little. It was more and it was less. Nell's lips began to quiver and something deep inside her chest clenched. Breathing was difficult. "Mamma," she whispered, feeling stupid and elated and vulnerable all at once.

THANK GOD the Central Reference Library was open late, for there was no way Nell could have waited until morning. Finally she knew her mother's name, Rose Elizabeth Mountrachet. Later, she would look back on that moment in the Tate Gallery as a birth of sorts. Swiftly, with neither warning nor fuss, she was someone's child, she knew her mother's name. She said the words over and over as she scurried along the darkening streets.

It was not the first time she'd heard them. The book she'd bought from Mr. Snelgrove with its entry on Eliza had mentioned the Mountrachet family. Eliza's maternal uncle, minor member of the aristocracy, owner of the grand estate in Cornwall, Blackhurst, where Eliza had been sent after her mother's death. It was the link she'd been looking for. The thread that tied the Authoress of Nell's memory to the face she now recognized as her mother's.

The woman at the library desk remembered Nell from the day before, when she'd come searching for information on Eliza.

"Did you find Mr. Snelgrove, then?" she said with a grin.

"I did," said Nell, rather breathlessly.

"And you lived to tell the tale."

"He sold me a book that was very helpful."

"That's our Mr. Snelgrove, always manages to make a sale." She shook her head fondly.

"I wonder," said Nell, "if you could help me again. I need to find some information on a woman."

The librarian blinked. "I'm going to need a little more to go on than that."

"Of course. A woman born sometime in the late nineteenth century."

"Was she a writer, too?"

"No, at least I don't think so." Nell exhaled, collected her thoughts. "Her name was Rose Mountrachet and her family were aristocrats of some kind. I thought perhaps I might find something in one of those books, you know the sort, with details of members of the peerage."

"Like *Debrett's*. Or *Who's Who*."

"Yes, exactly."

"Worth a look," said the librarian. "We've got both publications here, but *Who's Who* is probably easier to read. Hereditary peers are automatically invited for inclusion. She might not have an entry of her own but if you're lucky she'll be mentioned in someone else's, her father's, perhaps, or her husband's. Don't s'pose you know when she died?"

"No. Why?"

"Given that you don't know when she was entered, if at all, it might save you time if you just looked her up in *Who Was Who* first. Need to know when she died for that, though."

Nell shook her head. "I couldn't even guess. If you point me in the general direction I'll just check through the *Who's Who*—start this year and work backwards until I find mention of her."

"Might take a while, and the library's closing soon."

"I'll be quick."

The woman shrugged. Leaned over to pluck a small notepad from the typewriter beside her. She wrote down a shelf number and handed it to Nell. "Take the stairs to the first floor and you'll find the back files at the inquiry desk. The listings are alphabetical."

FINALLY, IN 1934, Nell struck gold. It wasn't Rose Mountrachet, but it was a Mountrachet nonetheless. Linus, the uncle who'd claimed Eliza Makepeace after Georgiana's death. She scanned the entry:

> *MOUNTRACHET,* Lord, Linus St. John Henry. *b.* 11 January 1860, *s.* of late Lord St. John Luke Mountrachet and late Margaret Elizabeth Mountrachet, *m.* 31 August 1888 Adeline Langley. One *d.* late Rose Elizabeth Mountrachet, *m.* late Nathaniel Walker.

Rose had married Nathaniel Walker. That meant, didn't it, that he was her father? She read the entry again. The *late* Rose and Nathaniel. So they'd both died earlier than 1934. Was that why she'd been with Eliza? Had Eliza been appointed her guardian because her parents were both dead?

Her father—that is, Hugh—had found her on the Maryborough wharf in late 1913. If Eliza had been appointed guardian after Rose and Nathaniel were killed, that meant, didn't it, that they must have died before then?

Suppose she were to look up Nathaniel Walker in *Who's Who* for that year? He was sure to have an entry. Better yet, if her theory was correct and he was no longer alive in 1913, she should go straight to *Who Was Who*. She hurried along the line of shelves and plucked out *Who Was Who 1897–1915*. Fingers trembling, she flicked through from the back, Z, Y, X, W. There he was:

> *WALKER,* Nathaniel James. *b.* 22 July 1883, *d.* 2 September 1913, *s.* of Anthony Sebastian Walker and Mary Walker, *m.* the late Hon. Rose Elizabeth Mountrachet, 3 March 1908. One *d.* the late Ivory Walker.

Nell stopped short. One daughter was correct, but what did they mean by late? She wasn't dead, she was very much alive.

Nell was aware suddenly of the library heating, felt she couldn't breathe. She fanned her face and looked back at the entry.

What could it possibly mean? Could they have got it wrong?

"Found her?"

Nell looked up. The woman from the front desk. "Are these ever wrong?" she said. "Do they ever get things wrong?"

The woman pursed her lips thoughtfully. "They're not the most reliable sources, I suppose. They're put together with information supplied by the subjects themselves."

"What about when the person is dead?"

"I'm sorry?"

"In *Who Was Who* the people are all dead. Who supplies the information then?"

She shrugged. "Remaining family, I expect. Most of it I guess they just copy from the last questionnaire the subject provided. Add the death dates and Bob's your uncle." She brushed a bit of lint from the top of the shelf. "We're closing in ten minutes. Let me know if there's anything else I can help you with."

There had been a mistake, that was all. It must happen often; after all, the person setting the type didn't know the subjects personally. It was possible, wasn't it, that a typesetter's mind might wander for a moment, the word "late" be inserted by error? A stranger consigned to early death in posterity's silent eyes?

It was little more than a typo. She knew she was the child of whom the entry spoke and she most certainly was not "late." All she needed to do was find a biography of Nathaniel Walker and she could prove the entry was wrong. She had a name now; her name had once been Ivory Walker. And if it didn't feel familiar, if it didn't slip over her like a well-worn coat, then that was as it was. There was no accounting for memory, which things stuck and which didn't.

She remembered suddenly the book she'd bought on her way

into the Tate, all about Nathaniel's paintings. It was bound to include a brief biography. She pulled it from her bag and flipped it open.

Nathaniel Walker (1883–1913) was born in New York to Polish immigrant parents, Antoni and Marya Walker (originally Walczwk). His father worked on the city wharves and his mother took in laundry and raised their six children, of whom Nathaniel was the third. Two of his siblings died of various fevers and Nathaniel was set to follow his father on to the wharves when a picture he had been sketching on a New York street was noticed by a passerby, Walter Irving Jnr, heir to the Irving oil fortune, who commissioned Nathaniel to paint his portrait.

Under his patron's wing, Nathaniel became a well-known member of New York's burgeoning society. It was at one of Irving's parties in 1907 that Nathaniel met the Honourable Rose Mountrachet, who was visiting New York from Cornwall. They were married the following year at Blackhurst, the Mountrachet estate near Tregenna, Cornwall. Nathaniel's reputation continued to grow after his marriage and relocation to the UK, and the pinnacle of his career was the commission in early 1910 for him to paint what would be King Edward VII's final portrait.

Nathaniel and Rose Walker had one daughter, Ivory, born in 1909. His wife and daughter were Nathaniel's frequent subjects and one of his best-loved portraits is that named Mother and Child. *The young couple were tragically killed in 1913 at Ais Gill when their railway train and another collided and caught fire. Ivory Walker died from scarlet fever days after her parents' deaths.*

It made no sense. Nell *knew* she was the child to whom this biography referred. Rose and Nathaniel Walker were her parents. She *re-*

membered Rose, had done so instantly. The dates fitted: her birth, even her voyage to Australia, tied in too neatly with Rose's and Nathaniel's deaths to be coincidence. Not to mention the further connection that Rose and Eliza must have been cousins.

Nell turned to the index and ran her finger down the list. She stopped at *Mother and Child* and flicked to the nominated page, heart thumping.

A tremor in her lower lip. She might not remember being called Ivory but there was no longer any doubt. She knew what she had looked like as a little girl. This was her. Sitting on her mother's lap, painted by her father.

Why, then, did history think her dead? Who had given such misinformation to *Who Was Who*? Was it a deliberate deception or had they believed it themselves? Not realizing that she had, instead, been boarded on a ship to Australia by a mysterious writer of fairy tales.

You mustn't speak your name. It's a game we're playing. That's what the Authoress had said. Nell could hear it now, the silvery voice, like a breeze off the ocean surface. *It's our secret. You mustn't tell.* Nell was four years old again, felt the fear, the uncertainty, the excitement. Smelled the river mud, so different from the wide blue sea, heard the hungry Thames gulls, the sailors calling to one another. A pair of barrels, a dark hiding space, a thread of dust-flecked light . . .

The Authoress had taken her. She hadn't been abandoned at all. She'd been kidnapped and her grandparents didn't know. That's why they hadn't come looking for her. They'd believed her dead.

But why had the Authoress taken her? And why had she then disappeared, leaving Nell alone on the boat, alone in the world?

Her past was like a Russian doll, question inside question inside question.

And what she needed to unravel these new mysteries was a person. Someone to whom she could speak, who might have known her then, or know someone who had. Someone who could shed light on the Authoress, and the Mountrachets, and Nathaniel Walker.

That someone, she figured, was not going to be found in the dusty vaults of a reference library. She would need to go to the heart of the mystery, to Cornwall, to this village, Tregenna. To the huge dark house, Blackhurst, where once her family had lived and she, as a little girl, had roamed.

NINETEEN

Ruby was late for dinner but Cassandra didn't mind. The waiter had given her a table by the large glass window and she was watching harried commuters hoofing their way home. All these people, the stars of lives unfolding quite outside the sphere in which Cassandra's own life took place. They came in waves. There was a bus stop right out front and across the street South Kensington station still wore its pretty coat of art nouveau tiles. Every so often the traffic current swept a wind-blown cluster of people inside the restaurant doors, where they would slide into seats or stand by the brightly lit deli awaiting white cardboard boxes of gourmet food to carry home for dinner.

Cassandra rubbed her thumb along the soft, worn edge of the notebook and ran the sentence through her mind once more, wondering whether it would sit more easily this time. Nell's father was Nathaniel Walker. Nathaniel Walker, painter to the royals, had been Nell's father. Cassandra's great-grandfather.

No, the truth still fitted like someone else's glove, just as it had when she'd first uncovered it that afternoon. She'd been sitting on the bench by the Thames, decoding Nell's scrawled account of her visit to the Battersea house in which Eliza Makepeace had been born, the Tate Gallery where Nathaniel Walker's portraits were on display. The breeze had picked up, skimming the river's surface and racing up the banks, and Cassandra had been about to leave when something drew her eye to the particularly scratchy passage on the facing page, an underlined sentence that read: *Rose Mountrachet was my mother. I recognize her portrait, and I remember her.* An arrow then, and Cassandra's attention leaped ahead to the title of a book, *Who Was Who,* under which was printed a hasty list of bullet points:

- Rose Mountrachet married Nathaniel Walker, painter, 1908
- one daughter! Ivory Walker (born sometime after—1909? Check. Scarlet fever?)
- Rose and Nathaniel both killed 1913, train crash, Ais Gill (same year I disappeared. Link?)

A piece of loose paper had been folded into the margins of the notebook, a photocopy taken from a book called *Great Rail Disasters of the Steam Age.* Cassandra pulled it out again now. The paper was thin and the text faded, but it was blessedly unmarked by the mold spots that were busy devouring the rest of the book. The title at the top read "The Ais Gill Railway Tragedy." As bistro noise hummed warmly around her, Cassandra scanned once more through the brief but enthusiastic account.

> *In the dark and early hours of 2 September 1913, two Midland Railway trains left Carlisle Station en route for London, all those aboard unaware that they were being spirited towards a scene of utter devastation. It was a steep line, traversing as it did the peaks and troughs of the rolling northern landscape, and the trains were hopelessly underpowered. Two facts conspired to drive the trains to their destruction that night: their engines were smaller than was recommended for the line's steep gradients, and each had been supplied with poorly screened coal, full of slack that prevented it from burning efficiently.*
>
> *After departing from Carlisle at 1.35 a.m., the first train laboured to reach the Ais Gill summit, the steam pressure began to plummet and the train ground to a halt. One can imagine the passengers would have been surprised by the train's*

sudden halt so soon after leaving the station, but not unduly alarmed. After all, they were in safe hands; the guard had reassured them that they'd only be sitting still a few minutes and then they'd be on their way again.

Indeed, the guard's certainty that the wait would be short was one of the fatal errors made that night. Conventional railway protocol suggests that if he'd known how long it would take for the driver and fireman to clean the grate and rebuild the steam pressure, he'd have laid some detonators or carried a lantern down the line to signal to any oncoming trains. But alas, he did not, and thus the fates of the good folk on board were sealed.

For further down the line the second engine was also straining. It pulled a lighter load but the small engine and inferior coal were nonetheless sufficient impediments to cause the driver difficulties. A few miles before Mallerstang, the driver made the fatal decision to leave the cab and inspect the engine in action. Though such practice seems unsafe by today's standards, it was quite a common occurrence in those days. Unfortunately, while the driver was absent from the cab, the fireman also encountered problems: the injector was stalling and the boiler level had begun to fall. When the driver returned to the cab, the task consumed their attention so fully that they both missed the red lantern being waved from the Mallerstang signal box.

By the time they finished and returned their attention to the line, the first stalled train was but a few yards away. There was no way the second train could stop in time. As can be imagined, the damage was extreme and the tragedy yielded unexpectedly high casualties. Additional to the collision impact, the parcels van's roof slid over the second engine and dissected the first-class sleeping accommodation behind. The gas from

the lighting system ignited and fire swept through the devas-
tated carriages, claiming the lives of those poor unfortunates
who stood in its way.

Cassandra shivered as images from a dark night in 1913 assailed her: the steep summit ride, the night-draped terrain through the window, the sensation of the train coming to an unexpected standstill. She wondered what Rose and Nathaniel had been doing at the moment of impact, whether they'd been asleep in their carriage, or engaged in conversation. Whether they'd even been speaking of their daughter, Ivory, waiting for them at home. How odd that she should be so moved by the plight of forebears she'd only just learned she had. How awful it must have been for Nell, to finally discover her parents only to lose them again in such a terrible way.

The door of Carluccio's pushed open, bringing with it a burst of cool air laced with exhaust fumes. Cassandra looked up to see Ruby bustling towards her, a thin man with a shiny bald head close behind.

"What an afternoon!" Ruby collapsed onto the seat across from Cassandra. "A group of students right at the last. I didn't think I'd ever extricate myself!" She indicated the thin neat man. "This is Grey. He's a lot more fun than he looks."

"Ruby, darling, what a charming introduction." He extended a smooth hand across the table. "Graham Westerman. Ruby's told me all about you."

Cassandra smiled. It was an interesting proposition given that Ruby had known her the sum total of two waking hours. Still, if anyone was capable of such a miracle, Cassandra suspected it was Ruby.

He slid into a seat. "What a stroke of luck inheriting a house."

"Not to mention a delicious family mystery." Ruby waved at a waiter and proceeded to order breads and olives for them all.

At mention of the mystery, Cassandra's lips tingled with her new-found knowledge, the identity of Nell's parents. The secret, though, sat lumpen in her throat.

"Ruby tells me you enjoyed her exhibition," said Grey, eyes twinkling.

"Of course she did, she's only human," said Ruby. "Not to mention an artist herself."

"Art historian." Cassandra blushed.

"Dad said you draw brilliantly. You illustrated a kids' book, didn't you?"

She shook her head. "No. I used to draw, but it was just a hobby."

"Bit more than a hobby from what I hear. Dad said—"

"I used to muck around with a sketchpad when I was younger. Not anymore. Not for years."

"Hobbies have a tendency to drop by the wayside," Grey said diplomatically. "I submit as evidence Ruby's mercifully short-lived infatuation with ballroom dancing."

"Oh, Grey, just because you've got two left feet . . ."

As her tablemates fell to debating Ruby's commitment to the finer points of salsa, Cassandra let her thoughts slip backwards to the afternoon, many years before, when Nell had tossed the sketchpad and pack of 2B pencils onto the table where Cassandra was busy drowning in algebra homework.

She'd been living with her grandmother for just over a year. Had started high school and was having as much trouble making friends as she was making equations balance.

"I don't know how to draw," she'd said, surprised and unsure. Unexpected presents had always made her wary.

"You'll learn," said Nell. "You've got eyes and a hand. Draw what you see."

Cassandra sighed patiently. Nell was full of unusual ideas. She was nothing at all like the other kids' mums and certainly nothing like Lesley, but she meant well and Cassandra didn't want to hurt her feelings. "I think there's more to it than that, Nell."

"Nonsense. It's just a matter of making sure you see what's really there. Not what you *think* is there."

Cassandra raised her eyebrows dubiously.

"Everything is made up of lines and shapes. It's like a code, you just need to learn to read and interpret it." Nell pointed across the room. "That lamp over there, tell me what you see."

"Um . . . a lamp?"

"Well, there's your problem," said Nell. "If all you see is a lamp, you've no chance of drawing it. But if you see that it's actually a triangle on top of a rectangle, with a skinny tube connecting them—well, you're halfway there, aren't you?"

Cassandra shrugged, uncertain.

"Humor me. Have a go."

Cassandra sighed again, a small sigh of extravagant tolerance.

"Never know, you might surprise yourself."

And she had. Not that she'd exhibited any great talent that first time. The surprise had been how much she enjoyed it. Time had seemed to disappear when she had the sketchpad on her lap and a pencil in her hand . . .

The waiter arrived and tossed two tins of bread onto the table with continental flair. Nodded as Ruby placed an order for Prosecco. As he left, Ruby reached for a wedge of focaccia. She winked at Cassandra and indicated the table. "Try the olive oil and balsamic. They're to die for."

Cassandra dunked some focaccia into the oil and vinegar.

"Come, Cassandra," said Grey, "save an old unmarried couple from bickering, tell us about your afternoon."

She picked up a crumb of bread that had fallen onto the table.

"Yes, anything exciting?" said Ruby.

Cassandra heard herself start speaking, "I found out who Nell's biological parents were."

Ruby squealed. "What? How? Who?"

She bit her lip, arresting its attempt to tremble into a smile of self-conscious pleasure. "Their names were Rose and Nathaniel Walker."

"Oh, my goodness," Ruby laughed, "it's the same as my painter, Grey! What are the odds of that, and us just speaking of him today, and he once living on the same estate as . . ." She froze as realization turned her face from pink to white. "You do mean my Nathaniel Walker?" She swallowed. "Your great-grandfather was Nathaniel Walker?"

Cassandra nodded, couldn't stop herself grinning. Felt vaguely ridiculous.

Ruby's mouth dropped open. "And you had no idea? Today, when I saw you at the gallery?"

Cassandra shook her head, still smiling like a fool. She spoke, if only to force the goofy grin from her face. "Not until this afternoon, when I read it in Nell's notebook."

"I can't believe you didn't say something as soon as we got here tonight!"

"With all your talk of salsa, I imagine she didn't have the opportunity," said Grey. "Not to mention, Ruby darling, that some people actually like to keep their private life private."

"Oh, Grey, no one really likes keeping secrets. The only thing that makes a secret fun is knowing that you weren't supposed to tell it." She shook her head at Cassandra. "You're related to Nathaniel Walker. Some people have all the bloody luck."

"It feels a little strange. It's very unexpected."

"Too right," said Ruby. "All those people searching through history in the hopes they're related to Winston bloody Churchill, and provenance drops unexpectedly into your lap in the shape of a famous painter."

Cassandra smiled again, couldn't help it.

The waiter reappeared and poured them each a glass of Prosecco.

"To solving mysteries," said Ruby, holding hers aloft.

They clinked glasses and all took a sip.

"Pardon my ignorance," said Grey, "my knowledge of art history isn't what it might be, but if Nathaniel Walker had a daughter who went missing, surely there'd have been a huge search?" He held his palms out towards Cassandra. "I'm not doubting your grandmother's research, but how on earth did the daughter of a famous artist go missing and no one knew it?"

Ruby, for once, had no ready answer. She looked to Cassandra.

"From what I can gather, reading Nell's notebook, all the records say Ivory Walker died when she was four. The same age Nell was when she turned up in Australia."

Ruby rubbed her hands together. "You think she was kidnapped and whoever did it made it look like she had died? How completely thrilling. So who was it? Why did they do it? What did Nell find out?"

Cassandra smiled apologetically. "It seems she never managed to solve that part of the mystery. Not for sure."

"What do you mean? How do you know?"

"I read the end of her notebook. Nell didn't find out."

"She must have found *something*, though, formed a theory?" Ruby's desperation was palpable. "Tell me she formed a theory! Left us something to go on?"

"There's a name," said Cassandra. "Eliza Makepeace. Nell wound up with a suitcase containing a book of fairy tales that sparked some memories. But if Eliza put Nell on the boat, she didn't make it to Australia herself."

"What happened to her?"

Cassandra shrugged. "There's no official record. It's like she disappeared into thin air right around the time Nell was being spirited to Australia. Whatever Eliza's plans, they must've gone wrong some-how."

The waiter topped up their glasses and asked whether they were ready to order their main course.

"I suppose we should," said Ruby. "Could you give us five min-utes, though?" She opened her menu with purpose and sighed. "It's all tremendously exciting. To think, tomorrow you're off to Cornwall to see your secret cottage! How can you bear it?"

"Are you staying in the cottage itself?" said Grey.

Cassandra shook her head. "The lawyer who's been holding the key said it's not really habitable. I've made a reservation at a nearby ho-tel, the Blackhurst Hotel. It's the house where the Mountrachet family used to live, Nell's family."

"Your family," said Ruby.

"Yes." Cassandra hadn't thought of that. Now her lips were at it again, acting against her wishes to form a trembling smile.

Ruby shivered theatrically. "I'm completely envious. I'd give any-thing for a mystery like that in my family's past, something exciting to unravel."

"I do feel quite excited. It's started to haunt me, I think. I keep seeing that little girl, little Nell, plucked from her family, sitting alone on the wharf. I can't get her out of my head. I'd love to know what re-ally happened, how she wound up on the other side of the world all alone." Cassandra felt self-conscious suddenly, realized she'd been do-ing a lot of talking. "It's silly, I suppose."

"Not at all. I think it's completely understandable."

And something in the sympathetic quality of Ruby's tone made Cassandra's skin cool. She knew what was coming. Her stomach tight-ened and her mind grasped for words to change the subject.

But she wasn't fast enough.

"There can't be much worse than losing a child," came Ruby's kind voice, her words cracking the thin protective shell of Cassandra's grief so that Leo's face, his smell, his two-year-old laugh, slipped free.

Somehow she managed to nod, to smile weakly, to hold back the memories as Ruby reached to take her hand.

"After what happened to your little boy, it's no wonder you're so intent on discovering your grandmother's past." Ruby gave a little squeeze. "Makes perfect sense to me: you lost a child and now you hope to find one."

TWENTY

❦

ELIZA knew who they were as soon as she saw them turn the corner into Battersea Church Road. She'd glimpsed them in the streets before, the old one and the young one, dressed to the nines, doing their good works with all the violent certainty as if God himself had come down from on high and bid them do so.

Mr. Swindell had been threatening to call the do-gooders ever since Sammy left them, had let no opportunity pass to remind Eliza that if she didn't find a way to earn the coins of two, she'd find herself in the workhouse. And though Eliza did her best to meet the rent and still leave a little spare for the leather pouch, her gift for rat-catching seemed to have deserted her, and week by week she slipped further behind.

Downstairs, a knock at the door. Eliza froze. She surveyed the room, cursing the tiny crack in the mortar, the blocked chimney. Being windowless and unobserved was all well and good when one wanted to spy upon the street, but not much use when gripped by an urgent need to escape.

The knock came again. A short sharp rap, urgent, and then a high trilling voice that pierced the brick wall. "Parish calling."

Eliza heard the door opening, the bell atop tinkling.

"I'm Miss Rhoda Sturgeon, and this is my niece, Miss Margaret Sturgeon."

Then Mrs. Swindell: "Charmed, I'm sure."

"My, what a lot of funny old things, and barely space to swing a cat."

Mrs. Swindell again, her tone soured: "Follow me, the girl's upstairs. And watch yourselves. Breakages must be paid for."

Footsteps, coming closer. The squeaky fourth step, then again, and again. Eliza waited, heart beating as fast as one of Mr. Rodin's captured rats. She could picture it, flickering away in her chest, like a flame in a light breeze.

Then the traitorous door was open, the two do-gooders framed by the jamb.

The older one smiled, eyes receding into folds of skin. "Ladies of the parish calling," she said. "I'm Miss Sturgeon, and this is my niece, Miss Sturgeon." She bent forward so that Eliza had to inch backwards. "And you must be little Eliza Makepeace."

Eliza didn't respond. She tugged slightly at Sammy's cap, which she was still wearing.

The old lady's gaze lifted to take in the dark and dingy room behind. "Oh my," she said, and made a clicking sound with her tongue, "your plight was not exaggerated." She raised an open hand and fanned her full chest. "No, it certainly was not exaggerated." She brushed past Eliza. "Is it any wonder ill health flourished here? No window to speak of."

Mrs. Swindell, offended by the scandalous affront to her room, scowled at Eliza.

The older Miss Sturgeon turned to the younger, who had not moved from the doorway. "I advise you to affix your handkerchief, Margaret, what with your delicate constitution."

The young woman nodded and plucked a lacy square from her sleeve, folded it in half to form a triangle, then clamped it over her mouth and nose while she ventured a step across the threshold.

Filled with the certainty of her own righteousness, the older Miss Sturgeon proceeded undeterred. "I'm delighted to announce that we've been able to find somewhere for you, Eliza. As soon as we heard of your situation, we immediately set about trying to help. You're a mite too young for service—and, I suspect, of the wrong character—but we've managed to do very well. With God's good grace, we've found you a place at the local workhouse."

Eliza's breath shortened, caught in her throat.

"So if you'll gather your things"—Miss Sturgeon's gaze flickered sideways beneath her blunt lashes—"such as they are, we'll be on our way."

Eliza didn't move.

"Come, now, don't tarry."

"No!" said Eliza.

Mrs. Swindell landed a slap on the back of Eliza's head and the old Miss Sturgeon's eyes widened. "You're a fortunate girl to be given a place, Eliza. I can assure you, there are worse things than the workhouse awaiting young girls left to their own devices." She sniffed knowingly and her nose went begging skywards. "Come along, now."

"I won't."

"Maybe she's dense," young Miss Sturgeon said through her handkerchief.

"She ain't dense," said Mrs. Swindell, "just wicked."

"The Lord claims all his lambs, even the wicked ones," said the older Miss Sturgeon. "Now, try to find some more suitable clothing for the girl, Margaret dear. And be careful not to breathe the foulness."

Eliza shook her head, she wasn't going to the workhouse and neither was she changing out of Sammy's clothing. It was part of her now.

This was when she needed her father to appear, heroic at the door. To scoop her up and take her with him, sailing across the seas in search of adventure.

"This'll do," said Mrs. Swindell, holding Eliza's tatty pinafore high. "She won't need any more than that where she's going."

Eliza thought suddenly of Mother's words. Her insistence that people need to rescue themselves, that with a strong enough will even the weak could wield great power. Suddenly she knew what must be done. Without another thought she leaped towards the door.

The older Miss Sturgeon, with advantageous heft and surprisingly fast reactions, blocked her way. Mrs. Swindell moved to form a second line of defense.

Eliza bucked her head and her face hit fulsome Sturgeon flesh. She bit with all her might. Miss Sturgeon let out a scream, clutched at her thigh. "Why, you little wildcat!"

"Aunt! She'll have given you the rabies!"

"I told you she were a menace," said Mrs. Swindell. "Here, forget about the clothes. Let's get her downstairs."

They each took an arm and the young Miss Sturgeon hovered nearby, offering useless advice as to the presence of stairs and doorways, while Eliza thrashed this way and that.

"Be still, girl!" said Old Miss Sturgeon.

"Help!" yelled Eliza, almost breaking free. "Someone help me."

"You'll get a walloping," Mrs. Swindell hissed as they reached the bottom of the stairs.

Then, suddenly, an unexpected ally.

"A rat! I saw a rat!"

"There's no rats in my house!"

The young Miss Sturgeon screamed, leaped atop a chair and sent an assortment of green bottles scuttling.

"Clumsy girl! Breakages must be paid for."

"But it was your own fault. If you hadn't been harboring rats—"

"I never did! There ain't a rat within a hair's breadth—"

"Auntie, I saw it. A horrid thing, large as a dog, with beady black eyes and long, sharp claws . . ." Her voice tapered off and she slumped against the chair back. "I've come over all faint. I'm not made for such horrors."

"There, now, Margaret, courage to the sticking place. Think of Christ's forty days and forty nights."

The older Miss Sturgeon proved her own impressive constitution by keeping a tight grip on Eliza's arm while leaning in to bolster her collapsing niece, who was now sniveling: "But its beady little eyes, the horrible twitchy nose—" She gasped. "Arggghhh! There it is!"

All eyes turned in the direction of Margaret's pointing finger. Crouched behind the coal scuttle, a quivering rat. Eliza willed him freedom.

"Come here, you little blighter!" Mrs. Swindell seized a cloth rag and started chasing the rodent about the room, swiping in all directions.

Margaret was squealing, Miss Sturgeon shushing, Mrs. Swindell cursing, glass shattering, and then, from nowhere, a new voice. Loud and low.

"Stop immediately."

All sound evaporated as Eliza, Mrs. Swindell and the two Misses Sturgeon turned to see whence the words came. Standing in the open doorway was a man dressed all in black. Behind him, a shiny carriage. Children were gathered around it, touching the wheels and marveling at the glowing lanterns up front. The man allowed his gaze to pass over the tableau before him.

"Miss Eliza Makepeace?"

Eliza nodded in a jerky fashion, unable to find words. Too dismayed that her point of escape was now blocked to wonder at the identity of this stranger who knew her name.

"Daughter of Georgiana Mountrachet?" He handed a photograph to Eliza. It was Mother, much younger, dressed in the fine clothing of a lady. Eliza's eyes widened. She nodded, confused.

"I am Phineas Newton. On behalf of Lord Mountrachet of Blackhurst Manor, I have come to collect you. To bring you home to the family estate."

Eliza's jaw dropped, though not so low as those belonging to the Misses Sturgeon. Mrs. Swindell collapsed onto a chair, victim of a sudden bout of apoplexy. Her mouth opened and closed like a mudskipper as she bleated confusedly, "Lord Mountrachet . . . ? Blackhurst Manor . . . ? Family estate . . . ?"

Old Miss Sturgeon straightened. "Mr. Newton, I'm afraid I cannot let you walk in here and take this girl without seeing some sort of order. We at the parish take our responsibilities—"

"All should be contained herein." The man presented a piece of paper. "My employer has applied for and been granted wardship of this minor." He turned to Eliza, barely flinched at her unusual outfitting. "Come, then, miss. There's a storm approaching and we've a way to go."

It took but a split second for Eliza to decide. Never mind that she had never heard of Georgiana Mountrachet or Blackhurst Estate. Never mind that she had no idea whether this Mr. Newton spoke the truth. Never mind that Mother had remained resolutely tight-lipped about her family, that a dark shadow had fallen across her face whenever Eliza pressed her for further mention. Anything was better than the workhouse. And in going along with this man's story, escaping the clutches of the Misses Sturgeon, waving good-bye to the Swindells and their cold, lonely rooftop room, it seemed to Eliza that she was helping to rescue herself just as surely as if she'd managed to break free and sprint out of the door.

She hurried towards Mr. Newton, stood behind his cloaked arm and sneaked a glance at his face. At such close range, he was not so large as he had seemed when silhouetted in the doorway. He was barrel-shaped and of medium height. His skin was ruddy and beneath his tall black hat Eliza could see a small amount of hair that the years were bleaching from brown to silver.

While the Misses Sturgeon were scrutinizing the wardship order, Mrs. Swindell finally regained her composure. She pushed forward, thrusting a thin, ropy finger in the direction of Mr. Newton's chest, punctuating every third word. "This is *nothing* but a *trick* and you, *sir,* are a *trickster*." She shook her head. "I don't know what it is you want with the girl, though I can imagine well enough, but you won't steal her from me by your wicked tricks."

"I assure you, madam," said Mr. Newton, swallowing a lump of rather apparent distaste, "there is no trick afoot."

"Oh no?" Her brows leapt and her lips stretched around a salivary smile. "Oh no?" She turned triumphantly towards the Misses Sturgeon. "It's lies, all lies, and he a nasty liar. This girl ain't got no family, she's an orphan, she is. An orphan. And she's mine, mine to do with as I please." Her lips took on a victorious curl as she reached a position she thought unassailable. "She were left me when the girl's mother died because there were nowhere else for her to go." She paused triumphantly. "That's right, the girl's own ma told me herself: she had no family to speak of. Not one mention of no family in the thirteen years I knowed her. This man's a shyster."

Eliza glanced upwards at Mr. Newton, who emitted a short sigh and raised his eyebrows. "Though it surprises me little that Miss Eliza's mother failed to divulge the details of her family's existence, it does not alter the fact that it is so." He nodded at the older Miss Sturgeon. "It's all in those papers." He stepped outside and held the carriage door wide. "Miss Eliza?" he said, indicating that she should climb inside.

"I'll call my husband," said Mrs. Swindell.

Eliza hesitated, hands opening and closing.

"Miss Eliza?"

"My husband'll set you right."

Whatever the truth about her family, Eliza realized the choice was simple: carriage or workhouse. She had no further control over her own destiny, not at this point. Her only option was to throw herself upon the mercy of one of the people gathered here. With a deep breath, she took a step towards Mr. Newton. "I have nothing packed . . ."

"Someone fetch Mr. Swindell!"

Mr. Newton smiled grimly. "I can think of nothing here that could possibly have a place at Blackhurst Manor."

A small crowd of neighbors had gathered now. Mrs. Barker stood to one side, mouth agape, basket of wet laundry nursed across her middle; little Hatty leaned her snotty cheek against Sarah's dress.

"If you would be so kind, Miss Eliza." Mr. Newton stood to the side of the door and swept his hand before the open space.

With a final glance at the panting Mrs. Swindell and the two Misses Sturgeon, Eliza climbed up the small ladder that had folded down to meet the gutter and disappeared into the dark cavity of the carriage.

IT WASN'T until the door was closed behind her that Eliza realized she wasn't alone. Sitting across from her, in the dark fabric folds of the other side, was a man she recognized. A man wearing pince-nez and a neat suit. Her stomach clenched. She knew instantly that this was the Bad Man that Mother had warned them about and she knew she had to escape. But as she turned desperately towards the closed door, the Bad Man hit the wall behind him and the carriage lurched forward.

PART TWO

PART TWO

TWENTY-ONE

THE ROAD TO CORNWALL, 1900

As they hurtled along Battersea Church Road, Eliza studied the carriage door. Perhaps if she turned one of the knobs, pressed one of the grooves, it would spring open and she could tumble to safety. The quality of that safety was dubious; if she survived the fall, she'd then have to find a way to avoid the workhouse, but it was better, surely, than being spirited away by the man who'd terrified Mother.

Heart fluttering like a trapped sparrow within her rib cage, she reached out carefully, closed her fingers around the lever and—

"I wouldn't do that if I were you."

She looked up sharply.

The man was watching her, eyes magnified behind the lenses of his pince-nez. "You'll fall beneath the carriage and the wheels will slice you through." He smiled thinly, revealing a gold tooth. "And how would I explain that to your uncle? Thirteen years of hunting only to deliver you in halves?" He made a noise then, rapid sucking sounds that Eliza recognized as laughter only by the upturned corners of his mouth.

As quickly as it started, the noise stopped and the man's mouth rearranged itself along sour lines. He brushed his bushy moustache, which sat like the tails of two small squirrels above his lips. "Mansell is my name." He leaned back and closed his eyes. Folded together his pale, damp-looking hands on the polished top of a dark cane. "I work for your uncle and I sleep very lightly."

The carriage wheels danced metallic down one cobblestone lane after another, brick buildings fled by, grey and grey as far as the eye could see, and Eliza sat stiffly, desperate not to wake the sleeping Bad Man. She tried to match her own breathing to the thuds of the galloping horses. Willed her spinning thoughts to straighten. Concentrated on the seat's cold leather beneath her. It was all she could do to stop her legs from shaking. She felt transported, like a character who'd been cut from the pages of one story, where rhythm and context were known, and glued rather carelessly into another.

When they reached the speckled outskirts of London and emerged finally from the forest of buildings, Eliza was able to see the angry sky. The horses were doing their best to outrun the dark grey clouds, but what chance had horses against God's own wrath? The first drops of rain spat spitefully on the carriage roof and the world outside was soon blanketed in white. It lashed against the windows and dripped through the thin gaps at the top of the carriage doors.

They drove on thus for hours and Eliza sought refuge in her thoughts, until suddenly they rounded a bend in the road and a trickle of icy water landed on her head. She blinked through waterlogged lashes, looked down at the drenched patch on her shirt. Felt a strong urge to cry. Strange that in a day of tumult, it should be something so innocuous as a dribble of water that prompted a person to tears. But she wouldn't let herself cry, not here, not with the Bad Man sitting just across the way. She swallowed the hard lump in her throat.

Without seeming to open his eyes, Mr. Mansell plucked a white handkerchief from his breast pocket and held it towards Eliza. Motioned for her to take it.

She patted her face dry.

"Such a fuss," he said, in a voice so thin his lips were barely parted. "Such a lot of fuss."

Eliza thought at first that he referred to her. It seemed unfair, as she had made very little fuss, but she didn't dare say as much. "So many years devoted," he continued, "so little reward." His eyes opened, cool and appraising; her skin tightened. "To such lengths will a broken man go."

Eliza wondered who the broken man was, waited for Mr. Mansell to make his meaning clear. But he did not speak again. Merely took back his handkerchief and held it between two pallid fingers before discarding it on the seat beside him.

The carriage jerked suddenly and Eliza gripped the seat to steady herself. The horses had changed their gait and the carriage was slowing. Finally, it stopped.

Had they arrived? Eliza looked out of the window but she could see no house. Only a vast, sodden field, and beside it a small stone building with a rain-battered sign above the door: MACCLEARY'S INN, GUILDFORD.

"I have other business," said Mr. Mansell, as he disembarked. "Newton will take you further." Rain almost obscured his next command, but as the door slammed shut, Eliza heard him shout, "Deliver the girl to Blackhurst."

A SHARP TURN and Eliza was thrown against the hard, cold door. Shocked from sleep, it took her some moments to remember where she was, why she was alone in a darkened carriage, being spirited towards an unknown destiny. Patchily, heavily, it all came back to her. The summons of her mysterious uncle, escape from the clutches of Mrs. Swindell's do-gooders, Mr. Mansell . . . She wiped condensation from the window and peered outside. Since she'd boarded the carriage they'd sped through day and night, stopping only occasionally to change the horses; and now it was almost dark again. Evidently she had been asleep for some time; just how long, she couldn't tell.

It was no longer raining and a smattering of early stars was visible beyond the low cloud. The carriage lights were no match for the thick dusk of the countryside, quivering as the coachman navigated the bumpy road. In the dim, damp light Eliza saw the shapes of large trees, black branches scribbled along the horizon, and a set of tall iron gates. They entered a tunnel of huge brambles and the wheels bumped along the ditches, tossing sprays of muddy water against the window.

All was dark within the tunnel, the tendrils so dense that none of the dusk light was permitted entry. Eliza held her breath, waiting to be delivered. Waiting for her first glimpse of what must surely lie ahead. Blackhurst. She could hear her heart, a sparrow no longer but a raven with large, powerful wings, beating within her chest.

Suddenly, they emerged.

A stone building, the biggest Eliza had ever seen. Bigger even than the hotels in London where the toffs came and went. It was shrouded in dark mist, with tall trees and branches laced together behind it. Lamplight flickered yellow in some of the lower windows. Surely this could not be the house?

Movement and her gaze was drawn to a window near the top. A distant face, bleached by candlelight, was watching. Eliza moved closer to the window to get a better look, but when she did the face was gone.

And then the carriage passed the building, metal wheels continuing to clack along the cobblestones. They went beneath a stone arch and the carriage jerked to a halt.

Eliza sat alert, waiting, watching, wondering whether she was supposed to climb out of the carriage, find her own way inside.

Suddenly the door opened and Mr. Newton, drenched despite his raincoat, held out his hand. "Come, then, miss, we're late enough already. No time for dithering."

Eliza took the proffered hand and scrambled down the carriage steps. They'd outrun the rain while she was sleeping, but the sky promised it would catch up with them. Dark grey clouds drooped towards the earth, heavy with intention, and the air beneath was thick with fog, a different fog from that in London. Colder, less greasy; it smelled like salt and leaves and water. There was a noise, too, which she couldn't place. Like a train rushing repeatedly by. *Whoosha . . . whoosha . . . whoosha . . .*

"You're late. The mistress expected the girl at half two." A man was standing in the doorway, dressed a little like a toff. He spoke like one, too, and yet Eliza knew that he wasn't. His rigidity gave him away, the vehemence of his superiority. No one born to quality ever needed to try so hard.

"Couldn't be helped, Mr. Thomas," said Newton. "Wretched weather the whole way. Lucky we made it at all, what with the Tamar rising like it is."

Mr. Thomas was unmoved. He snapped closed his pocket watch. "The mistress is greatly displeased. Little doubt she'll require an audience on the morrow."

The coachman's voice turned lemon sour: "Yes, Mr. Thomas. Little doubt. Sir."

Mr. Thomas turned to take in Eliza, swallowed a barbed kernel of displeasure. "What is this?"

"The girl, sir. Just like I was told to fetch."

"That isn't any girl."

"Yes, sir, she's the one."

"But its hair . . . its clothes . . ."

"I only do what I'm instructed, Mr. Thomas. If you have any queries, I suggest you take them up with Mr. Mansell. He was with me when I fetched her."

This news seemed to mollify Mr. Thomas somewhat. He forced a sigh through tight lips. "I suppose if Mr. Mansell was satisfied . . ."

The coachman nodded. "If that's all, I'll be getting the horses stabled."

Eliza considered running after Mr. Newton and his horses, seeking refuge in the stables, hiding in a carriage and finding her way, somehow, back to London, but when she looked after him he'd already been enveloped by the fog and she was stranded.

"Come," said Mr. Thomas, and Eliza did as she was bade.

Inside was cool and dank, though warmer and drier than outside. Eliza followed Mr. Thomas along a short hallway, trying to keep
her feet from clipping on the grey flagstones. The air was thick with
the smell of roasting meat and Eliza felt her stomach flip over. When
had she last eaten? A bowl of Mrs. Swindell's broth two days before, a
piece of bread and cheese the coachman had given her many long
hours ago . . . Her lips grew dry with sudden hunger.

The smell was stronger as they walked through a huge, steamy
kitchen. A cluster of maids and a fat cook stopped their conversation
to observe. As soon as Eliza and Mr. Thomas had passed, they erupted
in a rush of excited whispering. Eliza could've wept for having been so
close to food. Her mouth watered as if she'd swallowed a handful of
salt.

At the end of the hall, a skinny woman with a face made stiff by
exactitude stepped from a doorway. "This is the niece, Mr. Thomas?"
Her direct gaze traveled slowly down Eliza's person.

"It is, Mrs. Hopkins."

"There has been no mistake?"

"Regrettably not, Mrs. Hopkins."

"I see." She drew in a slow breath. "She certainly has the look of
London about her."

This, Eliza could tell, was not to her advantage.

"Indeed, Mrs. Hopkins," said Mr. Thomas. "I was of a mind to
have her bathed before presenting her."

Mrs. Hopkins's lips tightened. A sharp, decisive sigh. "Though I
agree with your sentiment, Mr. Thomas, I'm afraid there isn't time. *She*
has already let us know of her displeasure at being kept waiting."

She. Eliza wondered who *she* was.

A certain agitation crept into Mrs. Hopkins's manner when the
word was spoken. She brushed quickly at her already smooth skirts.
"The girl is to be taken to the drawing room. *She* will be along presently. Meanwhile, I'll draw a bath, see if we can't remove some of that
horrid London filth before dinner."

So there was to be dinner. And soon. Eliza was light-headed with relief.

A giggle from behind and Eliza turned just in time to see a curly-haired maid disappear back towards the kitchen.

"Mary!" said Mrs. Hopkins, stalking after the maid. "You'll wake one morning and trip over your own ears if you don't learn to stop them flapping . . ."

At the very end of the hall a set of narrow stairs ran up, then turned towards a wooden door at the top. Mr. Thomas went briskly and Eliza followed, through the door and into a large room.

The floors were covered with pale rectangular flagstones, and a magnificent staircase swept up from the center of the room. A chandelier was suspended from the high ceiling, its candles tossing tissues of soft light onto all below.

Mr. Thomas crossed the entrance foyer and moved towards a door, thick with glistening red paint. He inclined his head and Eliza realized he meant for her to come.

His pale lips quivered as he looked down at her. Little lines puckered. "The mistress, your aunt, will be down to see you in a minute. Mind your p's and q's and call her 'my lady' unless she bids you do otherwise."

Eliza nodded. *She* was her aunt.

Mr. Thomas was still looking at her. He shook his head slightly without removing his gaze. "Yes," he said in a quick, quiet voice. "I *can* see your mother in you. You're a tatty little wench, no mistake about it, but she's in there somewhere." Before Eliza could try on for size the pleasant notion that she was somehow like Mother, there was a noise at the top of the grand staircase. Mr. Thomas stopped, straightened. He gave Eliza a little prod and she stumbled alone across the threshold into a large room with burgundy wallpaper and a fire raging in the hearth.

Oil lamps flickered on the tops of tables but despite their best efforts they couldn't hope to light the enormous room. Darkness whispered in the corners, shadows breathed along the walls. Back and forth, back and forth . . .

A noise behind and the door opened again. A gust of cold air set the fire to spitting in the grate, hurled jagged shadows against the walls.

With a shiver of anticipation, Eliza turned.

A TALL, THIN woman stood in the doorway, her body an elongated hourglass. Her long dress, blue silk as deep as the midnight sky, clung to her figure.

A huge dog—no, not a dog, a hound—stood by her, long legs prancing as he worried close, stalking about the hem of her dress. He lifted his knobbled head every so often to rub against her hand.

"Miss Eliza," announced Mr. Thomas, who had hurried in behind the woman and now stood to attention.

The woman did not respond but studied Eliza's face. She was silent for a minute before her lips parted and a flinty voice emerged. "I must speak with Newton tomorrow. She comes later than expected." She spoke so slowly, so surely, that Eliza could feel the sharp corners of her words.

"Yes, my lady," said Thomas, cheeks flaming. "Shall I bring the tea, my lady? Mrs. Hopkins has—"

"Not now, Thomas." Without turning, she gave a vague flutter of her pale, fine hand. "You should know better than that, it's far too late for tea."

"Yes, my lady."

"If word should travel that tea had been taken at Blackhurst Manor after dark—" A tight crystal-breaking laugh. "No, we'll wait for dinner now."

"In the dining room, my lady?"

"Where else?"

"Set for two, my lady?"

"I will dine alone."

"And Miss Eliza, ma'am?"

The aunt inhaled sharply. "A light supper."

Eliza's stomach groaned. Please God that her meal would contain some warm meat.

"Very good, my lady," said Mr. Thomas, bowing as he left the room. The door sealed glumly behind him.

The aunt drew a long, slow breath and blinked at Eliza. "Come closer, then, child. Let me look at you."

Eliza obeyed, walked towards her aunt and stood, trying to silence breaths that had grown unaccountably quick.

Close up, the aunt was beautiful. It was the type of beauty exemplified in each feature but diminished somehow by the whole. Her face was like that in a painting. Skin as white as snow, lips as red as blood, eyes of palest blue. Looking into her eyes was like staring at a mirror with a light shone upon it. Her dark hair was smooth and shiny, swept back from her face and gathered richly at the crown of her head.

The aunt's gaze picked over Eliza's face and her eyelids seemed to flicker slightly. Cold fingers lifted Eliza's chin, all the better to observe her. Eliza, unsure where to look, blinked at those impassable eyes. The giant dog stood by his mistress, breathing warm, damp air onto Eliza's arms.

"Yes," the aunt said, the s sound lingering on her lips and a nerve twitching at the side of her mouth. It was as if she answered a question that had not been asked. "You are her daughter. Reduced in all ways, but hers nonetheless." She shivered slightly as a scud of rain hit the windows. The foul weather had finally found them. "We must only hope your nature is not the same. That with timely intervention we can arrest any similar tendencies."

Eliza wondered what these tendencies might be. "My mother—"

"No," the aunt raised her hand. "No." She steepled her fingers before her mouth, strangled her lips into a thin smile. "Your mother brought shame upon her family's name. Offended against all who live in this house. We do not speak of her here. Ever. This is the first and most important condition of your accommodation at Blackhurst Manor. Do you understand?"

Eliza bit her lip.

"Do you understand?" An unexpected tremor had entered the aunt's voice.

Eliza nodded slightly, more from surprise than agreement.

"Your uncle is a gentleman. He understands his responsibilities." The aunt's eyes flickered in the direction of a portrait by the door. A man of middle years with ginger hair and a foxlike expression. But for his red hair, he was nothing like Eliza's mother. "You must remember always how fortunate you are. Work hard that you might someday deserve your uncle's generosity."

"Yes, my lady," said Eliza, remembering what Mr. Thomas had said.

The aunt turned and pulled a small lever on the wall.

Eliza swallowed. Dared to speak. "Excuse me, my lady," she said softly. "Am I to meet my uncle?"

The aunt's left eyebrow arched. Thin pleats appeared briefly on her forehead before smoothing once more to give the appearance of alabaster. "My husband has been in Scotland, taking photographs of Brechin Cathedral and is not due back until tomorrow." She came close and Eliza was aware of tension emanating from her body. "Although he has offered you accommodation your uncle is a busy man, an important man, a man not given to the interruptions of children." She pressed her lips so tightly that their color was briefly bleached. "You must stay out of his way always. It is kindness enough that he has brought you here, do not be seeking more. Do you understand?" The lips quivered. "Do you understand?"

Eliza nodded quickly.

Then, blessedly, the door was open and Mr. Thomas was there again.

"You rang, my lady?"

The aunt's eyes were still focused on Eliza. "The child needs cleaning."

"Yes, my lady, Mrs. Hopkins has already fetched the water."

The aunt shivered. "Have her put some carbolic in it. Something strong. Sufficient to remove that London grime." She spoke under her breath. "Would that it removed all else with which I fear she's been tainted."

STILL RAW from the scrubbing she'd received, Eliza followed the flickering of Mrs. Hopkins's lantern up a flight of cold wooden stairs and into another hallway. Long-dead men leered at them from heavy gilt frames and Eliza thought how ghastly it must be to have one's portrait painted, to sit still for so long, all so that a layer of oneself could be left forever on a canvas, hung lonely in a darkened corridor.

She slowed. The final painting's subject she recognized. It was different from that in the room downstairs: in this one he was younger. His face was fuller and there was little hint of the fox that would later gnaw its way to the surface. In this portrait, in this young man's face, Eliza saw her mother.

"That there's your uncle," said Mrs. Hopkins without turning. "You'll meet him in the flesh soon enough." The word *flesh* made Eliza aware of the flecks of pink and cream paint that lingered on the portrait in the grooves of the artist's final strokes. She shivered, remembering Mr. Mansell's pale, moist fingers.

Mrs. Hopkins stopped before a door at the dim end of the hallway and Eliza hurried after, still clutching Sammy's clothing to her chest. The housekeeper withdrew a large key from a fold in her dress and inserted it into the lock. Pushed open the door and started through, lantern held aloft.

The room was dark; the lantern cast only the dimmest light across its threshold. In the center Eliza could make out a bed of shiny black wood with four posts that looked to have engraved upon them figures climbing towards the ceiling.

On the bedside table was a tray with a piece of bread and a bowl of soup from which steam no longer rose. No meat to be seen, but beggars couldn't be choosers, as Mother used to say. Eliza fell upon the bowl and spooned the soup into her mouth so fast she swallowed a set of hiccups. She ran the bread around the bowl so as not to waste a smear.

Mrs. Hopkins, who had been watching with a somewhat stunned expression, made no comment. She continued stiffly, set down the lantern on a wooden box at the foot of the bed and pulled back the heavy blanket. "There you are, then, climb in. I haven't all night."

Eliza did as she was told. The sheets were cold and damp beneath her legs, sensitive after their fierce scouring.

Mrs. Hopkins took the lantern and Eliza heard the door close behind her. And then she was alone in the pitch-dark room, listening as the house's tired old bones creaked beneath its shiny skin.

The darkness of the bedroom had a sound, Eliza thought. A low, distant rumbling. Ever present, always threatening, never coming close enough to be revealed as something harmless.

And then it started to rain again, heavy and sudden. Eliza shivered as a flash of lightning split the sky into two jagged halves and threw light across the world. In those moments of illumination, always followed by a crack of thunder that made the giant house shake, she scanned the room one wall at a time, trying to make out her surroundings.

Flash . . . crack . . . dark wooden wardrobe beside the bed.

Flash . . . crack . . . fireplace against the far wall.

Flash . . . crack . . . ancient rocking chair by the window.

Flash . . . crack . . . a window seat.

On tiptoes, Eliza crossed the cold floor. Wind slipped through the cracks in the timbers and rushed along its surface. She climbed onto the window seat that had been built into the nook and looked out across the dark grounds. Angry clouds had shrouded the moon and the garden sat beneath a cloak of troubled night. Needles of driving rain pelted the sodden ground.

Another flash of lightning and the room was lit once more. As the light faded, Eliza caught a glimpse of her reflection in the window. Her face, Sammy's face.

Eliza reached out but the image had already faded and her fingers merely brushed the icy glass. She knew, in that moment more than any before, that she was a long way from home.

She went back to bed and slid between the cold, damp, unfamiliar sheets. Placed her head on Sammy's shirt. Closed her eyes and drifted among the reedy fringe of sleep.

Suddenly she sat bolt upright.

Her stomach turned and her heart beat faster.

Mother's brooch. How could she have forgotten? In all the hurry, with all the drama, she had left it behind. High up in the chimney cavity, in Mr. and Mrs. Swindell's house, Mother's treasure waited.

TWENTY-TWO

CASSANDRA dropped a tea bag into a cup and switched on the kettle. As it worked itself up to steaming, she gazed towards the window. Her room was at the back of the Blackhurst Hotel, facing out to sea, and though it was dark Cassandra could still make out some of the rear gardens. A clipped kidney-shaped lawn sloped away from the terrace towards a line of tall trees, blue beneath the moon's silvery light. That was the cliff face, Cassandra knew, those trees the last line of defense on this particular piece of earth.

Somewhere beyond the cove was the town itself. Cassandra hadn't seen much of it yet. The train trip had taken most of the day and by the time the taxi wove its way through the back hills of Tregenna, daylight was fading quickly to darkness. Only briefly as the car mounted a crest had she glimpsed a circle of twinkling lights in the cove below, like a fairy village materializing with the dusk.

As she waited for the water to boil, Cassandra thumbed the dog-eared edge of Nell's notebook. She'd had it out during much of the train trip, had imagined that her time could be well spent unraveling the next stage of Nell's journey, but she had been mistaken. The theory was sound, its practice not so easily accomplished. She'd been in company most of the trip with her own thoughts, had been so ever since the dinner with Ruby and Grey. Though Nick and Leo were never far from Cassandra's mind, having the fact of their deaths remarked upon so openly, so unexpectedly, had brought the fracturing moment crashing back.

It had been so sudden. She supposed such things always were. One moment she was a wife and mother, the next she was alone. And all for the sake of an uninterrupted hour in which to draw. She'd thrust a thumb-sucking Leo into Nick's arms and sent them to the shops for groceries they didn't need. Nick had grinned at her as he'd started the car down the driveway, and Leo had waved a chubby little hand, still clutching the silk pillowcase he'd taken to carrying everywhere. Cassandra had waved back absently, her mind already in her studio.

Worst of all was how much she'd relished the hour and a half before the knock came on her door. She hadn't even noticed how long they'd been gone . . .

Nell had been Cassandra's savior for a second time. She'd come straightaway, brought Ben with her. He'd been able to explain what had happened, the words that had made no sense from the policeman's lips: an accident, a swerving truck, a collision. A ghastly sequence of events so mundane, so ordinary, it was impossible to believe that they were happening to her.

Nell hadn't told Cassandra it would be all right. She'd understood better than that, had known that it would never, could never, be all right. She'd come armed instead with pills to help Cassandra sleep. To deliver a blessed blow to her racing mind and make it all disappear, if only for a few hours. And then she'd taken Cassandra home with her.

It was better back at Nell's; the ghosts weren't as comfortable there. Nell's place had its own set and the ones Cassandra brought didn't have quite the same free run.

Time afterwards was a haze. Of grief and horror and nightmares that couldn't be shed with the new day. She wasn't sure which were worse, the nights that Nick filled her thoughts, his ghost asking, over and over, why did you make us go? Why did you make me take Leo? Or the nights when he wouldn't come, when she was alone and the dark hours threatened to stretch interminably, the partial salvation of the dawn rushing away from her faster than she could ever hope to chase it. And then there was the dream. The hateful field with its promise of finding them.

During the days it was Leo who trailed her, the noise of his toys, a cry, a little hand grabbing at her skirt, begging to be lifted into her arms and held. Oh, the flicker of unabated joy in her heart, momentary, fractured, but real nonetheless. The split second in which she forgot. Then the thud of reality when she turned to scoop him up and he wasn't there.

She had tried going out, had thought she might escape them that way, but it hadn't worked. There'd been so many children everywhere she went. The parks, the schools, the shops. Had there always been so many? So she'd stayed home, spent the days in Nell's yard, lying on her back beneath the old mango tree and watching the clouds waft overhead. The perfect blue sky behind the frangipani leaves, the fluttering of the palm fronds, tiny star-shaped seeds dislocated by the breeze to rain over the path below.

Thinking of nothing. Trying to think of nothing. Thinking of everything.

That was where Nell had found her on an afternoon in April. The season had just begun to turn, summer's swelter had lifted and there was a hint of impending autumn in the air. Cassandra's eyes were closed.

The first she realized that Nell was standing nearby was by the loss of warmth from the skin on her arms and the slight darkening inside her eyelids.

Then a voice: "Thought I'd find you out here."

Cassandra said nothing.

"D'you think it might be time you started doing something, Cass?"

"Please, Nell. Leave it alone."

Slower, more clearly enunciated: "You need to start doing something."

"Please . . ." To pick up a pencil made her physically ill. As for opening one of her sketchbooks . . . How could she bear to risk glimpsing the swell of a plump cheek, the tip of an upturned nose, the arc of kissable baby lips . . . ?

"You need to do something."

Nell was just trying to help and yet there was a part of Cassandra that wanted to scream and shake her grandmother, punish her for this failure to understand. Instead, she sighed. Her lids, still closed, fluttered a little. "I hear it enough from Dr. Harvey. I don't need it from you, too."

"I don't mean therapeutically, Cass." A brief hesitation before Nell continued. "I mean you need to start contributing."

Cassandra's eyes opened, she lifted a hand to block the glare. "What?"

"I'm not a spring chicken, my love. I need some help. Around the house, in the shop, financially."

The offending sentences shimmered in the bright air, sharp edges refusing to dissipate. How could Nell be so cold? So thoughtless? Cassandra shivered. "My family is gone," she managed finally, her throat aching with the effort. "I'm grieving."

"I know that," said Nell, easing herself down to sit by Cassandra. She reached out and clutched her hand. "I know that, my darling girl. But it's been six months. And *you* are not dead."

Cassandra was crying now. It was saying the words out loud that did it.

"You are here," said Nell softly, squeezing Cassandra's hand, "and I need help."

"I can't."

"You can."

"No—" Her head was throbbing; she was tired, so tired. "I mean I *can't*. I have nothing to give."

"I don't need you to give me anything. I just need you to come with me and do as I ask. You can hold a polishing cloth, can't you?"

Nell had reached out then to stroke Cassandra's hair from her cheeks, sticky with tears. Her voice was low, unexpectedly steely. "You'll beat this. I know it doesn't feel like it, but you will. You're a survivor."

"I don't want to survive it."

"I know that, too," Nell had said. "And it's fair enough. But sometimes we don't have a choice . . ."

The hotel kettle switched itself off with a triumphant *click* and Cassandra poured water over the tea bag, hand shaking a little. Stood for a moment as it drew. She realized now that Nell really had understood, that she knew all too well the sudden, blinding emptiness of having one's ties cut.

She stirred her tea and sighed quietly as Nick and Leo retreated once more. Forced herself to focus on the present. She was at the Blackhurst Hotel in Tregenna, Cornwall, listening as the waves of an unfamiliar ocean crashed upon the sands of an unfamiliar beach.

Beyond the dark heads of the tallest trees, a lone bird cut black across an inky sky and moonlight rippled on the faraway ocean surface. Tiny lights winked at the shore. Fishing boats, Cassandra figured. Tregenna was a fishing village, after all. Strange, in this modern world it was a surprise to find a pocket where things were still done in the old way, on a small scale, as they had been done for generations.

Cassandra took a sip and exhaled warmly. She was in Cornwall, just as Nell had been before her. Rose and Nathaniel and Eliza Makepeace before that. As she whispered their names to herself, she felt an odd tingling beneath her skin. Like tiny threads all being pulled at the same time. She had a purpose here, and it was not to wallow in her own past.

"Here I am, Nell," she said softly. "Is this what you wanted me to do?"

Twenty-three

When Eliza woke the next morning, it took her a moment to remember where she was. She seemed to be lying in a huge wooden sleigh with a deep blue canopy suspended above. Her nightdress was of the type to have Mrs. Swindell rubbing her hands together with glee and Sammy's dirty clothing was bunched beneath her head. Then she remembered: the do-gooders, Mr. Newton, the carriage ride, the Bad Man. She was at her uncle and aunt's house, there had been a storm, lightning, thunder and rain. Sammy's face in the window.

Eliza scrambled onto the window seat and looked outside. Was forced to squint. The rain and thunder of the night before had been rolled away by the dawn, and the light, the air, all was washed clean. Leaves and branches lay strewn across the lawn and a garden seat directly beneath the window had been blown over.

Her attention was drawn to a distant corner of the garden. Someone, a man, moved among the greenery. He had a black beard and was dressed in overalls, a strange little green hat and black galoshes.

A noise from behind and Eliza turned. The door to the room was open and a young maid with emphatically curly hair was placing a tray on the bedside table. It was the same maid who'd received a scolding the night before.

"Morning, miss," she said. "My name's Mary and I've brought you some breakfast. Mrs. Hopkins said you could have it in your room this morning on account of the long journey you took these past days."

Eliza hurried to sit at the little table. Her eyes widened as she took in the contents of the tray: hot bread rolls with lashings of melting butter, white pots filled to the brim with the fruitiest conserves she had ever seen, a pair of kippers, a pile of fluffy egg, a fat, glistening sausage. Her heart sang.

"That were quite a storm you brought with you last night," said Mary, strapping the curtains back. "I almost didn't make it home. Thought for a time I were going to need to stay here the night!"

Eliza swallowed a lump of bread. "You don't live here?"

Mary laughed. "No fear. Might be all right for the rest of them but I shouldn't like to live—" She glanced at Eliza, a pink glow warming her cheeks. "That is, I live in the village. With my ma and pa and my brothers and sister."

"You have a brother?" As Eliza thought of Sammy the emptiness yawned inside her.

"Oh yes, indeed, three of them. Two older and one younger, though Patrick, the eldest, don't live at home no more. Still works on the fishing boats with my pa, though. He, Will and Pa go out every day, whatever the weather. The younger, Roly, he's only three, he stays at home with my ma and little May." She plumped the cushions on the window seat. "We Martins have always worked on the sea. My great-grandfather were one of the Tregenna pirates."

"The what?"

"The Tregenna pirates," said Mary, eyes widening with incredulity. "Have you not heard of them?"

Eliza shook her head.

"The Tregenna pirates were the most fearsome bunch you'd ever find. They ruled the seas in their time, bringing back whisky and pepper when the folk at home couldn't get them otherwise. Only ever took from the rich, mind you. Just like what's-his-name, except on the ocean, not in the forest. There's passages winding right the way through these hills. One or two reach all the way to the sea."

"Where is the sea, Mary?" said Eliza. "Is it near?"

Mary looked at her strangely again. "Well, of course it is, poppet! Can't you hear it?"

Eliza paused and listened. Could she hear the sea?

"Listen," said Mary. "*Whoosha . . . whoosha . . . whoosha . . .* That there's the sea. Breathing in and out as it always does. Could you really not hear it?"

"I could hear it," said Eliza. "I just didn't know it was the sea."

"Didn't know it was the sea?" Mary grinned. "What on God's earth did you think it was?"

"I thought it was a train."

"A train!" Mary erupted into laughter. "You are the ticket. The station's a way off from here. Thought the sea were a train, indeed. Just you wait until I tell my brothers."

Eliza thought of the few stories Mother had told about sand and silver shingles and wind that smelled like salt. "Could I go and look at the sea, Mary?"

"I reckon you could. So long as you make sure and be back when Cook rings the luncheon bell. The mistress is out visiting this morning, so she won't be here to notice." A cloud came across Mary's cheerful face when she mentioned the mistress. "Just you mind you're back before she is, you hear? She's one for rules and order, and not to be crossed."

"How do I get there?"

Mary beckoned Eliza towards the window. "Come over here, poppet, and I'll show you."

THE AIR was different here, and the sky. It seemed brighter and further away. Not like the grey lid that hung low over London, threatening, always threatening, to close upon it. This sky was lifted high by sea breezes, like a great white sheet on laundering day, with the air caught beneath it, billowing higher and higher.

Eliza stood at cliff's edge looking out across the cove towards the deep blue sea. The very same sea her father had sailed upon, the beach her mother had known when she was a girl.

The storm of the night before had left driftwood scattered across the pale shore. Elegant white branches, gnarled and polished by time, emerged from the pebbles like the antlers of some great ghostly beast.

Eliza could taste salt in the air, just as Mother had always said. Out of the confines of the strange house she felt suddenly light and free. She took a deep breath and started down the wooden steps, scuttling faster and faster, eager to be at the bottom.

Once she reached the shore, she sat on a smooth rock and unlaced her boots, fingers tripping over themselves to complete the task. She rolled the hems of Sammy's breeches so that they sat above her knees, then she picked her way towards the water's edge. Stones, smooth and spiky alike, were warm beneath her feet. She stood for a moment, observing as the great blue mass heaved in and out, in and out.

Then, with a deep, salty breath, she skipped forward so that her toes, her ankles, her knees were wet. She followed the shoreline, laughing at the cool bubbles between her toes, picking up shells that took her fancy and, once, a piece of sea debris shaped like a star.

It was a small cove with a deep curve and it didn't take long for Eliza to travel the entire length of its shore. When she reached the end, proximity gave a third dimension to what had seemed, at a distance, a mere dark patch. A huge black crag emerged from the bluff and charged into the sea. It was shaped like a mighty puff of angry black smoke that had been frozen in time, cursed to an eternal solidity. Properly part of neither land nor sea nor air.

The black rock was slippery but Eliza found a ledge at its rim just deep enough to stand on. She hunted out jagged footholds and scrambled up the rock's side, didn't stop until she'd made it to the very top. She was so high, she couldn't look down without feeling that her head was filled with bubbles. On hands and knees, she inched forward. It became narrower and narrower until finally she was at the furthest point. She sat on the rock's raised fist and laughed, breathlessly.

It was like being at the top of a great ship. Beneath her, the white froth of duelling waves; before her, the open sea. The sun had set hundreds of lights to shimmering on its surface, rising and rippling with the breeze, all the way towards the clear unbroken horizon. Directly in front, she knew, was France. Beyond Europe was the East—India, Egypt, Persia and the other exotic places she'd heard humming on the lips of the Thames rivermen. Beyond even that was the Far East, the other side of the earth. Watching the vast ocean, the flickering sunlight, thinking of distant lands, Eliza was enveloped by a feeling quite unlike any she'd experienced before. A warmth, a glimpse of possibility, an absence of wariness—

She leaned forward and squinted. The horizon was unbroken no more. Something had appeared: a big black ship with full sails, balanced on the line where sea met sky, as if about to slip over the rim of the world. Eliza blinked and when her eyes opened again the ship was gone. It had disappeared; into the distance, she supposed. How swiftly ships must move in the open sea, how strong their wide white sails. That was the sort of ship her father would have sailed upon, she thought.

Eliza allowed her attention to drift skywards. A gull was circling above, calling out, camouflaged against the white sky. She followed its path until something on the cliff top caught her eye. There was a cottage, almost hidden by trees. She could just make out its roof and a funny little window that stuck out on top. She wondered what it would be like to live in such a place, right on the edge of the world like that. Would it always feel as if you were about to topple over and slide into the ocean?

Eliza started as cold water sprayed her face. She looked down at the swirling sea. The tide was coming in, the water rising quickly. The ledge she had first stepped upon was underwater now.

She crawled back along the ridge of the rock and went carefully down, keeping to the deepest edge so she could wrap her fingers around the craggy side.

When she was almost at water level she paused. From this angle she could see that the rock wasn't solid. It was as if someone had carved out a great hole.

A cave, that's what it was. Eliza thought of Mary's Tregenna pirates, their tunnels. That's what this cave was, she was sure of it. Hadn't Mary said the pirates used to traffic their loot through a series of caves that ran beneath the cliffs?

Eliza shimmied around the front of the rock and scrambled onto the flattish platform. She took a few steps inside: it was dark and moist. "Hello-o-o-o-o?" she called out. Her voice echoed pleasingly, lapped against the walls before fading to nothing.

She couldn't see far beyond but felt a thrill of excitement. Her very own cave. She would come back here one day, she determined, with a lantern so that she could see what lay inside—

A thudding sound, distant but drawing near. *Ker-thud, ker-thud, ker-thud* . . .

Eliza's first thought was that it issued from within the cave. Fear glued her feet to the spot, as she wondered what sort of sea monster was coming for her.

Ker-thud, ker-thud, ker-thud . . . Louder now.

She backed away slowly, started picking her way to the side of the rock.

Then, tearing along the ridge of the cliff, she saw a pair of shiny black horses dragging a carriage behind them. Not a sea monster after all, but Newton and his carriage on the cliff road, the sound amplified as it bounced between the rock walls of the cove.

She remembered Mary's warning. The aunt had gone out for the morning but was expected back for luncheon; Eliza was not to be late.

She clambered along the rock and jumped clear onto the pebbly shore. Ran through the shallow water, then back up the beach. Eliza laced her boots and bounded up the steps. The bottom of her breeches were wet, and the hems slapped heavily against her ankles as she wound her way back along the track between the trees. The sun had shifted since she'd come down to the cove, and now the path was dim and cool. It was like being in a burrow, a secret bramble burrow, home to fairies and goblins and elves. They were hiding, watching her as she tiptoed through their world. She scrutinized the underbrush as she went, tried not to blink, in the hopes she might catch one unawares. For everybody knew, a fairy glimpsed was bound to grant her finder's wishes.

A noise and Eliza froze. Held her breath. In the clearing before her was a man, a real live man. The one with the black beard whom she'd seen from her bedroom window that morning. He was sitting on a log, unwrapping a checked piece of cloth. Inside was a meaty wedge of pastry.

Eliza drew herself to the side of the path and watched him. The tips of tiny naked branches caught the ends of her short hair as she climbed cautiously onto a low bough, all the better to observe. The man had a barrow beside him, full of earth. Or so it seemed. Eliza knew that was a mere ruse, that beneath the earth he had his treasures stored. For he was a pirate king, of course. One of the Tregenna pirates, or the ghost of a Tregenna pirate. An undead seafarer, waiting to take revenge for the deaths of his comrades. A ghost with unfinished business, waiting in his lair to capture little girls to take home for his wife to bake into pies. That was the ship she'd seen out at sea, the big black ship that had disappeared in the blink of an eye. It was a ghost ship, and he—

The branch she was perched upon snapped and Eliza tumbled to the ground, landed in a mound of moist leaves.

The bearded man barely moved a muscle. His right eyeball seemed to swivel slightly in Eliza's direction as he continued to chew his pastry.

Eliza stood, rubbed at her knee, then straightened. Pulled a dry leaf from her hair.

"You're the new little lady," he said slowly, masticated pastry turning to glue inside his mouth. "I heard talk you'd come. Though if you don't mind me saying, you don't look much of a lady. What with those lad's clothes and your hair all torn up like that."

"I came last night. I brought the storm with me."

"That's quite a power you've got for such a small thing."

"With a strong enough will, even the weak can wield great power."

A furry-caterpillar eyebrow twitched. "Who told you that?"

"My mother."

Eliza remembered too late that she wasn't supposed to mention her mother. Heart flickering, she waited to see what the man would say.

He stared at her, chewing slowly. "I dare say she knew what she were talking about. Mothers tend towards right on most things."

The warm pins and needles of relief. "My mother died."

"So did mine."

"I'm living here now."

He nodded. "I'd say you are."

"My name is Eliza."

"And mine is Davies."

"You're very old."

"As old as me little finger and a bit older than me teeth."

Eliza took a deep breath. "Are you a pirate?"

He laughed, a deep chuffing sound like smoke from a dirty chimney. "Sorry to disappoint you, my girl, I'm a gardener, just like my daddy afore me. Maze keeper to be particular about it."

Eliza wrinkled her nose. "Maze keeper?"

"I keep the maze tended." When Eliza's face showed no dawn of clarity, Davies pointed at the tall twin hedges behind him, bridged by an iron gate. " 'Tis a puzzle made from hedges. The object, to find a way through without winding up lost."

A puzzle that could fit a person inside? Eliza had never heard of such a thing. "Where does it lead?"

"Oh, it weaves back and forth. If you're lucky enough to follow it right the way through you'll find yourself on the other side of the estate. If you're not so lucky"—his eyes widened ominously—"you'll likely perish of starvation before anyone knows you're missing." He leaned towards her, lowered his voice. "I ofttimes come across the bones of such unlucky souls."

Thrill squeezed Eliza's voice to a whisper. "And if I made it through? What would I find at the other end?"

"Another garden, a special garden, and a little cottage. Right on the edge of the cliff."

"I saw the cottage. From the beach."

He nodded. "I'd say you probably did."

"Whose house is it? Who lives there?"

"No one now. Lord Archibald Mountrachet—your great-grandfather, he'd have been—he had it built when he were in charge. There's some what says it were built as a lookout, a signaling post."

"For the smugglers, the Tregenna pirates?"

He smiled. "I can tell young Mary Martin's had your ear."

"Can I go and see it?"

"You'll never find it."

"I will."

His eyes twinkled as he teased. "Never, you'll never find your way through the maze. Even if you do, you'll never work out how to get through the secret gate and into the cottage garden."

"I will! Let me try, please, Davies."

"I'm afraid it ain't possible, Miss Eliza," Davies said, sobering somewhat. "There's no one been right the way through the maze in quite a time. I keep it maintained to a point, but I only go so far as I'm allowed. It's bound to be grown over in parts beyond."

"Why has no one been through?

"Your uncle had it closed some time past. No one's been through since." He leaned towards her. "Your mother, now there's someone who knew the maze like the back of her hand. Almost as well as I."

A bell sounded in the distance.

Davies took his hat off and wiped his sweaty forehead. "You'd better be off like star-shot, then, miss. That's the luncheon bell."

"Are you coming to have your luncheon, too?"

He laughed. "The staff don't eat luncheon, Miss Eliza, that's not proper. They have their dinner now."

"Are you coming up to have your dinner, then?"

"I don't eat inside the house. Haven't done for a long time."

"Why not?"

"It's not a place I like to be."

Eliza didn't understand. "Why not?"

Davies stroked his beard. "I'm happier when I stick to my plants, Miss Eliza. There's some that are made for the society of men, others that ain't. I'm one of the latter: happy on me own dungheap."

"But why?"

He exhaled slowly, like a great weary giant. "Certain places make a man's hairs stand on end, disagree with a man's way of being. Do you see what I'm saying?"

Eliza thought of her aunt in the burgundy room the night before, the hound and the shadows and the candlelight lashing angrily at the walls. She nodded.

"Young Mary, now, she's a good lass. She'll look out for you up at the house." He frowned a little as he stared down at her. "It doesn't do to trust too easily, Miss Eliza. Doesn't do at all, you hear?"

Eliza nodded solemnly because solemnity seemed to be called for.

"Now be off with you, young miss. You'll be late for luncheon and the mistress will have your heart on a supper tray. She don't like her rules broken, and that's a fact."

Eliza smiled, though Davies did not. She turned to go, stopped when she saw something in the upper window, something she'd seen the day before. A face, small and watchful.

"Who's that?" she said.

Davies turned and squinted up towards the house. Nodded slightly in the direction of the upper window. "I reckon that's Miss Rose."

"Miss Rose?"

"Your cousin. Your aunt and uncle's girl."

Eliza's eyes widened. Her cousin?

"We used to see quite a lot of her about the estate, bright young thing she was, but some years ago she took ill and that was the end of that. The mistress spends all her time and a fair bit of money trying to fix whatever's wrong, and the young doctor from town's always coming and going."

Eliza was still staring up at the window. Slowly she raised her hand, fingers wide like the starfish from the beach. She waved back and forth, watched as the face disappeared quickly into the dark.

A slight smile pulled at Eliza's face. "Rose," she said, tasting the sweetness of the word. It was just like the name of a princess in a fairy tale.

Twenty-four

CLIFF COTTAGE, 2005

THE wind whipped through Cassandra's hair, twirling her ponytail inside out, outside in, like streamers on a wind sock. She pulled her cardigan tight around her shoulders and paused a moment to catch her breath, looked back down the narrow coastal road to the village below. Tiny white cottages clung like barnacles to the rocky cove, and red and blue fishing boats dotted the denim harbor, bobbing on the swell as gulls swooped and spiraled above their hauls. The air, even at this height, was laden with salt licked from the sea's surface.

The road was so narrow and so close to the cliff's edge that Cassandra wondered how anyone ever worked up the courage to drive along it. Tall, pale sea grasses grew on each side, shivering as the wind rushed through. The higher she went, the more mist seemed to hang in the air.

Cassandra glanced at her watch. She'd underestimated how long it would take to reach the top, not to mention the weariness that would turn her legs to jelly midway up. Jetlag and good old-fashioned lack of sleep.

She'd slept terribly the night before. The room, the bed, were both comfortable enough, but she'd been plagued with strange dreams, the sort that lingered upon waking but slithered away from memory as she tried to grasp them. Only the tendrils of discomfort remained.

At some point during the night she'd been woken by a more material cause. A noise, like the sound of a key in her bedroom door.

216

She'd been sure that's what it was, the insertion and jiggling as the person on the other side tried to make it turn, but when she'd mentioned it at the front desk this morning, the girl had looked at her strangely before saying, in a rather chilly voice, that the hotel used key cards, not metal keys. What she'd heard was only the wind toying with the old brass fitting.

Cassandra started up the hill again. It couldn't be much further, the woman in the village grocery shop had said it was only a twenty-minute walk and she'd been climbing now for thirty.

She rounded a corner and saw a red car pulled over by the side of the road. A man and woman stood watching her: he was tall and thin while she was short and stout. For a moment Cassandra thought they might be sightseers enjoying the view, but when each lifted a hand in unison and waved, she knew who they must be.

"Hello there!" called the man, coming towards her. He was middle-aged, though his hair and beard, white as icing sugar, gave the initial impression of a much older face. "You must be Cassandra. I'm Henry Jameson and this"—he indicated the beaming woman—"is my wife, Robyn."

"Lovely to meet you," said Robyn, hot on her husband's heels. Her greying hair was cut in a neat bob that grazed cheeks pink and polished and plump as apples.

Cassandra smiled. "Thanks for meeting me on a Saturday, I really appreciate it."

"Nonsense." Henry ran a hand across his head to tidy fine wind-blown hairs. "No trouble at all. I only hope you don't mind Robyn coming along—"

"Of course she doesn't, why would she mind?" said Robyn. "You don't mind, do you?"

Cassandra shook her head.

"What did I tell you? She doesn't mind a bit." Robyn clutched Cassandra's wrist. "Not that he had any chance of stopping me. He'd have been risking the divorce courts if he'd so much as tried."

"My wife is the secretary of the local historical society," Henry said, a hint of apology threading through his voice.

"I've published a number of little booklets on the area. Histories mainly, about local families, important landmarks, great houses. My most recent is about the smuggling trade. We're actually in the middle of putting all of the articles onto a website—"

"It's her sworn aim to take tea in every stately home in the county."

"But I've lived in this village all my life and I've never so much as set foot inside the old place." Robyn smiled so that her cheeks shone. "I don't mind telling you, I'm about as curious as a cat."

"We would never have guessed, my love," said Henry wearily, indicating the hill. "We have to go on foot from here, the road goes no further."

Robyn led the way, striding purposefully along the narrow path of windswept grass. As they climbed higher, Cassandra began to notice the birds. Masses of tiny brown swallows calling to one another as they scuttled from one spindly branch to another. She had the oddest sensation of being watched, as if the birds were jostling to keep an eye on the human interlopers. She shivered a little, then admonished herself for being childish, inventing mystery where only atmosphere existed.

"It was my father who handled the sale to your grandmother," said Henry, shortening his long strides to walk just behind Cassandra. "Back in '75. I'd just started with the firm as a junior conveyancer, but I remember the sale."

"Everyone remembers the sale," called Robyn. "It was the last part of the old estate to go. There were folk in the village who swore the cottage'd never be sold."

Cassandra looked out to sea. "Why is that? The house must have beautiful views . . ."

Henry glanced at Robyn, who had stopped walking and was

catching her breath, hand on the middle of her chest. "Well, now, that's true enough," he said, "but—"

"There were bad stories about town," said Robyn, between pants. "Rumors and the like . . . about the past."

"What sort of things?"

"Silly rumors," said Henry firmly, "lots of nonsense, the sort you'd find in any English village."

"There was talk that it was haunted," Robyn continued, sotto voce.

Henry laughed. "Find me a house in Cornwall that isn't."

Robyn rolled her pale blue eyes. "My husband is a pragmatist."

"And my wife is a romantic," said Henry. "Cliff Cottage is stone and mortar, just like all the other houses in Tregenna. It's no more haunted than I am."

"And you call yourself a Cornishman." Robyn tucked a strand of wayward hair behind her ear and squinted up at Cassandra. "Do you believe in ghosts, Cassandra?"

"I don't think so." Cassandra thought of the strange feeling the birds had given her. "Not the sort that go bump in the night."

"Then you're a sensible girl," said Henry. "The only thing that's been in or out of Cliff Cottage in the past thirty years is the odd local lad wanting to give himself and his mates a fright." Henry took a monogrammed handkerchief from his trouser pocket, folded it in half and gave his forehead a pat. "Come now, Robyn dear. We'll be all day if we don't keep moving and that sun's got a bite. A bit of leftover summer this week."

The steep incline and narrowing track made further conversation difficult, and they walked the last hundred yards in silence. Wispy strands of pale grass shimmered as the wind sighed gently through.

Finally, after passing through a clump of straggly shrubs, they reached a stone wall. It was at least ten feet high and seemed incongruous after they'd come so far without seeing a single man-made structure. An iron arch framed the entrance gate and wiry tendrils of creeper had plaited themselves through, been calcified by time. A sign that must once have been attached to the gate now dangled by a corner. Pale green and brown lichen had grown scablike across its surface, filling greedily the curly lettered grooves. Cassandra inclined her head to read the words: KEEP OUT OR THE RISK BE ALL YOURS.

"The wall is a relatively new addition," said Robyn.

"By new, my wife means it's only a hundred years old. The cottage must be three times that." Henry cleared his throat. "Now you realize, don't you, that the old place is in a state of some disrepair?"

"I have a photograph." She pulled it from her handbag.

He raised his eyebrows as he looked it over. "Taken before the time of sale, I'd say. It's changed a bit since then. It's been untended, you see." He extended his left arm to push aside the iron gate and motioned with his head. "Shall we?"

A stone path led beneath an arbor of ancient roses with arthritic joints. The temperature cooled as they crossed the garden's threshold. The overall impression was one of darkness and gloom. And quiet, an odd, still quiet. Even the noise of the irrepressible sea seemed dulled in here. It was as if the grounds within the stone wall were asleep. Waiting for something, or someone, to wake them.

"Cliff Cottage," said Henry, as they reached the path's end.

Cassandra's eyes widened. Before her was a huge tangle of brambles, thick and knotted. Ivy leaves, deep green and jagged, clung on all sides, stretching across the spaces where windows must be hidden. She would have been hard-pressed to make out the building that lay beneath the creepers had she not known it was there.

Henry coughed, apology again coloring his face. "For sure, it's been left to its own devices."

"Nothing a good cleanup wouldn't fix," said Robyn, with a forced cheerfulness that could have resurrected sunken ships. "No need for despondence. You've seen what they do on those renovation shows, haven't you? You get them in Australia?"

Cassandra nodded absently, trying to make out the roofline.

"I'll let you do the honors," said Henry, reaching into his pocket to withdraw a key.

It was surprisingly heavy, long with a decorative end, a swirl of brass in a beautiful pattern. As she clasped it, Cassandra felt a flash of recognition. She'd held a key like this before. When, she wondered? In the antique center? The image was so strong but the memory wouldn't come.

Cassandra stepped onto the stone tread by the door. She could see the lock but a web of ivy had strung itself across the doorway.

"These ought to do the trick," said Robyn, plucking a pair of secateurs from her handbag. "Don't look at me like that, dear," she said as Henry raised an eyebrow. "I'm a country girl, we're always prepared."

Cassandra took the proffered tool and snipped the strands, one by one. When they all hung loose she paused a moment and ran her hand lightly over the salt-scarred wood of the door. A part of her was loath to proceed, content to linger a while on the threshold of knowledge, but when she glanced over her shoulder both Henry and Robyn nodded encouragement. She pushed the key into the lock and, using both hands, turned hard.

The smell was the first thing to hit her, damp and fecund, and rich with animal droppings. Like the rain forests back home in Australia, whose canopies concealed a separate world of moist fertility. A closed ecosystem, wary of strangers.

She took a tiny step inside the hall. The front door admitted enough light to reveal mossy flecks floating lazily in the stale air, too light, too tired to fall. The floors were made of wood and with each step her shoes made soft, apologetic sounds.

She came to the first room and peered around the door. It was dark, the windows coated by decades-old grime. As her eyes adjusted Cassandra saw it was a kitchen. A pale wooden table with tapered legs stood at center, two cane chairs tucked obediently beneath. There was a black range set into an alcove on the far wall, cobwebs forming a furry curtain before it, and in the corner a spinning wheel was still threaded with a piece of dark wool.

"It's like a museum," whispered Robyn. "Only dustier."

"I don't think I'll be offering you a cup of tea anytime soon," said Cassandra.

Henry had wandered over beyond the spinning wheel and was pointing to a stone nook. "There's a set of stairs over here."

A narrow flight ran up directly before turning abruptly at a small landing. Cassandra put her foot on the first step, testing its strength. Sturdy enough. Cautiously, she began climbing.

"Go carefully, now," said Henry, following, hands hovering behind Cassandra's back in a vague, kindly attempt at protection.

Cassandra reached the little landing and stopped.

"What is it?" said Henry.

"A tree, a huge tree, completely blocking the way. It's come right through the roof."

Henry peered over her shoulder. "I don't think Robyn's secateurs are going to be much help," he said, "not this time. You need a tree lopper." He started back down the stairs. "Any ideas, Robyn? Who would you call to clear a fallen log?"

Cassandra followed him and arrived at the bottom as Robyn said, "Bobby Blake's lad ought to do the trick."

"Local boy." Henry nodded at Cassandra. "Runs a landscaping business. Does most of the work up at the hotel, too, and you won't get a better recommendation than that."

"I'll give him a call, shall I?" said Robyn. "Find out how he's placed later in the week? I'll just take myself out to the point and see if I can pick up mobile reception. Mine's been dead as a doorknob since we set foot in here."

Henry shook his head. "Over a hundred years since Marconi received his signal, and now look where technology's taken us. You know the signal was sent from just round the coast a little way? Poldhu Cove?"

"Was it?" As the extent of the cottage's dereliction dawned on her, Cassandra was beginning to feel increasingly overwhelmed. Grateful though she was to Henry for meeting her, she wasn't sure she'd be able to feign interest in a lecture on early telecommunications. She brushed aside a woven shawl of spiderweb and leaned against the wall, offered him a stoic smile of polite encouragement.

Henry seemed to sense her mood. "I'm terribly sorry the cottage is in such a state," he said. "I can't help but feel some responsibility, being the lawyer in charge of the key."

"I'm sure there was nothing you could have done. Particularly if Nell asked your father not to." She smiled. "Besides, it would've been trespassing and the sign out front is pretty clear about that."

"True enough, and your grandmother was adamant about us not calling in tradesmen. She said the house was very important to her and she wanted to see to the restoration personally."

"I think she had plans to move here," said Cassandra. "For good."

"Yes," said Henry. "I had a look back over the old files when I knew I'd be meeting you this morning. All her letters mention coming here herself until one written in early 1976. She said her circumstances had changed and she wouldn't be back, not for a time at any rate. She asked my father to hold the key, though, so she'd know where to find it when the time came." He looked around the room. "But it never did."

"No," said Cassandra.

"But you're here now," Henry said with renewed enthusiasm.

"Yes."

A noise at the door and they both looked up. "I got through to Michael," said Robyn, tucking her phone away. "He said he'd pop over on Wednesday morning to see what needs doing." She turned to Henry.

"Come now, my love, we're expected at Marcia's for lunch and you know how she gets when we're late."

Henry raised his eyebrows. "Our daughter has many virtues but patience is not chief among them."

Cassandra smiled. "Thanks for everything."

"Now, don't you be thinking of trying to move that log yourself," he said. "No matter how keen you are to get a look upstairs."

"I promise."

As they made their way along the path to the front gate, Robyn turned back to Cassandra. "You look like her, you know."

Cassandra blinked.

"Your grandmother. You have her eyes."

"You met her?"

"Oh yes, of course, even before she bought the cottage. One afternoon she came into the museum where I was working. She asked questions about local history. Some of the old families in particular."

Henry's voice from the cliff edge. "Come on, Robyn love. Marcia will never forgive us if the roast burns."

"The Mountrachet family?"

Robyn waved at Henry. "That's them. The ones who used to live up at the grand house. The Walkers, too. The painter and his wife, and the lady writer who published fairy tales."

"Robyn!"

"Yes, yes. I'm coming." She rolled her eyes at Cassandra. "He's got about as much patience as a firecracker on a fire, that husband of mine." And then she bustled after him, instructions for Cassandra to call on them anytime floating back after her on the sea breeze.

Twenty-five

THE Tregenna Museum of Fishing and Smuggling was nestled in a small whitewashed building on the rim of the outer harbor, and though the handwritten sign posted in the front window was clear about the opening hours, Nell had been in the village for three days before she finally glimpsed a light inside.

She turned the handle and pushed open the low, lace-draped door.

Behind the desk sat a prim woman with shoulder-length brown hair. Younger than Lesley, thought Nell, but with a bearing infinitely older. The woman stood when she saw Nell, so that the tops of her legs pulled the lace cloth and a pile of papers towards her. She had the look of a child caught raiding the cake tin. "I—I wasn't expecting visitors," she said, peering over the top of her large glasses.

Nor did she seem particularly pleased to see any. Nell held out her hand. "Nell Andrews." She glanced at the name plaque on the desk. "And you must be Robyn Martin?"

"We don't get many visitors, not in the off season. I'll just find the key." She worried the papers on the desk, tucked a strand of hair behind her ear. "The displays are a little dusty," she said, a note of accusation in her voice. "But it's through that way."

Nell's gaze followed the sweep of Robyn's arm. Beyond the closed glass door was a small adjoining room, host to various nets and hooks and rods. Black-and-white photographs had been hung upon the wall, boats and crews and local coves.

"Actually," said Nell, "I'm looking for particular information. The fellow at the post office thought you might be able to help."

"My father."

"Pardon me?"

"My father's the postmaster."

"Yes," Nell said, "well, he thought you might be able to help me. The information I'm after isn't anything to do with fishing or smuggling, you see. It's local history. Family history, to be precise."

The change in Robyn's countenance was instant. "Why ever didn't you say so? I work here at the fishing museum to do my bit for the community, but Tregenna social history is my life. Here." She riffled through the pieces of paper she'd been busy with on her desk and thrust one into Nell's hand. "This is the text for a tourist pamphlet I'm putting together, and I'm just finishing the draft of a little article on great houses. I've had interest from a publisher in Falmouth." She looked at her fine silver-chained wristwatch. "I'd be happy to speak with you only I have to be somewhere—"

"Please," said Nell. "I've come a long way and I won't take much of your time. If you could just spare me a few minutes."

Robyn's lips tightened and she fixed Nell with her mouselike gaze. "I can do better than that," she said, nodding decisively. "I'll take you with me."

A THICKENING LAYER of fog had blown in with the high tide and conspired with dusk to leach the village of color. As they climbed higher along the narrow streets, everything was turned a shade of grey. The swift change in conditions had brought an agitation to Robyn's manner. She walked at a clipped pace so that Nell, despite her own naturally spruce gait, had to work to keep up. Though Nell wondered where it was they were going so fast, the pace was such an impediment to conversation that she couldn't ask.

At the top of the street, they reached a little white house with a sign that read Pilchard Cottage. Robyn rapped on the door and waited. There were no lights on inside and she lifted her wrist closer to her eyes to make out the time. "Still not home. We tell him always to come home early when the fog sets in."

"Who?"

Robyn glanced at Nell as if she'd forgotten for a moment that the other woman was with her. "Gump, my grandfather. He goes each day to watch the boats. He was a fisherman himself, you see. He's been re-tired twenty years but he's not happy unless he knows who's been out and where they were catching." Her voice snagged. "We tell him not to stay out when the fog's on the rise, but he won't be told—"

She broke off and squinted into the distance.

Nell followed her gaze, watched as a patch of thick mist seemed to darken. A figure loomed towards them.

"Gump!" called Robyn.

"No fuss, my girl," came a voice from the fog. "No fuss." He appeared in the gloom, climbed his three concrete steps and turned the key in the lock. "Well, don't just stand there shivering like a pair of winnards," he said over his shoulder. "Come on in and we'll have a nice drop of warm."

In the narrow hallway, Robyn helped the old man out of his salt-encrusted mackintosh and black Wellington boots, then stowed them on a low wooden bench. "You're damp, Gump," she fussed, clutching a handful of his checked shirt. "Let's get you into some dry clothes."

"Pah," said the old man, tapping his granddaughter's hand. "I'll sit a time by the fire and be dry as a bone by the time you bring me some tea."

Robyn raised her eyebrows slightly in Nell's direction as Gump hobbled into the front room: Can you see what I have to deal with? said the gesture.

"Gump's almost ninety but he refuses to move out of his house," she said quietly. "Between us we make sure someone has supper with him every night. I'm Monday to Wednesday."

"He seems well for ninety."

"His eyesight's starting to fail and his hearing isn't the best, but he still insists on making sure "his boys" get back safely into port, no thought for his own frailties. God help me if he comes to harm on my watch." She peered through the glass, wincing as her grandfather tripped over the rug on his way to the armchair. "I don't suppose . . . That is, I wonder whether you'd sit with him while I light the fire and put the kettle on. I'll feel better once he's all dried out."

Lured by the exquisite promise of finally learning something of her family, there was little Nell wouldn't agree to. She nodded and Robyn smiled with relief before hurrying through the door after her grandfather.

Gump had sat himself in the tan leather armchair, a homely quilt spread across his lap. For a moment, as she looked at that quilt, Nell thought of Lil and the quilts she'd made for each of her daughters. She wondered what her mother would think about this quest she was on, whether she'd understand why it was so important to Nell to reconstruct the first four years of her life. Probably not. Lil had always believed that a person's duty was to make the best of the hand they were dealt. No use wondering what might have been, she used to say, all that matters is what is. Which was all very well for Lil, who knew the truth about herself.

Robyn pushed herself to standing, new flames leaping eagerly from paper to paper on the grate behind her. "I'm going to fetch some tea now, Gump, put the supper on to cook. While I'm in the kitchen my friend here . . ." She looked searchingly at Nell. "I'm sorry . . ."

"Nell, Nell Andrews."

"Nell is going to sit with you, Gump. She's a visitor to Tregenna and interested in the local families. Perhaps you can tell her a bit about the old town while I'm gone."

The old man held open palms upon which a lifetime of hauling ropes and threading hooks had written its tale. "Ask me anything," he said, "and I'll tell you all I know."

As Robyn disappeared through a low doorway, Nell looked about for somewhere to sit. She settled on a green wingback chair by the fire, enjoying the surge of warmth as firelight yawned across her side.

Gump looked up from the pipe he was busy loading and nodded encouragement. Apparently the floor was hers.

Nell cleared her throat and shifted her feet a little on the rug, wondering where to begin. She decided there was no point beating around the bush. "It's the Mountrachet family I'm interested in."

Gump's match sizzled and he puffed vigorously to start his pipe.

"I've been asking about in the village but it seems that no one knows anything about them."

"Oh, they know about them, all right," he said on a smoky exhalation. "They just don't talk about them."

Nell's eyebrows lifted. "Why is that?"

"The folk in Tregenna like a good yarn, but we're a superstitious bunch by and large. We'll chat happily on just about any subject you care to name, but ask about the happenings up there on the cliff and people clam up."

"I noticed," said Nell. "Is it because the Mountrachets were titled aristocrats? Upper class?"

Gump snorted. "They had money, but don't you go talking about class." He leaned forward. "That was a title paid for by the spilled blood of innocents. It was 1724. A wild storm blew up late one afternoon, the fiercest in years. The lighthouse lost its roof and the new oil-lamp flame was snuffed out as if it were little better than a candle. The moon was in hiding and the night was black as my boots." Pale lips tightened around his pipe. He sucked long and hard, warming to his tale. "Most of the local fishing boats had come in early but there was a single sloop still out in the strait, a double-master with a foreign crew.

"The crew of that sloop never stood a chance. They say there were waves breaking halfway up the Sharpstone Cliffs and she was thrown so hard against the rocks that she started to fall to pieces before she even reached the cove. There were newspaper reports and a government inquiry, but they never recovered much more than a few pieces of tattered red cedar from the hull. They blamed the local free traders, of course."

"Free traders?"

"Smugglers," said Robyn, who had appeared with the tea tray.

"But it wasn't them who stripped the ship of its cargo," said Gump. "No fear. It was the family that did it, the Mountrachet family."

Nell took a proffered cup from Robyn. "The Mountrachets were smugglers?"

Gump laughed a dry, whiskery laugh and took a swig of tea. "They were nothing so dignified as that. Smugglers do their share of liberating overtaxed items from ships that come to grief, but they also do their bit rescuing the crews. What happened that night in the Blackhurst cove was the work of thieves. Thieves and murderers. They killed every single one of that crew, stole the cargo from her hull, then early next morning, before anyone had a chance to learn what had happened, they dragged the ship and its bodies out to sea and sank it. Made themselves a fortune: crates of pearls, and ivory, fans from China, jewelry from Spain."

"Over the next few years, Blackhurst underwent massive renovations." Robyn took up the story, perching on the faded velvet of her grandfather's footstool. "I've just been writing about it for my *Great Houses of Cornwall* pamphlet. That's when it acquired the third story and a number of the garden follies. And Mr. Mountrachet was given an ennoblement by the king."

"Amazing what a few well-chosen gifts can do."

Nell shook her head and shifted uncomfortably. Now was not the time to mention that these murderers and thieves were her ancestors. "To think they got away with it."

Robyn glanced at Gump, who cleared his throat. "Well now," he muttered, "I wouldn't say that."

Nell looked between them, confused.

"There's worse punishments than those doled out by the law. Mark my words, there's worse punishments than that." Gump exhaled through tight lips. "After what happened in the cove, the family up there was cursed, every last one of them."

Nell leaned back against her seat, disappointed. A family curse. Right when she'd thought herself on the verge of actual information.

"Tell her about the ship, Gump," said Robyn, seeming to sense Nell's deflation. "The black ship."

Happy to oblige, Gump raised his volume a notch as a show of narrative commitment. "The family might've sunk that ship but they couldn't rid themselves of her, not for long. She still appears sometimes on the horizon. Usually before or after a storm. A large black sloop, a phantom ship, stalking the cove. Haunting the descendants of those responsible."

"You've seen it? The ship?"

The old man shook his head. "I thought I might have once but I was mistaken, thank God." He leaned forward. "It's an ill wind blows that ship into view. They say a person who sights the phantom ship pays penance for its loss. If you see it, it sees you. And all I know is that those who admit to having seen it attract more ill fortune than anyone should bear. The sloop's proper name was the *Jacquard*, but around here we call it the *Black Hearse*."

"Blackhurst estate," said Nell. "Not a coincidence, I take it?"

"She's a bright penny," said Gump, smiling around his pipe at Robyn. "A bright penny, this one. And there's some that would agree that's where the estate got its name."

"Not you?"

"I've always thought it had more to do with the big black rock up there in the Blackhurst Cove. There's a passage runs right the way through it, you know. It used to lead from the cove to somewhere on the estate and back into the village. A blessing for the smugglers, but a temperamental one at that. Something in the angles and shapes of the tunnel: if the tide rose higher than expected, a man inside the caves had little hope of survival. That rock's been hearse to plenty of brave souls over the years. If you've ever looked down onto the estate beach you'll have seen it. Monstrous jagged thing."

Nell shook her head. "I haven't seen the cove, not yet. I tried to visit the house yesterday but the front gates were locked. I'm going back tomorrow to drop a letter of introduction in the letter box. Hopefully the owners will let me take a look. Any idea what they're like?"

"New people," said Robyn sagely. "Out-of-towners, talk of turning it into a hotel." She leaned forward. "They say the young woman's a paperback writer, romances and the like. She's very glamorous and the books are quite racy." Her gaze slipped sideways to her grandfather and she flushed. "Not that I've read them myself."

"I saw part of the property advertised in the estate agent's office," said Nell. "A little house called Cliff Cottage is for sale."

Gump laughed drily. "And always will be. There's no one fool enough to buy it. Take more than a coat of paint to clear that place of all the misfortune it's seen."

"What sort of misfortune?"

Gump, who had heretofore spun his stories with abounding relish, was suddenly silent, chewing over this last question. A flicker seemed to pass through his eyes. "That place should've been burned down years ago. There were things went on there that weren't right."

"What sort of things?"

"Never you mind about that," he said, lips trembling. "Just you take my word for it. There's some places can't be made new with a fresh coat of paint."

"I didn't mean to buy it," said Nell, surprised by his vehemence. "I just thought it might be a way of getting a look at the estate."

"No need to go through the Blackhurst estate to get a look at the cove. You can see it from the cliff top." He raised his pipe in the direction of the coast. "Take the path from the village up around the bluff and look towards Sharpstone; that's it below you. Prettiest little cove in all of Cornwall except for that brutish rock. No sign of the blood spilled across its beach long ago."

The smell of beef and rosemary had grown thick and Robyn fetched bowls and spoons from the kitchen. "You'll stay for supper, won't you, Nell?"

"Course she will," said Gump, leaning back into his chair. "Wouldn't think of sending her out on a night like this one. Black as your hat out there and twice as thick."

THE STEW was delicious and Nell took little convincing to have a second bowl. Afterwards, Robyn excused herself to wash the dishes, and Nell and Gump were alone again. The room was warm now, and his cheeks red. He sensed her gaze and nodded convivially.

There was something easy about William Martin's company, something insulating about sitting in his front room. This was the power of the story weaver, Nell realized. An ability to conjure color so that all else seemed to fade. And William Martin was a born storyteller, there was little doubt about that. Just how much of his tales to believe was another question. He had an obvious gift for spinning straw into gold, but nonetheless he was likely to be the only person she'd find who had lived through the years that interested her.

"I wonder," she said, the fire warming her side so that it itched pleasingly, "when you were younger, did you ever know Eliza Makepeace? She was a writer, the ward of Linus and Adeline Mountrachet."

There was a perceptible pause. William's voice was whisker-muffled. "Everyone knew of Eliza Makepeace."

Nell drew breath. Finally. "Do you know what happened to her?" she said, all in a rush. "In the end, I mean?"

He shook his head. "I don't know that."

A new reticence had crept into the old man's bearing, a guardedness that had been absent until now. While the implications of this made her heart swell with hope, Nell knew she'd have to tread carefully. She didn't want to send him into his shell, not now.

"What about earlier, when she lived at Blackhurst? Can you tell me anything?"

"I said I knew of her. I had no occasion to know her well, I wasn't welcome at the big house. Those in charge up there would've had something to say about that."

Nell persisted. "From what I can gather, Eliza was last seen in London in late 1913. She was with a small girl, Ivory Walker, who was four years old. Rose Mountrachet's daughter. Can you think of any reason, any reason at all, why Eliza might have been planning a trip to Australia with someone else's child?"

"No."

"Any idea why the Mountrachet family might have told people their granddaughter was dead when she was very much alive?"

The reed of his voice split. "No."

"So you knew that Ivory was alive despite contrary reports?"

The fire crackled. "I didn't know that, because it isn't so. That child died of scarlet fever."

"Yes, I know that's what was said at the time." Nell's face was warm, her head throbbing. "I also know that it's not true."

"How would you know a thing like that?"

"Because I was that child." Nell's voice cracked. "I arrived in Australia when I was four. Was put on a boat by Eliza Makepeace while everyone thought that I was dead and no one seems to be able to tell me why."

William's expression was difficult to interpret. He seemed about to answer but didn't.

Instead, he rose, stretched out his arms so that his belly thrust forward. "I'm tired," he said gruffly. "It's about time I went up to my bed." He called out, "Robyn?" And again, louder, "Robyn!"

"Gump?" Robyn returned from the kitchen, tea towel in hand. "What is it?"

"I'm turning in." He started for the narrow stairs that curved an exit path from the room.

"You don't want another cup of tea? We were having such a nice time."

William placed his hand on Robyn's shoulder as he passed her. "Put the wood in the hole on your way out, won't you, my girl? We don't want the mist settling inside."

As bewilderment widened Robyn's eyes, Nell fetched her own coat. "I should go."

"I'm very sorry," said Robyn. "I don't know what's come over him. He's old, he gets tired . . ."

"Of course." Nell finished doing up her buttons. She knew she should apologize, it was her fault, after all, that the old man had been upset, and yet she couldn't. Disappointment sat like a wedge of lemon in her throat. "Thank you for your time," she managed to say, stepping out of the front door and into the oppressive damp.

Nell glanced back when she reached the bottom of the hill and saw that Robyn was still watching. She raised an arm to wave when the other woman did so.

William Martin may have been old and tired, but there was more to his sudden departure than that. Nell ought to know; she had held on to her own thorny secret long enough to recognize a fellow sufferer. William knew more than he was letting on and Nell's need to uncover the truth outranked her respect for his privacy.

She pressed her lips together and bowed her head against the cold. Determined to convince him into telling her all he knew.

TWENTY-SIX

ELIZA was right: the name "Rose" was well suited to a fairy-tale princess, and certainly Rose Mountrachet enjoyed the uncommon privilege and beauty befitting the part. Sadly, though, for little Rose, the first eleven years of life had been anything but a fairy story.

"Open wide." Dr. Matthews plucked a reedy paddle from his leather bag and flattened Rose's tongue. He leaned forward to peer down her throat, his face so close that she was granted an unwelcome opportunity to conduct reciprocal inspection of his nasal hairs. "Hmmm," he said, setting the hairs to quivering.

Rose coughed weakly as the retracting paddle scraped her throat.

"Well, Doctor?" Mamma stepped from the shadow, tapered fingers pale against her deep blue dress.

Dr. Matthews stood to full height. "You did well to call, Lady Mountrachet. There is, indeed, an inflammation."

Mamma sighed. "I thought as much. You have a preparation, Doctor?"

As Dr. Matthews outlined his recommended mode of treatment, Rose turned her head to the side and closed her eyes. Yawned lightly. For as long as she could remember, she'd known she wasn't long for this world.

Sometimes, in weaker moments, Rose allowed herself to imagine what life might be like if she didn't know her end, if the future stretched before her indefinitely, a long road with twists and turns she couldn't anticipate. With milestones that might include a society debut, a husband, children. A grand home of her own with which to impress other ladies. For, oh, if she were honest, how earnestly she longed for such a life.

She didn't let herself imagine this too often, though. What use was there in lamenting? Instead, she waited, convalesced, worked on her scrapbook. Read, when she was able, of places she'd never see, and facts she'd never use, in conversations she'd never have. Waiting for the next inevitable episode that brought her closer to The End, hoping that the next ailment might be a little more interesting than the last. Something with less pain and more reward. Like the time she'd swallowed Mamma's thimble.

She hadn't meant to, of course. If it hadn't been so shiny, so pretty in its silver acorn holder, she wouldn't have thought to touch it. But it had and she did. What eight-year-old would have done differently? She'd been trying to balance it on the tip of her tongue, somewhat like the clown in her Meggendorfer's *International Circus* book, the one who balanced the red ball on his silly pointed nose. Inadvisable, certainly, but she'd only been a child, and besides had been performing the feat for some months without mishap.

The thimble episode had turned out pretty well by all accounts. The doctor had been called immediately, a new young physician who'd only recently taken over the village practice. He'd poked and prodded and done what doctors do, before making quivering suggestion that a certain new diagnostic tool might be of some use. By taking a photographic exposure he'd be able to look right within Rose's stomach without so much as lifting a scalpel. Everyone had been pleased with this suggestion: Father, whose skill with a camera meant he was called upon to take the modern exposure; Dr. Matthews, because he was able to publish the photographs in a special journal called the *Lancet;* and Mamma, because the publication sent a ripple of excitement through her society circles.

As for Rose, the thimble was passed (most indecorously) some forty-eight hours later and she was able to bask in the certain knowledge that she'd finally managed to please Father, if only briefly. Not that he said as much, that was not his way, but Rose was perspicacious when it came to recognizing the moods of her parents (if not yet their divining causes). And Father's pleasure had made Rose's own spirits rise as high and as light as one of Cook's soufflés.

"With your permission, Lady Mountrachet, I'll finish my examination."

Rose sighed as Dr. Matthews lifted her nightgown to expose her stomach. She closed her eyes tighter as cold fingers pressed on her skin, and she thought about her scrapbook. Mamma had arranged for a periodical from London with pictures of the latest bridal fashions and, using lace and ribbons from her craft box, Rose was decorating the scrapbook page beautifully. Her bride was coming along splendidly: a veil of Belgian lace, little seed pearls glued around the rim, pressed flowers for her bouquet. The groom was rather a different matter: Rose didn't know much about gentlemen. (And neither should she. It wouldn't be proper for a young lady to know such things.) But it seemed to Rose that the specifics of the groom were of little importance, as long as the bride was pretty and pure.

"All looks satisfactory," said Dr. Matthews, patting Rose's nightgown back into place. "Fortunately the infection is not general. Might I suggest, though, Lady Mountrachet, that I speak with you further regarding the best possible treatment?"

Rose opened her eyes in time to catch the doctor's sycophantic smile at Mamma. How tiresome he was, always angling for an invitation to tea, the opportunity to meet and treat more of the county's gentry. The published photos of Rose's thimble in situ had garnered him a certain cachet among the county's well-heeled, and he'd been quick to capitalize upon it. As he tucked his stethoscope carefully inside his big black bag, patted it into place with his neat little fingers, Rose's tedium turned to irritation.

"Am I not yet headed to heaven, then, Doctor?" she said, blinking plainly at his reddening face. "Only I'm working on a page for my scrapbook and it would be a shame to leave it unfinished."

Dr. Matthews laughed girlishly and glanced at Mamma. "Well, now, child," he stammered, "there's no need for worry. In time we shall all be welcomed at God's table . . ."

Rose watched for a while as he launched into an uncomfortable lecture on life and death, before turning her head to conceal a faint smile.

The prospect of an early death sits differently upon each person. In some it gifts maturity far outweighing their age and experience: calm acceptance blossoms into a beautiful nature and soft countenance. In others, however, it leads to the formation of a tiny ice flint in their heart. Ice that, though at times concealed, never properly melts.

Rose, though she would have liked to be one of the former, knew herself deep down to be one of the latter. It wasn't that she was nasty, rather that she'd developed a gift for dispassion. An ability to step outside herself and observe situations without the distraction of sentiment.

"Dr. Matthews." Mamma's voice interrupted his increasingly desperate description of God's little girl angels. "Why don't you go downstairs and wait for me in the morning room? Thomas will fetch the tea."

"Yes, Lady Mountrachet," he said, relieved to be delivered from the sticky conversation. He avoided Rose's eyes as he left the room.

"Now, Rose," said Mamma, "that was ill-mannered of you."

The admonition was diluted by Mamma's recent concern and Rose knew she wouldn't suffer castigation. She never did. Who could be cross with a little girl waiting for death to find her? Rose sighed. "I know, Mamma, and I'm sorry. Only I feel so light-headed, and listening to Dr. Matthews makes it so very much worse."

"A weak constitution is a dreadful cross to bear." Mamma took up Rose's hand. "But you are a young lady, a Mountrachet. And ill health is no excuse for manners less than perfect."

"Yes, Mamma."

"I must go and speak with the doctor now," she said, laying cool fingertips on Rose's cheek. "I'll look in on you again when Mary brings your tray."

She swept towards the door, dress rustling as she crossed from rug to floorboards. "Mamma?" called Rose.

Her mother turned back. "Yes?"

"There's something I wanted to ask you." Rose hesitated, unsure how to proceed. Aware how curious her question was. "I saw a boy in the garden."

Mamma's left eyebrow briefly broke formation. "A boy?"

"This morning, I saw him from the window when Mary moved me to my chair. He was standing behind a rhododendron bush speaking with Davies, a naughty-looking boy with shaggy red hair."

Mamma pressed a hand against the pale skin beneath her neck. Exhaled slowly and steadily so that Rose's interest was further piqued. "That was no boy you saw, Rose."

"Mamma?"

"That was your cousin, Eliza."

Rose's eyes widened. This was unexpected. Principally because it couldn't be so. Mamma had no brothers or sisters, and with Grand-mamma's passing, Mamma, Papa and Rose were the only Mountra-chets left. "I have no such cousin."

Mamma straightened, spoke unusually swiftly. "Unfortunately, you do. Her name is Eliza and she has come to live at Blackhurst."

"For how long?"

"Indefinitely, I fear."

"But, Mamma . . ." Rose felt more light-headed than ever. How could such a tatty urchin be *her* cousin? "Her hair . . . her manner . . . her clothes were all wet, and she was dirty and wind-blown . . ." Rose shuddered. "There were leaves all over her person . . ."

Mamma lifted a finger to her lips. She turned to face the window and the dark curl at the nape of her neck shivered. "She had nowhere else to go. Father and I agreed to take her in. An act of Christian charity she'll never appreciate, let alone deserve, but one must always be seen to do the right thing."

"But, Mamma, what is she to *do* here?"

"Cause us great vexation, I've little doubt. But we could hardly turn her away. Failure to act would have looked dreadful, thus must we turn necessity to virtue." Her words had the sound of sentiments being forced through a sieve. She seemed to sense their emptiness herself and said nothing further.

"Mamma?" Rose poked cautiously at her mother's silence.

"You asked what she is to do here?" Mamma turned to face Rose and a new edge entered her voice. "I am giving her to you."

"Giving her to me?"

"As a project of sorts. She will be your protégée. When you are well enough, you will be responsible for teaching her how to behave. She's little better than a savage, not one whit of grace or charm. An orphan who's had little if any guidance as to living in polite society." Mamma exhaled. "Of course, I have no illusions and don't expect you to work miracles."

"Yes, Mamma."

"You can only imagine, child of mine, the influences to which this orphan has been exposed. She has been living in London among such dreadful decadence and sin."

And then Rose knew just who this girl must be. Eliza was the child of Papa's sister, the mysterious Georgiana, whose portrait Mamma had banished to the attic, of whom nobody dared speak.

Nobody, that is, except Grandmamma.

In the old woman's final months, when she had returned like a wounded bear to Blackhurst and retired to the turret room to do her dying, she drifted in and out of wakefulness, speaking in fits and starts about a pair of children called Linus and Georgiana. Rose knew Linus was her father, thus, she gathered, Georgiana must be his sister. The one who had disappeared before Rose was born.

It was a summery morning and Rose was resting in the armchair by the window with a warm sea breeze tickling the back of her neck. Rose liked to sit by Grandmamma, to study her as she slept, each breath possibly her last, and had been watching curiously as beads of sweat glazed the old woman's forehead.

Suddenly Grandmamma's eyes blinked open: they were wide and pale, bleached by a lifetime of bitterness. She stared at Rose a moment but her gaze remained untouched by recognition and slid sideways. Transfixed, or so it seemed, by the gentle billowing of the summer curtains. Rose's first instinct was to ring for Mamma—it had been hours since Grandmamma last awoke—but just as she reached for the bell the old woman heaved a sigh. A long, wearied sigh, so thoroughly deflating that thin skin sagged into hollows between her bones.

Then out of nowhere a wizened hand clutched Rose's wrist. "Such a beautiful girl," she said, so quietly that Rose had to lean close to hear the words that were spoken next. "Too beautiful, a curse. Had all the young men's heads turning. He couldn't help himself, followed her everywhere, thought we didn't know. She ran away and didn't come back, not a word from my Georgiana . . ."

Now, Rose Mountrachet was a good girl who knew the rules. How could she be anything other? Her entire life, confined to her sickbed, she'd been captive to her mother's episodic lecture on the rules and nature of good society. Rose knew all too well that a lady must never wear pearls or diamonds in the morning; must never "cut" someone socially; must never, under any circumstances, call on a gentleman alone. But most importantly of all. Rose knew that scandal was to be avoided at all costs, that it was an evil whose very hint could smite a lady where she stood. Smite, at least, her good name.

And yet this mention of her errant aunt, the tantalizing whiff of family scandal, did no such thing to Rose. On the contrary, it sent a wicked thrill racing down her spine. For the first time in years she felt her fingertips tingle with excitement. She leaned closer still, willing

Grandmamma to continue, eager to follow the flow of conversation as it swirled into dark uncharted waters.

"Who, Grandmamma?" prodded Rose. "Who was it followed her? Who did she run away with?"

But Grandmamma didn't answer. Whatever the scenarios that played across her mind, they refused manipulation. Rose persisted but to no avail. And in the end she had to be content with turning the questions over and over in her mind, the name of her aunt becoming for her a symbol of dark and testing times. Of all that was unfair and wicked in the world . . .

"Rose?" Mamma's brows were knitted into a slight frown. One she tried to conceal but which Rose had become practiced at recognizing. "Are you saying something, child? You were whispering." She reached out a hand to gauge Rose's temperature.

"I'm all right, Mamma, just a little distracted by my thoughts."

"You seem flushed."

Rose pressed her own hand against her forehead. Was she flushed? She couldn't tell.

"I shall send Dr. Matthews up again before he leaves," said Mamma. "I'd sooner be careful than sorry."

Rose closed her eyes. Another visit from Dr. Matthews, two in the one afternoon. It was beyond her capacity to bear.

"You're too weak today to greet our new project," said Mamma. "I'll speak with the doctor and, if he deems it suitable, you may meet Eliza tomorrow. Eliza! Imagine bestowing a Mountrachet family name on the daughter of a sailor!"

A sailor, this was new. Rose's eyes snapped open. "Mamma?"

Mamma grew flushed herself then. She'd said more than she intended, an unusual chink in her armor of propriety. "Your cousin's father was a sailor. We do not speak of him."

"My uncle was a sailor?"

Mamma gasped and her thin hand leaped to her mouth. "He was

not your uncle, Rose, he was nothing to you or me. He was no more married to your Aunt Georgiana than I was."

"But, Mamma!" It was more scandalous than Rose had ever been able to invent for herself. "Whatever can you mean?"

Mamma's voice was low. "Eliza may be your cousin, Rose, and we have little choice but to have her in this house. But she's low-born, make no mistake of that. She is fortunate indeed that her mother's death has brought her back to Blackhurst. After all the shame this family suffered at the hands of her mother." She shook her head. "It nearly killed your father when she left. I can't bear to think what might have happened had I not been here to see him through the scandal." She looked directly at Rose. Her voice contained the slightest tremble. "A family can bear only so much shame before its good name is irreparably tarnished. That is why it's so important that you and I live spotlessly. Your cousin Eliza will present a challenge, of that I've little doubt. She will never be one of us, but through our best efforts we will at least elevate her from the London gutter."

Rose pretended absorption in the ruffled sleeve of her nightdress. "Can a girl of low birth never be taught to pass herself off as a lady, Mamma?"

"No, my child."

"Not even if she were taken in by a noble family?" Rose glanced at Mamma from beneath her eyelashes. "Married a gentleman, perhaps?"

Mamma turned sharp eyes upon Rose and hesitated before speaking slowly, carefully. "It is possible, of course, that a rare girl of humble but proper beginnings, who works ceaselessly to improve herself, may effect an elevation." She drew a quick breath designed to settle her composure. "But not, I fear, in the case of your cousin. We must lower our expectations, Rose."

"Of course, Mamma."

The real reason for her mother's discomfort sat between them, though Mamma, if she'd suspected Rose knew, would have been mortified. It was another family secret that Rose had managed to glean from her dying grandmother. A secret that explained so much: the animosity between the two matriarchs, and even more than that, Mamma's obsession with manners. Her devotion to the rules of society, her commitment to presenting always as a paragon of propriety.

Lady Adeline Mountrachet may have attempted to banish all mention of the truth long ago—most who knew it had been terrified into wiping it from their memories, and those who hadn't were too mindful of their position to dare breathe a word about Lady Mountrachet's origins—but Grandmamma had felt no such compunction. She'd been only too happy to remember the Yorkshire girl whose pious parents, fallen on hard times, had leaped at the opportunity to pack her off to Blackhurst Manor, Cornwall, where she might serve as a companion for the glorious Georgiana Mountrachet.

Mamma paused at the door. "One last thing, Rose, the most important thing of all."

"Yes, Mamma?"

"The girl *must* be kept out of Father's way."

A task that shouldn't be difficult; Rose could count on one hand the number of times she'd seen Father during the past year. All the same, her mother's vehemence was intriguing. "Mamma?"

A slight pause that Rose noted with growing interest, then the reply that raised more questions than it answered. "Your father is a busy man, an important man. He doesn't need to be reminded constantly of the stain on his family's good name." She inhaled quickly and her voice dropped to a grey whisper. "Believe me when I tell you, Rose, none in this house shall benefit should the girl be allowed near Father."

ADELINE PRESSED gently at her fingertip and watched as the red bead of blood appeared. It was the third time she'd pricked her finger in as many minutes. Embroidery had always served to calm her nerves but their fraying this day had been complete. She set the petit point aside. It was the conversation with Rose that had her rattled, and the distracted tea with Dr. Matthews, but beneath it all, of course, lay the arrival of Georgiana's girl. Though physically a mere scrap of a child, she had brought something with her. Something invisible, like the atmospheric shift that precedes a mighty storm. And that something threatened to bring to an end everything for which Adeline had strived; indeed, it had already started its insidious work; for all day Adeline had been beset with memories of her own arrival at Blackhurst. Memories she'd worked hard to forget, and to ensure that others did, too . . .

When she'd arrived in 1886, Adeline had been met by a house that seemed empty of inhabitants. And what a house it was, bigger than anything she'd ever set foot inside. She'd stood for ten minutes at least, waiting for some direction, for someone to receive her, until finally a young man, wearing a formal suit and a haughty expression, had appeared in the hall. He'd stopped, surprised, then checked his pocket watch.

"You're early," he said, in a tone that left Adeline in little doubt as to his opinion of those who arrived before their time. "We're not expecting you until tea."

She stood silently, unsure what was expected of her.

The man huffed. "If you wait here, I'll find someone to show you to your room."

Adeline was aware of being troublesome. "I could take a walk through the garden if you prefer?" she said in a meek voice, more conscious than ever of her northern accent, grown thicker in this glorious, airy room of white marble.

The man nodded curtly. "That would do well."

A footman had whisked her trunks away, so Adeline was unencumbered as she went back down the grand stairs. She stood at the bottom, looking this way and that, trying to shake the uncomfortable sense that she had somehow failed before she'd even begun.

Reverend Lambert had mentioned the Mountrachet family's wealth and stature numerous times during his afternoon visits with

Adeline and her parents. It was an honor for the entire diocese, he'd said earnestly and often, that one of their own had been selected to undertake such an important task. His Cornish counterpart had searched far and wide, under direct instruction from the lady of the house, in order to select the most suitable candidate, and it was up to Adeline to ensure that she was worthy of so great an honor. Not to mention the generous fee that would be paid to her parents for their loss. And Adeline had been determined to succeed. All the way from Yorkshire she'd given herself stern little lectures on topics like "The Appearance of Quality Is Akin to the Fact" and "A Lady Is as a Lady Does," but inside the house her faithless convictions had withered weakly away.

A noise above drew her attention to the sky, where a family of black rooks was tracing an intricate pattern. One of the birds fell steeply in flight before following the others in the direction of a stand of tall trees in the distance. For want of another destination, Adeline set off after them, lecturing herself all the way about new beginnings and starting as one meant to go on.

So involved was Adeline in her self-haranguing that she had little power of observation left with which to absorb the wondrous gardens of Blackhurst. Before she'd even made a start on her affirmations about rank and the aristocracy, she had cleared the dark coolness of the woods and was standing on the edge of a cliff, dry grasses rustling at her feet. Beyond the cliff, tossed out flat like a hank of velvet, was the deep blue sea.

Adeline clutched a nearby branch. She had never been one for heights and her heart was racing.

Something in the water directed her gaze back towards the cove. A young man and woman in a little boat, he seated while she stood rocking the boat from side to side. Her dress of white muslin was wet from the ankles to her waist and clung to her legs in a manner that made Adeline gasp.

She felt that she should turn away but she couldn't take her eyes from them. The young woman had red hair, such bright red hair, hanging loose and long, turning to wet tendrils at the end. The man had on a straw boater, a black box-shaped contraption strung around his neck. He was laughing, flicking water in the girl's direction. He started crawling towards her, reached out to grab at her legs. The boat rocked more violently, and just when Adeline thought he would touch her, the girl turned and dived in one long, fluid motion into the water.

Nothing in Adeline's experience had prepared her for such behavior. What could have possessed the young woman to do such a thing? And where was she now? Adeline craned to see. Scanned the glistening water until finally a figure in white became visible, gliding to the surface near the great black rock. The girl pulled herself from the sea, dress glued to her body, water dripping, and without turning back climbed the rock and disappeared up a hidden path in the steep hill, towards a little cottage on the cliff top.

Fighting to control her shallow breaths, Adeline turned her attention to the young man, for surely he was equally shocked? He had also watched the girl disappear and was now rowing the boat back to the cove. He pulled it out along the pebbles, picked up his shoes and started up the steps. He had a limp, she noticed, and a cane.

The man passed so close by Adeline and yet he didn't see her. He was whistling to himself, a tune Adeline didn't know. A happy, jaunty tune, full of sunshine and salt. The antithesis of the gloomy Yorkshire she was so desperate to escape. This young man seemed twice as tall as the fellows back home and twice as bright.

Standing alone on the cliff top, she was aware suddenly of the heat and weight of her traveling suit. The water below looked so cool; the shameful thought was hers before she could control it. What might it feel like to dive beneath the surface and emerge, dripping wet, as the young woman, as Georgiana, had done?

Later, many years later, when Linus's mother, the old witch, lay dying, she confessed her reason for selecting Adeline as Georgiana's companion. "I was looking for the dullest little dormouse I could find, with piety a great plus, in the hopes that some of it would rub off on my daughter. I didn't suspect for a moment that my rare bird would take flight and the dormouse usurp her place. I suppose I should congratulate you. You won in the end, didn't you, Lady Mountrachet?"

And so she had. From humble beginnings, with hard work and determination, Adeline had risen in the world, higher than her parents could ever have imagined when they permitted her departure for an unknown village in Cornwall.

And she had continued working hard, even after her marriage and assumption of the title Lady Mountrachet. She'd run a tight ship so that no matter the mud thrown, none would stick to her family, her grand home. And that was not about to change. Georgiana's girl was here now, that could not be helped. It was up to Adeline to ensure that life at Blackhurst Manor went on as ever.

She just needed to free herself from the niggling fear that by Eliza's accommodation at Blackhurst Rose would somehow be the loser . . .

Adeline shook away the misgivings that continued to prick her skin and concentrated on regaining her composure. She had always been sensitive where Rose was concerned, that was what came of having a delicate child. Beside her, the dog, Astrigg, whimpered. He, too, had been unsettled all day. Adeline reached down and stroked the knobbled head. "Shhh," she said. "All will be well." She scratched his raised eyebrows. "I'll see to that."

There was nothing to fear, for what risk could this interloper, this skinny girl with cropped hair and skin sallow from a life of poverty in London, possibly present to Adeline and her family? One needed only to glance at Eliza to see that she was no Georgiana, God be thanked. Why, perhaps these disquieting feelings weren't fear at all, but relief. Relief at having faced her worst fears and had them dissipate. For with Eliza's arrival came the additional comfort of knowing for certain that Georgiana was really gone, never to return. And in her place a waif with none of her mother's peculiar power for bending people to her will without so much as trying.

The door opened, admitting a gust to tussle with the fire.

"Dinner is served, ma'am."

How Adeline despised Thomas, despised them all. For all their yes and no, ma'am, dinner is served, ma'am, she knew what they really thought of her, what they'd always thought of her.

"The master?" Her coldest, most authoritative voice.

"Lord Mountrachet is on his way from the darkroom, ma'am."

The wretched darkroom, of course that's where he was. She'd heard his carriage arrive on the driveway while she was enduring tea with Dr. Matthews. Had kept one ear trained on the entrance hall waiting for her husband's signature stride—heavy, light; heavy, light—but nothing. She should have guessed that he'd gone straight to his infernal darkroom.

Thomas was still watching her, so Adeline screwed her composure to the sticking place. She'd sooner suffer at the hands of Lucifer himself than grant Thomas the satisfaction of noting marital disharmony. "Go," she said, with a wave of her wrist, "and see to it personally that the master's boots are cleaned of the ghastly Scottish mud."

LINUS WAS already seated when Adeline arrived at the table. He'd started on his soup and didn't look up as she entered. He was too busy studying the black-and-white prints that were laid out over his end of the long table: moss and butterflies and bricks, the spoils of his recent trip.

Seeing him, Adeline suffered a warm shot of air to the brain. What would others say if they knew that the Blackhurst dinner table was host to such behavior? She glanced sideways at Thomas and the footman, each focused on the distant wall. But Adeline wasn't fooled, she knew that behind their glazed expressions their minds were busy: judging, noting, preparing to tell their counterparts in other houses about the slipping standards at Blackhurst Manor.

Adeline sat stiffly in her place, waited as the footman placed her soup in front of her. She took a small mouthful and burned her tongue. Watched as Linus, head bowed, continued his inspection of the photographic prints. The little patch at the very crown of his head was thinning. It looked like a sparrow had been at work, laying the first scanty threads for a new nest.

"The girl is here?" he said, without looking up.

Adeline felt her skin prickle: the wretched girl. "She is."

"You've seen her?"

"Of course. She has been accommodated upstairs."

Finally he lifted his head, took a sip of his wine. Then another. "And is she . . . is she like . . . ? "

"No," Adeline's voice was cold. "No, she is not." In her lap, her fists balled tight.

Linus exhaled shortly, broke a piece of bread and began to eat it. He spoke with his mouth full, surely just to spite her. "Mansell said as much."

If anyone was to blame for the girl's arrival it was Henry Mansell. Linus may have sought Georgiana's return, but it was Mansell who'd kept the hope alive. The detective, with his thick moustache and fine pince-nez, had taken Linus's money and sent him frequent reports. Every night Adeline had prayed that Mansell would fail, that Georgiana would stay away, that Linus would learn to let her go.

"Your trip went well?" said Adeline.

No answer. His eyes were on the prints again.

Adeline's pride prevented another sideways glance at Thomas. She composed her features in a mask of contented calm and attempted another spoonful of soup, cooler by now. Linus's rejection of Adeline was one thing—he'd begun his drift soon after their marriage—but his complete denial of Rose was something other. She was his child; his blood coursed through her veins, the blood of his noble family. How he could remain so detached, Adeline couldn't fathom.

"Dr. Matthews has been again today," she said. "Another infection."

Linus looked up, eyes drawn with the familiar veil of disinterest. Ate another mouthful of bread.

"Nothing too serious, thank goodness," said Adeline, buoyed by his lifted gaze. "No need for grave concern."

Linus swallowed his piece of bread. "I head for France tomorrow," he said blankly. "There's a gate at Notre Dame . . ." His sentence faded away. Commitment to keeping Adeline informed of his movements only went so far.

Adeline's left brow peaked slightly before she caught it and ironed it smooth. "Lovely," she said, winding her lips back into a tight smile, smothering the image from nowhere, of Linus in the little boat, camera pointed at a figure dressed all in white.

TWENTY-SEVEN

THERE it was, the black rock of William Martin's story. From the top of the cliff, Nell watched as white sea froth swirled about the base before rushing inside the cave and being sucked back out on the tide. It didn't take much to imagine the cove as the site of thrashing storms and sinking ships and midnight smuggling raids.

Across the cliff top a line of trees stood soldierlike, blocking Nell's view of the house at Blackhurst, her mother's house.

She dug her hands deeper into the pockets of her coat. The wind was strong up here and it took all her strength to maintain balance. Her neck was numb, her cheeks simultaneously warm with chafing and cool with the breeze. She turned to follow the path of flattened grass back from the cliff edge. The road didn't come this far and the way was narrow. Nell went cautiously: her knee was swollen and bruised after the rather impromptu entrance she'd made to the Blackhurst estate the previous day. She'd gone intending to deliver a letter saying that she was an antiques dealer visiting from Australia, and requesting that she might come and see the house at a time convenient to its owners. But as she'd stood by the tall metal gates, something had overcome her, a need every bit as strong as that to breathe. The next she knew she'd abandoned all dignity and was clambering gracelessly up the gate, seeking footholds in the decorative metal curls.

Ridiculous behavior for a woman half her age, but that was as it was. To stand so close to her family home, her own birthplace, and be denied as much as a glimpse was intolerable. It was only regrettable

253

that Nell's physical dexterity had been no match for her tenacity. She'd been embarrassed and grateful in equal measure when Julia Bennett chanced upon her trespass attempt. Thankfully the new owner of Blackhurst had accepted Nell's explanation and invited her to take a look.

It had been such an odd feeling, seeing inside the house. Strange, but not in the way she'd expected. Nell had been speechless with anticipation. She'd walked across the entrance hall, climbed the stairs, peered around doorways, telling herself over and over: your mother sat here, your mother walked here, your mother loved here; and she had waited for the enormity to hit her. For some wave of knowing to launch itself from the house's walls and crash over her, for some deep part of herself to recognize that she was home. But no such knowingness had come. A foolish expectation, of course, and not like Nell at all. But there it was. Even the most pragmatic person fell victim at times to a longing for something other. At least she could now add texture to the memories she was trying to rebuild; imagined conversations would take place in real rooms.

In the long, shimmery grass Nell spied a stick just the right length. There was something immeasurably pleasant in walking with such a stick; it added a sense of industry to a person's journey. Not to mention it would take some pressure off her swollen knee. She reached to pick it up and continued carefully down the slope, past the tall stone wall. There was a sign on the front gate, just above that which threatened trespassers. *For Sale,* it read, and then a phone number.

This, then, was the cottage belonging to the Blackhurst estate, the one Julia Bennett had mentioned the day before, and that William Martin had wished burned to the ground, that had stood witness to things that "weren't right," whatever they might be. Nell leaned against the gate. There didn't look to be much threatening about it. The garden was overgrown and the approaching dusk spilled into every corner, settled for the night in cool, dim pockets. A narrow path led towards the cottage before scurrying left at the front door and continuing its windy way through the garden. By the far wall stood a lonely statue plastered with green lichen. A small naked boy in the middle of a garden bed, wide eyes turned eternal on the cottage.

No, not a garden bed, the boy stood in a fish pond.

The correction came swiftly and certainly, surprising Nell so that she held tighter to the locked gate. How did she know?

Then before her eyes the garden changed. Weeds and brambles, decades in the growing, receded. Leaves lifted from the ground, revealing paths and flower beds and a garden seat. Light was permitted entry once more, tossed dappled across the surface of the pond. And then she was in two places at once: a sixty-five-year-old woman with a sore knee, clinging to a rusty gate, and a little girl, long hair plaited down her back, sitting on a tuft of soft, cool grass, toes dangling in the pond . . .

The plump fish bobbed to the surface again, golden belly shining, and the little girl laughed as he opened his mouth and nibbled her big toe. She loved the pond, had wanted one at home, but Mamma had been fearful that she'd fall in and drown. Mamma was often fearful, especially where the little girl was concerned. If Mamma knew where they were today, she'd be very cross. But Mamma didn't know, she was having one of her bad days, was lying in the dark of her boudoir with a damp flannel on her forehead.

A noise and the little girl looked up. The lady and Papa had come back outside. They stood for a moment and Papa said something to the lady, something the little girl couldn't hear. He touched her arm and the lady started walking slowly forwards. She was watching the little girl in a strange way, a way that reminded her of the boy statue who stood by the pond all day, never so much as blinking. The lady smiled, a magical smile, and the little girl pulled her feet from the pond and waited, waited, wondering what the lady would say . . .

A rook flew close overhead and with it time was restored. The brambles and creepers re-formed, leaves dropped and the garden was once more a damp, moist place at the mercy of the dusk. The boy statue green with age, just as he should be.

Nell was aware of an ache in her knuckles. She loosened her grip on the gate and watched the rook, broad wings beating the air as he soared towards the top of the Blackhurst trees. In the west a flock of clouds had been lit from behind and glowed pink in the darkening sky.

Nell glanced dazedly at the cottage garden. The little girl was gone. Or was she?

As Nell dug the stick in before her and started back towards the village, a peculiar sense of duality, not unwelcome, followed her all the way.

Twenty-eight

Next morning, as pale wintry light rippled the glass of the nursery windows, Rose smoothed the ends of her long, dark hair. Mrs. Hopkins had brushed it until it shone, just the way Rose liked, and it sat perfectly against the lace of her very finest dress, the one that Mamma had sent for from Paris. Rose was feeling tired and a little tetchy, but that was her wont. Little girls with weak constitutions weren't expected to be happy all the time and Rose had no intention of performing against type. If she were honest, she rather liked having people walk on eggshells around her: it made her feel a little less miserable when others were similarly stifled. Besides, Rose had good reason for weariness today. She had lain awake all night, tossing and turning like the princess with her pea, only it hadn't been a lump in the mattress that had kept her awake, rather Mamma's astonishing news.

After Mamma had left the bedroom, Rose had fallen to pondering the precise nature of the stain on her family's good name, exactly what sort of drama had erupted after her Aunt Georgiana's flight from home and family. All night she had wondered about her wicked aunt, and the thoughts had not evaporated with the dawn. During breakfast, and later while Mrs. Hopkins dressed her, even now as she waited in the nursery, her mind was so engaged. She was watching the firelight flickering against the pale hearth bricks, wondering whether the dusky orange shadows resembled the door to hell through which her aunt must surely have passed, when suddenly—footsteps in the hallway!

Rose jumped a little in her seat, smoothed the lamb's wool blanket across her knees, and quickly arranged her face along the lines of placid perfection she'd learned from Mamma. Cherished the little thrill that worked its way down her spine. Oh, what an important task it was! The assignment of a protégée. Her very own wayward orphan to remake in her own image. Rose had never had a friend before, nor been allowed a pet of any kind (Mamma had grave concerns about rabies). And despite Mamma's words of caution, she harbored great hopes for this cousin of hers. She would be turned into a lady, would become a companion for Rose, someone to mop Rose's brow when she was ill, stroke her hand when she was peevish, brush her hair when she was bothered. And she would be so grateful for Rose's instruction, so happy to have been granted insight into the ways of ladies, that she would do exactly as Rose ordered. She would be the perfect friend—one who never argued, never behaved tiresomely, never so much as ventured a disagreeable opinion.

The door opened, the fire sputtered crossly at the disturbance and Mamma strode into the room, blue skirts swishing. There was an agitation to Mamma's manner today that piqued Rose's interest, something in the set of her chin that suggested her misgivings about the project were greater and more varied than she had revealed. "Good morning, Rose," she said rather curtly.

"Good morning, Mamma."

"Allow me to present your cousin," the slightest pause, "Eliza."

And then, from somewhere behind Mamma's skirts, was thrust forth the skinny sapling Rose had glimpsed from the window the day before.

Rose couldn't help it, she drew back a little into the safe arms of her chair. Her gaze slid from top to bottom, taking in the child's short, shaggy hair, the ghastly attire (breeches!), her knobbly knees and scuffed boots. The cousin said nothing, merely stared in a wide-eyed way Rose found exceptionally rude. Mamma was right. This girl (for surely she wasn't expected to think of her as a cousin!) had been deprived of even the most basic education on manners.

Rose recaptured her flagging composure. "How do you do?" Her tone was a little weak, but a nod from Mamma assured her that she had performed well. She awaited a return greeting, but none was forthcoming. Rose glanced at Mamma, who indicated that she should push on regardless. "And tell me, Cousin Eliza," she tried again, "are you enjoying your time here with us?"

Eliza blinked at her as one might a curious, foreign animal in the London Zoo, then nodded.

Another set of footsteps in the hall and Rose was granted brief respite from the challenge of summoning up further pleasantries to converse with this strange, silent cousin.

"I'm sorry to interrupt you, my lady," came Mrs. Hopkins's voice from the door, "only Dr. Matthews is downstairs in the morning room. He says he's brought the new tincture you were asking after."

"Have him leave it for me, Mrs. Hopkins. I have other business to attend to at present."

"Of course, my lady, and I suggested as much to Dr. Matthews, but he was most definite about giving it to you himself."

Mamma's eyelashes performed the slightest of flutters, so subtle that only one whose life's work had involved observation of her moods would have noticed. "Thank you, Mrs. Hopkins," she said grimly. "Advise Dr. Matthews that I will be down directly."

As Mrs. Hopkins's footsteps disappeared down the hallway, Mamma turned to the cousin and said, in a clear, authoritative voice, "You will sit silently on the rug and listen carefully as Rose instructs you. Do not move. Do not speak. Do not touch a thing."

"But, Mamma—" Rose had not expected to be left alone so soon.

"Perhaps you will begin your lessons by giving your cousin some guidance as to proper dress."

"Yes, Mamma."

And then the billowing blue skirts were receding again, the door was closed and the room's fire ceased spitting. Rose met the cousin's gaze. They were alone together and the work would begin.

"PUT THAT down. Put it down at once." Things were not going at all as Rose had imagined. The girl would not listen, would not obey, did not fall into line even when Rose raised the threat of Mamma's wrath. For five whole minutes now Eliza had been wandering around the nursery, picking things up, inspecting them, putting them down again. No doubt leaving sticky fingerprints everywhere. At this moment she was shaking the kaleidoscope that some great-aunt or another had sent for Rose's birthday one year. "That's precious," Rose said sourly. "I insist that you leave it. You're not even doing it right."

Too late, Rose realized she had said the wrong thing. Now the cousin was coming towards her, holding out the kaleidoscope. Coming so close Rose could glimpse the dirt beneath her fingernails, the dreaded dirt that Mamma promised would make her ill.

Rose was horrified. She shrank back against her chair, head spinning. "No," she managed to say, "shoo. Get away."

Eliza stopped at the arm of the chair, seemed about to perch herself right there on the velvet.

"Get away, I said!" Rose flapped a pale, weak hand. Did it not understand the Queen's English? "You mustn't sit right by me."

"Why not?"

So it did have words. "You've been outside. You're not clean. I could catch something." Rose collapsed back against the cushion. "I'm awfully dizzy now, and it's all your fault."

"It's not my fault," said Eliza plainly. Not even the tiniest note of proper supplication. "I'm dizzy, too. It's because this room's as hot as a furnace."

She was dizzy, too? Rose was speechless. Dizziness was her own special weapon to deploy. And what was the cousin doing now? She was on her feet again, moving towards the nursery window. Rose watched, eyes wide with fear. Surely she didn't intend to—

"I'll just get this open." Eliza jiggled the first lock loose. "Then we'll be all right."

"No," Rose felt terror surge within her. "No!"

"You'll feel much better."

"But it's winter. It's come over all dark and cloudy outside. I might catch a chill."

Eliza shrugged. "You might not."

Rose was so shocked by the girl's cheek that indignation outweighed fear. She adopted Mamma's voice. "I demand that you stop."

Eliza wrinkled her nose, seemed to be digesting this instruction. As Rose held her breath, the cousin's hands dropped from the window lock. She shrugged again, but the gesture was somehow less impertinent this time. As she wandered back towards the center of the room, Rose thought she detected a pleasing despondence in the set of Eliza's shoulders. Finally, the girl stopped in the center of the rug and pointed to the cylinder in Rose's lap. "Can you show me how it works? The telescope? I couldn't see through it."

Rose exhaled, weary, relieved and increasingly confused by this strange creature. Really, to have turned her attention back to the silly trinket again, just like that! Still, the cousin had been obedient and surely that deserved some small encouragement . . . "First of all," she said primly, "it's not a telescope at all. It's a *kaleido*scope. You're not supposed to see through it. You look inside and the pattern changes." She held it up and performed the action before laying the toy on the floor and rolling it towards her cousin.

Eliza picked it up and put it to her eye, turned the end. As the pieces of colored glass rattled this way and that, her mouth spread into a wide smile, which broadened until she was laughing.

Rose blinked with surprise. She hadn't heard much laughter before, only the servants occasionally when they thought she wasn't near. The sound was lovely. A happy, light, girlish sound, quite at odds with her cousin's appearance.

"Why do you wear those clothes?" said Rose.

Eliza continued to peer through the kaleidoscope. "Because they're mine," she said eventually. "They belong to me."

"They look as if they belong to a boy."

"Once upon a time they did. Now they're mine."

This was a surprise. Things were becoming more curious with each passing minute. "Which boy?"

There came no answer, just the jiggling of the kaleidoscope.

"I said, which boy?" A little louder this time.

Slowly, Eliza lowered the toy.

"It's very bad manners to ignore people, you know."

"I'm not ignoring you," said Eliza.

"Then why don't you answer?"

Another shrug.

"It's rude to lift your shoulders like that. When someone speaks to you, you must provide them with an answer. Now tell me, why were you ignoring my question?"

Eliza looked up and stared at her. As Rose watched, something seemed to change in her cousin's face. A light that hadn't been there before seemed now to glow behind her eyes. "I didn't speak, because I didn't want *her* to know where I was."

"Her? Who?"

Carefully, slowly, Eliza came a little closer. "The Other Cousin."

"What other cousin?" Really the girl spoke no sense. Rose was beginning to think she truly was simple. "I don't know what you're talking about," she said. "There is no other cousin."

"She's a secret. They keep her locked upstairs."

"You're making it up. Why would anyone keep her a secret?"

"They kept me a secret, didn't they?"

"They didn't keep you locked upstairs."

"That's because I wasn't dangerous." Eliza tiptoed to the nursery door, prised it open a crack and peered outside. She gasped.

"What?" said Rose.

"Shhh!" Eliza held a finger to her lips. "We can't let her know we're in here."

"Why?" Rose's eyes were wide.

Eliza tiptoed back to the edge of Rose's chair. The flickering fire-light in the darkening room gave her face an eerie glow. "Our Other Cousin," she said, "is insane."

"Mad?"

"As a hatter." Eliza lowered her voice so that Rose had to lean close to hear. "She's been locked in the attic since she was small, but someone's let her out."

"Who?"

"One of the ghosts. The ghost of an old woman, a very fat old woman."

"Grandmamma," whispered Rose.

"Shhh!" said Eliza. "Listen! Footsteps."

Rose could feel her poor feeble heart leaping like a frog in her chest.

Eliza jumped onto the arm of Rose's chair. "She's coming!"

The door opened and Rose screamed. Eliza grinned and Mamma gasped.

"What are you doing up there, wicked girl?" Mamma hissed, gaze flitting from Eliza to Rose. "Young ladies do not sit astride the furniture. You were told not to move." Her breathing was loud. "Are you harmed, my Rose?"

Rose shook her head. "No, Mamma."

For just an instant, Mamma seemed at a rare loss; Rose almost feared that she might cry. Then she seized Eliza by the upper arm and marched her towards the door. "Wicked girl! You'll have no supper to-night." A familiar steel had returned to her voice. "And no supper any night thereafter. Not until you learn to do as you are told. I am mistress of this house and you *will* obey me . . ."

The door closed and Rose sat alone once more. Wondering at this peculiar turn of events. The thrill of Eliza's story, the curious enjoyable fear that had stalked up her spine, the terrible, wonderful specter of the mad Other Cousin. But it was the crack that had appeared in Mamma's usually cast-iron composure that intrigued Rose most of all. For in that moment, the stable borders of Rose's world had seemed to shift.

All was not as it had been. And that knowledge made Rose's heart thump—strongly now—with unexpected, unexplained, unadulterated joy.

TWENTY-NINE

THE colors were different here. Cassandra had never realized how sharp the Australian glare was until she met the gentle Cornish light. She wondered how she'd go about replicating it in watercolors, surprised herself for having wondered. She took a bite of buttery toast and chewed thoughtfully, looked at the line of trees that stood on the cliff edge. Closing one eye, she lifted her index finger to trace along their tops.

A shadow fell across her table and there was a voice right beside her. "Cassandra? Cassandra Ryan?" A woman in her early sixties was standing by the table, silver-blond and shapely, with eye makeup whose application had left no corner of the shadow compact unexplored. "I'm Julia Bennett, I own the Blackhurst Hotel."

Cassandra wiped a buttery finger on her napkin and shook hands. "Nice to meet you."

Julia indicated the vacant chair. "Mind if I . . . ? "

"Of course not, please."

Julia sat down and Cassandra waited uncertainly, wondering whether this was part of the personalized service threatened in the brochure.

"I hope you're enjoying your stay with us."

"It's a lovely spot."

Julia looked at her and smiled so that dimples appeared in each cheek. "You know, I can see your grandmother in you. But I bet you hear that all the time."

Behind Cassandra's polite smile, a flock of questions resisted shepherding. How did this stranger know who she was? How did she know Nell? How had she put the two of them together?

Julia laughed and leaned forward conspiratorially. "A little birdie told me the Australian girl who'd inherited the cottage was in town. Tregenna is a small place. You sneeze on the Sharpstone Cliffs and the fellows in the harbor know all about it."

Cassandra realized who the bird in question was. "Robyn Jameson."

"She was here yesterday, trying to enlist me for the festival committee," said Julia. "Couldn't resist imparting the local comings and goings while she was at it. I put two and two together and connected you with the lady who came to call some thirty years ago, saved my skin by taking the cottage off my hands. I always wondered when your grandmother would return, kept an eye out for her for some time. I liked her. She was a straight shooter, wasn't she?"

The description was so accurate that Cassandra couldn't help wondering what Nell had said or done to earn it.

"You know, the first time I met your grandmother, she was hanging from a rather thick wisteria near the front entrance."

"Really?" Cassandra's eyes widened.

"She'd scaled the front wall and was having difficulty getting down on the other side. Lucky for her I'd just had an argument with my husband, Richard, number ninety-seven for the day, and I was stalking around the grounds trying to cool down. I hate to think how long she'd have been hanging there otherwise."

"She was trying to see the house?"

Julia nodded. "Said she was an antiques dealer interested in Victoriana and wondered if she could take a peek inside."

Cassandra felt a fierce flame of affection for Nell as she imagined her scaling walls and telling half-truths, refusing to take no for an answer.

"I told her she was welcome to come in, just as soon as she'd finished swinging from my wisteria!" Julia laughed. "The house was in pretty poor condition, it'd been roundly neglected for decades by then, and Rick and I had dismantled things to the point that they looked far worse than they had done to begin with, but she didn't seem to mind. She walked through, stopping at each and every room. It was like she was trying to commit them to memory."

Or retrieve them from memory. Cassandra wondered how much Nell had told Julia about the reason for her interest. "Did you show her the cottage, too?"

"No, but I sure as hell mentioned it to her. Then I crossed my fingers and everything else I could manage to cross." She laughed. "We were that desperate for a buyer! We were going broke just as surely as if we'd dug a hole beneath the house and tossed every last pound into it. We'd had the cottage on the market for a while, you see. Almost sold it twice to Londoners looking for a holiday home, but both contracts fell through. Rotten luck. We dropped the price but there was no way we could get anyone local to buy it, not for love nor money. Spectacular views and no one interested because of some silly old rumors."

"Robyn told me."

"As far as I can see, there's something wrong with your house in Cornwall if it isn't haunted," said Julia lightly. "We've got our very own ghost at the hotel. But you already know that, I hear you met her the other night?"

Cassandra's puzzlement must have shown on her face, for Julia continued, "Samantha on the front desk told me you reported a key in your door?"

"Oh," said Cassandra, "yeah. I thought it was another guest, but it must've been the wind. I didn't mean to cause any—"

"That's her, all right, that's our ghost." Julia laughed at Cassandra's expression of perplexity. "Oh, now, don't you be alarmed, she won't do you any harm. She's not an *unfriendly* ghost exactly. I wouldn't keep an unfriendly ghost."

Cassandra had the feeling that Julia was pulling her leg. All the same, she'd heard more talk of ghosts since she'd arrived in Cornwall than she had since she was twelve years old and went to her first slumber party. "I suppose every old house needs one," she ventured.

"Precisely," said Julia. "People expect it. I'd have had to invent one if there hadn't been one here already. An historic hotel like this . . . Why, a resident ghost is as important to guests as clean towels." She leaned forward. "Ours even has a name. Rose Mountrachet: she and her family used to live here, back at the start of the twentieth century. Well, before that if you consider the family went back hundreds of years. That's her in the picture hanging by the bookcase in the foyer, the young woman with pale skin and dark hair. Have you seen it?"

Cassandra shook her head.

"Oh, you must," said Julia. "It's a John Singer Sargent, painted a few years after he did the Wyndham sisters."

"Really?" Cassandra's skin cooled. "An actual John Singer Sergeant?"

Julia laughed. "Incredible, isn't it? Another of the house's secrets. I didn't realize its value myself until a few years ago. We had a fellow out from Christie's to look at another painting and he spotted it. I call it my nest egg, not that I could ever bear to part with it. Such a beauty was our Rose, and such a tragic life! A delicate child who overcame ill health only to die at twenty-four in a dreadful accident." She sighed romantically. "Have you finished your breakfast? Come with me and I'll show you."

ROSE MOUNTRACHET at eighteen was fair indeed: white skin, a cloud of dark hair swept back in a loose braid and the full bosom so fashionable in the period. Sargent was renowned for his ability to discern and capture the personality of his sitters, and Rose's gaze was soulful. Red lips relaxed in repose but eyes that remained watchful, fixed on the artist. It was a seriousness of expression that fitted with what Cassandra imagined of a girl who'd spent her entire childhood imprisoned by ill health.

She leaned closer. The portrait's composition was interesting. Rose was seated on a sofa, a book in her lap. The sofa was angled away from the frame so that Rose was in the right-hand foreground and behind her was a wall papered in green but with little other detail. The way the wall was rendered gave it a sense of being pale and feathery, more impressionistic than the realism for which Sargent was known. It was not unheard of for Sargent to use such techniques, but this seemed somehow lighter than his other work, less careful.

"She was a beauty, wasn't she?" said Julia, sashaying over from the reception desk.

Cassandra nodded distractedly. The date on the painting was 1907, not long before he swore off portraiture. Perhaps he had been growing tired of rendering the faces of the wealthy even then.

"I see she's worked her spell on you. Now you know why I was so keen to enlist her as our ghost." She laughed, then noticed Cassandra hadn't. "Are you all right? You look a little peaky. Glass of water?"

Cassandra shook her head. "No, no, I'm fine, thanks. It's just the painting . . ." She pressed her lips together, heard herself say, "Rose Mountrachet was my great-grandmother."

Julia's eyebrows leaped.

"I only found out recently." Cassandra smiled at Julia, embarrassed. No matter that it was the truth, she felt like an actor speaking soap opera lines, bad soap opera lines. "I'm sorry. This is the first time I've seen a picture of her. It all feels very real suddenly."

"Oh, my dear," said Julia. "I hate to be the one to break it to you, but I'm afraid you must be mistaken. Rose couldn't be your great-grandmother. She couldn't be anyone's great-grandmother. Her only child died when she was practically still a baby."

"Of scarlet fever."

"Poor little cherub, only four years old—" She looked sideways at Cassandra. "If you know about the scarlet fever, you must know that Rose's daughter died."

"I know people think that, but I also know it's not what really happened. It can't be."

"I've seen the headstone in the estate cemetery," said Julia gently. "Sweetest lines of poetry, so sad. I can show it to you if you'd like."

Cassandra could feel her cheeks flushing as they always did when she sensed the outskirts of disagreement. "There may be a headstone, but there's no little girl buried there. Not Ivory Walker, at any rate."

Julia's expression vacillated between interest and concern. "Go on."

"When my grandmother was twenty-one, she found out her parents weren't really her parents."

"She was adopted?"

"Sort of. She was found on a wharf in Australia when she was four years old, with nothing but a child's suitcase. It wasn't until she was sixty-five that her dad finally gave her the case and she was able to start searching for information about her past. She came to England and spoke with people and researched, and all the while she kept a journal."

Julia smiled knowingly. "Which you have now."

"Exactly. That's how I know she found out that Rose's daughter didn't die. She was kidnapped."

Julia's blue eyes searched Cassandra's face. Her cheeks had taken on a sudden flush. "But if that were the case, wouldn't there have been a search? Wouldn't it have been all over the newspapers? Like what happened with the Lindbergh boy?"

"Not if the family kept it quiet."

"Why would they have done that? They'd have wanted everyone to know, surely?"

Cassandra was shaking her head. "Not if they wanted to avoid scandal. The woman who took her was the ward of Lord and Lady Mountrachet, Rose's cousin."

Julia gasped. "*Eliza* took Rose's daughter?"

It was Cassandra's turn to look surprised. "You know of Eliza?"

"Of course, she's quite famous in these parts." Julia swallowed. "Let me get this straight. You think Eliza took Rose's daughter to Australia?"

"Put her on the boat to Australia but didn't go herself. Eliza went missing somewhere between London and Maryborough. When my great-grandfather found Nell, she was all by herself on the wharf. That's why he took her home, he couldn't leave a child that age alone."

Julia was clicking her tongue. "To think of a little girl abandoned like that. Your poor grandma, terrible not to know one's origins. Certainly explains her eagerness to take a look at this place."

"That's why Nell bought the cottage," said Cassandra. "Once she discovered who she was, she wanted to own a piece of her past."

"Of course." Julia lifted her hands, then dropped them again. "That part makes perfect sense, I just don't know about the rest."

"What do you mean?"

"Well, even if what you say is correct, if Rose's daughter survived, was kidnapped, wound up in Australia, I just can't believe Eliza had anything to do with it. Rose and Eliza were so close. More like sisters than cousins, the very best of friends." She paused, seemed to run the equation once more through her mind, then exhaled decisively. "No, I just can't believe Eliza capable of such betrayal."

Julia's faith in Eliza's innocence didn't seem that of a dispassionate observer discussing a historical hypothetical. "What makes you so certain?"

Julia indicated a pair of wicker chairs arranged in the bay window. "Come, sit for a moment. I'll have Samantha organize some tea."

Cassandra glanced at her watch. Her appointment with the gardener was drawing near but she was curious about Julia's strength of conviction, the way she spoke of Eliza and Rose as one might of dear friends. She sat in the proffered chair while Julia mouthed "Tea?" in Samantha's glazed direction.

As Samantha disappeared, Julia continued, "When we bought Blackhurst it was in a complete mess. We'd always dreamed of running a place like this but the reality resembled something out of a nightmare. You have no idea how much can go wrong in a house this size. It took us three years to make any headway at all. We worked solidly, nearly lost our marriage in the process. Nothing like rising damp and endless holes in the roof to drive a couple apart."

Cassandra smiled. "I can imagine."

"It's sad, really. The house was lived in and loved by the one family for so long, but in the twentieth century, particularly after the First War, it was virtually abandoned. Rooms were boarded up, fireplaces sealed, not to mention the damage done by the army when they were here in the 1940s.

"We sank every penny we had into the house. I was a writer way back when, a series of romantic novels in the 1960s. Not exactly Jackie Collins, but I did all right. My husband was in banking and we were confident we had enough to get this place up and running." She laughed. "Huge underestimation. *Huge*. By our third Christmas, we'd almost run out of money and had little to show for it other than a marriage hanging by a few threads. We'd already sold most of the smaller parts of the estate and by Christmas Eve 1974 we were just about ready to throw in the towel, head back to London with our tails between our legs."

Samantha appeared with a heavily loaded tray, jolted it onto the table, then hesitated before reaching for the teapot handle.

"I can pour it myself, Sam," said Julia, waving her away with a laugh. "I'm not the queen. Well, not yet." She winked at Cassandra. "Sugar?"

"Please."

Julia handed a cup of tea to Cassandra, took a sip of her own, then resumed her story. "It was freezing cold that Christmas Eve. A storm had blown in off the sea and was terrorizing the headland. We'd lost power, our turkey was going off in a warm fridge and we couldn't remember where we'd put the new batch of candles. We were hunting in one of the upstairs rooms when a flash of lightning bathed the room in light and the two of us noticed the wall." She rubbed her lips together in anticipation of her own punch line. "In the wall, there was a hole."

"Like a mouse hole?"

"No, a square hole."

Cassandra frowned uncertainly.

"A little cavity in the stone," said Julia. "The sort of thing I dreamed of as a kid whenever my brother found my diaries. It had been hidden behind a tapestry that the painter pulled down earlier in the week." She took a large slurp of tea before continuing. "I know it sounds silly, but finding that hidey-hole was like a good-luck charm. Almost like the house itself was saying, 'All right, you've been here long enough with your banging and clanging. You've proved your intentions are true, so you can stay.' And I tell you, from that night onwards things seemed easier somehow. Started to go right more often than they went wrong. Your grandma turned up for one thing, eager to buy Cliff Cottage, a fellow named Bobby Blake began bringing the garden back to life and a couple of coach companies started busing tourists in for afternoon teas."

She was smiling at the memory and Cassandra almost felt bad for interrupting. "But what was it you found? What was in the hidey-hole?"

Julia blinked at her.

"Was it something belonging to Rose?"

"Yes," said Julia, swallowing an excited smile. "Yes, it was. Tied up with a ribbon was a collection of scrapbooks. One for each year from 1900 up until 1913."

"Scrapbooks?"

"Plenty of young ladies used to keep them back then. It was a hobby wholeheartedly approved of by the powers that were—one of the few! A form of self-expression in which a young lady might be permitted indulgence without fears that she'd lost her soul to the Devil." She smiled fondly. "Oh, Rose's scrapbooks are no different from any other you might find in museums or attics all across the country— they're full of pieces of fabric, sketches, pictures, invitations, little anecdotes—but when I found them I so identified with this young woman from almost a century before, her hopes and dreams and disappointments, that I've had a soft spot for her ever since. I think of her as an angel, watching over us."

"Are the scrapbooks still here?"

A guilty nod. "I know I should donate them to a museum or to one of those local history mobs, but I'm rather superstitious and can't bear to part with them. For a little while I put them on display in the lounge, in one of the glass cabinets, but every time I caught a glimpse I felt a wave of shame, as if I'd taken something private and made it public. I have them stored in a box in my room now, for want of somewhere better."

"I'd love to see them."

"Of course you would, my dear. And so you shall." Julia smiled brilliantly at Cassandra. "I'm expecting a group booking in the next half-hour and Robyn's got the rest of my week stitched up with festival arrangements. Can we say dinner, Friday night, up in my apartment? Rick will be away in London so we'll have a real girls" night. Pore over Rose's scrapbooks and have ourselves a good old weep. How does that sound?"

"Great," said Cassandra, smiling a little uncertainly. It was the first time anyone had ever invited her anywhere for a cry.

THIRTY

CAREFUL not to alter her position on the sofa and incur the portrait artist's wrath, Rose allowed her gaze to drop so she could look upon the most recent page of her scrapbook. She'd been working on it all week, whenever Mr. Sargent had allowed them a rest from posing. There was a piece of the pale pink satin from which her birthday dress had been sewn, a ribbon from her hair, and at the bottom, in her best hand, she'd written out the lines from a poem by Lord Tennyson:

> But who hath seen her wave her hand?
> Or at the casement seen her stand?
> Or is she known in all the land,
> The Lady of Shalott?

How Rose identified with the Lady of Shalott! Cursed to spend eternity in her chamber, forced always to experience the world at one remove. For hadn't she, Rose, spent most of her life similarly interred?

But not anymore. Rose had made a decision: no longer would she be shackled by the morbid prognoses of Dr. Matthews, the hovering concern of Mamma. Though still delicate, Rose had learned that frailty begot frailty, that nothing caused light-headedness so surely as day after day of stifling confinement. She was going to open windows when she was hot—she might catch a chill, but then again she might not. She was going to live with every expectation of marrying, having children, growing old. And at long last, on the occasion of her eighteenth birthday, Rose was to look down on Camelot. Better than that, walk through Camelot. For after years of pleading, Mamma had finally consented: today, for the first time, Rose was to accompany Eliza to the Blackhurst cove.

Ever since she'd arrived seven years before, Eliza had been bringing back tales from the cove. When Rose was lying in her warm, dark room, breathing the stale air of her latest illness, Eliza would burst through the door so that Rose could almost smell the sea on her skin. She would climb in beside Rose and put a shell, or a powdery cuttlefish, or a little piece of shingle in her hand, and then she would begin her story. And in her mind, Rose would see the blue sea, feel the warm breeze in her hair, the hot sand beneath her feet.

Some of the tales Eliza invented, some she learned elsewhere. Mary, the maid, had brothers who were fishermen, and Rose suspected she enjoyed chatting when she should be working. Not to Rose, of course, but Eliza was different. All the servants treated Eliza differently. Quite improperly, almost as if they fancied themselves her friends.

Just lately Rose had begun to suspect that Eliza was venturing beyond the estate, had maybe even spoken with a villager or two, for her tales had taken on a new edge. They were rich with the specifics of boats and sailing, mermaids and treasures, adventures across the sea, told in colorful language that Rose secretly savored; and there was a more expansive look in their teller's eyes, as if she'd tasted the wicked things of which she spoke.

One thing was certain, Mamma would be livid to learn that Eliza had been into the village, mixed with common folk. It riled Mamma enough that Eliza spoke with the servants—for that fact alone Rose was able to bear Eliza's friendship with Mary. If Mamma were to ask Eliza where she went, certainly Eliza wouldn't lie, though what Mamma could do Rose wasn't sure. In all the years of trying, Mamma had been unable to find a punishment that deterred Eliza.

The threat of being considered improper meant nothing to Eliza. Being sent to the cupboard beneath the stairs only gave her time and quiet to invent more stories. Denying her new dresses—punishment indeed for Rose—garnered nary a sigh: Eliza was more than happy to wear Rose's castoffs. When it came to punishments, she was like the heroine from one of her own stories, protected by a fairy charm.

Watching Mamma's thwarted attempts to discipline Eliza gave Rose illicit pleasure. Each bid was met with a blank blue-eyed blink, a carefree shrug and an unaffected, "Yes, Aunt." As if Eliza genuinely hadn't realized her behavior might cause offense. The shrug in particular drove Mamma to fury. She had long ago released Rose from any expectation that she might shape Eliza into a proper young lady, was pleased enough that Rose had succeeded in convincing Eliza to dress appropriately. (Rose had accepted Mamma's praise and silenced the little voice whispering that Eliza had shed the tatty breeches only when she no longer fitted them.) There was something broken inside Eliza, Mamma said, like a piece of mirror in a telescope that prevented it from functioning properly. Prevented her from feeling proper shame.

As if she read Rose's thoughts, Eliza shifted beside her on the sofa. They had been sitting still for almost an hour and resistance was emanating from Eliza's body. Numerous times Mr. Sargent had needed to remind her to stop frowning, to hold a position, while he amended part of his painting. Rose had heard him telling Mamma the day before that he'd have been finished already, only the girl with hair afire refused to sit still long enough for him to capture her expression.

Mamma had shivered distastefully when he said that. She would have preferred that Rose were Mr. Sargent's sole subject, but Rose had put her foot down. Eliza was her cousin, her only friend, of course she must be in the portrait. And then Rose had coughed a little, eyeing Mamma from beneath her lashes, and the matter had been closed.

And although the small icy part of Rose savored Mamma's displeasure, her insistence on Eliza's inclusion had been heartfelt. Rose had never had a friend before Eliza. The opportunity had never presented itself, and even if it had, what use did a girl not long for life have for friends? Like most children whom circumstance has accustomed to suffering, Rose had found she shared little in common with other girls her age. She had no interest in rolling hoops or tidying dolls' houses, and became quickly bored when faced with wearying conversations as to her favorite color, number or song.

But Cousin Eliza was not like other little girls. Rose had known that on the first day they met. Eliza had a way of seeing the world that was frequently surprising, of doing things that were completely unexpected. Things that Mamma couldn't bear.

The best thing about Eliza, though, even better than her ability to rile Mamma, was her storytelling. She knew so many wonderful tales the likes of which Rose had never heard. Frightening stories that made Rose's skin prickle and her feet perspire. About the Other Cousin, and the London river, and a wicked Bad Man with a glinting knife. And of course her tale about the black ship that haunted the Blackhurst cove. Even though Rose knew it to be another of Eliza's fictions, she loved to hear the story told. The phantom ship that appeared on the horizon, the ship that Eliza claimed to have seen and had spent many a summer's day in the cove hoping to see again.

The one thing Rose had never been able to get Eliza to tell tales about was her brother, Sammy. She'd let slip his name only once but had clammed up immediately when Rose probed further. It was Mamma who informed Rose that Eliza had been a twin, had once had a brother cut from the same cloth, a boy who had died in a tragic way.

Over the years, when she was lying alone in bed, Rose had liked to imagine his death, this little boy whose loss had done the impossible: robbed Eliza the storyteller of words. "Sammy's Death" had replaced "Georgiana's Escape" as Rose's daydream of choice. She'd imagined him drowning, she'd imagined him falling and she'd imagined him wasting away, the poor little boy who had come before her in Eliza's affections.

"Sit still," said Mr. Sargent, pointing his paintbrush in Eliza's direction. "Stop wriggling. You're worse than Lady Asquith's corgi."

Rose blinked, was careful not to let her expression change when she realized that Father had entered the room. He was standing behind Mr. Sargent's easel, watching intently as the artist worked. Frowning and tilting his head the better to follow the brushstrokes. Rose was surprised; she had never imagined her father had an interest in the fine arts. The only thing for which she knew him to bear fondness was photography, but even that he managed to make dull. Never photographing people, only bugs and plants and bricks. Yet here he was, transfixed by his daughter's portrait. Rose sat a little taller.

Only twice in her childhood had Rose had opportunity to observe her father at close quarters. The first instance was when she swallowed the thimble and Father had been called upon to take the photograph for Dr. Matthews. The second had not been so felicitous.

She'd been hiding. Dr. Matthews was expected and the nine-year-old Rose had taken it into her head she didn't feel like seeing him. She'd found the one place Mamma would never think to seek her: Father's darkroom.

There was a cavity beneath the big desk and Rose had taken a pillow to keep herself comfortable. And for the most part she was: if only the room hadn't had such a ghastly smell, like the cleaning lotions the servants used during the spring clean.

She had been there for fifteen minutes or so when the door to the room opened. A thin beam of light passed through a tiny hole in the center of a timber knot at the back of the desk. Rose held her breath and pressed her eye against the hole, dreading the sight of Mamma and Dr. Matthews coming for her.

But it wasn't Mamma or the doctor holding the door open, it was Father, dressed in his long black traveling cloak.

Rose's throat constricted. Without ever having been properly told, she knew that the threshold to Father's darkroom was one she should not cross.

Father stood for a moment, silhouetted black against the bright outside. Then in he came, peeling off his coat and discarding it on an armchair just as Thomas appeared, mortification paling his cheeks.

"Your Lordship," Thomas said, catching his breath, "we weren't expecting you until next—"

"My plans were changed."

"Cook is preparing luncheon, my lord," said Thomas, lighting the gas lamps on the wall. "I'll lay for two and tell Lady Mountrachet that you've returned."

"No."

The suddenness with which this command was issued caused Rose's breath to catch.

Thomas turned abruptly towards Father and the match between his gloved fingers was extinguished, victim of the sudden chill.

"No," said Father again. "The journey was long, Thomas. I need to rest."

"A tray, sir?"

"And a decanter of sherry."

Thomas nodded, then disappeared through the door, footsteps fading down the hall.

Rose could hear a thumping. She pressed her ear against the desk, wondering whether something in the drawer, some mysterious item belonging to Father, was ticking. Then she realized it was her own heart, pounding a warning against her chest. Jumping for its life.

But there was no escape. Not while Father sat in his armchair, blocking the door.

And so Rose, too, continued to sit, knees pulled tight against the traitorous heart which threatened to give her away.

It was the only time she could remember being alone with Father. She noticed how his presence filled the room so that a space, previously benign, now seemed charged with emotions and feelings Rose didn't understand.

Dull footsteps on the rug, then a heavy masculine exhalation that made the hairs on her arms stand on end.

"Where are you?" Father said softly, then again from between clenched teeth. "Where are you?"

Rose caught her breath and kept it prisoner behind tight lips. Was he speaking to her? Had her all-knowing father somehow divined that she was hidden where she should not be?

A sigh from Father—sorrow? love? weariness?—and then *"Poupée."* So softly, so quietly, a broken word from a broken man. Rose had been learning French from Miss Tranton, and she knew what *poupée* meant—little baby doll. *"Poupée,"* Father said again. "Where are you, my Georgiana?"

Rose released her breath. Relieved that he had not discerned her presence, aggrieved that such soft tones did not describe her name.

And, as she pressed her cheek against the desk, Rose promised herself that one day someone would speak her name that way . . .

"Put your hand down!" Mr. Sargent was exasperated now. "If you continue to move it, I'll paint you with three and that's how you'll be remembered evermore."

Eliza heaved a sigh, knotted her hands behind her back.

Rose's eyes were glazed from holding the one position and she blinked a few times. Father had left the room now, but his presence lingered, the same unhappy feeling that always trailed after him.

Rose let her gaze rest once more on her scrapbook. The fabric was such a pretty shade of pink, one she knew would suit her dark hair well.

Throughout her years of sickness, there was only one thing Rose had ever wanted and that was to grow up. To escape the bounds of childhood and live, as Milly Theale had put it so perfectly in Rose's favorite book, however briefly and brokenly. She longed to fall in love, to marry, to have children. To leave Blackhurst and begin a life all her own. Away from this house, away from this sofa that Mamma insisted she recline upon even when she felt quite well. "Rose's sofa," Mamma called it. "Put a new throw rug on Rose's sofa. Something that will pick up the paleness of her skin, make her hair look shinier."

And the day of her escape was drawing near, Rose knew it. At long last Mamma had agreed that Rose was well enough to meet a suitor. Over the past few months, Mamma had arranged luncheons with a procession of eligible young (and not so young!) men. They'd all been fools—Eliza had entertained Rose for hours after each visit with her reenactments and impersonations—but it was good practice. For the perfect gentleman was out there somewhere, waiting for her. He would be nothing like Father, he would be an artist, with an artist's sense of beauty and possibility, who didn't care two whits about bricks and bugs. Who was open and easy to read, whose passions and dreams brought light to his eyes. And he would love her, and only her.

Beside her, Eliza huffed impatiently. "Really, Mr. Sargent," she said, "I should paint myself faster."

Her husband would be like Eliza, Rose realized, a smile pulling at her placid expression. The gentleman she sought was the male incarnation of her cousin.

AND FINALLY their captor set them free. Tennyson was right, to rust unburnished was inconceivably dull. Eliza hurried out of the ridiculous dress Aunt Adeline had insisted upon for the portrait. It was one of Rose's from a season ago—lace that itched, satin that clung, and a shade of red that made Eliza feel like strawberry pulp. Such a pointless waste of time, losing a morning to a grumpy old man intent on capturing their images so that they, too, could be hung, lonely and static, upon some chilly wall.

Eliza hopped down on hands and knees and peered beneath her bed. Lifted the corner of the floorboard she'd loosened long ago. She reached her hand inside and pulled out the story, "The Changeling."

Ran her hand across the black-and-white cover, felt the ripples of her own penmanship beneath her fingertips.

It was Davies who had suggested she put her tales to paper. She'd been helping him plant new roses when a grey and white bird with a striped tail had flown to a low bough nearby.

"Cuckoo," said Davies. "Winters in Africa but returns here in the spring."

"I wish I were a bird," said Eliza. "Then I should simply run towards the cliff top and glide over the edge. All the way to Africa, or India. Or Australia."

"Australia?"

It was the destination that currently held her imagination in its grip. Mary's eldest brother, Patrick, had emigrated recently with his young family to a place called Maryborough, where his aunt Eleanor had settled some years before. Despite this family connection, Mary liked to think the name had also swayed his choice, and could often be probed for details of the exotic land, floating in a far-off ocean on the other side of the globe. Eliza had found Australia on the schoolroom map, a strange, giant continent in the Southern Ocean with two ears, one pointed, one broken.

"I know a fellow went to Australia," said Davies, pausing a minute in his planting. "Got himself a farm of a thousand acres and couldn't get a thing to grow."

Eliza bit her lip and tasted excitement. This extremism was in line with her own impression of the place. "They've got a giant sort of rabbit there, Mary says. Kangaroos, they call them. Feet as long as a grown man's leg!"

"I don't know what you'd do with yourself in a place like that, Miss Eliza. Nor Africa nor India, neither."

Eliza knew exactly what she'd do. "I'm going to collect stories. Ancient stories that no one here has heard before. I'll be just like the Brothers Grimm I was telling you about."

Davies frowned. "Why you'd want to be like your pair of grim old German fellows is beyond me. You should be writing down your own stories, not those belonging to others."

And so she had. She'd begun by writing a story for Rose, a birthday gift, a fairy story about a princess who was turned by magic into a bird. It was the first story she'd ever trapped on paper, and to see her thoughts and ideas turned concrete was curious. It made her skin seem unusually sensitive, strangely exposed and vulnerable. Breezes were cooler, the sun warmer. She couldn't decide whether the sensation was one she liked or loathed.

But Rose had always loved Eliza's stories and Eliza had no greater gift to give, thus was it the perfect choice. For in the years since Eliza had been plucked from her lonely London life and transplanted to the grand and mysterious Blackhurst, Rose had become a soul mate. She'd laughed and longed with Eliza, and gradually come to fill the space where Sammy once had lodged, the dark empty hole belonging to all single twins. In return, there was nothing Eliza would not do or give or write for Rose.

The Changeling

by Eliza Makepeace

In the olden time, when magic lived and breathed, there was a Queen who longed for a child. She was a sad Queen, for the King was oft away, leaving her with little to do but dwell upon her own loneliness, and wonder how it was that her husband, whom she loved so well, could bear to be parted from her so long and so often.

It happened that, many years before, the King had stolen the throne from its rightful ruler, the Fairy Queen, and the beautiful, peaceful land of Fairy had overnight become a desolate place in which magic no longer flourished and laughter was banished. So wrathful was the King that he determined to capture the Fairy Queen and force her back to the kingdom. A golden cage was prepared specially that he might imprison the Fairy Queen and impel her to make magic for his pleasure.

One winter's day, while the King was away, the Queen sat by an open window, gazing out across the snow-laden ground. She was weeping as she sat, for the desolation of the winter months had a habit of reminding the Queen of her own loneliness. As she took in the barren winter landscape, she thought of her own barren womb, empty, as ever, despite her longing. "Oh, how I wish for a child!" she cried. "A beautiful daughter with a heart of truth and eyes that never fill with tears. Then need I never be lonely again."

Winter passed, and the world around began to wake. The birds returned to the kingdom and set about readying their nests, deer could be seen once more grazing where the fields met the woods, and buds burst forth upon the branches of the kingdom's trees. As the new season's skylarks took to the air, the Queen's skirt began to tighten around her middle, and by and by she realized she was with child. The King had not been back to the castle and thus the Queen knew that a mischievous fairy, far from home and hidden in the winter garden, must have heard her weeping and granted her wish by magic.

The Queen grew and grew and winter came once more, and on Christmas Eve, as a deep snow fell across the land, the Queen began to pain. All night she labored, and on the last chime of midnight her daughter was born, and the Queen was able to look at last upon her baby's face. To think that this beautiful child, with pale unblemished skin, dark hair, and red lips in the shape of a rosebud, was all hers! "Rosalind," the Queen said. "I shall name her Rosalind."

The Queen was instantly smitten and refused to let the Princess Rosalind out of her sight. Loneliness had made the Queen bitter, bitterness had made her selfish, and selfishness had made her suspicious. At every turn the Queen worried that someone was waiting to steal the child from her. She is mine, thought the Queen, my salvation, thus must I keep her for myself.

On the morning of the Princess Rosalind's christening, the wisest women in all the land were invited to bring their blessings. All day the Queen watched as wishes for grace and prudence and wit rained upon the child. Finally, when night began its creep into the kingdom, the Queen bid the wise women farewell. Her back was turned but briefly, yet when she looked again upon her child, she saw that one guest remained. A traveler in a long cloak stood by the crib, staring down at the infant.

"It is late, wise woman," said the Queen. "The Princess has been blessed and must now be allowed her sleep."

The traveler pushed back her cloak and the Queen gasped, for the face was not that of a wise maiden, but a wizened crone with a toothless smile.

"I come with a message from the Fairy Queen," said the crone. "The girl is one of ours, thus must she come with me."

"No," cried the Queen, rushing to the crib-side. "She is my daughter, my precious baby girl."

"Yours?" said the crone. "This glorious child?" And she began to laugh, a cruel cackle that made the Queen draw back in horror. "She was yours only as long as we let you keep her. In your heart you have always known she was born of fairy dust and now must you give her up."

The Queen wept then, for the crone's pronouncement was all that she had feared. "I cannot give her up," she said. "Have mercy, crone, and let me keep her longer."

Now, it so happened that the crone liked to cause mischief and, at the Queen's words, a slow smile spread across her face. "I offer you a choice," she said. "Relinquish the child now and her life will be long and happy, spent at the Fairy Queen's knee."

"Or?" said the Queen.

"Or you may keep her here. But only until the morning of her eighteenth birthday, when her true destiny will come for her and she will leave you forever. Think carefully, for to keep her longer is to love her deeper."

"I don't need to think upon it," said the Queen. "I choose the second."

The crone smiled so that the dark gaps in her mouth showed. "She is yours, then, but only until the morning of her eighteenth year."

At that moment the baby Princess began to cry for the first time ever. The Queen turned to scoop the child into her arms, and when she looked back the crone was gone.

The Princess grew to be a beautiful little girl, full of joy and light. She bewitched the ocean with her singing and brought smiles to the faces of all throughout the land. All, that is, except the Queen, who was too plagued by fear to enjoy her child. When her daughter sang the Queen did not hear, when her daughter danced the Queen did not see, when her daughter reached out the Queen did not feel, for she was too busy calculating the time left before the child was to be taken from her.

As the years passed, the Queen grew ever more afraid of the cold, dark event that lurked around the corner. Her mouth forgot how to smile, and the lines about her forehead learned how to hold their creases. Then, one night, she had a dream in which the crone appeared. "Your daughter is almost ten," said the crone. "Do not forget that her destiny will find her on her eighteenth birthday."

"I've changed my mind," said the Queen. "I cannot let her go, I will not let her go."

"You gave your word," said the crone, "thus must it be honored."

The next morning, after making sure the Princess was safely under guard, the Queen put on her riding habit and sent for her horse. Although magic had been banished from the castle there was one place where spells and sorcery might still be found. In a black cave on the edge of the enchanted sea lived a fairy who was neither good nor bad. She had been punished by the Fairy Queen for using magic unwisely and had thus remained hidden while the rest of the magic folk had fled the land. And although the Queen knew it was dangerous to seek the fairy's help, she had no other hope.

The Queen rode for three days and three nights and when she finally arrived at the cave the fairy was waiting for her. "Come," she said, "and tell me what it is you seek."

The Queen told of the crone and her promise to return on the Princess's eighteenth birthday, and the fairy listened. Then, when the Queen was finished, the fairy said, "I cannot undo the crone's curse, but I may help you still."

"I order you to do so," said the Queen.

"I must warn you, my Queen, that when you hear what I propose, you may not thank me for my help." And the fairy leaned over and whispered in the Queen's ear.

The Queen did not hesitate, for surely anything was better than losing her child to the crone. "It must be done."

So the fairy handed the Queen a potion and instructed her to give the Princess three drops on each of three nights. "All will then be as I promised," she said. "The crone will trouble you no more, for only the Princess's true destiny will find her."

The Queen hastened home, her mind easy for the first time since her daughter's christening, and for the next three nights she placed three drops of the potion into her daughter's milk glass. On the third night, when the Princess drank of her glass she began to choke and, as she fell from her chair, she was changed from a Princess into a beautiful bird, just as the fairy had foretold. The bird fluttered about the room and the Queen called for her servant to fetch the golden cage from the King's quarters. The bird was shut inside, the golden door was closed and the Queen breathed a sigh of relief. For the King had been clever and his cage, once closed, could not be reopened.

"There now, my pretty," said the Queen. "You are safe and none shall ever take you from me." And then the Queen hung the cage from a hook in the highest turret of the castle.

With the Princess trapped in the cage, all light went out of the kingdom, and the subjects of Fairyland were sunk into an eternal winter in which crops and fertile lands failed. All that kept the people from despair was the Princess bird's songs—sad and beautiful—which drifted from the turret window and spilled across the barren land.

Time passed, as time must, and royal princes made brave by greed came from far and wide to release the trapped Princess. For it was said that in the arid kingdom of Fairyland there was a golden cage so precious it made their own fortunes seem humble, and a caged bird whose songs were so beautiful that gold pieces had been known to fall from the sky when she sang. But all who tried to open the cage dropped dead as soon as they touched it. The Queen, who sat day and night in her rocking chair, guarding the cage so that none might steal her prize, laughed when she saw the princes slain, for fear and suspicion had finally conspired to drive her mad.

Some years after, the youngest son of a woodcutter came to the forest from a distant land. While he was working, there arrived upon the breeze a melody so glorious that he stopped midstroke and remained as still as if he had been turned to stone, listening to every note. Unable to help himself, he laid down his axe and went in search of the bird that could sing so sadly and so splendidly. As he made his way through the overgrown forest, birds and beasts appeared to help him and the woodcutter's son made sure to thank them, for he was a gentle soul who could communicate with all in nature. He climbed through brambles, ran across fields, scaled mountains, slept at night in hollow trees, ate only fruits and nuts, until finally he arrived at the castle walls.

"How came you into this forsaken land?" said the guard.

"I followed the song of your beautiful bird."

"Turn back if you value your life," said the guard. "For all in this kingdom is cursed, and whosoever touches the sad bird's cage shall be lost."

"I have nothing to love nor lose," said the woodcutter's son. "And I must see for myself the source of such glorious singing."

It so happened that, just in that instant, the Princess bird attained her eighteenth year and she began to sing the saddest and most beautiful song of all, lamenting the loss of her youth and her freedom.

The guard stood aside, and the young man crossed into the castle and climbed the stairs to the highest turret.

When the woodcutter's son saw the trapped bird, his heart was full of care, for he liked to see neither bird nor beast imprisoned. He looked beyond the gold cage and saw only the bird inside. He reached for the cage door and, at his touch, it sprang open and the bird was set free.

At that moment, the bird was transformed into a beautiful woman with long hair that swirled about her, and a crown of glistening seashells upon her head. Birds came from distant trees and from their beaks showered her with pieces of shining flint that clung to her so that she was attired all in silver. Animals returned to the kingdom, and crops and flowers began instantly to grow from the barren soil.

The following day, as the sun rose brilliant over the ocean, a thundering sound could be heard, and six enchanted horses appeared at the castle gates dragging a golden carriage behind. The Fairy Queen stepped from inside and all her subjects bowed down. Following her was the fairy from the sea cave, who had proved herself most certainly good, by doing her true Queen's bidding and ensuring that the Princess Rosalind was ready when her destiny came for her.

Under the Fairy Queen's watchful eye, the Princess Rosalind and the woodcutter's son were married, and the joy of the young couple was so great that magic returned to the land and all in Fairyland were thenceforward free and happy.

Excepting, of course, the Queen, who was nowhere to be found. In her place was a huge ugly bird with a cry so horrid it made the blood of all who heard it curdle. It was chased from the land and flew to a distant wood, where it was killed and eaten by the King, who had been driven to madness and despair by his wicked and unfruitful hunt for the Fairy Queen.

THIRTY-ONE

THERE was a blunt knock at the door and Eliza hid "The Changeling" behind her back. Felt her cheeks flush with anticipation.

Mary hurried in, curls messier than ever. Her hair always gave fair indication of her mood and Eliza was left in little doubt that the kitchen was abuzz with birthday preparations.

"Mary! I was expecting Rose."

"Miss Eliza." Mary pressed her lips together. An unusually prim gesture and one that made Eliza laugh. "The master wishes to see you, miss."

"My uncle wishes to see me?" Though she had roamed far and wide across the estate, in the years she'd been at Blackhurst Eliza had barely encountered her uncle. He was a shadowy figure who spent most of his time touring the Continent in search of bugs, the images of which he stole for his darkroom.

"Come now, Miss Eliza," said Mary. "Look sharp."

Mary was more serious than Eliza had ever seen her. She went quickly along the hall and down the narrow back stairs, and Eliza had to scurry to keep up. At the bottom, instead of turning left to the main part of the house, Mary turned right and hurried along a quiet passageway, dim for having fewer whispering lanterns than elsewhere in the house. There were no pictures, either, Eliza noticed; indeed, little attempt at decoration had been made along the cool, dark walls.

When they reached the furthest door, Mary stopped. As she was about to open it she glanced over her shoulder and gave Eliza's hand a slight squeeze, completely unexpected.

Before Eliza could ask what the matter was, the door was open and Mary was announcing her.

"Miss Eliza, Your Lordship."

And then she was gone and Eliza was alone on the threshold to her uncle's lair, subject to a most peculiar smell.

He was seated behind a large wooden desk at the back of the room.

"You wished to see me, Uncle?" The door closed behind her.

Uncle Linus peered over his glasses. Once again Eliza found herself wondering that this blotchy old man could be related to her beautiful mother. The tip of his pale tongue appeared between his lips. "I hear you have performed well in the schoolroom during the years you've been at Blackhurst."

"Yes, sir," said Eliza.

"And according to my man Davies, you are fond of the gardens."

"Yes, Uncle." From her first morning at Blackhurst, Eliza had been enamored of the estate. Along with the passageways that ran beneath the cliffs, she knew the cleared part of the maze and the wider garden as well as she'd once known the foggy streets of London. And no matter how far and wide she explored, the garden grew and changed with each season.

"It is within our family. Your mother . . ." His voice cracked. "Your mother when she was a girl had a great fondness for the garden."

Eliza tried to accord this information with her own memories of Mother. Through the tunnel of time came fragmented images: Mother in the windowless room above Mrs. Swindell's shop; a small pot with a fragrant herb. It hadn't lasted long, there was little that could survive in such dim conditions.

"Come closer, child," her uncle said, beckoning with his hand. "Come into the light that I might see you."

Eliza went to the other side of the desk so that she was standing by his knees. The room's smell was stronger now, as if it were coming from her uncle himself.

He reached out a hand, trembling slightly, and caressed the golden ends of Eliza's long red hair. Lightly, so lightly. Withdrew his hand, as if scorched.

He shuddered.

"Are you unwell, Uncle? Should I fetch someone to help?"

"No," he answered quickly. "No." He reached out to stroke her hair once more, closed his eyes. Eliza was so near that she could see the eyeballs moving beneath his lids, could hear the tiny clicking noises in his throat. "We searched so long, so wide, to bring your mother . . . to bring our Georgiana home."

"Yes, sir." Mary had told Eliza as much. About Uncle Linus's attachment to his younger sister, his heartbreak when she left, his frequent trips to London. The searching that had consumed his youth and his little good humor, the eagerness with which he left Blackhurst each time, the inevitable disappointment of his return. The way he would sit alone in the darkroom, drinking sherry, refusing any counsel, even that of Aunt Adeline, until Mr. Mansell would appear once more with a new lead.

"We were too late." He was stroking harder now, wrapping Eliza's long hair around his fingers, this way and that, like ribbon. It was pulling, and Eliza had to hold the edge of the desk to save herself from stumbling. She was transfixed by his face; it was that of the wounded fairy-tale king whose subjects have all deserted him. "I was too late. But you are here now. By God's grace, I have been given another chance."

"Uncle?"

Her uncle's hand dropped to his lap and his eyelids peeled open. He pointed to a little bench on the far wall, shrouded in white muslin cloth. "Sit," he said.

Eliza blinked at him.

"Sit." He limped to a black tripod by the wall. "I wish to take your photograph."

Eliza had never had a photograph taken, had no interest in having one taken now. Just as she opened her mouth to tell him so, the door opened.

"The birthday luncheon—" Aunt Adeline's words ended with a shrill rise. Her thin hand leaped to her chest. "Eliza!" The word was passenger on a desperate exhalation. "Whatever are you thinking, girl? Upstairs at once. Rose is asking for you."

Eliza hurried towards the door.

"And stop bothering your uncle," hissed Aunt Adeline as Eliza passed her. "Can't you see he's exhausted from his travels?"

AND SO the day had come. Adeline hadn't known what form it would take, but the threat had always been there, lurking in dark places so she could never fully be at ease. She ground her back teeth, channeled her rage into the bones at the back of her neck. Willed herself to clear the image from her mind. Georgiana's girl, her hair hanging loose, looking for all the world like a ghost from the past, and the expression on Linus's face, his old face turned foolish by a young man's desire. To think he had been about to take the girl's photograph! To do what he had never done for Rose. Nor for Adeline.

"Close your eyes, Lady Mountrachet," said her maid, and Adeline did as she was asked. The other woman's breath was warm as she combed the hair from Adeline's brow, strangely comforting. Oh, to sit here forever, the warm, sweet breath of this dull, cheerful girl on her face, no other thoughts to plague her. "And open again, ma'am, while I fetch your pearls."

The maid bustled away and Adeline was left alone with her thoughts. She leaned forward. Her brows were smooth, her hair neat. She pinched each cheek, harder perhaps than was necessary, and sat back again to observe the whole. Oh, but to age was cruel! Little changes that slipped by unnoticed, that could never be arrested. The nectar of youth slipping through a blind sieve whose holes continued to widen. "And thus was friend turned to foe," whispered Adeline to the merciless mirror.

"Here you are, ma'am," said the maid. "I've brought the set with the ruby clasp. Nice and festive on such a happy occasion. Who could have imagined it, Miss Rose's birthday luncheon. Eighteen years old! A wedding next, you mark my words . . ."

As the maid babbled on, Adeline shifted her gaze, refusing to look any longer upon her own decay.

The photograph hung where it always had, beside the dressing table. How proper she looked in her bridal dress, how right. No one would guess by this photo at the fierce self-coaxing she'd suffered in order to affect this model of calm. Linus, for his part, looked every bit the gentleman groom. Glum, perhaps, but that was the custom.

They were married a year after Georgiana disappeared. From the moment of their engagement Adeline Langley had worked hard to re-invent herself. She determined to become a woman worthy of the grand old name of Mountrachet: cast off her Northern accent and small-town tastes, devoured *Debrett's,* and schooled herself in the twin arts of vanity and gentility. Adeline knew she had to be twice as much a lady as anyone else if she were to wipe from people's memories the reality of her origins.

"Would you like your green bonnet, Lady Mountrachet?" said the maid. "Only it always suits this dress so well, and you'll be wanting a hat if you're headed to the cove. I'll lay it out on the bed, shall I?"

Their wedding night had been nothing like Adeline expected. She couldn't tell, and certainly there were no words to ask, but she suspected it had disappointed Linus, too. They shared a marriage bed only rarely afterwards, even less when Linus started his roaming. Taking photographs, he said, but Adeline knew the truth.

How worthless she felt. How failed as a wife and as a woman. Worse still, failed as a society lady. For all her efforts, they were rarely invited out. Linus, when he was at Blackhurst, was such poor company, standing alone most of the time, answering questions when necessary with belligerent remarks. When Adeline grew sickly, pale and tired, she presumed it was despair. Only when her stomach began to swell did she realize she was with child.

"There you are, Lady Mountrachet. The hat's on the bed and you're all ready for the party."

"Thank you, Poppy." She managed a thin smile. "That will be all."

As the door closed, Adeline dismantled her smile and met her own gaze once more.

Rose was the rightful inheritor of the Mountrachet glory. This girl, Georgiana's daughter, was little more than a cuckoo, sent back to supplant Adeline's own child. To push her from a nest that Adeline had fought to make her own.

For a time order had been maintained. Adeline made sure to decorate Rose with darling new dresses, a pretty sofa to sit upon, while Eliza was clothed in the previous season's fashions. Rose's manners, her feminine nature, were perfect, where Eliza could not be taught. Adeline was calm.

But as the girls grew older, grew unstoppably towards womanhood, things were changing, slipping from Adeline's control. Eliza's prowess in the schoolroom was one thing—no one liked a clever woman—but now, with the time she spent outdoors in the fresh sea air, her complexion had taken on a healthy glow, her hair, that accursed red hair, had grown long, and she was filling out.

The other day Adeline had heard one of the servants talking about how beautiful Miss Eliza was, more beautiful even than her mother, Miss Georgiana. Adeline had frozen in her tracks when she'd heard the name spoken. After all these years of silence, the name now awaited her at every corner. Laughing at her, reminding her of her own inferiority, her own failure ever to match up, despite working so much harder than Georgiana.

Adeline felt a dull thump in her temple. She raised her hand and pressed lightly. Something was the matter with Rose. This spot on her temple was Adeline's sixth sense. Ever since Rose was a tiny baby, Adeline had pre-empted her daughter's maladies. It was a bond that couldn't be broken, mother to daughter.

And now her temple was once again throbbing. Adeline's lips tightened with resolve. She observed her stern face as if it belonged to a stranger, the lady of a noble house, a woman whose control was infrangible. She inhaled strength into that woman's lungs. Rose must be protected; poor Rose, who failed even to perceive Eliza as a threat.

An idea began to form in Adeline's mind. She couldn't send Eliza away, Linus would never permit it and Rose's sorrow would be too great, and besides, it was better to keep one's enemies close, but perhaps Adeline might find a reason to take Rose abroad for a time? To Paris, or New York? Give her an opportunity to shine without the unexpected glare of Eliza drawing everyone's attention, ruining Rose's every chance . . .

Adeline smoothed her skirt as she went towards the door. One thing was certain, there would be no visiting the cove today. It was a foolish promise to have made, a moment of weakness on Adeline's part. Thank God there was still time to correct her error in judgement. Eliza's wickedness would not be allowed to taint Rose.

She closed the door behind her and started down the hall, skirt swishing. As for Linus, he would be kept busy. She was his wife, it was her duty to ensure he was given no opportunity to suffer at the hands of his own impulses. He would be packed off to London. She would implore the wives of government ministers to enlist his services, suggest exotic photographic locations, send him far away. Satan would not be allowed to find mischief for his idle hands to do.

LINUS LEANED back against the garden seat and hooked his cane beneath the decorative arm. The sun was setting and dusk spilled, orange and pink, across the western edge of the estate. There had been plenty of rain throughout the month and the garden glistened. Not that Linus cared.

For centuries the Mountrachets had been keen horticulturalists. Forebear after forebear had traveled far and wide, spanning the globe in search of exotic specimens with which to augment their plot. Linus, however, had not inherited the green thumb. That had gone to his little sister—

Well, now, that wasn't completely true.

There had been a time, long ago, when he had cared for the garden. When, as a boy, he had followed Davies on his rounds, marveling at the spiky flowers in the antipodean garden, the pineapples in the hothouse, the way new shoots appeared overnight, taking the place of seeds he'd helped to lay.

Most miraculous of all, in the garden Linus's shame had disappeared. The plants, the trees, the flowers, cared not at all that his left leg had stopped growing inches short of his right. That his left foot was a useless appendage, stunted and curved, freakish. There was a place for everything and everyone in the Blackhurst garden.

Then, when Linus was seven, he'd become lost in the maze. Davies had warned him not to go inside alone, that the way was long and dark, full of obstacles, but Linus had been dizzy on the thrill of being seven years old. The maze, with its dense lush walls, its promise of adventure, had lured him. He was a knight, off to do battle with the fiercest dragon in the land, and he was going to emerge triumphant. To find his way to the other side.

Shadows came early to the maze. Linus had not foreseen how dark it would become, and how quickly. In the dusk, sculptures came to life, leering at him from their hiding places, tall hedges turned to hungry monsters, low hedges played nasty tricks: made him think he was heading in the right direction, when in fact he was doubling back. Or was he?

He had reached as far as the center before his slide to despair was complete. Then, to add injury to insult, a brass ring attached to a plat-form on the ground had leaped up and tripped him, tossed him to the ground so that his good ankle was twisted like that of a cheap rag doll. There'd been little choice for Linus but to sit where he was, ankle ach-ing, angry tears spilling hot down his cheeks.

Linus had waited and waited. Dusk became dark, cool became cold, and his tears dried up. He later learned that it was Father who had refused to send anyone in for him. He was a boy, Father said, and, lame or not, any boy worth his salt would find his own way out of the maze. Why, he—St. John Luke—had made it through when a mere four years old. The boy needed to toughen up.

Linus had shivered in the maze all night before Mother finally convinced Father to send Davies in after him.

It took a week before Linus's ankle healed, but every day for a fortnight thereafter, Father marched Linus back to the maze. Set him to finding his way through, then berated him for his inevitable failure. Linus began to dream of the maze and when he was awake drew maps from memory. He worked at it like a mathematical problem, for he knew there must be a solution. If he were worth his salt he'd find it.

After two weeks, Father gave up. On the fifteenth morning, when Linus appeared for his daily test, he didn't even lower his newspaper. "You're a great disappointment," he said. "A fool of a boy who will never amount to anything." He turned a page, shook the paper straight and scanned for headlines of note. "Remove yourself from my room."

Linus had never gone near the maze again. Unable to bring him-self to blame Father and Mother for his shameful failings—they were right, after all, what kind of a boy couldn't find his way through a maze?—he blamed the garden. He took to breaking the stems of plants, removing flowers, stepping on new shoots.

All are shaped by things beyond their control, traits inherited, traits learned. For Linus, the piece of his leg bone that had refused to lengthen defined him. As he grew, lameness begot shyness, shyness begot a stammer, and thus Linus grew into an unlikeable little boy who discovered that attention came his way only when he behaved badly. He refused to go outside, so his skin grew pallid and his good leg thin. He put insects in his mother's tea, thorns in his father's slippers, and gladly took whatever punishment came his way. And thus, in such predictable form, Linus's life continued.

Then, when he was ten years old, a baby sister was born.

Linus despised her on sight. So soft and fair and bonny. And, as Linus discovered when he peered beneath her long lacy frock, perfectly formed. Both legs the same length. Dear little feet, not a useless, wizened piece of flesh among them.

Worse than her physical perfection, though, was her happiness. Her pink smile, her musical laugh. What business did she have being so happy when he, Linus, was miserable?

Linus determined to do something about it. Whenever he could get away from his governess, he would sneak into the nursery and kneel by the edge of the bassinet. If the baby slept, he would make a sudden noise to startle her. If she reached for a toy, he would move it away. If she held out her arms, he would cross his own. If she smiled, he would arrange his features into a mask of appalling horror.

Yet she remained unaffected. Nothing Linus did could make her cry, nothing dinted her sunny disposition. It perplexed him, and he set his mind to inventing sly and singular punishments for his little sister.

As Linus grew into his teens, became even more awkward, with long gangly arms and odd ginger hairs sprouting from his spotty chin, Georgiana blossomed into a beautiful child, beloved of all on the estate. She brought a smile to the face of even the most hardened tenants, farmers who hadn't had a kind word for the Mountrachet family in years would send baskets of apples to the kitchen for Miss Georgiana to enjoy.

Then one day Linus was sitting on the window ledge in the library, using his treasured new magnifying glass to turn ants to ash, when he slipped and fell. He was unharmed, but his precious glass shattered into a hundred tiny pieces. So cherished was his new toy, so used to disappointing himself was he, that despite his thirteen years Linus burst into tears of rage, great hulking sobs. He reproached himself for having fallen in such a clumsy way, for not being clever enough, for having no friends, for being unlovable, for being born imperfect.

His tears were so blinding that Linus didn't realize his fall had been observed. Not until he felt the tap against his arm. He looked up and saw his little sister standing there, holding something towards him. It was Claudine, her favorite dolly.

"Linus sad," she said. "Poor Linus. Claudine make Linus happy."

Linus had been speechless, had taken the doll, still staring at his little sister as she sat beside him.

With an uncertain sneer he pushed one of Claudine's eyelids so that it was dented. Looked to see what effect his vandalism had had on his little sister.

She was sucking her thumb, watching him, big blue eyes full of empathy. After a moment she reached out and dented Claudine's other lid.

From that day forth, they were a team. Without complaint, without so much as a frown, she weathered her brother's rages, his cruel humor, all the things that rejection had wrought in him. She let him fight her, and berate her and, later, cuddle her.

If only they'd been left alone everything would have turned out well. But Mother and Father couldn't bear that someone loved him. He heard them speaking in low voices—too much time together, not proper, not healthy—and within a matter of months he was packed off to boarding school.

His grades were appalling, Linus made sure of that, but Father had once hunted with the Master of Balliol College and thus a place was found for him at Oxford. The only positive thing to come out of his university days was his discovery of photography. A sensitive young English tutor had allowed him use of his camera, then advised him on his own purchase.

And finally, when he was twenty-three, Linus returned to Blackhurst. How his *poupée* had grown! Thirteen and so tall. The longest red hair he had ever seen. For a time he was shy of her: she was so changed, he had to learn her again. But one day, when he was photographing near the cove, she had appeared in his viewfinder. Sitting on top of the black rock, facing out to sea. The salty breeze was weaving through her hair, her arms were wrapped around her knees, and her legs, her legs were bare.

Linus could hardly breathe. He blinked, continued to watch as she turned her head slowly, looked directly at him. Where other subjects couldn't conceal the knowingness in their eyes, Georgiana was completely unself-conscious. She seemed to be looking beyond the camera directly into his eyes. Hers were the same empathetic eyes that had watched him crying all those years before. Without thinking, he squeezed the camera button. Her face, her perfect face, was his to capture.

CAREFULLY LINUS pulled the photographic print from his coat pocket. He was gentle, for it was old now, rough around the edges. The last of the sun's light was almost gone, but if he held it at the right angle . . .

How many times had he sat like this and gazed upon it, pored over it after she disappeared? It was the only print he had, for when Georgiana left, someone—Mother? Adeline? One of their minions?—had sneaked into his darkroom and removed his negatives. Only this one remained, spared because Linus carried it always on his person.

But now, a second chance, and this one Linus wouldn't lose. He was no longer a child, but master of Blackhurst. Mother and Father were both in their graves. Only that tiresome wife of his and her sickly daughter remained, and who were they to stand in Linus's way? He had courted Adeline to punish his parents for Georgiana's flight, and the engagement had delivered such a final, brutal blow that the woman's accommodation in his house had seemed a small price to pay.

And so it had been. So would it continue to be. She was easily ignored. He was master and what he wanted he would have.

Eliza. He allowed the sound of it to escape across his lips, lodge within the curls of his beard. His lips were trembling and his skin had cooled.

He was going to make a gift to her. Something to inspire gratitude. Something he knew she'd love, for how could she not when her mother had loved it so before her?

Thirty-two

CASSANDRA stepped through the gate and was struck once more by the strange, heavy silence that lay around the cottage. There was something else, too, something she felt but couldn't name. An odd sense of collusion. As if by entering the gates she was agreeing to a pact whose rules she did not know.

It was earlier in the day than the last time she'd come and flecks of sunlight flickered in the garden. The landscaper wasn't due for another fifteen minutes, so Cassandra put the key back in her pocket and decided to explore a little.

A narrow stone path, almost obscured by lichen, wound along the front before disappearing around the corner. The weeds at the side of the house were tall and thick and she had to pull them away from the wall before stepping through.

There was something about the garden that reminded her of Nell's backyard in Brisbane. Not the plants so much as the mood. As long as Cassandra could remember, Nell's yard had been a jumble of cottage plants, herbs and brightly colored annuals. Little concrete paths winding their way through the growth. So different from the other suburban backyards, with their stretches of sunburned grass and the occasional thirsty rosebushes inside white-painted car tires.

Cassandra reached the back of the cottage and stopped. A dense tangle of thorny brambles, at least ten feet high, had grown across the path. She stepped closer and craned to see over the top. The shape was uniform, linear, almost as if the plants themselves had formed a wall.

She made her way along the hedge, trailing her fingers lightly over jagged ivy leaves. It was slow going, the undergrowth was as high as her knees and threatened to trip her at each step. Midway along she noticed a gap in the brambles, a small gap but enough to see that no light shone through, that there was something solid behind it. Careful not to be pricked by the thorns, Cassandra reached a hand in and leaned closer as the hedge devoured her arm, all the way to her shoulder. Her fingers scraped against something hard and cold.

A wall, a stone wall, coated with moss if the damp green smears on her fingertips were anything to go by. Cassandra wiped her hand on her jeans and pulled the title deeds from her back pocket, turned to the property map. The cottage was clearly marked, a small square towards the front of the block. According to the map, though, the rear property line extended quite a way beyond. Cassandra refolded the map and tucked it away. If the map was correct, this wall was part of Nell's property, not its boundary. It belonged to Cliff Cottage, as did whatever was on the other side.

Cassandra continued her obstacle course along the wall, hoping to find a gate or a door, anything permitting entry. The sun was rising in the sky and the birds had relaxed their singing. The air was heavy with the sweet, swooning perfume of a climbing rose. Although it was autumn, Cassandra was becoming hot. To think she had once imagined England a cold country to which the sun was a stranger. She stopped to wipe sweat from her brow and bumped her head on something low-hanging.

The gnarled bough of a tree reached armlike over the wall. An apple tree, Cassandra realized, when she saw that the branch bore fruit—shiny, golden apples. They were so ripe, so deliciously fragrant, that she couldn't resist picking one.

Cassandra checked her watch and, with a longing glance at the bramble hedge, started back the way she'd come. She could continue her search for a door later, didn't want to risk missing the gardener. Such was the odd sense of dense seclusion surrounding the cottage,

Cassandra had the feeling she might not hear him from back here, even if he called out.

She unlocked the front door and went inside.

The house seemed to be listening, waiting to see what she would do. She ran her hand lightly along the inside wall. "My house," she said softly. "This is my house."

The words pressed dully into the walls. How strange it was, how unexpected. She wandered through the kitchen, past the spinning wheel and into the little sitting room at the very front. The house felt different now that she was alone. Familiar somehow, like a place she'd visited long ago.

She eased herself into an old rocker. Cassandra was comfortable enough with antique furniture to know that the chair wasn't about to collapse, and yet she felt wary. As if the chair's rightful owner was somewhere nearby and might return at any time to find an intruder in their place.

As she polished the apple on her shirt, Cassandra turned her head to look through the dusty window. Creepers had plaited themselves together across the glass, but she could still see enough to make out the rambling garden beyond. There was a little statue she hadn't noticed before, a child, a boy, perched on a stone, staring at the house with wide-open eyes.

Cassandra lifted the apple to her lips. The sunny scent was strong as she bit into it. An apple, from a tree in her very own garden, a tree planted many years before that still produced fruit. Year in, year out. It was sweet. Were apples always so sweet?

She yawned. The sun had made her very drowsy. She would sit, just for a little while longer, until the gardener arrived. She took another bite of the apple. The room felt warmer than it had before. As if the range had suddenly begun to work, as if someone else had joined her in the cottage and was beginning to make lunch. Her lids were heavy and she closed her eyes. A bird somewhere sang, a lovely, lonely tune; breeze-blown leaves tapped against the window, and in the distance the ocean breathed steadily, in and out, in and out, in and out . . .

. . . IN AND out of her head all day. She paced again across the kitchen, stopped at the window but forbade herself another glance outside. She looked at her little mantel clock instead. He was late. He had said half past the hour. She wondered whether his tardiness meant anything of consequence, whether he'd been caught up, fallen victim to second thoughts. Whether he was still coming.

Her cheeks were warm. It was very warm in here. She went back to the range and turned the damper to slow the burning. Wondered whether she should have prepared some sort of meal.

A noise outside.

The floors of her composure dissolved. He was here.

She opened the door and wordlessly he came inside.

He seemed so large in the narrow hall, and though she knew him well by now, she was shy, couldn't meet his eyes.

He was nervous, too; she could see that, though he did his best to conceal it.

They sat opposite one another at the kitchen table and the lamp-light quivered between them. A strange place to sit on such a night, but that was as it was. She looked at her hands, wondered how to proceed. It had all seemed so simple at first. But now the way forward seemed crisscrossed by threads just waiting to trip them up. Perhaps such meetings were always thus.

He reached out.

She drew breath as he caught a long thread of her hair between two fingers. Looked at it for what seemed an age. Looked not at the hair so much as the strange fact of *her* hair in *his* fingers.

Finally, his gaze lifted and met her own. His hand came to rest lightly on her cheek. He smiled then, and so did she. Sighed with relief and something else. He opened his mouth and said—

"HELLO?" A loud rapping sound. "Hello? Anyone there?"

Cassandra's eyes flicked open. The apple in her hand dropped to the floor.

Heavy footsteps and then a man was standing in the doorway, a tall, solidly built man in his midforties. Dark hair, dark eyes, wide smile.

"Hello there," he said, holding his hands in an attitude of surrender. "You look as if you've seen a ghost."

"You frightened me," said Cassandra defensively, pulling herself out of the chair.

"Sorry." He stepped forward. "The door was open. Didn't realize you were having a kip."

"I wasn't. I mean, I was, but I didn't mean to. I only meant to sit for a while but . . ." Cassandra's explanation trailed off as her mind returned to the dream. It had been a long time since she'd dreamed anything even remotely erotic, a long time since she'd *done* anything remotely erotic. Not since Nick. Well, not so that it counted, not so that she wanted to remember. Where on earth had it come from?

The man grinned and extended his hand. "I'm Michael Blake, landscaper extraordinaire. You must be Cassandra."

"That's right." She blushed as he closed his large, warm hand around hers.

He shook his head slightly, smiling. "My mate told me Australian girls were the prettiest but I never believed him. Now I know he was telling the truth."

Cassandra didn't know where to look, settled for a spot just beyond his left shoulder. Such open flirtation made her uncomfortable at the best of times, but her dream had left her doubly unsettled. She could still sense it, lingering in the room's corners.

"I hear you've got a problem with a tree?"

"Yes." Cassandra blinked and nodded as she pushed the dream aside. "Yes, I have. Thanks for coming."

"Never could resist a damsel in distress." He smiled again, a broad, easy smile.

She pulled her cardigan a little tighter round her middle. Tried to smile back but managed only to feel prim. "It's over this way. On the stairs."

Michael followed her along the hall, leaned to see around the curve of the stairwell. He whistled. "One of the old pines. Looks like she's been lying here a while. Probably came down in the big storm of '95."

"Can you move it?"

"Course we can." Michael looked over his shoulder, past Cassandra. "Get the chain saw, will you, Chris?"

Cassandra turned; she hadn't been aware there was anyone else in the room with them. Another man stood behind her, leaner than the first, a little younger. Sandy brown hair curled roughly around his neck. Olive skin, brown eyes. "Christian," he said, nodding slightly. He extended his hand a little, hesitated, then wiped it on his jeans. Held it out again.

Cassandra reached to meet it.

"Chain saw, Chris," said Michael. "Come on, speed it up."

Michael raised his eyebrows at Cassandra as Christian left. "I'm due at the hotel in a half-hour or so, but never fear, I'll get the main work done and leave my trusty sidekick to finish up." He smiled at Cassandra with the sort of direct gaze she found impossible to hold. "So this is your place. I've lived in the village my whole life and never thought it was owned by anyone."

"I'm still getting used to the idea myself."

Michael cocked an eyebrow as he took in the dereliction of the room. "What's a nice Aussie girl like you doing in a house like this?"

"I inherited it. My grandmother left it to me."

"Your grandmother was English?"

"Australian. She bought it in the 1970s when she was on holiday."

"Some souvenir. Couldn't she find a tea towel she liked?"

A noise at the door and Christian was back carrying a large chain saw. "This the one you're after?"

"It's a saw with a chain," said Michael, winking at Cassandra. "I'd say it's the right one."

The hall was narrow and Cassandra turned sideways to let Christian pass. She didn't meet his eyes, rather pretended interest in a loose baseboard at her feet. The way that Michael spoke to Christian made her feel embarrassed.

"Chris is new to the business," said Michael, oblivious to Cassandra's discomfort. "Doesn't know his chain saw from his drop-saw yet. He's a bit of a greenie but we'll turn him into a woodcutter yet." He grinned. "He's a Blake, it's in his blood." He gave his brother a playful punch and the two men turned their attention to the task at hand.

Cassandra was relieved when the chain saw started up and she was free, finally, to escape back to the garden. Although she knew her time would be better spent clearing creepers from inside the house, her interest had been piqued. She was determined to find a way through that wall if it took all day.

THE SUN was high now and shade was at a premium. Cassandra unwrapped her cardigan and laid it on a nearby rock. The sun's tiny footprints danced across her arms and the top of her head was soon hot to the touch. She wished she'd remembered to bring a hat.

As she searched the brambles, poked her hand gingerly through one gap after another, avoiding thorns, her thoughts drifted back to her dream. It had been particularly vivid and she could remember every detail—sights, smells, even the dream's pervasive mood. Undeniably erotic, laced with forbidden desire.

Cassandra shook her head a little, shooing away the tendrils of confusing and unwanted emotion. She turned her thoughts instead to Nell's mystery. The night before, she'd sat up late reading the notebook. A task that was easier said than done. If the rash of mold didn't make things difficult enough, Nell's deplorable handwriting had deteriorated further when she arrived in Cornwall. Longer, loopier, scratchier. Written faster, Cassandra was willing to bet, more excitedly.

Nonetheless, Cassandra was managing. She'd been spellbound by the account of Nell's returning memories, her certainty that she'd visited the cottage as a little girl. Cassandra couldn't wait to see the scrapbooks Julia had found, the diaries that Nell's mother had once filled with her most private thoughts. For surely they would shed further light on Nell's childhood, maybe even offer vital clues as to her disappearance with Eliza Makepeace.

A whistle, loud and shrill. Cassandra looked up, expecting a bird of some kind.

Michael was standing by the corner of the house, watching her work. He indicated the brambles. "Impressive crop you've got there."

"Nothing a bit of weeding won't solve," she said, standing awkwardly. She wondered how long he'd been watching.

"A year of weeding and a chain saw." He grinned. "I'm off up to the hotel now." He cocked his head towards the cottage. "We've made some good headway. I'll leave Chris to tie up loose ends. He should be able to manage, just make sure he leaves it how you'd like." He paused and smiled again in that artless way of his. "You've got my number, right? Give me a call. I'll show you a few of the local sights while you're in town."

It wasn't a question. Cassandra smiled slightly and regretted it immediately. She suspected Michael was the sort to read any response as agreement. Sure enough, he gave her a wink as he headed back towards the front of the house.

With a sigh, Cassandra turned back towards the wall. Christian had climbed through the hole made by the tree and was now perched on the roof, using a handsaw to cut the branches into lengths. Where Michael was easygoing, there was an intensity about Christian that seemed to spill into everything he did and touched. He shifted position and Cassandra looked away quickly, feigned an avid interest in her wall.

They continued working, and the silence strung between them amplified every other sound: Christian's saw dragging back and forth; the pitter-patter of birds on the roof tiles; the faint noise of running water somewhere. Ordinarily, Cassandra was happy to work without speaking, she was used to being alone, preferred it for the most part. Only this wasn't being alone, and the longer they pretended it was, the more static-filled the silence grew.

Finally she could stand it no longer. "There's a wall behind here," she said, voice loud and somewhat more strident than she'd intended. "I found it earlier."

Christian looked up from his stack of wood. Stared at her as if she'd just started quoting from the periodic table.

"I don't know what's on the other side, though," she rushed on. "I can't find a gate and the plan my grandmother got with the sale gives no indication. I know there's a heap of creepers and branches, but I thought you might be able to see from up there."

Christian glanced down at his hands, seemed about to speak.

A thought popped into Cassandra's mind: he has nice hands. She pushed it right back where it came from. "Can you see what's over the wall?"

He pressed his lips together, dusted his hands on his jeans and nodded a little.

"You can?" This she hadn't really expected. "What is it? Can you tell me?"

"I can do better than that," he said, holding on to the eave so that he could jump down from the roof. "Come on, I'll show you."

THE HOLE was very small, right at the bottom of the wall, and concealed so that Cassandra might have searched for a year and not found it. Christian was on his hands and knees, pulling the undergrowth aside. "Ladies first," he said, sitting back.

Cassandra looked at him. "I thought maybe there'd be a gate."

"You find one, I'll follow you through it."

"You want me to . . ." She glanced at the hole. "I don't know if I can, if I even know how to . . ."

"On your stomach. It's not as tight as it looks."

Of this Cassandra had some doubt. It looked very tight. All the same, the day's fruitless searching had only strengthened her resolve: she *needed* to know what lay on the other side. She hopped down so she was eye level with the hole and looked sidelong at Christian. "Are you sure this is safe? You've done it before?"

"At least a hundred times." He scratched his neck. "Sure, I was younger and smaller, but . . ." His lips twitched sideways. "I'm joking. I'm sorry, you'll be fine."

There was some relief once her head was free and she realized she wasn't going to perish with her neck jammed beneath a brick wall. Not on the way in, at any rate. She shimmied the rest of her body through, as fast as possible, and stood up. Dusted her hands together and looked around, wide-eyed.

It was a garden, a walled garden. Overgrown but with beautiful bones visible still. Someone had cared for this garden once. The remains of two paths snaked back and forth, intertwined like the lacing on an Irish dancing shoe. Fruit trees had been espaliered around the sides, and wires zigzagged from the top of one wall to the top of another. Hungry wisteria branches had woven themselves around to form a sort of canopy.

Against the southern wall, an ancient and knobbled tree was growing. Cassandra went closer. It was the apple tree, she realized, the one whose bough had reached over the wall. She lifted her hand to touch one of the golden fruit. The tree was about sixteen feet high and shaped like the Japanese bonsai plant Nell had given Cassandra for her twelfth birthday. Over the decades, the short trunk had adopted a sideways angle, and someone had gone to the effort of propping a crutch beneath a large limb to absorb some of its weight. A scorch mark midway along suggested a lightning strike many years before. Cassandra reached out to run her fingers along the burn.

"It's magical, isn't it, this place?" Christian was standing in the center of the garden by a rusted iron bench. "Even when I was a kid I could feel that."

"You used to come here?"

"All the time. It felt like my secret spot. No one else knew about it." He shrugged. "Well, hardly anyone else."

Beyond Christian, on the other side of the garden, Cassandra noticed something glinting against the creeper-covered wall. She went closer. It was metal, shining in the sun. A gate. Ropelike tendrils draped across it, a giant web blocking the entrance to the spider's lair. Or exit, as the case may be.

Christian joined her and together they pulled some of the creepers loose. There was a brass handle turned black with time. Cassandra gave it a rattle. The door was locked.

"I wonder where it goes."

"There's a maze on the other side that leads all the way through the estate," said Christian. "It ends over near the hotel. Michael's been working to restore it these past months."

The maze, of course. She had known that. Where had Cassandra read about the maze? Was it Nell's notebook? One of the tourist brochures at the hotel?

A quivering dragonfly hovered near before darting away, and they turned back towards the center of the garden.

"Why did your grandmother buy the cottage?" said Christian, brushing a fallen leaf from his shoulder.

"She was born around here."

"In the village?"

Cassandra hesitated, wondering how much she should tell. "The estate, actually. Blackhurst. She didn't know until her adoptive father died, when she was in her sixties. She found out her parents were Rose and Nathaniel Walker. He was—"

"An artist, I know." Christian picked up a small stick from the ground. "I've got a book with his illustrations in it, a book of fairy tales."

"*Magical Tales for Girls and Boys*?"

"Yeah." He looked at her, surprised.

"I have a copy, too."

He raised his eyebrows. "There weren't many printed, you know, not by today's standards. Did you know Eliza Makepeace used to live right here in the cottage?"

Cassandra shook her head. "I knew she grew up on the estate . . ."

"Most of her stories were written here in this garden."

"You know a lot about her."

"I've been rereading the fairy tales lately. I used to love them when I was a kid, ever since I found an old copy in the local charity shop. There was something bewitching about them, more than met the eye." He scuffed at the dirt with his boot. "It's a bit sad, I guess—a grown man reading children's fairy tales."

"I don't think so." Cassandra noticed that he was raising and lowering his shoulders, hands in pockets. Almost as if he were nervous. "Which one's your favorite?"

He tilted his head, squinted a little in the sun. " 'The Crone's Eyes.' "

"Really? Why?"

"It always seemed different from the others. More meaningful somehow. Plus I had a wild eight-year-old crush on the princess." He smiled shyly. "What's not to like about a girl whose castle is destroyed, her royal subjects vanquished, who nonetheless plucks up enough courage to embark on a quest and uncover the old crone's missing eyes?"

Cassandra smiled, too. The tale of the brave princess who didn't know she was a princess was the first of Eliza's fairy tales she'd read. On that hot Brisbane day, when she was ten years old and had disobeyed her grandmother's instruction, discovered the suitcase under the bed.

Christian broke his stick in half and tossed the pieces aside. "I suppose you're going to try and sell the cottage?"

"Why? Interested in buying it?"

"On the wage Mike's paying me?" Briefly their eyes met. "Don't hold your breath."

"I don't know how I'm going to get it ready," she said. "I didn't realize how much work there'd be. The garden, the house itself." She gestured over the southern wall. "There's a hole in the bloody roof."

"How long are you here for?"

"I'm booked at the hotel for another three weeks."

He nodded. "That ought to be enough time."

"You reckon?"

"Sure."

"Such faith. And you haven't even seen me wield a hammer."

He reached up to plait a stray piece of wisteria in with the others. "I'll help you."

Cassandra felt a flush of embarrassment: he thought she'd been hinting. "I didn't mean . . . I don't have . . ." She exhaled. "There's no restoration budget, none at all."

He smiled, the first proper smile she'd seen him give. "I'm earning peanuts already. Might as well earn nothing working in a place I love."

THIRTY-THREE

NELL looked out over the churning sea. It was the first overcast day she'd struck since arriving in Cornwall and the whole landscape was shivering. The white cottages clinging to cold crags, the silvery gulls, the grey sky reflecting the swollen sea.

"Best view in all of Cornwall," said the estate agent.

Nell didn't dignify the inanity with comment. She continued to watch the roiling waves from the little dormer window.

"There's another bedroom next door. Smaller, but a bedroom nonetheless."

"I need longer to inspect," said Nell. "I'll join you downstairs when I'm done."

The agent seemed happy enough to be dismissed and, within a minute, Nell saw her appear outside the front gate, huddling into her coat.

Nell watched as the woman did battle with the wind to light a cigarette, then she let her gaze drift down towards the garden. She couldn't see much from up here, had to look through a frayed tapestry of creepers, but she could just make out the stone head of the little-boy statue.

Nell leaned on the dusty window frame, felt the salt-roughened wood beneath her palms. She had been in this cottage before, as a child, she knew that now. She had stood at this very spot, in this room, watching the same sea. She closed her eyes and willed her memory into sharper focus.

A bed had stood where she was now, a single bed, simple, with brass ends, dulled knobs that needed polishing. From the ceiling, an inverted cone of netting fell, like the white mist that hung from the horizon when storms were stirring the distant sea. A patchwork quilt, cool beneath her knees; fishing boats bobbing on the tide, flower petals floating on the pond below.

Sitting in this window that jutted out from the rest of the cottage was like hanging from the top of the cliff, like the princess in one of her favorite fairy tales, turned to a bird and left swinging in her golden cage—

Raised voices downstairs, her papa and the Authoress.

Her name, Ivory, sharp and jagged like a star cut from cardboard with pointed scissors. Her name as a weapon.

There were other angry words being hurled. Why was Papa shouting at the Authoress? Papa who never raised his voice.

The little girl felt frightened, she didn't want to hear.

Nell clenched her eyes tighter, tried to hear.

The little girl blocked her ears, sang songs in her mind, told stories, thought about that golden cage, the princess bird swinging and waiting.

Nell tried to push aside the child's song, the image of a golden cage. In the cold depths of her mind, the truth was lurking, waiting for Nell to clutch it and drag it to the surface . . .

But not today. She opened her eyes. Those tendrils were too slippery today, the water around them too murky.

Nell took herself back down the narrow stairs.

The agent locked the gate and together they started in silence down the path to where the car was parked.

"So, what did you think?" said the agent in the perfunctory tone of one who thought she knew the answer.

"I'd like to buy it."

"Perhaps there's something else I can—" The agent looked up from the car door. "You'd like to buy it?"

Nell gazed again across the stormy sea, the misty horizon. She enjoyed a bit of inclemency in her weather. When the clouds hung low and rain threatened, she felt restored. Breathed more deeply, thought more clearly.

She had no idea how she'd pay for the cottage, what she'd have to sell in order to do so. But as sure as black and white made grey, Nell knew she had to own it. From the moment she'd remembered that little girl by the fish pond, the little girl who was Nell in a different lifetime, she'd known.

THE AGENT drove all the way back to the Tregenna Inn with breathless promises to walk round with the contracts just as soon as she had them typed up. She had the name of a good lawyer Nell could use, too. Nell closed the car door and went up the steps to the foyer. She was so intent on her attempt to calculate the time difference—was it add three hours and change a.m. to p.m.?—so she could call her bank manager and attempt to explain the sudden acquisition of a Cornish cottage, she didn't see the person coming towards her until they almost collided.

"I'm sorry," said Nell, stopping with a jolt.

Robyn Martin was blinking quickly behind her glasses.

"Were you waiting for me?" said Nell.

"I brought you something." Robyn handed Nell a pile of papers clipped together. "It's research for the article I've been working on about the Mountrachet family." She shifted awkwardly. "I heard you asking Gump about them, and I know he wasn't able to . . . that he wasn't much help." She smoothed already smooth hair. "It's an odd assortment, really, but I thought they might be of interest to you."

"Thank you," said Nell, meaning it. "And I'm sorry if I . . ."

Robyn nodded.

"Is your grandfather . . . ?"

"Much better. In fact, I was wondering whether you might come to dinner again, one night next week. At Gump's house."

"I appreciate you asking me," said Nell, "but I don't think your grandfather will."

Robyn shook her head, hair swinging neatly. "Oh no, you've misunderstood."

Nell's eyebrows lifted.

"It was his idea," said Robyn. "He said there was something he needed to tell you. About the cottage and Eliza Makepeace."

THIRTY-FOUR

Miss Rose Mountrachet
Cunard Liner, *Lusitania*

Miss Eliza Mountrachet
Blackhurst Manor
Cornwall, England

9 September 1907

My Dearest Eliza,

Oh!—What wonder the *Lusitania*! As I write this letter, cousin of mine, I am seated on the upper deck—a dainty little table on the Veranda Café—gazing out across the wide blue Atlantic, as our great "floating hotel" spirits us towards New York.

There is an atmosphere of tremendous celebration on board, with everyone positively overbrimming with hope that the *Lusitania* will take back the Blue Riband from Germany. At the landing stage in Liverpool, as the great ship moved slowly from her moorings & began proper her maiden voyage, the crowd on deck were singing "Britons never, never, never shall be slaves" & waving flags, so many & so quickly, that even as we pulled further away & the folk ashore were diminished into tiny dots, I could see the flags still moving. When the boats bade us farewell by tooting their horns, I confess to goose bumps on my arms & a sensation of swelling pride in my heart. What joy to be involved in such momentous events! Will history remember us, I wonder? I do hope so—to imagine that one might do something, touch an event somehow, & thereby transcend the bounds of a single human lifetime!

I know what you will say with regards to the Blue Riband—that it's a silly race invented by silly men trying to prove little more than that their boat can outrun that belonging to even sillier men! But dearest Eliza, to be here, to breathe the spirit of excitement & conquest—Well, I can only say that it's invigorating. I feel more alive than I have done in an age, & though I know you will be rolling your eyes, you must allow me to profess my deepest wish that we *do* make the trip in record speed & win back our rightful place.

The entire ship is appointed in such a way that it is difficult at times to remember that one is at sea. Mamma & I are staying in one of two "Regal Suites" on board—it comprises two bedrooms, a sitting room, dining room, private bath, lavatory & pantry, & is beautifully decorated, reminding me a little of the pictures of Versailles in Miss Tranton's book, the one she brought to the schoolroom that summer long ago.

I overheard a beautifully dressed lady commenting that it is more like a hotel than any ship she has ever before traveled aboard. I do not know who that lady was, but I feel sure she must be Very Important, for Mamma suffered a rare bout of speechlessness when we found ourselves within her orbit. Never fear, 'twas not abiding—Mamma cannot be repressed for long. She quickly found her tongue & has been making up for lost time ever since. Our fellow passengers are a veritable who's who of London society, according to Mamma, & thus they must be "charmed." I am under strict instructions to be always at my best—thank goodness I have two wardrobes full of armaments with which to dress for battle! For once Mamma & I are of a mind, though certainly not of a taste!—she is forever pointing out a gentleman she considers an excellent match & I am frequently dismayed. But enough—I fear I will lose the audience of my dearest cousin if I tarry too long on such subjects.

Back to the ship, then—I have been carrying out certain explorations, sure to make my Eliza proud. Yesterday morning I managed briefly to escape Mamma, & passed a lovely hour in the roof garden. I thought of you, dearest, & how amazed you would be to see that such vegetation could be grown on board a ship. There are tubs at every turn, filled with green trees & the most beautiful flowers. I felt quite joyous sitting among them (no one knows better than I the healing properties of a garden) & gave myself over to all kinds of silly daydreams. (You will be able to imagine well enough the paths down which my fancies rambled . . .)

Oh! but how I wish you had relented & come with us, Eliza. I shall make time here for a brief but gentle scold, for I simply cannot understand. It was you, after all, who first raised the notion that the two of us might someday travel to America, witness firsthand the skyscrapers of New York & the great Statue of Liberty. I cannot think what induced you to forsake the opportunity so that you might stay at Blackhurst with only Father for company. You are, as always, a mystery to me, dearest, but I know better than to argue with you when your mind is made up, my dear, stubborn Eliza. I will say only that I miss you already & find myself frequently imagining how much mischief might be had were you here with me. (How we would wreak havoc on poor Mamma's nerves!) It is strange to think upon a time when you were unknown to me, it seems we have always been a pair & the years at Blackhurst before you arrived but a horrid waiting period.

Ah—Mamma is calling. It seems we are expected yet again in the dining room. (The meals, Eliza! I am having to stroll about the deck between times in order to stand any hope at all of making a polite attempt at the next sitting!) Mamma has no doubt managed to harpoon the earl of so-and-so, or the son of some wealthy industrialist as tablemate. A daughter's work is never done, & she is right in this: I shall never meet My Fate if I keep myself locked away.

I bid you good-bye, then, my dear Eliza, & close by saying that though you are not with me in person, you most certainly are in spirit. I know that when I first catch sight of the famed lady of Liberty, standing vigilant over her port, it will be my cousin Eliza's voice I hear, saying, "Just look at her & think of all she's seen."

I remain always, your beloved cousin, Rose

ELIZA TIGHTENED her fingers around the brown-paper-wrapped parcel. Standing on the doorstop of the Tregenna general store, she watched as a dark grey blanket of cloud sagged towards the mirror below. Haze on the horizon spoke of storms at sea, and the air in the village vacillated with anxious flecks of moisture. Eliza had brought no bag, as when she'd left the house she hadn't intended a trip to the village. It was sometime during the morning that the story had crept up on her and demanded immediate attention. The five pages left in her current notebook had been sorely inadequate, the need for a new one pressing, thus had she embarked on this impromptu shopping expedition.

Eliza glanced once more at the sullen sky and set off quickly along the harbor. When she reached the point where the road forked, she ignored the main branch and started instead up the narrow cliff track. She had never followed it before, but Davies had once told her that a shortcut from the estate to the village ran along the cliff edge.

The way was steep and the grass long but Eliza proceeded apace. She paused only once to look out across the flat, granite sea, on which a fleet of tiny white fishing boats was coming home to roost. Eliza smiled to see them, like baby sparrows returning to the nest, hurrying in after a day spent exploring the rim of a vast world.

One day she would cross that sea, all the way to the other side, just as her father had done. There were so many worlds waiting beyond the horizon. Africa, and India, Arabia, the antipodes, and in such faraway places would she discover new stories, magical tales from long ago.

Davies had suggested she write down her own tales, and write Eliza had. She'd filled twelve notebooks and still she hadn't stopped. Indeed, the more she wrote, the louder the stories seemed to grow, swirling in her mind, pressing against her head, anxious for release. She didn't know whether they were any good and in truth she didn't care. They were hers, and writing them made them real somehow. Characters who'd danced around inside her mind grew bolder on the page. They took on new mannerisms she hadn't imagined for them, said things she didn't know they thought, began to behave unpredictably.

Her stories had a small but receptive audience. Each night after supper, Eliza would crawl into bed beside Rose, just as she had when they were younger, and there she would begin her most recent fairy tale. Rose would listen, wide-eyed, gasping and sighing in all the right places, laughing gleefully at certain gruesome moments.

It was Rose who had cajoled Eliza into sending one of her tales away to the London office of the *Children's Storytime* journal.

"Don't you want to see them in print? They will be real stories then, and you a real writer."

"They're already real stories."

Rose had taken on a slightly devious look. "But if they're published, you will earn a little income."

An income of her own. This *did* interest Eliza, and Rose well knew it. Up until this point Eliza had been fully dependent on her aunt and uncle, but lately she'd been wondering how she was going to fund the travels and adventures she knew the future held.

"And it certainly wouldn't please Mamma," said Rose, clasping her hands together beneath her chin, biting her lip to stop from smiling. "A Mountrachet lady earning a living!"

Aunt Adeline's reaction, as always, meant little of consequence to Eliza, but the idea of other people reading her tales . . . Ever since Eliza had discovered the book of fairy tales in Mrs. Swindell's rag and bottle shop, had disappeared inside its faded pages, she'd understood the power of stories. Their magical ability to refill the wounded part of people.

Drizzle was turning now to light rain and Eliza began to run, hugging the notebook to her chest as wet strands of grass brushed against her damp skirt. What would Rose say when Eliza told her the children's journal was going to publish "The Changeling," that they had asked to see more? She smiled to herself as she ran.

A week to go before Rose was finally home, and Eliza could barely wait. How she longed to see her cousin! Rose had been rather remiss with correspondence—there had been one letter composed en route to America, but nothing since, and Eliza found herself waiting impatiently for news of the great city. She would have loved to visit it herself but Aunt Adeline had been clear.

"Ruin your own prospects, by all means," she said one evening when Rose had retired to bed. "But I will not allow you to ruin Rose's future with your uncivilized ways. She'll never meet Her Fate if she's not given opportunity to shine." Aunt Adeline had drawn herself to her full height. "I have booked two passages to New York. One for Rose and one for myself. I wish to avoid unpleasantness, thus it would be best if she thought the decision had been yours."

"Why would I lie to Rose?"

Aunt Adeline inhaled and her cheeks hollowed. "To make her happy, of course. Don't you want her to be happy?"

A thunderclap echoed between the cliff walls as Eliza reached the hilltop. The sky was darkening and the rain growing heavier. In the clearing stood a cottage. The same little cottage, Eliza realized, that crouched on the other side of the walled garden that Uncle Linus had given her to plant. She hurried to shelter beneath the entrance portico, huddled against the door as rain spilled, thicker and faster, over the eaves.

It had been almost two months since Rose and Aunt Adeline had left for New York, and though time was dragging now, the first month had passed swiftly in a whirl of fine weather and splendid story ideas. Eliza had split each day between her two favorite places on the estate: the black rock down in the cove, on top of which millennia of tides had washed smooth a seat-sized platform; and the hidden garden, her garden, at the end of the maze. What a delight it was to have a place of one's own, an entire garden in which to Be. Sometimes Eliza liked to sit on the iron seat, perfectly still, and just listen. To the windblown leaves tapping against the walls, the muffled ocean breathing in and out, and the birds singing their stories. Sometimes, if she sat still enough, she almost fancied she could hear the flowers sighing in gratitude to the sun.

But not today. The sun had withdrawn and beyond the cliff edge sky and sea were merged in grey agitation. Rain continued to pour and Eliza sighed. There was no point yet attempting to make her way to the garden and through the maze, not unless she wanted a thorough drenching for herself and her new notebook. If only a hollow tree could be found in which to shelter! A story idea began to flutter on the edge of Eliza's imagination; she snatched at it, refused to let it go, held on as it grew arms, legs and a clear destination.

She reached inside her dress and withdrew the lead pencil she always kept tucked beneath her bodice. Leaned the new notebook against her bent knee and began to scribble.

The wind blew stronger up here in the realm of the birds, and rain had begun to swirl inside her hiding place, tossing splotches on her pristine pages. Eliza turned towards the door but still the rain found her.

This was no good! Where would she write when the wet weather set in for the season? The cove and the garden would not be fair shelter then. There was her uncle's house, of course, with its hundred rooms, but Eliza found it difficult to write when there was always someone nearby. It was possible to think oneself alone, only to discover a housemaid had been knelt by the fire, raking coals all the while. Or her uncle, sitting silent in a dim, dark corner.

A scud of heavy rain landed at Eliza's feet, drenching the portico. She closed the notebook and tapped her heel impatiently against the stone floor. She needed better shelter than this. Eliza glanced at the red door behind her. How had she not noticed before? Emerging from the lock was the ornate handle of a big brass key. Without further hesitation, Eliza twisted it to the left. The mechanism shifted with a clunk. She lay her hand on the doorknob, smooth and unaccountably warm, and turned it. A click, and the door was open, as if by magic.

Eliza stepped across the threshold into the dark, dry womb.

BENEATH THE black umbrella Linus sat waiting. He hadn't caught a glimpse of Eliza all day and agitation possessed his every mannerism. She would come, though, he knew that, Davies said she had intended to visit the garden and there was only one way back from there. Linus allowed his eyes to close and his mind to fall backwards through the years to a time when Georgiana had disappeared daily into the garden. She had asked him again and again to come, to see the planting she had done, but Linus always declined. He had waited for her, though, kept vigil until his *poupée* reappeared each day from between the hedges. Remembered sometimes his entrapment by the maze all those years before. What an exquisite feeling it had been, the curious mixture of old shame mixed with joy at his sister's emergence.

He opened his eyes and drew breath. Thought at first he was subject to a wishful fantasy, but no, it was Eliza, coming this way and deep in thought. She hadn't seen him yet. His dry lips moved around the words he wished to speak. "Child," he called out.

She looked up, surprised. "Uncle," she said, smiling slowly. She held her hands out to the side; in one was a brown package. "How sudden the rain!"

Her skirt was wet, the transparent rim clinging to her legs. Linus couldn't look away. "I—I was afraid you might be caught in the weather."

"And I very nearly was. I found shelter, though, in the cottage, the little cottage on the other side of the maze."

Wet hair, wet hem, wet ankles. Linus dug his cane into the damp earth and pushed himself to standing.

"Is the cottage used by anyone, Uncle?" Eliza came closer. "It appeared unused."

Her smell—rain, salt, soil. He leaned against his cane and almost fell. She reached to steady him. "The garden, child, tell me of the garden."

"Oh, Uncle, how it grows! You must come one day and sit among the flowers. See for yourself the planting I have done."

Her hands on his arm were warm, her grip firm. He would give the remaining years of his life to stop time and remain forever in this moment, he and his Georgiana—

"Lord Mountrachet!" Thomas was flustering towards them from the house. "My Lord, you should have said you needed help."

And then Eliza was no longer holding him, Thomas was in her place. And Linus could only watch as she disappeared up the steps and into the entrance hall, paused fractionally at the stand to collect the morning's post, before being swallowed by his house.

Miss Rose Mountrachet
Cunard Liner, *Lusitania*

Miss Eliza Mountrachet
Blackhurst Manor
Cornwall, England

7 November 1907

Dearest Eliza,

What a time! So much has happened since last we met, I can barely think where to start. First, I must apologize for the dearth of letters in recent weeks. Our last month in New York was such a whirlwind, & when I first sat down to write to you, as we left the great American port, we fell victim to such a storm I almost believed myself back in Cornwall. The thunder, & Oh! the squalls! I was laid up in my cabin for a full two days, & poor Mamma was quite green. She required frequent tending—what a turnup it was, Mamma ill and Sickly Rose her nurse!

After the storm finally subsided, the mist remained for many days, floating about the ship like a great sea monster. It put me in mind of you, dear Eliza, & the stories you used to spin when we were girls, about the mermaids & the ships lost at sea.

The skies have cleared now, as we draw ever closer towards England—

But wait. Why am I giving you weather reportage when I have so much else to relate? I know the answer to that: I am dancing around my true intentions, hesitating before giving voice to my real news, for Oh! where to begin . . .

You will remember, Eliza dear, from my last letter, that Mamma & I had made the acquaintance of certain Important people? One, Lady Dudmore, turned out to be a person of some consequence indeed; what's more, it would seem she took a shine to me, for Mamma & I were issued many a letter of introduction & were thus inducted into a circle of New York's finest society. What glittering butterflies we were, flitting from one party to another—

But still I tarry—for you need not hear of every soirée, every game of bridge! Eliza dearest, with no further ado, I will hold my breath & write it plain—I am engaged! Engaged to be married! & dear Eliza, I am so bursting with joy & wonder that I hardly dare open my mouth to speak for fear I will have little to say except to gush about my Love. And that I will not do—not here, not yet. I refuse to diminish these fine feelings through inadequate attempt to capture them in words. Instead, I will wait until we meet again & then tell you all. Let it be enough, my cousin, to say that I am floating in a great & glittering cloud of happiness.

I have never felt so well, and I have you to thank, my dear Eliza—from Cornwall you have waved your fairy wand & granted me my dearest wish! For my fiancé (what thrill to write those two words—my fiancé!) may not be what you imagine. Though in most everything he is of the highest order—handsome, clever & good—in matters of finance, he is quite a poor man! (And now you will begin to intuit just why I suspect you of the gift of prophecy—). He is just as the match you invented for me in "The Changeling"! How did you know, dearest, that I would have my head turned by such a one!

Poor Mamma is in a state of some shock (though improved somewhat by now), indeed, she barely spoke to me for some days after I informed her of my engagement. She, of course, had her heart set on a greater match & will not see that I care not one whit for money or title. Those are *her* desires for me, & while I confess I once shared them, I do so no longer—How can I when my Prince has come for me and unlatched the door to my golden cage?

I ache to see you again, Eliza, & to share with you my joy. I have missed you tremendously and can hardly bear to think that once I arrive in England there will be another week to wait before we're together. I will post this letter as soon as we dock in Liverpool: would that I were accompanying it directly to Blackhurst, rather than languishing in the dreary company of Mamma's family!

I remain yours, lovingly now & evermore, cousin Rose

If she were honest, Adeline blamed herself. Had she not, after all, been present with Rose at each glittering event during their visit to New York? Had she not appointed herself chaperone at the ball given by Mr. and Mrs. Irving in their grand house on Fifth Avenue? Worse still, had she not given Rose a nod of encouragement when the dashing young man with dark hair and full lips made his approach and requested the pleasure of a dance?

"Your daughter is a beauty," Mrs. Frank Hastings had said, leaning over to whisper in Adeline's ear as the handsome couple took to the floor. "Fairest of them all tonight."

Adeline had shifted—yes, proudly—on her seat. (Was that the moment of her undoing? Had the Lord noted her hubris?) "Beauty equaled by her purity of heart."

"And Nathaniel Walker is a handsome man indeed."

Nathaniel Walker. It was the first time she'd heard his name.

"Walker," she said thoughtfully: the name had a solid ring to it, surely she'd heard tell of a family called Walker who'd made their fortune in oil? New money, but times were changing, there was no longer any shame in a match of title with treasure. "Who are his people?"

Did Adeline imagine the hint of barely concealed glee that briefly animated Mrs. Hastings's bland features? "Oh, no one of consequence." She raised one bald eyebrow. "An artist, you know, befriended, most ludicrously, by one of the younger Irving boys."

Adeline's smile had grown stale around the edges but still she held it. All was not yet lost, painting was a perfectly noble hobby after all . . .

"Rumor has it," came Mrs. Hastings's crushing blow, "the Irving chappie met him on the street! Son of a pair of immigrants, Poles at that. Walker may be what he calls himself, but I doubt that's what was written on the immigration papers. I hear tell he makes sketches for a living!"

"Oil portraits?"

"Oh, nothing so grand as that. Scratchy charcoal things, from what I understand." She sucked in one cheek in an attempt to swallow her glee. "Quite a rise indeed. Parents are Catholics, father worked on the wharves."

Adeline fought the urge to scream as Mrs. Hastings leaned back against her gilt chair, face pinched at the edges by one of Schadenfreude's smiles. "No harm in a young girl dancing with a handsome man, though, is there?"

A smooth smile to mask her panic. "No harm at all," said Adeline.

But how could she believe it when her mind had already tossed up the memory of a young girl standing atop a Cornish cliff, eyes wide and heart open as she looked upon a handsome man who appeared to promise so much? Oh, there was harm indeed for a young lady flattered by the brief attentions of a handsome man.

The week passed, and that was the best that could be said of it.

Night after night, Adeline paraded Rose before an audience of suitable young gentlemen. She waited and she hoped, longing to see a spark of interest brighten her daughter's face. But each night, disappointment. Rose had eyes only for Nathaniel, and he, it seemed, for her. Like one in the grip of dangerous hysteria, Rose was trapped and unreachable. Adeline had to fight the urge to slap her cheeks, cheeks that glowed more fervently than a delicate young woman's cheeks had any right to.

Adeline, too, was haunted by Nathaniel Walker's face. At each dinner, dance or reading they attended she would scan the room, seeking him out. Fear had created a template in her mind and all other faces were blurred: only his features clear. She began to see him even when he wasn't there. She had dreams of wharves and boats and poor families. Sometimes the dreams took place in Yorkshire, and her own parents played the part of Nathaniel's family. Oh, her poor addled brain; to think that she could be brought to this.

Then one evening the worst finally happened. They had been at a ball and the entire carriage ride home Rose was very quiet. The particular type of quiet which presages a firming of heart, a clearing of view. Like someone nursing a secret, keeping it close for a time before unleashing it to do its worst.

The horrid moment came when Rose was dressing for bed.

"Mamma," she said, as she brushed her hair, "there's something I wish to tell you." Then the words, the dreaded words. Affection . . . fate . . . forever . . .

"You are young," Adeline said quickly, cutting Rose off. "It is understandable that you should confuse friendship with affection of another kind."

"It isn't friendship alone that I feel, Mamma."

Heat rose beneath Adeline's skin. "It would be a disaster. He brings nothing—"

"He brings himself and that's all I need."

Her insistence, her infuriating confidence. "Evidence of your naivety, my Rose, and your youth."

"I am not too young to know my mind, Mamma. I am eighteen now. Did you not bring me to New York so that I might meet My Fate?"

Adeline's voice was thin. "This man is not Your Fate."

"How do you know that?"

"I am your mother." How feeble it sounded. "You are beautiful, from an important family, and yet you would settle for so little?"

Rose sighed softly, in a way that seemed to signal a close to the conversation. "I love him, Mamma."

Adeline closed her eyes. Youth! What chance had the most reasonable arguments against the arrogant power of those three words? That her daughter, her precious prize, should utter them so easily, and about such a one as he!

"And he loves me, Mamma, he told me so."

Adeline's heart tightened with fear. Darling girl, blinded by foolish thoughts of love. How to tell her that the hearts of men were not so easily won. If won, rarely kept.

"You'll see," Rose said. "I shall live happily ever after, just like in Eliza's story. She wrote this, you know, almost as if she knew what would happen."

Eliza! Adeline seethed. Even here, at this distance, the girl continued her menace. Her influence extended across the oceans, her ill whisperings sabotaged Rose's future, goaded her into making the biggest mistake of her life.

Adeline pressed her lips together tightly. She hadn't overseen Rose's recovery from countless ailments and illnesses in order to watch her throw herself away on a poor marriage. "You must break it off. He will understand. He must have known it would never be allowed."

"We are engaged, Mamma. He has asked and I have accepted him."

"Break it off."

"I will not."

Adeline felt her back against the wall. "You will be shunned from society, unwelcome in your father's home."

"Then I will stay here where I *am* welcome. In Nathaniel's home."

How had it come to this? Her Rose, saying such things. Things she must have known would break her mamma's heart. Adeline's head was spinning, she needed to lie down.

"I'm sorry, Mamma," Rose said quietly, "but I won't change my mind, I can't. Don't ask me to."

They didn't speak for days after, excepting, of course, such banal social pleasantries as would have been unthinkable for either of them to ignore. Rose thought Adeline was sulking, but she was not. She was deep in thought. Adeline had always been able to bend passion towards logic.

The current equation was impossible, thus some factor must be changed. If it wasn't going to be Rose's mind, it would have to be the fiancé himself. He must become a man deserving of her daughter's hand, the sort of man people spoke about with awe and, yes, with envy. And Adeline had a feeling she knew just how such a change might be effected.

In each man's heart there lies a hole. A dark abyss of need, the filling of which takes precedence over all else. Adeline suspected that Nathaniel Walker's hole was pride, the most dangerous pride, that of the poor man. A hunger to prove himself, to rise above his birth and make of himself a better man than his father. Even without the biography so greedily supplied by Mrs. Hastings, the more Adeline saw of Nathaniel Walker the more she knew this to be true. She could see it in the way he walked, the careful shine of his shoes, the keenness of his smile and the volume of his laugh. These were the traits of a man who had come from little and glimpsed the gleaming world swirling far above his own. A man whose finery was hung upon a poor man's skin.

Adeline knew his weakness well, for it was her own. She also knew exactly what she had to do. She must ensure that he received every advantage; she must become his greatest champion, promote his art to the best in society, ensure that his name became synonymous with portraiture of the elite. With her ringing endorsement, with his good looks and charm, not to mention Rose for a wife, he couldn't fail to impress.

And Adeline would make sure that he never forgot who was responsible for his good fortune.

ELIZA DROPPED the letter beside her on the bed. Rose was engaged, was going to be married. The news shouldn't have come as such a surprise. Rose had spoken often of her hopes for the future, her desire for a husband and family, a grand house and a carriage of her own. And yet Eliza felt odd.

She opened her new notebook and ran her fingers lightly over the first page, blistered by raindrops. She drew a line with her pencil, watched absently as it switched from dark to light according to whether its base was damp or dry. She began a story, scribbled and scratched out for a time before pushing the book aside.

Finally, Eliza leaned back against her pillow. There was no denying it, she felt unusual: something sat deep within her stomach, round and heavy, sharp and bitter. She wondered whether she had taken ill. Perhaps it was the rain? Mary had often warned against staying outdoors too long.

Eliza turned her head to look at the wall, at nothing. Rose, her cousin, hers to entertain, willing coconspirator, was to be married. With whom would Eliza share the hidden garden? Her stories? Her life? How was it that a future so vividly imagined—years stretching ahead, filled with travel and adventure and writing—could prove so suddenly, so emphatically, a chimera?

Her gaze slipped sideways to rest on the cold glass of the mirror. Eliza didn't often glance at the looking glass and in the time that had elapsed since last she met her echo, something had gone missing. She sat up and moved closer. Appraised herself.

Realization came fully formed. She knew just what it was she'd lost. This reflection belonged to an adult, there was no place in its angles for Sammy's face to hide. He was gone.

And now Rose was going, too. Who was this man who had stolen her dearest friend in the blink of an eyelid?

Eliza could not have felt so ill had she swallowed one of the Christmas decorations Mary made, one of the oranges spiked with cloves.

Envy, that's what this lump was called. She envied the man who had made Rose well, who had done so easily what Eliza sought to do, who had caused her cousin's affections to shift so swiftly and completely. *Envy.* Eliza whispered the sharp word and felt its poisoned barbs prick the inside of her mouth.

She turned away from the mirror and closed her eyes, willed herself to forget the letter and its awful news. She didn't want to feel envious, to harbor this barbed lump. For Eliza knew from her fairy tales the fate awaiting wicked sisters bewitched by envy.

THIRTY-FIVE

JULIA'S apartment was at the very top of the house, accessed by an incredibly narrow set of stairs at the end of the second-floor hallway. When Cassandra left her room the sun had already begun to melt into the horizon, and the hall was now almost completely dark. She knocked and waited, tightening her grip on the neck of the bottle of wine she'd brought with her. A last-minute decision as she'd walked home with Christian through the village.

The door opened and Julia was there, wrapped in a shiny pink kimono. "Come, come," she said, gesturing for Cassandra to follow as she swept across the room. "I'm just titivating our dinner. Hope you like Italian!"

"Love it," said Cassandra, hurrying behind.

What had once been a warren of tiny bedrooms housing an army of housemaids had been opened and reconfigured to create a large loft-style apartment. Dormer windows ran all the way along both sides and must have given incredible views across the estate during the day.

Cassandra stopped at the entrance to the kitchen. Every surface was covered with mixing bowls and measuring cups, tomato tins with their lids hanging off, gleaming pools of olive oil and lemon juice and other mysterious ingredients. For want of somewhere to put it, she held out her offering.

"Aren't you a darling?" Julia popped the cork, then plucked a lone goblet from the rack above the bench, gurgled wine into it from a theatrical height. She licked a drop of shiraz from her finger. "Personally, I never drink anything but gin," she said with a wink. "Keeps you youthful; it's pure, you know." She handed the goblet of sinful red liquid to Cassandra and swept from the kitchen. "Now, come on in and make yourself comfortable."

She indicated an armchair in the center of the room and Cassandra sat down. Before her was a wooden chest, doubling as a coffee table, and at its center sat a stack of old scrapbooks, each wearing a faded brown leather jacket.

A shot of excitement spread quickly through Cassandra's body and her fingertips tingled with desire.

"You sit and have a little flick through while I put the finishing touches to our dinner."

Cassandra didn't need to be told twice. She reached for the top scrapbook and ran her palm ever so lightly over its surface. The leather had lost all hint of its grain and was smooth and soft as velvet.

Inhaling her anticipation, Cassandra opened the cover and read, in a pretty and precise script: *Rose Elizabeth Mountrachet Walker, 1909.* She traced the words with a fingertip and felt the faint marks in the paper. Imagined the nibbed pen which had made them. Carefully, she turned the pages until she arrived at the first entry.

A new year. And one in which such tremendous events are promised. I have barely been able to concentrate since Dr. Matthews arrived and gave me his verdict. I confess, the fainting spells of late had me gravely worried, and I was not the only one. I only needed glance at Mamma's face to see anxiety writ large across her features. While Dr. Matthews was examining me I lay still, eyes focused on the ceiling, forcing my mind away from fear by recalling the happiest moments of my life so far. My wedding day, of course; my

trip to New York; the summer Eliza first came to Blackhurst
. . . How bright such memories seem when the life they catalogue is threatened!

Afterwards, when Mamma and I sat side by side on the
sofa awaiting Dr. Matthews's diagnosis, her hand reached
for mine. It was cold. I glanced at her but she would not
meet my eyes. It was then that I began to worry in earnest.
Through all my childhood ailments, Mamma was the one
to keep a positive mind. I wondered why her confidence
had now deserted her, what it was she had intuited that
gave her cause for such concern. When Dr. Matthews
cleared his throat, I squeezed Mamma's hand and waited.
What he said, though, was more shocking than anything I
could have dreamed.

"You are with child. Two months gone, I'd say. God
willing, you will deliver in August."

Oh, but are there words to explain the joy those words
provoked? After so long hoping, the terrible months of
disappointment. A baby to love. An heir for Nathaniel, a
grandchild for Mamma, a godchild for Eliza.

Cassandra's eyes stung. To think that this baby whose conception
Rose celebrated was Nell, this desperately wanted baby-in-waiting was
Cassandra's dear, displaced grandmother. Rose's hopeful sentiments
were especially moving, written as they were in ignorance of all that
would come afterwards.

She flicked quickly through the journal pages, past snippets of
lace and ribbon, brief notes reporting doctor's visits, invitations to various dinners and dances around the county, until finally, in December
1909, she found what she was looking for.

She is here—I make this record a little later than expected.
The past months have been more difficult than anticipated,

and I have had little time or energy for writing, but all has been worth it. After so many months of hoping, long spells of illness and worry and confinement, I hold in my arms my darling child. Everything else fades away. She is perfect. Her skin so pale and creamy, her lips so pink and plump. Her eyes are a deep blue, but the doctor says that is always so and they may darken with time. Secretly I hope he is wrong. I wish for her the true Mountrachet coloring, like Father and Eliza: blue eyes and red hair. We have decided to name her Ivory. It is the color of her skin and, as time will doubtless prove, her soul.

"Here we are." Julia was juggling two steaming bowls of pasta and had an enormous pepper mill tucked beneath her arm. "Ravioli with pine nuts and Gorgonzola." She handed one to Cassandra. "Careful, the plate's a bit warm."

Cassandra took the proffered bowl and set the scrapbook aside. "Smells delicious."

"If I hadn't become a writer, then a renovator, then a hotelier, I'd have been a chef. Cheers." Julia lifted her glass of gin, took a sip, then sighed. "I sometimes feel my entire life is a series of accidents and chances—not that I'm complaining. One can be very happy having relinquished all expectation of control." She speared a ravioli square. "But enough about me—how goes it at the cottage?"

"Really well," said Cassandra. "Except the more I do, the more I realize needs doing. The garden's quite wild and the house itself is a mess. I'm not even sure it's structurally sound. I suppose I should have a builder come and look at it for me, but I haven't had time yet, there's been so much else to keep me busy. It's all very . . ."

"Overwhelming?"

"Yeah, it's definitely overwhelming, but more than that. It's"— Cassandra paused, searched for the right word, surprised herself when she found it—"exciting. I've found something at the cottage, Julia."

"Found something?" Her brows shot up. "As in hidden treasure something?"

"If you like your treasure green and fertile." Cassandra bit her bottom lip. "It's a hidden garden, a walled garden at the back of the cottage. I don't think anyone's been inside for decades, and no wonder, the walls are really high, completely covered by brambles. You'd never guess it was there."

"How did you find it?"

"By accident, really."

Julia shook her head. "No such thing as accidents."

"I honestly had no idea it was there."

"I'm not suggesting that you did. I'm just saying, perhaps the garden only hid from those it didn't wish to see."

"Well, I'm certainly glad it showed itself to me. The garden is incredible. It's really overgrown, but underneath the brambles all kinds of plants have survived. There are paths, garden seats, bird feeders."

"Like Sleeping Beauty, fast asleep until the enchantment is broken."

"That's the thing, though; it hasn't been asleep. The trees have kept growing, bearing fruit, even though there's been no one there to appreciate it. You should see the apple tree, it looks to be a hundred years old."

"It is," said Julia suddenly, sitting upright and pushing her bowl aside. "Or it very nearly is." She flicked through the scrapbooks, running her finger down page after page, turning back and forth. "Aha," she said, tapping an entry. "Here it is. Just after Rose's eighteenth birthday, before she went to New York and met Nathaniel." Julia propped a pair of turquoise and mother-of-pearl glasses on the end of her nose and began to read:

Twenty-first of May 1907. What a day it has been! And to think when it started I thought I was to suffer yet another interminable day inside. (After Dr. Matthews mentioned a

few cases of sniffles in the village, Mamma has become terrified that I will fall ill and jeopardize the country weekend
we are to attend next month.) Eliza, as always, had other
ideas. Just as soon as Mamma had left by carriage for Lady
Phillimore's luncheon, she appeared at my door, cheeks
aglow (how I envy her the time she spends out of doors!),
and insisted that I put aside my scrapbook (for I was working on you, dear diary!) and come with her through the
maze: there was something there that I must see.

My first instinct was to demur—I feared that one of
the servants might report back to Mamma and I don't fancy
an argument, certainly not with the New York trip on the
horizon—but then I realized that Eliza had the "look" in
her eyes, the one she gets when she has concocted a plan
and will suffer no hesitations, the "look" that has led me
into more scrapes than I care to remember over the past
seven years.

So excited was my dear cousin that it was impossible
not to be swept up in her enthusiasm. I sometimes think
she has enough spirit for the two of us, which is just as well
seeing as I am so often dispirited. Before I knew it we were
hurrying along together, arms linked, giggling. Davies was
waiting for us at the maze gate, lumbering beneath the weight
of an enormous potted plant, and all the way through Eliza
kept doubling back with offers of help (which he always
declined) before leaping back beside me, seizing my hand
and pulling me further along. We continued thus through
the maze (with whose routes Eliza was extremely au fait),
crossing the center sitting area, passing the brass ring that
Eliza says heralds the entrance to an underground passage,
until we arrived, finally, at a metal door with a large brass
lock. With a flourish, Eliza withdrew a key from the pocket
of her skirt and, before I had time to ask her where on earth

she'd found such a thing, it was inserted. She turned the lock and pushed so that the door swung slowly open.

Inside was a garden. Similar and yet somehow different from the other gardens on the estate. For a start, it is walled completely. Tall stone walls around all four sides, broken only by two opposing metal doors, one on the northern and one on the southern wall—

"So there is another door," said Cassandra. "I couldn't see it."

Julia looked over the top of her glasses. "There were renovations made, back around 1912 . . . 1913 . . . The brick wall out front, for one, maybe they removed the door then? But wait. Listen to this:

The garden itself was neat and rather under-planted. It had the look of a fallow field, waiting to be sown after the winter months have passed. In its center, an ornate metal bench sat by a stone birdbath, and on the ground were several wooden crates loaded with small potted plants.

Eliza ran inside with all the grace of a schoolboy.

"What is this place?" I said in wonder.

"It's a garden, I've been tending it. You should have seen the weeds when first I started. We've been so busy, haven't we, Davies?"

"We certainly have at that, Miss Eliza," he said, depositing the potted plant by the southern wall.

"It's going to be ours, Rose, yours and mine. A secret place where we can be together, just the two of us, just as we imagined when we were younger. Four walls, locked gates, our very own paradise. Even when you're unwell you can come here, Rose. The walls keep it protected from the rough sea winds, so you'll still be able to listen to the birds, smell the flowers, feel the sun on your face."

Her enthusiasm, the intensity of her feeling, was such that I couldn't help but long for such a garden. I gazed upon the tamed garden beds, the potted flowers that were just beginning to bud, and I could imagine the paradise she described. "I heard talk when I was very small about a walled garden hidden on the property, but I thought it must be a story."

"It's not," said Eliza, eyes shining. "It was all true, and now we're bringing it back to life."

They had certainly worked hard. If the garden had been untended all this time, ever since . . . I frowned, the talk I'd heard as a girl was coming back to me. Then realization struck: I knew exactly whose garden this had been—

"Oh, Liza," I said quickly. "You must be careful, *we* must be careful. We must leave this place and never come back. If Father were to find out—"

"He already knows."

I looked at her sharply, more sharply than I intended. "What do you mean?"

"It was Uncle Linus who instructed Davies that I should have the garden. He had Davies clear the last part of the maze and told him that we should give the garden new life."

"But Father forbade anyone to go inside the walled garden."

Eliza shrugged, that gesture of hers that comes so readily and which Mamma so despises. "He must have had a change of heart."

A change of heart. How uneasily the sentiment sat with my image of Father. It was the word "heart" that did it. Except for the one time in his study, when I was hidden beneath the desk and heard him weep for his sister, his *poupée,* I cannot think that I have ever seen Father behave in a way that suggested a heart. Suddenly, I knew, and I felt a strange heaviness in the very base of my stomach. "It is because you are her daughter."

But Eliza did not hear me. She had left my side and was dragging the propagating pot towards a large hole by the wall.

"This is our first new tree," she called. "We're going to have a ceremony. That's why it was so important that you be here today. This tree will continue to grow, no matter where our lives take us, and it will remember us always: Rose and Eliza."

Davies was by my side then, holding out a small spade. "It's Miss Eliza's wish that you should be the first to toss earth onto the roots of the tree, Miss Rose."

Miss Eliza's wish. Who was I to argue with so great a force?

"What sort of tree is it?" I asked.

"An apple tree."

I should have known. Eliza has always had an eye to symbolism, and apples are, after all, the first fruit.

Julia looked up from the scrapbook and a tear slipped from eyes that were brimming. She snuffled and smiled. "I just love Rose so much. Can't you feel her here with us?"

Cassandra smiled back. She had eaten an apple from a tree her great-grandmother had helped to plant, nearly a hundred years before. She blushed slightly as thoughts of the apple brought back echoes of the strange dream. All week as she'd worked close by Christian, she'd managed to block it out. She had thought she was rid of it.

"And now you're cleaning up the same garden all over again. What lovely symmetry. What would Rose say if she knew?" Julia plucked a tissue from a nearby box and blew her nose. "Sorry," she said, dabbing mascara from beneath each eye. "It's just so romantic." She laughed. "It's a shame you don't have a Davies to help you."

"He's not a Davies, but I do have someone helping me," said Cassandra. "He's been every afternoon this week. I met him and his brother, Michael, when they came to clear a fallen tree from the cottage. You know them, I think. Robyn Jameson said they do the gardens here, too."

"The Blake boys. They most certainly do, and I must say I enjoy watching them. That Michael's easy on the eye, isn't he? Quite the charmer, too. If I were still writing, it'd be Michael Blake I'd picture when I was describing my ladies' man."

"And Christian?" Despite her best attempt at nonchalance, Cassandra felt her cheeks warm up.

"Oh, he'd definitely be the smarter, younger, quieter brother who surprises everyone by saving the day and winning the heroine's heart."

Cassandra smiled. "I'm not even going to ask who I'd be."

"And I have no doubts who I'd be," Julia said with a sigh. "The ageing beauty who doesn't have a chance with the hero so channels her energy into helping the heroine realize her fate."

"Life'd be a lot easier if it were like a fairy tale," said Cassandra, "if people belonged to stock character types."

"Oh, but people do, they only *think* they don't. Even the person who insists such things don't exist is a cliché: the drear pedant who insists on his own uniqueness!"

Cassandra took a sip of wine. "You don't think there's any such thing as uniqueness?"

"We're all unique, just never in the ways we imagine." Julia smiled, then waved her hand, bangles clattering. "Listen to me. What a dreadful absolutist I am. Of course there are variations in character. Take your Christian Blake, for instance, he's not a gardener by trade, you know. He works at a hospital in Oxford. That is, he did. Some kind of doctor, I forget the proper name—they're so long and confusing, aren't they?"

Cassandra sat up straighter. "What's a doctor doing lopping trees?"

"What's a doctor doing lopping trees?" Julia echoed meaningfully. "My point exactly. When Michael told me his brother was starting with him I didn't ask questions, but I've been curious as the proverbial ever since. What makes a young man swap vocations, just like that?"

Cassandra shook her head. "Change of heart?"

"Pretty big change, I'd say."

"Maybe he realized he didn't enjoy it."

"Possible, but you'd think he might have got the hint at some time during the interminable years of study." Julia smiled enigmatically. "I think it's likely far more interesting than that, but then, I was a writer and old habits die hard. I can't stop my imagination running away with me." She pointed a gin-clutching finger at Cassandra. "That, my dear, is what makes a character interesting, their secrets."

Cassandra thought of Nell and the secrets she'd kept. How could she have stood it, finally discovering who she really was and not telling a soul? "I wish my grandmother had seen the scrapbooks before she died. They would have meant so much to her, the closest thing possible to hearing her mother's voice."

"I've been thinking about your grandmother all week," said Julia. "Ever since you told me what happened I've been wondering what made Eliza take her."

"And? What do you reckon?"

"Envy," said Julia. "I come back to it every time. It's a bloody powerful motivator, and Lord knows there was enough to envy about Rose: her beauty, her talented husband, her birthright. Throughout their childhoods Eliza must have seen Rose as the little girl who had everything, particularly the things she didn't have. Wealthy parents, a beautiful house, a kind nature that people admired. Then, in adulthood, to see Rose marry so quickly, and to a man who must've been quite a catch, then fall pregnant, have a beautiful baby girl . . . Hell, *I* feel jealous of Rose! Imagine what it was like for Eliza—a bit of an odd bird by all accounts." She drained her drink, put the glass down emphatically. "I'm not excusing what she did, not at all, I'm just saying it doesn't surprise me."

"It's the most obvious answer, isn't it?"

"And the most obvious answer is usually the right one. It's all there in the scrapbooks—well, it's all there if you know what you're looking for. From the moment Rose found out she had a baby on the way, Eliza grew more distant. There's very little mention of Eliza after Ivory was born. It must've plagued Rose—Eliza was like a sister, and suddenly, in such a special time, she withdrew. Packed up and took herself away from Blackhurst."

"Where did she go?" said Cassandra, surprised.

"Overseas somewhere, I think." Julia frowned. "Though now you mention it, I'm not sure that Rose actually says"—she waved her hand—"and it's beside the point, really. The fact is, she went away while Rose was pregnant and didn't come back until after Ivory was born. Their friendship was never the same again."

CASSANDRA YAWNED and readjusted her pillow. Her eyes were tired but she was almost at the end of 1907 and it seemed a shame to put the scrapbook aside with only a handful of pages left to go. Besides, the sooner she read them, the better: while Julia had kindly agreed to the loan, Cassandra suspected that the separation would only be borne for a short time. Thankfully, where Nell's writing was scrawled, Rose's hand was steady and considered. Cassandra took a sip of tea, lukewarm now, and passed over pages filled with fabric, ribbon samples, wedding tulle and flourished autographs reading: *Mrs. Rose Mountrachet Walker, Mrs. Walker, Mrs. Rose Walker.* She smiled—certain things never changed—and turned to the last page.

I have just finished rereading *Tess of the D'Urbervilles.* It is a perplexing novel, and one which I cannot truly say that I enjoy. There is so much that is brutal in Hardy's fiction. It is too wild, I suppose, for my tastes: I am my mother's daughter, after all, despite my best intentions. Angel's conversion to Christianity, his marriage to Liza Lu, the death of poor baby Sorrow: these occurrences bother me, all. Why should Sorrow have been deprived of a Christian burial—babies aren't to blame for the sins of their parents, surely? Does Hardy approve of Angel's conversion or is he a Skeptic? And how could Angel transfer his affections so simply from Tess to her sister?

Ah well, such issues have perplexed greater minds than mine, and my purpose in turning again to the sad tale of poor, tragic Tess was not literary criticism. I confess I consulted Mr. Thomas Hardy in the hopes that he might offer some insight into what I might expect when Nathaniel and I are wed. More particularly, what might be expected of me. Oh! how it heats my cheeks even to think such questions in my mind! Certainly I could never find words to speak them. (Imagine Mamma's face!)

Alas, Mr. Hardy did not provide the answers I so hopefully sought. I had remembered incorrectly, Tess's defilement is covered in no great detail. So there it is. Unless I can think of somewhere else I might turn (not Mr. James, I think, nor Mr. Dickens), I will have little choice but to go blind into that dark abyss. My greatest fear is that Nathaniel will have cause to look upon my stomach. Surely it won't be so? Vanity is indeed a great sin, but alas I cannot help myself. For my marks are so ugly, and he so fond of my pale skin.

Cassandra read the last few lines over. What were these marks of which Rose spoke? Birthmarks perhaps? Scars? Had she read anything else in the scrapbooks that might elucidate the entry? Try as she might, Cassandra couldn't remember. It was too late and she too tired, her thoughts as blurred as her vision.

She yawned again, rubbed at her eyes and closed the scrapbook. Probably she'd never know, and in all likelihood it didn't matter. Cassandra ran her fingers again over the worn cover, just as Rose must have done many times before her. She placed the book on her bedside table and switched off the light. Closed her eyes and slid into a familiar dream about long grass, an endless field and, suddenly, unexpectedly, a cottage on the edge of an ocean cliff.

Thirty-six

NELL waited by the door, wondering whether she should knock again. She'd been standing on the doorstep for over five minutes and had begun to suspect that William Martin knew nothing of her impending arrival at his dinner table, that the invitation might have been little more than a ploy of Robyn's to smooth the waters after their previous encounter. Robyn seemed the type for whom social unpleasantness, no matter what its cause or consequence, might be intolerable.

She knocked again. Affected an expression of blithe dignity for the benefit of any of William's neighbors who might be wondering at the strange woman on his doorstep who seemed content to knock all night.

It was William himself who finally unhooked the latch. Tea towel over his knobbly shoulder, wooden spoon in hand, he said, "I hear you've gone and bought yourself that cottage."

"Good news travels fast."

He pressed his lips together, regarding her. "You're a bloody-minded lass, I could tell that a mile away."

"As God made me, I'm afraid."

He nodded, gave a little huff. "Come on, then. You'll catch your death out there."

Nell peeled off her waterproof jacket and found a peg on which to hang it. She followed William through the main door and into the sitting room.

The air was heavy, damp with steam, the smell at once nauseating and delicious. Fish and salt and something else.

"Got a pot of my morgy broth on the stove," said William, disappearing at a shuffle into the kitchen. "Couldn't hear you knocking over the bloody spits and spurts." A racket of pots and pans, a gruff curse. "Robyn'll be along shortly." Another clatter. "Got held up a time with that fellow of hers."

The last he uttered with some distaste. Nell followed him into the kitchen and watched as he stirred the lumpy broth. "You don't approve of Robyn's fiancé?"

He leaned his ladle on the countertop, replaced the saucepan lid and picked up his pipe. Plucked a lone strand of tobacco from the rim. "Nothing wrong with the lad. Nothing bar the fact he's not perfect." Hand supporting the small of his stooped back, he headed for the sitting room. "You have children? Grandchildren?" he said as he passed Nell.

"One of each."

"Then you know what I'm talking about."

Nell smiled grimly to herself. Twelve days had passed since she'd left Australia; she wondered whether Lesley had noticed her absence. It was unlikely—all the same, it struck Nell that she might send a postcard. The girl would like that, Cassandra. Children liked that sort of thing, didn't they?

"Come on, then, lass." William's voice from the sitting room. "Keep an old man company."

Nell, creature of habit, chose the same velvet chair as she had on the previous occasion. She nodded at William.

He nodded back.

They sat for a minute or so, in a performance of companionable silence. The wind had picked up outside and the windowpanes rattled periodically, accentuating the dearth of conversation within.

Nell indicated the painting above the fireplace, a fisherman's boat with a red-and-white-striped hull and her name printed in black along the side. "That's yours? The *Piskie Queen*?"

" 'Tis indeed," said William. "Love of my life, I sometimes think. Saw each other through some mighty storms, she and I."

"You still have her?"

"Not for a few years now."

Another silence stretched out between them. William patted his shirt pocket, then withdrew a pouch of tobacco, started refilling his pipe.

"My father was portmaster," said Nell. "I grew up around ships." She had a sudden image of Hugh, standing on the Brisbane wharf sometime after the war, the sun behind him and he in eclipse, long Irish legs and large strong hands. "Gets into your blood, doesn't it?"

"That it does."

The windowpanes chattered again and Nell exhaled. Enough was enough, it was now or never, and numerous other handy clichés: the air needed clearing and Nell was the one to do it, there was only so much small talk she was prepared to make. "William," she said, leaning forward to rest her elbows on her knees, "about the other night, what I said. I didn't mean to—"

He raised a work-hardened palm, slightly shaky. "No matter."

"But I shouldn't have—"

" 'Twas nothing." He clamped his pipe between his back teeth and thereby closed the matter. He struck a match.

Nell leaned back into her chair: if that was the way he wanted it, so be it, but she was determined, this time, not to leave without another piece of the puzzle. "Robyn said there was something you wanted to tell me."

The sweet scent of fresh tobacco as William sucked a couple of times, then puffed to get his pipe smoking. He nodded slightly. "Should have told you the other night, only"—he was focused on something beyond her and Nell fought the urge to turn and see what it was—

"only, you caught me by surprise. It's been a long time since I heard her name spoke."

Eliza Makepeace. The unspoken sibilant shimmered its silver wings between them.

"Been more than sixty years since last I saw her, but I can picture her right enough, coming down the cliff from the cottage up there, striding into the village, hair loose behind her." His eyelids had closed as he spoke, but now he opened them and eyeballed Nell. "I expect that doesn't mean much to you, but back then . . . Well, it wasn't often that one of the folk from the grand house lowered themselves to mix among the villagers. Eliza, though"—he cleared his throat a little, repeated the forename—"Eliza behaved as if it were the most natural thing in the world. She wasn't like the rest of them."

"You met her?"

"Knew her well, as well as one could know the likes of her. Met her when she was just eighteen. My little sister, Mary, worked up at the house and brought Eliza with her for one of her afternoons off."

Nell fought hard to contain the thrill. Finally to be speaking with someone who had known Eliza. Better yet, to have his description confirm the illicit sense that flirted on the rim of her own patchy memories. "What was she like, William?"

He pressed his lips together and scratched at his chin: the whiskery sound caught Nell by surprise. For a split second she was five years old again, sitting on Hugh's lap, head resting against his bristled cheek. William smiled broadly, teeth large and rimmed with tobacco brown. "Like no one you've met before, an original. We all of us around here like to tell stories, but hers were something else. She was funny, courageous, unexpected."

"Beautiful?"

"Yes, and beautiful." His eyes met hers fleetingly. "She had this red hair. Long it was, all the way to her waist. Strands that turned golden in the sun." He indicated with his pipe. "She liked to sit on that black rock in the cove, looking out to sea. On a clear day, we'd be able to see her as we were coming back to port. She'd lift her hand and wave, looking for all the world like the Queen of the Piskies."

Nell smiled. The *Piskie Queen*. "Like your boat."

William pretended fascination with the corduroy grooves of his trousers, grunted a little.

Realization crowned: this was no coincidence.

"Robyn should be here soon." He didn't glance at the door. "We'll have us some tea."

"You named your boat for her?"

William's lips parted, closed again. He sighed, the sigh of a young man.

"You were in love with her."

His shoulders sagged. "Course I was," he said. "Just like every fellow who ever laid eyes on her. I told you, she was different from anyone you'd ever met. The things that govern the rest of us didn't matter one whit to her. She did as she felt, and she felt a great deal."

"And did she, were you and she ever—"

"I was engaged to someone else." His attention shifted to a photograph on the wall, a young couple in wedding clothes, she sitting, he standing behind. "Cecily and I, we'd been steady for a couple of years by then. A village like this, that's what happens. You grow up next door to a girl, and one day you're kids rolling stones off the cliff, next thing you know you're three years married with another baby on the way." He sighed so that his shoulders deflated and his sweater seemed too large. "When I met Eliza the world shifted. Can't describe it better than that. Like a magic spell, she was all I could think of." He shook his head. "I was that fond of Cec, loved her true, but I'd have left her in a moment." His gaze met Nell's before shifting quickly away. "Doesn't make me proud to say that, sounds awful disloyal. And it was, it was." He looked at Nell. "But you can't blame a young man for his honest feelings, can you?"

His eyes searched hers and Nell felt something inside her buckle.

She understood: he'd been seeking absolution a long time. "No," she said. "No, you can't."

He breathed a sigh, spoke so softly that Nell had to turn her head to the side to hear. "Sometimes the body wants things the mind can't explain, can't even accept. My every foolish thought was of Eliza, I couldn't help myself. It was like a, like an—"

"Addiction?"

"Just like that. I figured I could only ever be happy if it were with her."

"Did she feel the same way?"

He raised his brows and smiled ruefully. "You know, for a time I thought she did. She had a way about her, an intensity. A habit of making you feel that there was nowhere she'd rather be and no one she'd rather be with." He laughed, a little unkindly. "Soon enough learned my error."

"What happened?"

He pressed his lips together and for an awful second Nell thought the story had dried up. She breathed a sigh of relief when he continued. "A spring night, it was. Must've been 1908 or 1909. I'd had a big day on the boats, brought in a huge haul and I'd been out celebrating with some of the other lads. I'd got a bit of Dutch courage into me and on my way home I found myself heading up along the cliff edge. Foolhardy thing to do—it was just a narrow path back then, hadn't yet been turned into a road and was barely fit for a mountain goat, but I didn't care. I'd got it into my head that I was going to ask her to marry me." His voice quivered. "But when I got near the cottage I saw through the window . . ."

Nell leaned forward.

He sat back. "Well, you've heard this tale before."

"She was with someone else?"

"Not just any someone else." His lips trembled a little around the words. "One that was family to her." William rubbed at the edge of his eye, checked his finger for a phantom irritant. "They were . . ." He glanced at Nell. "Well, you can imagine right enough."

A noise outside and a burst of cool air. Robyn's voice drifted in from the hallway. "It's grown cold out there." She stepped into the sitting room. "Sorry I'm late." She looked hopefully between the two of them, running her hands over mist-damp hair. "Everything all right in here?"

"Couldn't be better, my girl," said William, with a quick glance at Nell.

Nell nodded slightly. She had no intention of divulging an old man's secret.

"Just about to dish up my broth," said William. "Come and give your Gump's sore old eyes a sight of you."

"Gump! I told you I'd fix the tea. I brought everything with me."

"Humph," he grumbled, pushing himself out of the chair and catching his balance. "Once you and that fellow get going, there's no telling when you'll remember your old Gump, if at all. Figured if I didn't look out for myself I stood a good chance of going hungry."

"Oh, Gump," she scolded as she carried her shopping bag to the kitchen. "Really, you are the limit. When have I ever forgotten you?"

"It's not you, my dear." He shuffled after her. "It's that fellow of yours. Like all lawyers, he's a windbag."

While the two of them argued familiarly about whether or not it was beyond William's physical abilities to cook and dish up broth, Nell sorted mentally through all that William had told her. She understood now why he was so adamant about the cottage being tainted somehow, sad; and no doubt for him it was. But William had become sidetracked by his own confession and it was up to Nell to steer him back in the direction she needed to go. And no matter her own curiosity as to whom Eliza had been with that night, it was beside the point and pushing William would only cause him to withdraw. She couldn't risk that, not before she found out why Eliza might have taken her from Rose and

Nathaniel Walker, why she'd been sent to Australia and a completely different life.

"Here we go." Robyn appeared carrying a tray loaded with three steaming bowls.

William followed, somewhat sheepishly, and eased himself into his chair. "I still make the best morgy broth this side of Polperro."

Robyn raised her eyebrows at Nell. "No one's disputing that, Gump," she said, handing a bowl across the coffee table.

"Just my ability to carry it from kitchen to table."

Robyn sighed theatrically. "Let us help you, Gump, that's all we ask."

Nell ground her teeth; she needed to keep this argument from escalation, she couldn't risk losing William again to pique. "Delicious," she said loudly, tasting the broth. "Perfect amount of Worcestershire sauce."

William and Robyn both blinked at her, spoons hovering at half-mast.

"What?" Nell looked between them. "What is it?"

Robyn opened her mouth, closed it again like a fish. "The Worcestershire sauce."

"It's our secret ingredient," said William. "Been in the family for generations."

Nell shrugged apologetically. "My mum used to make morgy broth, so did her mum. They always used Worcestershire sauce. I guess it was our secret ingredient, too."

William inhaled slowly through wide nostrils and Robyn bit her lip.

"It's delicious, though," said Nell taking another slurp. "Getting the amount right, that's the trick."

"Tell me, Nell," said Robyn, clearing her throat, assiduously avoiding William's eyes. "Was there anything of use in those papers I gave you?"

Nell smiled gratefully. Robyn to the rescue. "They were very interesting. I enjoyed the newspaper article about the *Lusitania* launch."

Robyn beamed. "It must have been so exciting, an important launch like that. Terrible to think of what happened to that beautiful ship."

"Germans," said Gump, through a mouthful of broth. "Sacrilege, that was, a mighty act of barbarism."

Nell imagined the Germans felt much the same way about the bombing of Dresden, but now was neither the time nor the place, and William not the person with whom to have such a discussion. So she bit her tongue and carried on pleasant, pointless conversation with Robyn about the history of the village and the house at Blackhurst until, finally, Robyn excused herself to clear the plates and fetch some pudding.

Nell watched her bustle from the room, then, aware that it might be her last chance to speak with William alone, she seized the opportunity. "William," she said, "there's something I have to ask you."

"Ask away."

"You knew Eliza . . ."

He sucked on his pipe, nodded once.

". . . So why do you think she took me? Did she want a child, do you think?"

William exhaled so that smoke plumed. He clenched the pipe in his back teeth and spoke around it. "Doesn't sound right to me. She was a free spirit. Not the sort to welcome domestic responsibility, let alone steal it."

"Was there any talk in the village? Did anyone have a theory?"

"We all believed that the child, that you, had fallen to the scarlet fever. No one questioned that part." He shrugged. "As for Eliza's disappearance, no one thought much of that, either. It wasn't the first time."

"No?"

"She'd done the same a few years before." He glanced quickly towards the kitchen and lowered his voice, avoided Nell's eyes. "Always blamed myself a bit for that. It was soon after—soon after the other thing I was telling you about. I confronted her, told her what I'd seen; called her all manner of names. She made me promise not to tell any-one, told me that I didn't understand, that it wasn't as it seemed." He laughed bitterly. "All the usual things a woman says when caught in such a situation."

Nell nodded.

"I did as she asked, though, and kept her secret. Not long after that I learned in the village that she'd gone away."

"Where did she go?"

He shook his head. "When she finally got back—a year or so later, it was—I asked her over and over, but she never would say."

"Pudding's up," came Robyn's voice from the kitchen.

William leaned forward, pulled his pipe from his mouth and pointed it at Nell. "That's why I had Robyn ask you here tonight, that's what I wanted to tell you: find out where Eliza went, and I reckon you'll be some of the way to figuring out your riddle. Because I can tell you something, wherever it was she disappeared to, she was different when she came back."

"Different how?"

He shook his head at the memory. "Changed, less herself some-how." He exhaled, clenched his teeth on his pipe. "There was some-thing missing and she was never the same again."

PART THREE

THIRTY-SEVEN

ON the morning scheduled for Rose's return from New York, Eliza went early to the hidden garden. The November sun was still shrugging off sleep and the way was dim, light just enough to reveal the grass, silver with dew. She went quickly, arms wrapped across her front against the chill. It had rained overnight and puddles lay all about; she stepped around them as best she could, then creaked open the maze gate and started through. It was darker still within the thick hedge walls, but Eliza could have navigated the maze in her sleep.

Ordinarily she loved the brief moment of twilight as night anticipated dawn, but today she was too distracted to pay it any heed. Ever since she'd received Rose's letter announcing her engagement, Eliza had battled with her emotions. The spiked barb of envy had lodged in her stomach and refused to grant her rest. Each day, when her thoughts turned to Rose, when she reread the letter, felt her imaginings slide towards the future, fear prickled her insides. Filled her with their dread poison.

For with Rose's letter, the color of Eliza's world had changed. Like the kaleidoscope in the nursery that had so delighted her when she first came to Blackhurst, one twist and the same pieces were rearranged to create a vastly different picture. Where a week ago she had felt secure, enveloped in the certainty that she and Rose were irrevocably tied, now she feared herself alone again.

By the time she entered the hidden garden, early light was sifting through the autumn-sparse canopy. Eliza took a deep breath. She'd come to the garden because it was the place in which she always felt settled, and today more than ever she needed it to work its magic.

She ran her hand along the little iron seat, beaded with rain, and perched on its damp edge. The apple tree was fruiting, shiny globes of orange and pink. She could pick some for Cook, or perhaps she should tidy the borders, or trim the honeysuckle. Apply herself in some way that would take her mind from Rose's arrival, the resistant fear that her cousin would be somehow changed when she returned.

For in the days since Rose's letter, as Eliza had grappled with her envy, she had realized that it wasn't the man, Nathaniel Walker, whom she feared; it was Rose's love for him. The marriage she could bear, but not a shift in Rose's affection. Eliza's greatest worry was that Rose, who had always loved her best, had found a replacement and would no longer need her cousin most of all.

She forced herself to stroll casually and appraise her plants. The wisteria was shedding its final leaves, the jasmine had long lost its flowers, but the autumn had been mild and the pink roses were still in bloom. Eliza went closer, took a half-opened bud between her fingers and smiled at the perfect raindrop caught within its inner petals.

The thought was sudden and complete. She must make a bouquet, a welcome-home gift for Rose. Her cousin was fond of flowers, but more than that, Eliza would select plants that were a symbol of their bond. There must be ivy for friendship, pink rose for happiness, and some of the exotic oak-leaved geranium for memories . . .

Eliza chose each sprig carefully, making sure to pick only the finest stems, the most perfect blooms, then she gathered the little bouquet together with a pink satin ribbon torn from her hem. She was tightening the bow when she heard the familiar sound of metal wheels jangling on the distant driveway stones.

They were back. Rose was home.

With her heart in her throat, Eliza hitched up her damp-hemmed skirts, clutched the bouquet, and began to run. Zigzagging back and forth through the maze. She splashed through puddles in her haste, pulse hammering apace with the horses' hooves.

She emerged from the gates just in time to see the carriage draw to a stop in the turning circle. Paused a moment to catch her breath. Uncle Linus was sitting, as always, on the garden seat by the maze gate, his little brown camera beside him. But when he called to her, Eliza pretended not to hear.

She arrived at the turning circle as Newton was opening the carriage door. He winked and Eliza waved back. Pressed her lips together as she waited.

Since receiving Rose's letter, long days had bled into longer nights, and now the moment was finally upon her. Time seemed to slow: she was aware of her hurried breaths, her pulse still racing in her ears.

Did she imagine the change in Rose's facial expression, the shift in her bearing?

The bouquet slipped from Eliza's fingers and she picked it up from the wet lawn.

The motion must have caught their peripheral vision, for both Rose and Aunt Adeline turned; one smiled, the other did not.

Eliza raised her hand slowly and waved. Lowered it again.

Rose's eyebrows lifted with amusement. "Well, aren't you going to welcome me home, Cousin?"

Relief spread instantly beneath Eliza's skin. Her Rose was back and all would surely be well. She started forward, began to run, arms outstretched. Wrapped Rose in an embrace.

"Stand back, girl," said Aunt Adeline. "You're covered in mud splatter. You'll mark Rose's dress."

Rose smiled and Eliza felt the sharp edges of her worry retract. Of course Rose was unaltered. She had been away only two and a half months. Eliza had allowed fear to conspire with absence and effect an impression of change where there was none.

"Cousin Eliza, how wonderful it is to see you!"

"And you, Rose." Eliza presented the bouquet.

"How delightful!" Rose lifted it to her nose. "From your garden?"

"It's ivy for friendship, oak-leaved geranium for memories—"

"Yes, yes, and rose, I see. How darling of you, Eliza." Rose held the bouquet out towards Newton. "Have Mrs. Hopkins find a vase, won't you, Newton?"

"I've so much to tell you, Rose," said Eliza. "You'll never guess what's happened. One of my stories—"

"Goodness me!" Rose laughed. "I haven't even reached the front door and my Eliza is telling me fairy tales."

"Stop tiring your cousin," said Aunt Adeline sharply. "Rose needs to rest." She glanced towards her daughter and a quaver of hesitation entered her voice. "You should consider lying down."

"Of course, Mamma. I intend to retire directly."

The change was subtle, but Eliza noted it nonetheless. There was something unusually tentative in Aunt Adeline's suggestion, something less pliant in Rose's response.

Eliza was still pondering this slight shift when Aunt Adeline started into the house and Rose leaned close, whispered in Eliza's ear, "Now, come upstairs, dearest. There's so much *I* have to tell *you*."

AND TELL Rose did. She recounted every moment spent in Nathaniel Walker's company and, more tediously, the anguish of each moment spent away from him. The epic tale began that afternoon and continued through night and day. In the beginning Eliza was able to feign interest—indeed, at the very first she *had* been interested, for the feelings Rose described were like none she'd ever felt herself—but as the days wore on, grouped themselves into weeks, Eliza began to flag. She tried to interest Rose in other things—a visit to the garden, the newest story she had written, even a trip to the cove—but Rose had ears only for tales of love and forbearance. Specifically, her own . . .

So it was, as the weeks cooled towards midwinter Eliza sought more frequently the cove, the hidden garden, the cottage. Places into which she could disappear, where servants would think twice before bothering her with their dreaded messages, always the same: Miss Rose requires Miss Eliza's presence immediately on a matter of dire import. For it seemed that no matter how spectacularly Eliza failed to grasp the virtues of one wedding dress over another, Rose never tired of tormenting her.

Eliza told herself that all would settle down, that Rose was just excited: she had always loved fashions and decorations, and here was her chance to play the fairy princess. Eliza just needed to be patient and all would return to normal between them.

Then it was spring again. The birds returned from the bright beyond, Nathaniel arrived from New York, the wedding was upon them, and next thing Eliza knew she was waving at the rear of Newton's carriage as it drew the happy couple towards London and a ship to the Continent.

LATER THAT night, as she lay in her own bed in the bleak house, Eliza felt Rose's absence sharply. The knowledge formed clearly and simply: Rose would never again come to her room at night, neither would Eliza go to Rose. They would no longer lie together and giggle and tell stories while the rest of the house slept. A special room was being prepared for the newlyweds in a distant wing of the house. A larger room, with a view of the cove, far more befitting a married couple. Eliza turned onto her side. In the darkness she glimpsed finally how unbearable it would be to know herself beneath the same roof as Rose and yet be unable to seek her out.

The next day, Eliza sought her aunt. Found her in the morning room, writing at the narrow desk. Aunt Adeline made no acknowledgment of Eliza's presence, but Eliza spoke regardless.

"I wondered, Aunt, whether certain items might not be spared from the attic."

"Items?" said Aunt Adeline, without shifting her attention from the letter she was penning.

"It is only a desk and chair that I require, and a bed—"

"A bed?" Cold eyes narrowed as her gaze swept sideways to meet Eliza's.

In the clarity of night, Eliza had realized that it was better to make changes for oneself than try to mend holes torn by the decisions of others. "Now that Rose is married, it occurs to me that my presence might be less required in the house. That I might take up residence in the cottage."

Eliza's expectations were low: Aunt Adeline drew particular pleasure from issuing denials. She watched as her aunt signed her letter with a careful signature, then scratched sharp fingernails on her hound's head. Her lips stretched into what Eliza took to be a smile, albeit slight, then she stood and rang the bell.

THE FIRST night in her new abode Eliza sat by the upstairs window, watching the ocean swelling and subsiding like a great drop of mercury beneath the moon's lambent light. Rose was across that sea, somewhere on the other side. Once more her cousin had traveled by ship and Eliza had been left behind. Someday, though, Eliza would set sail on her own journey. The magazine didn't pay much for her fairy tales, but if she kept writing and saved for a year, then surely she would be able to afford the voyage. And there was the brooch, of course, with its colored gems. Eliza had never forgotten Mother's brooch, tucked away inside the Swindells' fireplace. One day, somehow, she intended to retrieve it.

She thought of the advertisement she'd seen in the newspaper the week before. *People wanted to travel to Queensland,* it had said. *Come and begin a new life.* Mary had often spun tales of her brother's adventures in the town of Maryborough. To hear her tell it, Australia was a land of open spaces and blinding sun, where the rules of society were flouted by most and opportunity abounded for all to start afresh. Eliza had always imagined that she and Rose might travel together, they had spoken of it many times. Or had they? Looking back, she realized Rose's voice had been quiet when conversation touched upon such imagined adventures.

Eliza stayed at the cottage every night. She bought her own produce from the market in the village; her young fisherman friend, William, made sure she was well supplied with fresh whiting; and Mary dropped by most afternoons on her way home from work at Blackhurst, always bringing a bowl of Cook's soup, some cold meat from the luncheon roast, and news from the house.

Apart from such visits, for the first time in her life Eliza was truly alone. In the beginning, unfamiliar sounds, nocturnal sounds, disturbed her, but as the days passed she came to know them: soft-pawed animals under the eaves, the ticking of the warming range, floorboards shivering in the cooling nights. And there were unexpected benefits to her solitary life: alone in the cottage, Eliza discovered that the characters from her fairy tales became bolder. She found fairies playing in the spiders' webs, insects whispering incantations on the windowsills, fire sprites spitting and hissing in the range. Sometimes in the afternoons, Eliza would sit in the rocking chair listening to them. And late at night, when they were all asleep, she would spin their stories into her own tales.

One morning in the fourth week, Eliza took her writing pad into the garden and sat in her favorite spot, the tuft of soft grass beneath the apple tree. A story idea had gripped her and she began to scribble it down: a brave princess who forsook her birthright and accompanied her maid on a long journey, a dangerous voyage to a wild and wicked land where danger thrived. Eliza was just about to send her heroine into the webbed cave of a particularly spiteful piskie, when a bird flew to perch in the branch above her and began to sing.

"Is that so?" said Eliza, laying down her pen.

The bird sang again.

"I agree, I'm rather peckish myself." She plucked one of the few remaining apples from a low branch, polished it on her dress and took a bite. "It really is delicious," she said as the bird flew away. "You're most welcome to try one."

"I might take you up on that."

Eliza paused midcrunch and sat very still, staring at the place where the bird had been.

"I should have brought my own, only I didn't think I'd be here so long."

She scanned the garden, and blinked when she saw a man sitting on the iron garden seat. He was so utterly out of context that, though they'd met before, it took her a moment to place him. The dark hair and eyes, the easy smile . . . Eliza inhaled sharply. It was Nathaniel Walker, who had married Rose. Sitting in *her* garden.

"You certainly look to be enjoying your apple," he said. "Watching you is almost as satisfying as having one myself."

"I don't like to be watched."

He smiled. "Then I shall avert my eyes."

"What are you doing here?"

Nathaniel held up a pristine novel. "*Little Lord Fauntleroy.* Ever read it?"

She shook her head.

"Neither have I, despite hours of trying. And I hold you partly to blame, Cousin Eliza. Your garden is too distracting. I've been sitting here all morning and still I haven't ventured much beyond the first chapter."

"I thought you were in Italy."

"And so we were. We returned a week early."

A chill shadow fell instantly across Eliza's skin. "Rose is home?"

"Of course." He smiled openly. "I hope you don't suggest I might have lost my wife to the Italians!"

"But when did she—" Eliza swiped loose strands of hair from her forehead, tried to understand. "When did you arrive back?"

"Monday afternoon. A mightily choppy sea voyage."

Three days. They had been back three days and Rose had not sent word. Eliza's stomach tightened. "Rose. Is Rose all right?"

"Never better. The Mediterranean climate agreed with her. We'd have stayed the full week, only she wanted to be involved with the garden party." He raised his brows with affectionate theatricality. "To hear Rose and her mother speak, I fear it's going to be something of an extravaganza."

Eliza hid her confusion behind another bite of apple, then tossed the core away. She'd heard mention of a garden party but had presumed it was one of Adeline's society things: nothing to do with Rose.

Nathaniel lifted the book again. "Hence my choice of reading matter. Mrs. Hodgson Burnett will be in attendance." His eyes widened. "Why, you must be looking forward to meeting her. I imagine there'd be great pleasure gained from speaking with another authoress."

Eliza rolled the corner of her piece of writing paper between her thumb and forefinger, didn't meet his eyes. "Yes . . . I expect so."

A note of apology curled the edges of his voice. "You are coming, of course? I'm certain Rose spoke of you attending. The party is to be held on the oval lawn, Saturday afternoon at two."

Eliza scribbled a vine around the margin of her page. Rose knew she did not care for parties, that's all it was. Thoughtful Rose, sparing Eliza the agony of Aunt Adeline's society.

Nathaniel's voice was gentle. "Rose speaks often of you, Cousin Eliza. I feel that I know you myself." He gestured with his hand. "She told me of your garden, that's why I came today. I had to see for myself whether it was really as beautiful as she painted it with words."

Eliza met his eyes briefly. "And?"

"It is everything she said and more. As I say, I blame the garden for distracting me from my reading. There is something in the way the light falls that makes me want to render it on paper. I have scribbled all over my book's frontispiece." He smiled. "Don't tell Mrs. Hodgson Burnett."

"I planted the garden for Rose and myself." Eliza's voice was odd to her own ears, she had become used to being alone. She felt ashamed, too, of the transparent sentiments she was expressing, and yet had no power to stop herself speaking them. "So that we might have a secret place, a place where no one else could find us. Where Rose might have an outside place to sit even when she was unwell."

"Rose is fortunate indeed to have a cousin who cares for her as you do. I must extend my eternal gratitude that you kept her so well for me. We are something of a team, you and I, are we not?"

No, Eliza thought, we are not. Rose and I are a pair, a team. You are additional. Temporary.

He stood, brushed off his trousers and held the book before his heart. "And now I must bid you fond farewell. Rose's mother is one for rules and I suspect will not gladly tolerate my tardy appearance at the dinner table."

Eliza, who had followed him to the gate, watched him go. She closed it behind him, then sat on the edge of the seat. Shifted along so as not to sit where he had left the metal warm. There was nothing to dislike in Nathaniel and for that she disliked him. Their encounter left a cold weight on her chest. It was his mention of the garden party, and Rose, his confidence in the quality of her affection. The gratitude he had extended to Eliza, though perfectly kindly expressed, left her in little doubt that he considered her an adjunct. And now, to have penetrated her garden, found his way so easily through her maze—

Eliza shook such thoughts from her mind. She would return to her fairy tale. The princess was just about to follow her faithful maid down into the piskie's cave. By such means would this unsettling meeting be forgotten.

But try as she might, Eliza's enthusiasm had fled and taken her inspiration with it. A plot that had filled her with glee when she began was now revealed as flimsy and transparent. Eliza scratched out what she'd written. It would not do. And yet, whichever way she twisted the plot, she couldn't make it work, for which fairy-tale princess ever chose her maid over her prince?

THE SUN shone just as brilliantly as if Adeline had put in an order with the Lord. The extra lilies arrived on time and Davies raided the gardens for more exotic species with which to gild the arrangements. The nocturnal shower that had kept Adeline awake and anxious had succeeded only in adding sparkle to the garden, so that each leaf looked to have been polished specially, and across the spill of new-pressed lawn, cushioned chairs were artfully perched. Hired waiters stood in lines by the stairs, models of calm and control, while in the kitchen, far from sight and mind, Cook and her team worked apace.

The guests had been arriving in the turning circle for the past quarter of an hour, and Adeline had been on hand to greet them and usher them in the direction of the lawn. How grand they looked in their fine hats—though none so fine as Rose's, brought back specially from Milan.

From where she now stood, concealed by a giant rhododendron, Adeline surveyed the guests. Lord and Lady Ashfield sitting with Lord Irving-Brown; Sir Arthur Mornington sipping tea by the croquet set, while the young Churchills laughed and played; Lady Susan Heuser involved in a tête-à-tête with Lady Caroline Aspley.

Adeline smiled to herself. She had done well. Not only was the garden party a fitting way to welcome home the newlyweds, Adeline's careful selection of connoisseurs, gossips and social climbers ensured the best opportunity for disseminating word of Nathaniel's portraiture. Along the walls of the entrance hall she'd had Thomas hang the works she deemed finest, and later, when tea had been served, she planned to usher select guests through. In this way would her new son-in-law be introduced as subject matter for the ready pens of art's critics and the quick tongues of society's fashion makers.

All Nathaniel had to do was charm the guests half as comprehensively as he had charmed Rose. Adeline scanned the group and spotted her daughter sitting with Nathaniel and the American, Mrs. Hodgson Burnett. Adeline had debated inviting Mrs. Hodgson Burnett, for where one divorce was unfortunate, two seemed terribly close to godlessness. But the writer was indubitably well connected on the Continent, and therefore, Adeline had decided, her potential assistance outweighed her infamy.

Rose laughed at something the woman said and warm waves of satisfaction welled inside Adeline. Rose was looking spectacularly beautiful today, as radiant as the wall of roses that provided her a glorious backdrop. She looked joyous, Adeline thought, as a young woman ought when marriage sat newly upon her, and the vows of commitment had only shortly crossed her lips.

Her daughter laughed again and Nathaniel pointed in the direction of the maze. Adeline hoped they weren't wasting precious time discussing the walled garden or some other of Eliza's nonsense when they should be speaking of Nathaniel's portraiture. For, oh, what an unexpected gift from providence, the removal of Eliza!

During the weeks of party preparation, Adeline had lain awake night after night wondering how best to prevent the girl upsetting the day. What blessed surprise the morning she had appeared by Adeline's writing desk, requesting relocation to the distant cottage. To her credit, Adeline had managed to keep veiled the joy she felt. Eliza safely ensconced in the cottage was an eminently more desirable arrangement than anything Adeline would have managed to contrive, and the removal had been complete. Adeline had seen neither hide nor hair of the girl since she'd left; the entire house was lighter and more spacious. Finally, after seven long years, she was freed from the suffocating gravity of that girl's orbit.

The greatest sticking point had been determining how to convince Rose that Eliza's exclusion was for the best. Poor Rose had always been blind where Eliza was concerned, had never perceived in her the threat Adeline knew was there. Indeed, one of the first things the dear girl did upon returning from her honeymoon was to inquire about her cousin's absence. When Adeline provided a judicious explanation as to why Eliza was now living in the cottage, Rose had frowned—it seemed so sudden, she said—and resolved to call on Eliza first thing the following day.

Such a visit was unthinkable, of course, if Adeline's small deception was to play out as planned. So it was, immediately after breakfast the following morning, that Adeline sought out Rose in her new room, where she was busy assembling a delicate arrangement of flowers. While Rose plucked a cream clematis from among the others, Adeline asked, casually and calmly, "Do you think Eliza should be invited to attend the garden party?"

Rose turned, the clematis dripping water from the end of its stalk. "But of course she must come, Mamma. Eliza is my dearest friend."

Adeline pressed her lips together: it was the response she had anticipated and thus she was prepared. The appearance of capitulation is always a calculated risk, and Adeline deployed it knowingly. A sequence of lines she'd prepared earlier, repeated over and over beneath her breath so that they fell naturally from her lips. "Of course, my dear. And if you desire her presence, so it shall be. We will have no further discussion on the matter." Only after such generous and sweeping concession did she allow herself a wistful little sigh.

Rose had her back turned, a potent gardenia in her hand. "What is it, Mamma?"

"Nothing at all, dearest."

"Mamma?"

Carefully, carefully. "I was merely thinking of Nathaniel."

This drew Rose's gaze, sparked a blush. "Nathaniel, Mamma?"

Adeline stood, smoothing the front of her skirt. She smiled

brightly at Rose. "Never mind. I'm sure things will go just as well for him with Eliza in attendance."

"Of course they will." Rose hesitated before threading the gardenia into the arrangement. She didn't look again at Adeline but she didn't need to. Adeline could picture the uncertainty that creased her pretty face. Sure enough, the cautious question came: "Why ever should Nathaniel benefit from Eliza's absence?"

"Only that I had hoped to direct a certain amount of attention towards Nathaniel and his artworks. Eliza, blessed girl, has a way of stealing the focus. I was hoping the day might belong to Nathaniel, and to you, my darling. But of course you shall have Eliza there if you think it best." She laughed then—a light, gay laugh, practiced to perfection. "Besides, I dare say once Eliza learns you're home early she'll be over here so often that one of the servants will be bound to let slip about the party. And despite her aversion to society, her devotion to you, my dear, is such that she'll insist upon attending."

Adeline had left Rose then, had smiled to herself when she noted the stiff set to her daughter's shoulders. A clear sign that the shot had reached its mark.

Sure enough, Rose had appeared at Adeline's boudoir later the same day, had suggested that seeing as Eliza didn't enjoy parties, perhaps she might be spared attendance on this occasion. She'd continued in a quieter voice, said that she'd thought better of calling on her cousin today. She'd wait until after the garden party, when things had settled down and the two could have a longer visit.

An eruption of applause at the croquet drew Adeline's attention. She clapped her gloved hands and called up a gregarious smile, made her way back across the lawn. As she approached the sofa, Mrs. Hodgson Burnett stood and opened a white parasol. She nodded farewell to Rose and Nathaniel, and started off in the direction of the maze. Adeline hoped she didn't intend to enter; the maze gate had been closed earlier as an obvious discouragement, but it was just like an American to form her own ideas. Adeline increased her pace a little—searching for a lost guest had no place in her plans for the day—and intercepted Mrs. Hodgson Burnett before she managed to achieve a great distance. She bestowed on her guest a most gracious smile. "Good day, Mrs. Hodgson Burnett."

"Why, good day, Lady Mountrachet. And what a fine day it is, too."

That accent! Adeline smiled indulgently. "We couldn't have wished for better. And I see you've met the happy couple."

"Monopolized, more like. Your daughter is a most glorious creature."

"Thank you. I'm rather partial to her."

Polite laughter on both sides.

"And her husband clearly dotes," said Mrs. Hodgson Burnett. "Isn't young love grand?"

"I was *delighted* by the match. Such a talented gentleman"— the shadow of a pause—"of course, Nathaniel mentioned his portraits?"

"He did not. I dare say I didn't give him a chance. I was too busy quizzing them on the secret garden they say is hidden on this grand estate of yours."

"A trifle of a thing." Adeline smiled thinly. "A plot of flowers with a wall surrounding. There's one like it on every estate in England."

"Not with such romantic tales attached, I'm sure. A garden raised from ruins to help bring a delicate young lady back to health!"

Adeline laughed with brittle cheer. "Goodness! It would appear my daughter and her husband have told you quite a fairy tale. Rose owes her health to the efforts of a fine physician, and I must assure you the garden really is very ordinary. Nathaniel's portraits, on the other—"

"Nonetheless, I should love to see it. The garden, I mean. My interest has been piqued."

There was little Adeline could say to that. She nodded with as much grace as she could muster and cursed beneath her smile.

Adeline was all set to give Nathaniel and Rose a stern talking-to, when in her peripheral vision she caught a flurry of white fabric through the maze gates. She turned, just in time to see Eliza open the gate right into Mrs. Hodgson Burnett.

Her hand leaped to her mouth, caught the shriek before it was launched. Of all the days and of all the moments. That girl: always rushing, regrettably attired, certainly unwelcome. With her rude good health, flushed cheeks, tangled hair, ungainly hat, and—Adeline noted with horror—bare hands. Small mercy, she was wearing shoes.

Mouth tightening at the sides like that of a wooden puppet, Adeline glanced about, trying to assess the extent of the disturbance. A servant was at Mrs. Hodgson Burnett's side, helping her to a nearby chair. All else seemed calm, the day was not yet lost. Indeed, only Linus, sitting beneath the maple tree and ignoring old Lord Appleby's conversation, had paid the arrival any notice, lifting his boxy little photographic contraption to point it at Eliza. Eliza, for her part, was staring in Rose's direction, her face a study in consternation. Surprised, no doubt, to see her cousin home from the Continent so soon.

Adeline turned quickly, determined to spare her daughter upset. But Rose and Nathaniel were oblivious to the intrusion, too absorbed each with the other. Nathaniel had shifted to the edge of his chair and was seated so that his knees reached almost to touch (or did they make slight contact? Adeline couldn't tell) Rose's own. Between two fingertips he held one of Davies's hothouse strawberries by its stalk, was twirling the fruit this way and that, bringing it close to Rose's lips before withdrawing it once more. Each time Rose laughed, her chin tilted so that dappled sunlight stroked her bare throat.

Flushing, Adeline lifted her fan to block the sight. Such unsuitable display! What would people think? She could just imagine that gossip Caroline Aspley setting pen to paper as soon as she arrived home.

Adeline knew it was her duty to head off such wanton behavior, and yet . . . She lowered her fan once more, blinked over its rim. Try as she might, she couldn't turn away. Such ripeness! The freshness of the image was magnetic. Even though she knew Eliza was causing havoc behind her, even though her husband was behaving with no thought for propriety, it was as if the world had slowed and Adeline stood alone at its center, aware only of her own heartbeat. Her skin tingled, her legs grew unexpectedly weak, her breathing was shallow. The thought was hers before she had the chance to stop it: what must it be like, to be so loved?

THE SMELL of mercury vapor filled his nose and Linus breathed it deeply. He held it in, felt his mind expand, his eardrums burn, before finally exhaling. Alone in his darkroom, Linus was six feet tall, each leg as straight and as strong as the other. Using his silver tongs, he slid the photographic paper back and forth, watched closely as the image began to materialize.

She would never consent to pose. In the beginning he had insisted, then he had pleaded, then in time he had discerned the nature of her game. She enjoyed the chase, and it had been up to Linus to rethink his tactics.

Rethink them he had. Mansell had been dispatched to London for an Eastman Kodak Brownie—an ugly little thing, the province of unskilled amateurs, photographic quality nothing to his Tourograph, but it was light and portable and that was the thing. So long as Eliza continued her teasing, Linus knew it was the only way to catch her.

Her removal to the cottage was a bold step and one for which Linus gave her credit. He had gifted her the garden so that she might come to love it as her mother had before her—nothing had put light in his *poupée*'s eyes quite like the walled garden—but Linus had not foreseen this recent repatriation. Eliza hadn't been near the house for weeks. Day after day he waited by the maze gates, but she continued to torment him with her absence.

And now, to complicate matters further, Linus found he had an adversary. Three mornings ago, while maintaining his vigil, he'd been confronted with a most unpleasant sight. While he awaited Eliza, who had he seen coming through the maze gates in her stead but the painter, the new husband? Linus had been shocked, for what did the man think he was doing, passing through those gates? Treading boldly where Linus himself could never bear to go? Linus simmered with questions. Had he seen her? Spoken with her? Looked into her eyes? It was unthinkable, the painter sniffing about his prize.

But Linus had won in the end. Today, finally, his patience had paid off.

He inhaled. The image was coming. With only the small red light to see by, Linus leaned close. Dark surrounds—the maze hedges—but paler in the middle where she had faltered into frame. She had noticed him straight away and Linus had felt his neck warm with pleasure. Her wide eyes, parted lips, like an animal unexpectedly cornered.

Linus squinted into the pan of developing lotion. There she was. The white of her dress, the narrow waist—oh, how he longed to lay his fingers around it, feel her light breaths fluttering fearfully beneath her rib cage. And that neck, the pale, pale neck, its pulse flecking just like her mother's before her. Linus closed his eyes briefly and pictured his *poupée*'s neck with the red slice across it. She had tried to leave him, too.

HE'D BEEN in the darkroom when Georgiana had come that final time. He'd been cutting backing card in order to mount his newest selection of prints: grasshoppers of the West Country. He'd been excited about the photographs, had even considered asking Father whether he might permit a little exhibition, and would have tolerated very few interruptions. But Georgiana was an exception to most rules.

How ethereal, how perfect she'd looked, framed in his doorway, the lamp's flame enlivening her features. She'd lifted a finger to her lips and bade him catch his words before he spoke them, eased the door closed behind her. He'd watched her walking slowly towards him, a slight smile animating her lips. Her secrecy was one of the things that most excited him, being alone with his *poupée* provoked a tantalizing sense of collusion, rare for Linus, who had little time for others. For whom others had little time.

"You'll help me, won't you, Linus?" she'd said, eyes wide and clear. And then she'd started speaking about a man she'd met, a sailor. They were in love, going to be together, a secret from Mother and Father, he would help her, wouldn't he? Those eyes, imploring, uncomprehending of his pain. Time had stretched out between them, her words swirling in his mind, growing and shrinking, louder and softer. A lifetime of loneliness had gathered in an instant.

Without thinking twice, he'd lifted his hand, still clutching the penknife, and drawn it swiftly along her milky skin, made his pain her own . . .

LINUS USED his tweezers to hold the print closer to the light. Squinted, blinked. Damnation! Where Eliza's face should be was only white light, grey-flecked. She had moved at the precise moment he depressed the shutter. He hadn't been quick enough and she had vanished beneath his fingertip. Linus clenched his fist. Brought to mind, as he always did in spots of bother, that little girl who'd sat by him on the library floor, offered up her dolly and with it the promise of herself. Before she disappointed him.

Never matter. A mere setback, that's all it was, a temporary twist in the game they were playing, the game he had played with her mother. He had lost that time: after the incident with the penknife his Georgiana had vanished, never to return. But this time he would be more careful.

Whatever it took, however long he had to wait, Linus would prevail.

ROSE PLUCKED petals from the white daisy until none was left: boy, girl, boy, girl, boy, girl. She smiled and closed her fingers around the daisy's golden heart. A little daughter for Nathaniel and herself, and then perhaps a son, and then another of each.

Ever since she could remember, Rose had wanted a family of her own. A family very different from the cold and lonely arrangement she had known as a child, before Eliza came to Blackhurst. There would be closeness and, yes, love between the parents, and many children, brothers and sisters who would always look after one another.

Though these were her desires, Rose had been privy to enough discussions by grown-up ladies to have gleaned that while children were a blessing, the act of begetting them was a trial. Consequently, on the night of her wedding, she had expected the worst. When Nathaniel unpeeled her dress, removed the lace that Mamma had ordered specially, Rose held her breath, watched his face carefully. She was very nervous. Fear of the unknown combined with worry over her marks, and she sat holding her breath. Waiting for him to speak yet frightened that he might. He cast aside her dress and slip, still silent. Did not meet her gaze. Looked her over slowly and closely as one might a piece of art that one had always longed to see. His dark eyes were focused, his lips slightly parted. He lifted his hand and Rose shivered in anticipation; a fingertip traced lightly along her larger mark. The touch sent chills across Rose's stomach, down her inner thighs as well.

Later they made love, and Rose discovered that the ladies had been right, it was painful. But Rose was no stranger to pain, was quite able to step outside herself, so that the experience became something she observed rather than felt. She concentrated instead on the curious fact of his face, so close to her own—his closed eyes, smooth dark lids; full mouth held in an attitude she'd rarely glimpsed before; breaths grown quick and heavy—and Rose realized she was powerful. In all her years of ill health she had never identified herself as possessing strength. She was poor Rose, delicate Rose, weak Rose. But in Nathaniel's face Rose read desire, and that made her strong.

While on honeymoon, time had seemed to drop away. Where once there had been hours and minutes, now only days and nights, sun and moon, existed. It was a shock when they returned to England and found the increments of time awaiting them. A shock, too, resuming life at Blackhurst. Rose had become used to privacy in Italy, and found that she now resented the presence of others. The servants, Mamma, even Eliza, someone was always lurking around corners, seeking to steal her attention from Nathaniel. Rose would have liked a house of their own, where no one would ever disturb them, but she knew there would be time enough for that. And she understood that Mamma was right: Nathaniel was better able to meet the right people from Blackhurst, and the house itself was large enough for twenty men to live comfortably.

Just as well. Rose laid her hand gently across her stomach. She suspected they would have need of a nursery before much longer. All morning Rose had felt curious, like one in possession of a special secret. She was sure that such a momentous event should be like that, a woman aware instantly of the miracle of new life inside her body. Clutching the daisy's golden center, Rose headed back to the house, sun glorious on her back. She wondered when she should share the secret with Nathaniel. Smiled at the thought. How excited he would be! For when they had a child, then they would be complete.

Thirty-eight

And finally it seemed autumn had realized it was September. The last lingering days of summer had been pushed offstage and in the hidden garden long shadows stretched towards winter. The ground was littered with spent leaves, orange and pale green, and chestnuts in spiky coats sat proudly on the fingertips of cold branches.

Cassandra and Christian had worked all week in the cottage—untangling creepers, scrubbing mold-spotted walls, mending rotten floorboards. But because it was Friday, because each was as eager as the other, they'd agreed that the hidden garden should have some attention.

Christian was digging a hole where the southern gate had been, trying to reach the bottom of exceptionally large sandstone footings, and Cassandra had been crouched by the northern wall for two hours, pulling bracken from what must once have been a garden bed. The task reminded her of childhood weekends spent helping Nell pull weeds from her garden in Paddington, and Cassandra felt infused by a comforting sense of familiarity. She'd assembled a decent pile of leaves and roots behind her, but her pace was slowing. It was difficult not to be distracted in the hidden garden. Sliding beneath the wall was like entering a place outside time. It was the walls that did it, she supposed, though the sense of enclosure went beyond the physical. Things sounded different in here: the birds were louder and the leaves whispered in the breeze. Smells were stronger—damp fertility, sweet apples—and the air was clearer. The longer she spent in the garden, the more certain Cassandra was that she'd been right. This garden wasn't sleeping; it was very much awake.

The sun moved slightly, casting shafts of streaky light through the creepers overhead, and a shower of tiny yellow confetti leaves rained down from a nearby tree. Watching them flutter, gold in the ribbons of light, Cassandra was seized by an overwhelming urge to sketch, to capture on paper this magical contrast between light and dark. Her fingers twitched, imagining the strokes necessary to render the shafts linear, the shading required to convey transparency. The desire to sketch caught her off guard.

"Tea break?" On the other side of the garden Christian tossed his shovel against the wall. Lifted the bottom of his faded T-shirt and wiped the sweat from his forehead.

"Sounds good." She patted her gloved hands against her jeans to shake free the dirt and fern flecks, tried not to stare at his exposed stomach. "Your boil or mine?"

"Mine." He knelt in the patch they'd cleared in the middle of the garden and filled a saucepan with the remains of his water bottle.

Cassandra sat gingerly. A week of cleaning had left her calves stiff and her thighs sore. Not that she minded. Cassandra drew perverse pleasure from her aching body. It was the indisputable proof of her own physicality. She no longer felt invisible or fragile; she was heavier, far less likely to blow away on the breeze. And at night she fell quickly through the thick layers of sleep, woke to find night lying behind her in one solid dreamless drift.

"How's the maze been going?" she said as Christian set the saucepan on the little camping stove he'd brought. "Over at the hotel?"

"Not bad. Mike reckons we'll have it cleared by winter."

"Even with you spending so much time here?"

Christian smiled. "Predictably, Mike's got quite a lot to say about that." He tossed the residue of morning tea from the mugs and dangled a fresh bag over each rim.

"I hope you're not in trouble for helping me."

"Nothing I can't handle."

"I really appreciate how much you've done, Christian."

"It's nothing. I made a promise to help and I meant it."

"I know, and I'm really glad." She pulled her gloves off slowly. "All the same, I'll understand if you're too busy with other things."

"With my real job, you mean?" He laughed. "Don't worry. Mike's still getting his pound of flesh."

His real job. And there it was, the topic Cassandra had been wondering about but hitherto found herself unable to broach. Somehow, though, being in the garden today, she felt infused by an unusual spirit of come-what-may. A spirit something like Nell's. She drew an arc in the dirt with her heel. "Christian?"

"Cassandra?"

"I was just wondering"—she drew over the arc, added an echo beneath—"there's something I've been meaning to ask you, something Julia Bennett mentioned." She met his gaze but didn't hold it for long. "Why are you here in Tregenna, working for Michael, instead of being a doctor in Oxford?"

When Christian didn't answer she dared look at him again. His expression was difficult to read. He shrugged a little, smiled slightly. "Why are you here in Tregenna renovating a new house without your husband?"

Cassandra inhaled sharply, surprised as much as anything else. Without thinking, her fingers began their habitual worrying of her wedding band. "I . . . I'm . . ." Any number of evasive answers popped like bubbles on the tip of her tongue, then she heard a voice, not quite her own: "I don't have a husband. I did once, I just . . . There was an accident, Nick was—"

"Sorry. Look, you don't have to. I didn't mean to—"

"It's okay, I—"

"No. It's not." Christian ruffled his own hair, held out the palm of his hand. "I shouldn't have asked."

"It's all right. I asked first." And in a strange way that Cassandra couldn't articulate, even to herself, some small part of her was glad to have said the words. To have spoken Nick's name was a relief, made her feel less guilty somehow, that she was still here and he was not. That she was here, now, with Christian.

The saucepan was jiggling on the stove top, the water spitting. Christian tipped it sideways to fill the mugs, then tossed a teaspoon of sugar into each and stirred quickly. He handed one to Cassandra.

"Thanks." She wrapped her fingers around the warm tin and blew gently across its surface.

Christian took a sip, wincing as he burned his tongue.

Noisy silence stretched between them and Cassandra clutched at topical threads to weave the conversation back together. Caught none that seemed suitable.

Finally Christian spoke. "I think your grandma was lucky not to know her past."

Cassandra used the tip of her little finger to drag a fallen leaf fragment from her tea.

"It's a gift, don't you reckon, to be able to look forward and not back?"

She pretended interest in the rescued leaf. "In some ways."

"In most ways."

"Awful to forget the past entirely, though."

"Why?"

She glanced sideways, trying to ascertain whether or not he was being serious. No humor lurked in his expression. "Because then it would be like it never happened."

"But it did, nothing can change that."

"Yeah, but you wouldn't remember it."

"So?"

"So . . ." She flicked the leaf aside and shrugged lightly. "You need memories to keep things from the past alive."

"That's what I'm saying. Without memories everyone could just get on with it. Move on."

Cassandra's cheeks flared and she hid behind a gulp of tea. Then another. Christian was coaching her on the importance of relegating the past to history. She expected it from Nell and Ben, had learned to nod somberly when any of the aunts expressed similar sentiments, but this was different. She had been feeling so positive, so much lighter than usual, her outlines clear where they were usually smudged. She'd been enjoying herself. She wondered when precisely he'd pegged her as a lost cause in need of help. She felt embarrassed and, more than that, disappointed somehow.

She took another sip of tea and sneaked a glance at Christian. His attention was occupied by a stick he was threading with dried autumn leaves, and his expression was difficult to read. Preoccupied, certainly, but more than that: distracted, distant, lonely.

"Christian—"

"I met Nell once, you know."

She was caught off guard. "My grandma, Nell?"

"I presume it was her. Can't think who else it would have been, and the dates seem about right. I was eleven, so it must've been 1975. I'd come up here to get away, and I was just disappearing under the wall when someone grabbed my foot. I didn't realize it was a person at first, I thought for a second that my brothers had been telling the truth when they said the cottage was haunted, that some ghost or witch was going to turn me into a toadstool." His lips twitched into a half-smile, and he crunched a leaf in his fist, sprinkling the debris on to the ground. "But it wasn't a ghost, it was an old woman with a strange accent and a sad face."

Cassandra pictured Nell's face. Had it been sad? Formidable, yes, not given to unnecessary warmth, but sad? She couldn't tell; its familiarity made such critique impossible.

"She had silver hair," he said, "tied up high."

"In a knot."

He nodded, smiled slightly, then tipped his mug upside down to empty the dregs. Tossed his threaded stick aside. "Are you any closer to solving her mystery for her?"

Cassandra exhaled slowly; there was definitely something unsettled about Christian this afternoon. His mood reminded her of the shafts of light filtering through the creepers. It was ungraspable, shimmering, changeable somehow. "Not really. Rose's scrapbooks didn't contain the revelation I hoped they might."

"No entry entitled: 'Why Eliza Might Someday Take My Child'?" He smiled.

"Unfortunately not."

"At least you've had some interesting bedtime reading."

"If only I didn't fall asleep as soon as my head hit the pillow."

"It's the sea air," said Christian, standing up and fetching his shovel once again. "It's good for the soul."

That felt true enough. Cassandra stood, too. "Christian," she said, shaking her gloves, "about the scrapbooks."

"Yeah?"

"There's something I hoped you might be able to help me with. A sort of mystery."

"Oh yeah?"

She glanced at him, a little wary given his earlier avoidance of the subject. "It's a medical question."

"Okay."

"Rose mentions some marks on her stomach. From what I can gather they're quite large, noticeable enough that they embarrass her, and early on she has a couple of consultations about them with her doctor, Ebenezer Matthews."

He shrugged apologetically. "Skin wasn't really my specialty."

"What was?"

"Oncology. Does Rose give you anything more to go on? Color, size, type, quantity?"

Cassandra shook her head. "She wrote in euphemisms for the most part."

"Typical Victorian prudery." He walked the shovel back and forth on the ground while he thought. "They could be anything, really. Scars, pigmentation marks—does she mention any surgery?"

"Not that I can remember. What sort of surgery?"

He lifted one hand to the side. "Well, off the top of my head, it could have been appendicitis, her kidneys or lungs may have needed operating on." He raised his eyebrows. "Hydatids maybe. Is it likely she'd been near any farms?"

"There were farms on the estate."

"It's definitely the most common reason a Victorian child would've had abdominal surgery."

"What is it, exactly?"

"A parasite, tapeworm. It lives in dogs but has a part of its cycle in humans or sheep. It usually settles in the kidney or liver, but sometimes winds up in the lungs." He looked up at her. "It fits, but I'm afraid, short of asking her or finding more information in the scrapbooks, I doubt you'll ever know for sure."

"I'll have another look this afternoon, see if I missed something."

"And I'll keep thinking about it."

"Thanks. But don't go to any trouble, it's really just my curiosity." She pulled her gloves on, locked the joins of her fingers together to tighten them.

Christian dug the shovel into the earth a few times. "There was too much death."

Cassandra looked at him.

"My job, oncology; it was too relentless. The patients, the families, the loss. I thought I'd be able to handle it, but it builds up, you know? Over time?"

Cassandra thought of Nell's last days, the ghastly sterile smell of the hospital, the cold, blank gaze of the walls.

"I was never cut out for it, really. I figured that much when I was still at university."

"You didn't think of changing your degree?"

"I didn't want to disappoint my mum."

"She wanted you to be a doctor?"

"I don't know." His eyes met hers. "She died when I was a kid."

And then Cassandra understood. "Cancer." Understood, too, why he was so eager to forget the past. "I'm so sorry, Christian."

He nodded, watched as a black bird flew low overhead. "Looks like rain. When the rooks swoop like that, there's rain coming." He smiled shyly, as if to apologize for the swift change of topic. "Meteorology has nothing on Cornish folklore."

Cassandra picked up her gardening fork. "I reckon we work another half-hour, then call it a day."

Christian looked at the ground suddenly and stubbed his boot against the earth. "You know, I was going to get a drink at the pub on the way home." He glanced at her. "I don't suppose—that is, I wonder if you'd like to come?"

"Sure," she heard herself say. "Why not?"

Christian smiled and his face seemed to relax. "Great. That's great."

A fresh, moist gust of salty breeze brought an elm leaf drifting down to land on Cassandra's head. She brushed it off and returned her attention to her bracken patch, dug the little gardening fork beneath a long thin root and tried to wrestle it from the ground. And she smiled to herself, though she wasn't quite sure why.

A BAND HAD been playing at the pub so they'd stayed and ordered pies and chips. Christian told self-deprecating stories about being back at home with his dad and stepmum, and Cassandra divulged some of Nell's eccentricities: her refusal to use a potato peeler because it couldn't trim as close as she could with a knife, her habit of adopting other people's cats, the way she'd had Cassandra's wisdom teeth set in silver and turned into a pendant. Christian had laughed, and the sound so pleased Cassandra that she found herself laughing, too.

It was dark when he finally dropped her back at the hotel, the air thick with mist so that the car's headlights glowed yellow.

"Thank you," said Cassandra as she hopped out. "I had a good time." And she had. An unexpectedly good time. Her ghosts had been with her, as ever, but they hadn't sat so close.

"I'm glad you came."

"Yeah. Me, too." Cassandra smiled against her shoulder, waited a moment, then closed the door. Waved as his car disappeared into the fog.

"Phone message," said Samantha, waving a small slip of paper as Cassandra entered the foyer. "Been out, have you?"

"The pub, yeah." Cassandra took the paper, ignored Samantha's raised brows.

Phone call from Ruby Davies, it read. *Coming to Cornwall on Monday. Booked to stay at the Blackhurst Hotel. Expecting progress report!*

Cassandra felt a wave of genuine pleasure. She would be able to show Ruby the cottage and the scrapbooks and the hidden garden. Ruby, she knew, was someone who would understand how special they all were. She would like Christian, too.

"Someone dropped you home, then, did they? Looked like Christian Blake's car."

"Thanks for the message," said Cassandra with a smile.

"Not that I got much of a look," Samantha called as Cassandra disappeared up the stairs. "I wasn't spying or anything."

Back in her room, Cassandra ran a hot, deep bath and tossed in some lavender salts Julia had found for her sore muscles. She took the scrapbooks with her and laid them on a dry towel spread across the tiled floor. Careful to keep her left hand dry for page turning, she eased into the tub, sighing with pleasure as the silky water surrounded her, then leaned against the porcelain side and opened the first scrapbook, hopeful that some missed detail about Rose's marks would jump out.

By the time the water was tepid and Cassandra's feet were pruned, she'd found little of any use. Just the same veiled mention by Rose of "marks" that embarrassed her.

But she had found something else interesting. Unrelated to the marks, but curious nonetheless. It wasn't just the words themselves, but the tone of the entry that struck Cassandra. She couldn't shake the feeling that it meant far more than it appeared to say.

April 1909. Work has started on the wall at the cottage. Mamma felt, and rightly, that it was best to do it while Eliza is away. The cottage is too vulnerable. It was all well and good for it to remain exposed in olden times when its use was more nefarious, but it no longer needs to signal out to sea. Quite the contrary: there is none among us now who wishes exposure. And one can never be too careful, for where there is much to gain, there is ever much to lose.

Thirty-nine

Rose was weeping. Her cheek was warm and her pillow wet, but still she wept. She clenched her eyes against the sneaking winter light and cried as she hadn't since she was a very little girl. Wicked, wicked morning! How dare the sun so surely rise to gloat over her misery? How dare other people go about their business as if God were in his heaven, when yet again Rose had woken to see the end to her hopes writ in blood? How much longer, she wondered, how many more times must she tolerate this monthly despair?

In some ghastly way it was better to know, for surely the worst days were those in between. The long days in which Rose allowed herself to imagine, to dream, to hope. *Hope,* how she had grown to hate the word. It was an insidious seed planted inside a person's soul, surviving covertly on little tending, then flowering so spectacularly that none could help but cherish it. It was hope, too, that prevented a person taking counsel from experience. For each month, after her bleeding week, Rose felt a resurgence of the foul creature, and her slate of experience was wiped clean. No matter that she promised herself that this time she wouldn't play along, wouldn't fall prey to the cruel, propitious whispers, she always did. Because desperate people cling to hope like sailors to their wreck.

In the course of a year there had been one small reprieve from the terrible cycle. A month when the bleeding hadn't come. Dr. Matthews had been duly summoned, had conducted an examination and uttered the blessed words: she was with child. What bliss to hear one's dearest wish spoken so calmly, with so little thought for the months of disappointment that had come before, with steadiness and confidence that all would continue. Her stomach would swell and a baby would be born. Eight days she had nursed the precious news, whispered words of love to her flat stomach, walked and spoken and dreamed differently. And then, on the ninth day—

A knock at the door but Rose didn't stir. Go away, she thought, go away and leave me be.

The door creaked and someone entered, took infuriating care to be quiet. A noise—something being placed on the bedside table—and then a soft voice by her ear. "I brought you some breakfast."

Mary again. As if it wasn't enough that Mary had seen the sheets, marked with their dark reproach.

"You must keep your spirits up, Mrs. Walker."

Mrs. Walker. The words made Rose's stomach tighten. How she'd longed to be Mrs. Walker. After she'd met Nathaniel in New York, had arrived at dance after dance with her heart pulsing in her chest, scanned the room until she spied him, held her breath until their eyes met and his lips spread into a smile, just for her.

And now the name was hers, yet she had proved herself unworthy of it. A wife who couldn't perform the most basic of a married woman's functions. Couldn't provide her husband with the very things a good wife must. Children. Healthy, happy children to run across the estate, turn cartwheels along the sand, hide from their governess.

"You mustn't cry, Mrs. Walker. It'll happen for you in good time."

Each well-meant word was a bitter barb. "Will it, Mary?"

"Of course, ma'am."

"What makes you so sure?"

"It's bound to, ain't it? A woman can't avoid it if she tries. Not for long. There's many I know would be glad to escape it if way were known."

"Ungrateful wretches," said Rose, face hot and wet. "Such women don't deserve the blessing of children."

Mary's eyes clouded with something Rose took for pity. Rather than slap the servant's plump, healthy cheeks, she turned away and curled up beneath her covers. Nursed her grief deep within her stomach. Surrounded herself with the dark and empty cloud of loss.

NATHANIEL COULD have drawn it in his sleep. His wife's face was so familiar to him he sometimes thought he knew it better than his own hand. He finished the line he was sketching and smudged it slightly with his thumb. Squinted and tilted his head. She was beautiful, he had been right in that. The dark hair and pale skin, pretty mouth. And yet he took no pleasure from it.

He filed the portrait sketch in his portfolio. She would be glad to receive it as she always was. Her requests for new portraits were so desperate he could never say no. If he didn't present a new one every few days she was likely to weep and beg him for assurances of love. He drew her from memory now, rather than from life. The latter was too painful. His Rose had vanished inside her own sorrow. The young woman he had met in New York had been eaten away, revealing this shadow Rose, with darkened eyes from lack of sleep, worry-faded skin, agitated limbs. Had any poet adequately described the wretched ugliness of a loved one turned inside out with grief?

Night after night she presented herself to him and he consented. But Nathaniel's desire had vanished. What had once excited him filled him now with dread and, worse, guilt. Guilt that when they made love he could no longer bear to look at her. Guilt that he could not give her what she wanted. Guilt that he did not want the baby as desperately as she did. Not that Rose would believe that. No matter how many times Nathaniel assured her that she was enough for him, Rose would not be convinced.

And now, most mortifying of all, her mother had come to see him in his studio. Had perused his portraits somewhat woodenly, before sitting in the chair by his easel and launching her oration. Rose was delicate, she started, had always been so. The animal drives of a husband were likely to cause her great harm and it would be best for all if he could desist for a time. So disquieting was it to conduct such a conversation with his mother-in-law, Nathaniel had been unable to find words or inclination to explain his own position.

Instead he had nodded his accession and taken to seeking solitude in the estate garden, rather than his studio. The gazebo had become his workplace. It was still cold in February, but Nathaniel was only too willing to forgo comfort. The weather made it less likely that anyone else would seek his counsel. Finally, he could be at ease. Being inside the house over the winter, with Rose's parents and her suffocating needs, had been oppressive. Her sorrow and disappointment had permeated the walls, the curtains, the carpets. It was the house of the dead: Linus locked away in his darkroom, Rose in the bedroom, Adeline lurking in the corridors.

Nathaniel leaned forward, attention caught by the spill of weak sunlight through the rhododendron branches. His fingers twitched, longed to capture the light and shade. But there was no time. The canvas of Lord Mackelby sat before him on the easel, beard painted in, blush-shot cheeks, lined forehead. Only the eyes remained. It was always the eyes that let Nathaniel down in oil.

He selected a brush and removed a loose hair. Was about to put paint to canvas when he felt his arms tingle, the strange sixth sense of solitude retreating. He looked over his shoulder. Sure enough a servant stood behind him. Agitation bristled.

"For goodness sake, man," said Nathaniel. "Don't sneak up like that. If there's something you'd like to say, come, stand before me and say it. There's no need, surely, for such stealth."

"Lady Mountrachet sends advice that luncheon is to be served early, sir. The carriage for Tremayne Hall will depart at two o'clock this afternoon."

Nathaniel cursed silently. He had forgotten about Tremayne Hall. Yet another of Adeline's wealthy friends looking to dress their walls in their own image. Perhaps, if he were very lucky, his subject would insist he also feature her three tiny dogs!

To think he had once been thrilled by such introductions, had felt his status rising like the sail on a new ship. He had been a blind fool, ignorant to the cost that such success would claim. His commissions had grown, but his creativity had been reduced commensurately. He was pumping out portraits just as surely as one of the new mass-production factories of which men in business were always speaking, rubbing their shiny hands together with glee. No time to pause, to improve, to vary his method. His work was not that of a craftsman, there was no longer dignity or humanity in his strokes.

Worst of all, while he was busy producing portraits, the time for sketching, his true passion, was slipping through his fingers. Since arriving at Blackhurst he had managed only one panel sketch and a clutch of studies of the house and its inhabitants. His hands, his skills, his spirits had all been stunted.

He had made the wrong choice, he saw that now. If only he had heeded Rose's requests and sought a new home for them after their marriage, perhaps things would have turned out differently. Perhaps they would be blissfully content, children at her feet, creative satisfaction at his fingertips.

Then again, perhaps all would be the same. He and she forced to endure similar torture in reduced circumstances. And that was the rub. How was a boy who'd tasted poverty ever expected to choose the poorer road?

And now Adeline, like Eve herself, had started whispering about a possible sitting with the king. And though he was tired of portraiture, though he hated himself for having forsaken so completely his passion, Nathaniel's skin prickled at the mere suggestion.

He laid down his brush and rubbed at a paint stain on his thumb. Was about to head in for luncheon when his portfolio snagged his attention. With a glance back towards the house, he pulled the secret sketches from within. He'd been working at them on and off for a fortnight now, ever since he'd come across Cousin Eliza's fairy tales among Rose's things. Though they were written for children, magical stories of bravery and morality, they had made their way beneath his skin. The characters had seeped inside his mind and come alive, their simple wisdom a balm for his swirling mind, his ugly adult troubles. He had found himself in moments of distraction scribbling lines that had turned themselves into a crone at a spinning wheel, the Fairy Queen with her long thick plait, the Princess bird trapped in her golden cage.

And what began as scribbles he was now turning into sketches. Darkening the shading, firming the lines, accentuating the facial features. He looked them over, tried not to notice the embossed parchment Rose had bought for him when they were newly married, tried not to think of happier times.

The sketches were not yet finished but he was pleased with them. Indeed, it was the only project that seemed to bring him pleasure anymore, grant him escape from the trial his life had become. With a quickening heart, Nathaniel clipped the pieces of parchment to the top of his easel. Lord Mackelby's gloomy eyes could wait. After luncheon he was going to allow himself to sketch, to draw without purpose as he had once done as a boy.

FINALLY, WITH Mary's help, Rose was dressed. She had been sitting in her convalescent chair all morning but had decided eventually to venture from her room. When had she last left its four walls? Two days before? Three? When she stood she almost fell. She was light-headed and weak-stomached, familiar sensations from her childhood. Back then Eliza had been able to hoist her spirits high again with fairy stories and tales dragged back from the cove. If only the remedy for adult affliction were so simple.

It had been some time since Rose had seen Eliza. She spied her

occasionally from the window, stalking through the garden or standing on the cliff top, a distant speck with long red hair streaming behind her. Once or twice Mary had come to the door with a message
that Miss Eliza was downstairs requesting an audience, but Rose always said no. She loved her cousin, but the battle she was waging
against grief and hope took all the energy she could muster. And Eliza
was so spirited, so full of vitality, possibility, health. It was more than
Rose could endure.

Weightless as a ghost, Rose drifted along the carpeted hall, hand
resting on the dado rail to keep her balance. This afternoon, when Nathaniel returned from his meeting at Tremayne Hall, she would join
him outside in the gazebo. It would be cold, of course, but she would
have Mary wrap her warmly, Thomas could move the daybed and a
blanket for her comfort. Nathaniel must be lonely out there, he would
be glad to have her by his side once more. He would be able to sketch
her reclining. Nathaniel did so like to draw her, and it was her duty as
a wife to offer comfort to her husband.

Rose had almost reached the stairs when she heard voices floating along the drafty corridor.

"She says she ain't going to say nothing, that it's no one's business
but hers." The words were punctuated by the striking of a broom's
head against the skirting board.

"The mistress won't be pleased when she finds out."

"The mistress won't find out."

"If she's got eyes in her head she will. There's not many can't tell
when a girl grows fat with child."

Rose pressed a cold hand against her mouth, crept quietly along
the hall, strained to hear further.

"She says all the women in her family carry small. She'll be able
to hide it beneath her uniform."

"Let's just hope for her sake she's right, else she'll be out on
her ear."

Rose arrived at the top of the stairs just in time to see Daisy disappearing into the servants hall. Sally was denied such fortunate reprieve.

The servant gasped and her cheeks flushed in most unbecoming blotches. "Sorry, ma'am." A fumbled curtsy, broomstick tangled in skirts. "I didn't see you there."

"Of whom do you speak, Sally?"

The blotches spread to the tips of the girl's ears.

"Sally," said Rose, "I demand you answer me. Who is with child?"

"Mary, ma'am." Little more than a whisper.

"Mary?"

"Yes, ma'am."

"Mary is with child?"

The girl nodded quickly, the lines of her face describing an urgent desire to disappear.

"I see." A deep black hole had opened in the center of Rose's stomach and threatened to pull her inside out. That stupid girl with her hideous, cheap fertility. Flaunting it for all to see, cooing over Rose, telling her everything would be well, then laughing behind her back. And she unwed! Well, not in this house. Blackhurst Manor was a house of ancient and sturdy moral standing. It was up to Rose to make sure standards were observed.

ADELINE RAN the brush through her hair, stroke by stroke by stroke. Mary was gone and though that left them woefully short-staffed for the coming weekend party, the girl's absence would just have to be managed. While ordinarily Adeline didn't encourage Rose to make decisions about staff without due consultation, these were exceptional circumstances and Mary quite the little sneak. An unmarried sneak, which made matters even more disgraceful. No, Rose had been right in her instincts, if not her method.

Poor dear Rose. Dr. Matthews had been to see Adeline earlier in the week, had sat across from her in the morning room and adopted his low voice, the one he always donned in times of worry. Rose was not well, he had said (as if Adeline couldn't see as much for herself), and he was gravely concerned.

"Unfortunately, Lady Mountrachet, my fears are not limited to her apparent decline. There are"—he coughed lightly into his neat fist—"other things."

"Other things, Dr. Matthews?" Adeline handed him a cup of tea.

"Emotional matters, Lady Mountrachet." He smiled primly and took a sip of tea. "When questioned on the physical aspects of her marriage, Mrs. Walker confessed to what would be considered, in my professional opinion, an unhealthy tendency towards physicality."

Adeline felt her lungs expand, she caught her breath and forced herself to exhale calmly. For want of something else to say or do, she stirred an additional lump of sugar into her own tea. Without meeting his eyes she bade Dr. Matthews continue.

"Be comforted, Lady Mountrachet. While certainly it's a serious condition, your daughter is not alone. I can report a rather high incidence of heightened physicality among young ladies currently, and feel certain it is a condition she will outgrow. More concerning to me is my suspicion that her physical tendency is contributing to her repeated failures."

Adeline cleared her throat. "Continue, Dr. Matthews."

"It is my sincere medical opinion that your daughter must cease physical relations until her poor body has had time adequately to recover. For 'tis all related, Lady Mountrachet, 'tis all related."

Adeline lifted her cup to her mouth and tasted the bitterness of fine china. She nodded almost imperceptibly.

"The Lord works in mysterious ways. So, too, through his design, the human body. It is reasonable to hypothesize that a young lady with heightened . . . appetites"—he smiled apologetically, eyes narrowed—"would present a less than ideal maternal model. The body knows such things, Lady Mountrachet."

"You are suggesting, Dr. Matthews, that with fewer attempts, my daughter may have greater success?"

"It is worth consideration, Lady Mountrachet. Not to mention the benefits such temperance will have for her general heath and well-being. Picture, if you will, Lady Mountrachet, a windsock."

Adeline arched her brows, wondered—not for the first time—why she had remained loyal to Dr. Matthews all this time.

"If a windsock is left suspended for years on end, without opportunity for rest or repair, the harsh winds will invariably tear holes in its fabric. So, too, Lady Mountrachet, your daughter must be allowed time to recuperate. Must be shielded from the strong winds that threaten to rend her asunder."

Windsocks aside, a certain sense had lurked behind Dr. Matthews's words. Rose was weak and unwell and without allowing herself proper time to heal could not be expected to make a full recovery. And yet her fierce longing for a child consumed her. Adeline had agonized over how best to convince her daughter to put her own health first, and finally she had realized it would be necessary to enlist Nathaniel in the attempt. Awkward though such conversation promised to be, his obedience had been assured. Over the past twelve months, Nathaniel had learned to toe Adeline's line, and now, with a royal portrait in the offing, there'd been little doubt he'd see things her way.

Although Adeline managed to keep a calm veneer, oh, how she raged in private. Why should other young women be granted children when Rose must go without? Why should she be blighted when others were made strong? How much more would Rose's weak body be forced to endure? In her darkest moments, Adeline wondered whether it was something *she* had done. Whether maybe God was punishing *her*. She had been too proud, gloated one too many times about Rose's beauty, her fine manners, her sweet nature. For what worse punishment than to see a beloved child suffering?

And now the thought of Mary, that ghastly, healthy girl with her broad, beaming face, her nest of unkempt hair, that she should be carrying a child. An unwanted child when others who craved so deeply were continually denied. There was no justice. Little wonder Rose had snapped: it was *her* turn. The happy news, the child, should belong to Rose. Not Mary.

If only some way could be found to grant Rose a child without physical toll. Of course, it was impossible. Women would be lined up if such a method existed.

Adeline paused midstroke. Looked at her reflection but saw nothing. Her mind was elsewhere, contemplating the topsy-turvy image of a healthy girl with no maternal instinct beside a delicate woman whose body failed her willing heart . . .

She lay down the brush. Pressed cold hands together in her lap.

Was it possible such contrariness might be righted?

It would not be easy. First, Rose must be convinced that it was for the best. Then there was the girl. She would need to be made to see that it was her duty. That she owed it to the Mountrachet family, after so many years of goodwill.

Difficult, certainly. But not impossible.

Slowly Adeline stood. Laid the brush lightly on the dressing table. Mind still honing her idea, she started down the hall towards Rose's room.

THE KEY to grafting roses was the knife. Razor sharp it had to be, Davies said, sharp enough to give the hairs on your arm a clean shave. Eliza had found him in the hothouse and he'd been only too happy to help her with the hybrid she was planning for her garden. He'd shown her where to make the cut, how to ensure that there were no splinters or bumps or imperfections that might prevent the scion binding to the new stock. In the end, she'd stayed all morning and helped with the repotting for spring. It was such a pleasure to sink one's hands into the warm earth, to feel at one's fingertips the possibilities of the new season.

When she left, Eliza walked the long way back. It was a cool day, thin clouds skimming quickly in the upper atmosphere, and she relished the chill breeze on her face after the muggy hothouse. Being so near, her thoughts turned, as they always did, to her cousin. Mary had reported that Rose was low in spirits lately, and though Eliza suspected she wouldn't be granted admission, she couldn't bear to come so close without trying. She knocked on the side door and waited until it opened.

"Good day, Sally. I've come to see Rose."

"You can't, Miss Eliza," said Sally, a sullen expression on her face. "Mrs. Walker is otherwise engaged and unavailable to guests." The lines had the melody of those learned by rote.

"Come now, Sally," Eliza said, smile straining, "I hardly qualify as a guest. I'm sure if you just let Rose know that I am here—"

From the shadows, Aunt Adeline's voice. "Sally is quite right. Mrs. Walker is otherwise engaged." The dark hourglass drifted into view. "We are about to begin luncheon. If you care to leave a calling card, Sally will ensure that Mrs. Walker knows you requested an audience."

Sally's head was bowed and her cheeks flushed. No doubt some fuss had occurred among the staff and Eliza would hear all about it from Mary later. Without Mary and her regular reports, Eliza would have little idea of what went on at the house.

"I have no card," said Eliza. "Tell Rose I called, won't you, Sally? She knows where to find me."

With a nod in her aunt's direction, Eliza set off once more across the lawn, pausing only once to gaze at the window of Rose's new bedroom, where early spring light bleached the surface to white. With a shiver, her thoughts turned to Davies's grafting knife: the ease with which a sharp enough blade might sever a plant so that no evidence of the former bond remained.

Around the sundial and further across the lawn, Eliza came to the gazebo. Nathaniel's painting equipment was set up inside, as it often was these days. He was nowhere to be seen, had probably gone inside for luncheon, but his work had been left pegged to the easel—

Eliza's thoughts fled.

The sketches on top were unmistakable.

She suffered the odd displacement of seeing figments from her own imagination brought to life. Characters, hitherto the province of her own mind, turned as if by magic to pictures. An unexpected ripple passed beneath her skin, hot and cold all at once.

Eliza went closer, up the stairs of the gazebo, and examined the sketches. She smiled, couldn't help herself. It was like discovering an imaginary friend had gained corporal existence. They were similar enough to her own imaginings to be instantly recognizable, yet different somehow. His hand was darker than her mind, she realized, and she liked it. Without thinking, she unclipped them.

Eliza hurried back: along the maze, across her garden, through the southern door, all the way mulling the sketches over in her mind. Wondering when he had drawn them, why, what he intended to do with them. It wasn't until she was hanging her coat and hat in the hallway of the cottage that her thoughts turned to the letter she had recently received from the publisher in London. Mr. Hobbins had opened by paying Eliza a compliment regarding her stories. He had a little daughter, he said, who awaited each Eliza Makepeace fairy tale with bated breath. Then he had suggested that Eliza might like to consider publishing an illustrated collection and to bear him in mind if such a time arose.

Eliza had been flattered but unconvinced. For some reason the concept hadn't progressed in her imagination from the abstract. Now, however, having seen Nathaniel's sketches, she found she could envisage such a book, could almost feel its weight in her hands. A bound edition containing her favorite stories, a volume for children to pore over. Just like the book she had discovered in Mrs. Swindell's rag and bottle shop all those years ago.

And though Mr. Hobbins's letter had not been explicit about remuneration, surely Eliza could expect payment more handsome than that she had received thus far? For an entire book must be worth far more than a single story. Perhaps she would finally have the money necessary to travel across the sea . . .

A fierce knocking at the door drew her attention.

Eliza pushed aside the irrational feeling that Nathaniel was waiting for her on the other side, come for his sketches. Of course he wasn't. He never came to the cottage, and besides, it would be hours before he realized they were missing.

All the same, Eliza rolled them up and tucked them within her coat pocket.

She opened the door. Mary stood there, cheeks stained with tidelines of tears.

"Please, Miss Eliza, help me."

"Mary, what is it?" Eliza ushered the girl inside, glancing over her shoulder before closing the door. "Are you hurt?"

"No, Miss Eliza." She swallowed a sob. " 'Tis nothing like that."

"Then tell me, what has happened?"

"It's Mrs. Walker."

"Rose?" Eliza's heart hammered against her chest.

"She's turned me out," Mary inhaled wetly, "told me to finish up immediately."

Relief that Rose was unharmed battled with surprise. "But, Mary, whatever for?"

Mary collapsed onto a chair and wiped the back of her wrist across her eyes. "I don't know how to say it, Miss Eliza."

"Then speak plainly, Mary, I implore you, and tell me what on earth has happened."

Fresh tears began to fall. "I'm with child, Miss Eliza. I'm going to have a baby, and though I thought I kept it hid, Mrs. Walker has found out and now says I'm not welcome."

"Oh, Mary," said Eliza, sinking onto the other chair, taking Mary's hands between her own. "Are you sure about the baby?"

"There's no doubting the fact, Miss Eliza. I didn't mean for it to happen, but it did."

"And who is the father?"

"A lad what lives in the neighboring street to ours. Please, Miss Eliza, he's not a bad fellow, and he says he wants to marry me, but I need to earn some money first, else there'll be naught to feed or clothe the babe. I can't lose my position, not yet, Miss Eliza, and I know I can still perform it well."

Mary's face was so desperate that Eliza could answer no other way. "I'll see what I can do."

"Will you speak with Mrs. Walker?"

Eliza fetched a glass of water from the pitcher and handed it to Mary. "I'll endeavor to do so. Though you know as well as I do that an audience with Rose is not easy to obtain."

"Please, Miss Eliza, you're my only hope."

Eliza smiled with a confidence she didn't feel. "I will give it a few days, enough time for Rose to settle down, and then I shall speak with her on your behalf. I'm certain she will be made to see reason."

"Oh, thank you, Miss Eliza. You know I didn't wish for this to happen. I've gone and made a mess of everything. I only wish I could turn the weeks back and have it undone."

"We have all wished for similar power at times," said Eliza. "Go home now, Mary dear, and try not to worry. Things will work out, I'm sure. I will send word when I have spoken with Rose."

ADELINE KNOCKED lightly on the bedroom door and pushed it open. Rose was sitting in the window seat, attention focused on the ground below. Her arms were so frail, her profile so gaunt. The room had grown listless in sympathy to its owner, cushions flat, curtains sagging in despondence. Even the air seemed to have staled within the streams of weak light.

Rose gave no indication that she noticed or minded the intrusion, so Adeline went to stand behind her. She looked through the window to see what it was that held her daughter's attention.

Nathaniel was seated at his easel in the gazebo, sifting through pages from his leather portfolio. There was an agitation in his manner, as if he had misplaced a vital tool.

"He will leave me, Mamma." Rose's voice was pale as the sunlight. "For what reason would he stay?"

Rose turned then, and Adeline tried not to let her face reflect her daughter's grey and terrible state. She laid a hand on Rose's bony shoulder. "All will be well, my Rose."

"Will it?"

Her tone was so bitter that Adeline winced. "Of course."

"I don't see how that can be, for it seems I am unable to make of him a man. Again and again I fail to give him an heir, a child of his own." Rose turned back to the window. "Of course he will leave. And without him I will fade away to nothing."

"I have spoken with Nathaniel, Rose."

"Oh, Mamma . . ."

Adeline lifted a finger to Rose's lips. "I have spoken with Nathaniel and I am confident that he, as I, wants nothing more than your return to good health. Children will come when you are well, and for that you must be patient. Allow yourself the time to recover."

Rose was shaking her head, her neck so thin that Adeline wanted to stop the gesture lest she damage herself. "I cannot wait, Mamma. Without a child I cannot go on. I would do anything for a baby, even at my own cost. I would rather die than wait."

Adeline sat gently on the window seat and took her daughter's pale, cool hands between her own. "It need not come to that."

Rose blinked large eyes at Adeline; within them flickered a pale flame of hope. Hope that a child never quite loses, faith that a parent can put things to right.

"I am your mother and I must look after your health, even if you won't, thus have I given your plight much thought. I believe there may be a way for you to have a child without endangering yourself."

"Mamma?"

"You may be reluctant at first, but I beg of you, cast aside your doubts." Adeline lowered her voice. "Pray listen carefully now, Rose, to all I have to say."

IN THE end, it was Rose who made contact with Eliza. Five days after Mary's visit, Eliza received word that Rose would like to meet. Even more surprising, Rose's letter suggested that the two should meet in Eliza's hidden garden.

When she saw her cousin, Eliza was glad she'd thought to fetch cushions for the iron seat, for dear Rose was reduced in every way. Mary had hinted at a decline but Eliza had never imagined such extreme diminishment. Though she fought to keep her face from registering shock, Eliza knew she must have failed.

"You are surprised by my appearance, Cousin," said Rose, smiling so her cheekbones turned to blades.

"Not at all," Eliza blustered. "Of course not, I merely . . . My face—"

"I know you well, my Eliza. I can read your thoughts as if they were my own. It is all right. I have been unwell. I have weakened. But I will recover, as I always do."

Eliza nodded, felt a warm shot stinging behind her eyes.

Rose smiled, a smile all the sadder for its attempt at certitude. "Come"—she gestured—"sit by me, Eliza. Let me have my dear cousin by my side. Do you remember the day you first brought me to the hidden garden and together we planted the apple tree?"

Eliza took Rose's thin, cold hand. "Of course I do. And just look at it now, Rose, look at our tree."

The sapling stem had thrived, so that the tree now reached almost to the top of the wall. Graceful naked branches swept sideways and willowy offshoots pointed towards the sky.

"It's beautiful," said Rose wistfully. "To think that we needed only plant it in the earth and it knew just what to do."

Eliza smiled gently. "It has done only what nature intended for it."

Rose bit her lip, left a red mark. "Sitting here, I almost believe myself eighteen again, on the verge of my trip to New York. Filled with excitement and anticipation." She smiled at Eliza. "It feels like an age since we've sat together, just you and I, as we used to when we were girls."

A wave of nostalgia washed away the year of envy and disappointment. Eliza clasped Rose's hand tightly. "Indeed, it does, Cousin."

Rose coughed a little and her frail body shook with the effort. Eliza was about to offer a shawl for her shoulders when Rose started speaking again: "I wonder, have you had news from the house lately?"

Eliza answered cautiously, wondering at the sudden change of topic. "I have seen Mary."

"Then you know." Rose met Eliza's gaze, held it for a time before shaking her head sadly. "She left me no choice, Cousin. I understand that you and she were fond of each other, but it was unthinkable that she should be kept on at Blackhurst in such a state. You must see that."

"She is a good and loyal girl, Rose," said Eliza gently. "She has behaved imprudently, I don't deny that. But surely you might relent? She is without income and the baby she is growing will have needs she must fulfil. Please think about Mary, Rose. Imagine her plight."

"I assure you, little else has been in my thoughts."

"Then perhaps you will see—"

"Have you ever longed for something, Eliza, something you wanted so much that without it you knew you could live no longer?"

Eliza thought of her imagined sea voyage. Her love for Sammy. Her need for Rose.

"I want a child more than anything. My heart aches, as do my arms. Sometimes I can feel the weight of the child I long to cradle. The warm head in the crook of my elbow."

"And surely one day—"

"Yes, yes. One day." Rose's faint smile belied her optimistic words. "But I have struggled and done without for so long. Twelve months, Eliza. Twelve months, and the road has been filled with such disappointment and denial. Now Dr. Matthews instructs me that my health may let me down. You must imagine, Eliza, how Mary's little secret made me feel. That she should have by accident the very thing I crave. That she, with nothing to offer, shall have that which I, with everything, have been denied. Why, surely you can see it isn't right? Surely God does not intend such contrary occurrences?"

Rose's devastation was so complete, her frail appearance so at odds with her fierce desire, that suddenly Mary's well-being was the least of Eliza's concerns. "How can I help you, Rose? Tell me, what can I do?"

"There is something, Cousin Eliza. I need you to do something for me, something that will in turn help Mary, too."

Finally. As Eliza had always known she must, Rose had realized that she needed Eliza. That only Eliza could help her. "Of course, Rose," she said. "Anything. Tell me what you need and so shall it be."

FORTY

THE weather came in late Friday night and fog sulked grey and general across the village all weekend. Given such resolute inclemency, Cassandra decided her weary limbs could do with a rest and took a well-earned break from the cottage. She spent Saturday curled up in her room with cups of tea and Nell's notebook, intrigued by her grandmother's account of the detective she'd consulted in Truro. A man named Ned Morrish, whose name she'd plucked from the local telephone book after William Martin suggested that she'd figure out her riddle if she learned where Eliza had disappeared to in 1909.

On Sunday Cassandra met with Julia for afternoon tea. Rain had fallen steadily all morning, but by midafternoon the deluge was reduced to drizzle and fog had been allowed to settle in the gaps. Through the mullioned windows, Cassandra could make out only the sober green of the drenched lawn; all else was mist, bare branches visible occasionally, like hairline fractures in a wall of white. It was the sort of day Nell had loved. Cassandra smiled, remembering how pulling on a raincoat and gum boots had infused her grandmother with enthusiasm. Perhaps, from somewhere deep inside, Nell's heritage had been calling her.

Cassandra leaned back into the cushions of her armchair and watched the flames flickering in the grate. People were gathered in all corners of the hotel lounge—some playing board games, others reading or eating—and the room was dense with the comforting low voices of the warm and dry.

Julia dropped a spoonful of cream onto her jam-laden scone. "So why the sudden interest in the cottage wall?"

Cassandra's fingers flattened warm around her mug. "Nell believed that if she found out where Eliza went in 1909, she'd discover the answer to her own mystery."

"But what's that got to do with the wall?"

"I don't know, maybe nothing. But something in Rose's scrapbook got me thinking."

"Which bit?"

"She makes an entry in April 1909 that seems to link Eliza's trip with the building of the wall."

Julia licked cream from her fingertip. "I remember," she said. "She writes that bit about being careful because when there's a lot to gain, there's also a lot to lose."

"Exactly. I just wish I knew what she meant."

Julia bit her lip. "How rude of her not to elaborate for the benefit of those of us who'd be reading over her shoulder some ninety years later!"

Cassandra smiled absently, played with a thread coming loose from the chair's arm. "Why would she have said that, though? What was there to gain? What was she so worried about losing? And what does the security of the cottage have to do with any of it?"

Julia took a bite of her scone and chewed it slowly, thoughtfully. She patted her lips with a hotel napkin. "Rose was pregnant at the time, right?"

"According to that entry in the scrapbook."

"So maybe it was hormones. That can happen, can't it? Women get all emotional and such? Maybe she was missing Eliza and worried that the cottage would be robbed or vandalized. Maybe she felt responsible. The two girls were still close at that point."

Cassandra thought about this. Pregnancy could account for some pretty crazy mood swings, but was it enough of an answer? Even allowing for a hormonal narrator, there was something curious about the entry. What was happening at the cottage that made Rose feel so vulnerable?

"They say it's going to clear up tomorrow," said Julia, laying her knife across a crumb-laden plate. She leaned back into her armchair, pulled the curtain edge aside and gazed into the misty glare. "I suppose you'll be back at work in the cottage?"

"Actually, no. I've got a friend coming to stay."

"Here at the hotel?"

Cassandra nodded.

"Lovely! You just let me know if there's anything I can do to help."

Julia was right and by Monday afternoon the mist had finally begun to lift and a tremulous sun promised to break through the clouds. Cassandra was waiting in the lounge when Ruby's car pulled into the car park outside. She smiled when she saw the little white hatchback, packed up the scrapbooks and hurried into the foyer.

"Phew!" Ruby took a step inside and dropped her bags. Then she pulled off her rain hat and shook her head. "Talk about a good old Cornish welcome! Not a drop of rain and I'm still soaking wet." She stopped still and stared at Cassandra. "Well, now, look at you!"

"What?" Cassandra patted her hair down. "What's the matter with me?"

Ruby grinned so that her eyes pleated at the corners. "Nothing at all, that's what I bloody well mean. You look fabulous."

"Oh. Well, thanks."

"The Cornish air must agree with you. You're hardly the same girl I met at Heathrow."

Cassandra started to laugh, surprising Samantha, who was eavesdropping from the main desk. "It's really good to see you, Ruby," she said, picking up one of the bags. "Let's get rid of these and go for a walk, check out the cove after all this rain."

CASSANDRA CLOSED her eyes, tilted her face skywards and let the sea breeze tickle her eyelids. Gulls engaged in conversation further along the beach, an insect flew close by her ear, gentle waves lapped rhythmically against the coast. She felt an enormous sense of calm descend as she matched her breath to that of the sea: in and out, in and out, in and out. The recent rain had stirred up the ocean brine and the strong smell laced the wind. She opened her eyes and looked slowly about the cove. The line of ancient trees atop the ridge, the black rock at the cove's end, the tall grassy hills that hid her cottage. She exhaled; deep pleasure.

"I feel just like I've stumbled into *Five Go to Smuggler's Top*," called Ruby from further along the beach. "I keep expecting Timmy the Dog to come running down the sand with a message-filled bottle in his mouth"—her eyes widened—"or a human bone; some nefarious thing he's dug up!"

Cassandra smiled. "I used to love that book." She started walking along the pebbles towards Ruby and the black rock. "When I was a kid, reading it on hot Brisbane days, I'd have given anything to be growing up on a foggy coast with smugglers' caves."

When they reached the end of the beach where pebbles met grass, the steep hill that bordered the cove rose before them.

"Good Lord," said Ruby, craning to see the top. "You actually intend for us to climb that, don't you?"

"It's not as steep as it looks, I promise."

Time and traffic had worn a narrow path, barely visible among the long silvery grasses and little yellow flowers, and they went slowly, stopping every so often for Ruby to catch her breath.

Cassandra relished the clear, rain-stirred air. The higher they got, the cooler it became. Each swirl of breeze was flecked with moisture, swept from the sea to pepper their faces. As she neared the top, Cassandra reached out to grasp the long, pale strands of grass, felt them slide through her closed hands. "Nearly there," she called back to Ruby. "It's just over this crest."

"I feel like a von Trapp," Ruby said between puffs. "But fatter, older and with absolutely no energy for singing."

Cassandra reached the summit. Above her, thin clouds fleeted across the sky, chased by strong autumn winds. She wandered towards the cliff edge and looked out across the broad and moody sea.

Ruby's voice from behind: "Oh, thank God. I'm alive." She was standing with her hands on her knees, catching her breath. "I'll let you in on a secret. I was not confident this moment would ever arrive."

She righted herself, shifted her hands to the small of her back and came to stand by Cassandra. Her expression lightened as her eyes scanned the horizon.

"It's beautiful, isn't it?" said Cassandra.

Ruby was shaking her head. "It's amazing. This is what birds must feel like when they're sitting in their nests." She took a step back from the cliff edge. "Except possibly a little more secure, given that they have wings in the event of a fall."

"The cottage used to be a lookout. Back in the days of the smugglers."

Ruby nodded. "I can believe that well enough. Not much you wouldn't see from up here." She turned, expecting to catch sight of the cottage. Frowned. "Shame about that great big wall. It must block a lot of the view."

"Yeah, from downstairs it does. But it wasn't always there. It went up in 1909."

Ruby wandered over towards the gate. "Why on earth would anyone wall it up like that?"

"Security."

"Against what?"

Cassandra followed Ruby. "Believe me, I'd love to know." She pushed open the creaky iron gate.

"Friendly." Ruby pointed at the sign threatening trespassers.

Cassandra smiled thoughtfully. *Keep out or the risk be all yours.* She had passed by the sign so often in recent weeks that she'd stopped seeing it. Now, in tandem with Rose's scrapbook entry, the words took on new significance.

"Come on, Cass." Ruby was standing at the other end of the path by the cottage door, stamping her little feet. "I went along with the hike with barely a complaint. Surely you don't expect me to scale the walls and find a window to climb through?"

Cassandra smiled and held up the brass key. "Never fear. No more physical challenges. Not for today, anyway. We'll save the hidden garden for tomorrow." She inserted the key in the lock and turned it to the left with a clunk, then pushed open the door.

Ruby stepped across the threshold and made her way along the hall towards the kitchen doorway. It was much lighter inside now that Cassandra and Christian had cleared the windowpanes of creepers and washed a century of grime from the glass.

"Oh my," Ruby whispered, eyes wide as she took in the kitchen, "it's unspoiled!"

"That's one way of putting it."

"No one's destroyed it under the guise of modernization. What an incredibly rare find." She turned to Cassandra. "It has a wonderful feel about it, doesn't it? Enveloping, warm somehow. I can almost feel the ghosts of the past moving about among us."

Cassandra smiled. She had known Ruby would feel it, too. "I'm so glad you could come, Ruby."

"I wouldn't have missed it," she said, crossing the room. "Grey's just about taken to wearing earplugs when we meet, he's so bloody sick of my talking about your Cornish cottage. Plus I had business in Polperro, so the whole thing couldn't have worked out better." Ruby leaned against the rocking chair to peer through the front window. "Is that a pond out there?"

"Yeah, just a little one."

"Cute statue. I wonder if he's cold." She let go of the rocking chair so that it was set in gentle motion. The treads squeaked softly against the floorboards. Ruby continued her inspection of the room, running her fingers lightly along the rim of the range shelf.

"What was your business in Polperro?" Cassandra sat cross-legged on the kitchen table.

"My exhibition ended last week and I was returning the Nathaniel Walker sketches to their owner. Just about broke my heart to part with them, I can tell you."

"No way she'd consider giving them to the museum on permanent loan?"

"That'd be nice." Ruby's head had disappeared into the bricked range alcove and her voice was muffled. "Perhaps you can sweet-talk her for me."

"Me? I've never met her."

"Well, not yet, of course you haven't. But I mentioned you to her when I was there. Told her all about your grandma being related to the Mountrachets, having been born here at Blackhurst, how she came back and bought the cottage. Clara was most interested."

"Really? Why would she care?"

Ruby stood up, bumping her head on the range shelf. "Bugger." She rubbed the spot furiously. "Always the bloody head."

"Are you all right?"

"Yes, yes, I'm fine. High pain threshold." She stopped rubbing, blinked her eyes clear. "Clara's mum used to work at Blackhurst, remember, as a domestic? Mary, the one who ended up making black puddings with her butcher husband?"

"Yeah, I remember now. So how did you know Clara was interested in Nell? What did she say?"

Ruby resumed her inspection of the range, opening the grate door. "She said there was something she wanted to talk to you about. Something her mum had told her before she died."

The skin on Cassandra's neck prickled. "What was it? Did she say anything else?"

"Not to me, and don't go getting too excited. Knowing the reverence in which she held her old mum, it may well be she thinks you'll be pleased to learn that Mary spent the best years of her life in service at the grand old house. Or that Rose once paid her a compliment on her silver polishing." Ruby closed the grate door, turned towards Cassandra. "I don't suppose the range still works?"

"It does, actually. We couldn't believe it."

"We?"

"Christian and I."

"Who's Christian?"

Cassandra ran her fingertips along the table's rim. "Oh, a friend. Someone who's been helping with the cleanup."

Ruby's brows arched. "A friend, huh?"

"Yeah." Cassandra shrugged. Tried to seem nonchalant.

Ruby smiled knowingly. "Nice to have friends." She made her way to the back of the kitchen, past the window with the broken pane, to the antique spinning wheel. "I don't suppose I'll get to meet him?" She reached out and turned the wheel.

"Careful," said Cassandra. "Don't prick your finger."

"No indeed." Ruby let her fingers skim the top of the turning wheel. "I don't want to be responsible for putting us both to sleep for a hundred years." She bit her bottom lip, eyes twinkled. "Though it would give your friend an opportunity to rescue us."

Cassandra felt her cheeks flush. She pretended casualness while Ruby took in the exposed beams of the ceiling, the blue and white tiles around the stove, the wide floorboards. "So," she said finally, "what do you think?"

Ruby rolled her eyes. "You know what I think, Cass, I'm jealous as hell! It's fabulous!" She came to lean against the table. "Still planning to sell it?"

"Yeah, I guess so."

"You're stronger than I am." Ruby shook her head. "I wouldn't be able to part with it."

From nowhere, a flash of possessive pride. Cassandra quelled it. "I have to. I can't just leave it sitting here. The maintenance would be too much, especially with me all the way on the other side of the world."

"You could keep it as a holiday house, rent it out when you're not using it. Then we'll always have somewhere to stay when we need some seaside." She laughed. "That is, *you'll* have somewhere to stay." She nudged Cassandra with her shoulder. "Come on, show me what's upstairs. I'll bet there's a killer view."

Cassandra led the way up the narrow stairs, and when they reached the bedroom Ruby leaned against the windowsill. "Oh, Cass," she said, as the wind plucked white tips on the surface of the sea, "you'd have people lining up to holiday here. It's unspoiled, close enough to the village for supplies, far enough away to feel private. It must be glorious at sunset, and then at night, when the distant lights of the fishing boats sparkle like little stars."

Ruby's comments both excited and frightened Cassandra, for she had given voice to Cassandra's secret wish, a sentiment she hadn't even realized she felt until she'd heard it expressed by someone else. She *did* want to keep the cottage, no matter that she knew the sensible thing was to sell it. The atmosphere of the place had made its way beneath her skin. There was its connection to Nell, but there was something more. A sense that all was well when she was in the cottage and its garden. Well with the world and well within herself. She felt whole and solid for the first time in ten years. Like a circle complete, a thought without dark edges.

"Oh, my God!" Ruby turned and clutched Cassandra's wrist.

"What!" Cassandra's stomach lurched. "What is it?"

"I've just had the most brilliant idea." She swallowed, motioned with her hand as she caught her breath. "A sleepover," she squealed finally. "You and me, tonight, here in the cottage!"

CASSANDRA HAD already been to the market and was leaving the hardware shop with a cardboard box full of candles and matches when she bumped into Christian. It had been three days since they'd had supper at the pub—there'd been far too much rain to even contemplate returning to the hidden garden over the weekend—and she hadn't seen or spoken to him since. She felt oddly nervous, could feel her cheeks flushing.

"Going camping?"

"Sort of. A friend has come to visit and wants to spend a night in the cottage."

He raised his eyebrows. "Don't let the ghosts bite."

"I'll try."

"Or the rats." He gave a lopsided smile.

She smiled, too, then pressed her lips together. The silence drew out like a rubber band, threatened to snap back. She started shyly: "Hey, you know . . . You could come up and have a bite of dinner with us? Nothing fancy, but it'll be fun . . . if you're free, I mean? I know Ruby would love to meet you." Cassandra flushed and cursed the thread of query that had lifted the end of her sentences. "It'll be fun," she said again.

He nodded, seemed to be considering. "Yeah," he said. "Sure. Sounds good."

"Great." Cassandra felt a ripple beneath her skin. "Seven o'clock? And no need to bring anything—as you can see, I'm well stocked."

"Oh, hey, give me that." Christian took Cassandra's cardboard box. She shifted the handles of her plastic grocery bag from around her wrist and scratched the red imprints they'd made. "I'll give you a lift up the cliff walk," he said.

"I don't want to put you out."

"You're not. I was on my way to see you anyway, about Rose and her marks."

"Oh, I couldn't find anything else in the scrap—"

"It doesn't matter, I know what they were and I know how she got them." He gestured towards his car. "Come on, we can talk while I drive."

Christian maneuvered his car out of the tight parking spot by the water's edge and drove along the main street.

"So what is it?" said Cassandra. "What did you find?"

The windows had fogged up, and Christian reached out to wipe the windscreen with his palm. "When you were telling me about Rose the other day there was something familiar. It was the doctor's name, Ebenezer Matthews. I couldn't for the life of me remember where I'd heard it, then early Saturday morning it came to me. At university I took a course on medical ethics, and as part of the assessment we had to write a paper on historical uses of new technologies."

He slowed the car at a T-intersection and fiddled with the heating. "Sorry, it plays up sometimes. Should be warm in a minute." He pushed the dial from blue to red, indicated left and started up the steep cliff road. "One of the benefits of living back home is that I've got ready access to the boxes my life was packed into when my stepmum turned my room into a gym."

Cassandra smiled, remembering the boxes of embarrassing high-school memorabilia she'd uncovered when she moved back in with Nell after the accident.

"Took me a while, but finally I found the essay, and sure enough there was his name, Ebenezer Matthews. I'd included him because he was from the same village I'd grown up in."

"And? Was there something in the essay about Rose?"

"Nothing like that, but after I realized who Rose's Dr. Matthews was, I e-mailed a friend up at Oxford who works in the medical library. She owed me a favor and agreed to send me anything she could on the doc's patients between 1889 and 1913. Rose's lifetime."

A friend. She. Cassandra pushed aside the unexpected surge of envy. "And?"

"Doc Matthews was quite a busy boy. Not at first: for someone who rose to such lofty heights, he came from humble beginnings. Doctor in a small town in Cornwall, doing all the things young doctors in small towns do. His big break, from what I can gather, was meeting Adeline Mountrachet of Blackhurst Manor. I don't know why she would have chosen a young doctor like him when her little girl was sick—aristocrats were much more likely to call upon the same old ghost who'd treated Great-uncle Kernow when he was a boy— but whatever the case, Ebenezer Matthews was summoned. He and Adeline must've hit it off, too, because after that first consultation he became Rose's regular doctor. Stayed that way all throughout her childhood, even after she was married."

"But how do you know? How did your friend find that sort of information?"

"A lot of doctors back then kept surgery logs. Records of the patients they saw, who owed them money, treatments they prescribed, articles they published, that sort of thing. Many of the logs wound up in libraries. They were donated, or sold, usually by the doctor's family."

They'd reached the end of the road where gravel gave way to grass and Christian pulled the car over onto the narrow parking strip by the lookout. Outside, the wind was buffeting the cliff and the tiny cliff birds huddled together glumly. He switched off the ignition, turned in his seat to face Cassandra. "In the last decade of the nineteenth century, Dr. Matthews began to make a bit of a name for himself. It seems he wasn't content with his lot as a country GP, even though his patient list was beginning to resemble a who's who of local society. He started publishing on various medical matters. It wasn't very difficult to cross-reference his publications with his log to find out that Rose appears as *Miss RM*. She becomes a frequent entry after 1897."

"Why? What happened then?" Cassandra realized she was holding her breath, her throat was tight.

"When Rose was eight she swallowed a sewing thimble."

"Why?"

"Well, I don't know, accident I expect, and it's beside the point. It wasn't a big deal—half the British currency has sat inside a child's stomach at one point or another. They pass through without too much difficulty if they're left alone."

Cassandra exhaled suddenly. "But it wasn't left alone. Dr. Matthews performed an operation."

Christian shook his head. "Worse than that."

Her stomach lurched. "What did he do?"

"He ordered an X-ray, a couple of X-rays, and then he published the pictures in the *Lancet*." Christian reached to the backseat and pulled out a photocopied piece of paper, handed it to her.

She glanced at the article, shrugged. "I don't get it, what's the big deal?"

"It's not the X-ray itself, it's the exposure." He pointed to a line at the top of the page. "Dr. Matthews had the photographer take a sixty-minute exposure. I guess he wanted to be sure he got his picture."

Cassandra could feel the cold outside her glass window, shimmering against her cheek. "But what does it mean? A sixty-minute exposure?"

"X-rays are radiation—haven't you ever noticed the way your dentist sprints from the room before pushing the X-ray button? An exposure of sixty minutes means that, between them, Dr. Matthews and the photographer fried her ovaries and everything inside them."

"Her ovaries?" Cassandra stared at him. "Then how did she conceive?"

"That's what I'm saying. She didn't, she couldn't. That is, she certainly couldn't have carried a healthy baby to term. As of 1897, Rose Mountrachet was, for all intents and purposes, infertile."

FORTY-ONE

DESPITE a ten-day delay before contracts were due to be exchanged, young Julia Bennett had been most obliging. When Nell requested early access to the cottage, she'd handed over the key with a wave of her jewelry-laden wrist. "Doesn't worry me a bit," she'd said, bangles clacking, "you make yourself at home. Lord knows, the key's so heavy I'll be happy to have it off my hands!"

The key *was* heavy. It was big and brass, with intricate swirls at one end, blunt teeth at the other. Nell looked at it, almost the length of her palm. She laid it on the wooden table in the kitchen. The kitchen of her cottage. Well, almost her cottage. Ten days to go.

Nell wouldn't be in Tregenna when they were exchanged. Her flight left London in four days' time and when she'd tried to change the booking she'd been told that such late alterations were possible only at exorbitant cost. So she'd decided to go home to Australia as planned. The local lawyers handling her purchase of Cliff Cottage were happy to hold the key for her until she returned. It wouldn't be long, she'd assured them, she just needed time to sort out her things and then she'd be back for good.

For Nell had decided she was going home to Brisbane for the last time. What had she there to keep her? A few friends, a daughter who didn't need her, sisters she perplexed. Her antiques shop she would miss, but perhaps she could start afresh here in Cornwall. And when she was here, with more time, Nell would get to the bottom of her mystery. She would learn why Eliza stole her and put her on the boat

430

to Australia. All lives needed purpose, and this would be Nell's. For otherwise, how would she ever know herself?

Nell walked slowly about the kitchen, making a mental inventory. The first thing she intended to do when she got back was to give the cottage a thorough clean. Dirt and dust had long been allowed free rein and every surface was coated. There would be repairs to make, too: the baseboards would need replacing in sections, there was bound to be wood rot, the kitchen would have to be brought to working order . . .

Of course a village like Tregenna would have any number of local tradesmen available to help, but Nell balked at the idea of employing strangers to work in her cottage. Although made of stone and wood, it was more than a house to Nell. And just as she had tended Lil when she was dying, had refused to pass responsibility into the hands of a kindly stranger, Nell knew she must tend the cottage herself. Use the skills that Hugh had taught her all those years before when she was a little girl and wide-eyed with love for her dad.

Nell stopped by the rocking chair. A little shrine in the corner caught her attention. She went closer. A half-empty drink bottle, a packet of digestive biscuits, a comic called *Whizzer and Chips*. They had certainly not been there when Nell made her purchasing inspection, which could only mean that someone had been in her cottage since. Nell flicked through the comic book: a young someone, by the looks of it.

A moist breeze brushed Nell's face and she looked to the back of the kitchen. The window was missing a pane of glass from one of its four square frames. Making a mental note to bring plastic and tape to mask it before she left Tregenna, Nell peered through. A huge hedge ran parallel to the house, blunt and even, almost like a wall. A flash of color and Nell thought she saw movement at the corner of her vision. When she looked again there was nothing. A bird, probably, or a squirrel.

Nell had noticed on the map sent to her by the lawyer that the property extended quite a way beyond the house. That meant, presumably, that whatever lay on the other side of the tall, thick hedge was hers, too. She decided to take a look.

The path that wound around the side of the house was narrow, and dim from lack of sun. Nell went cautiously, pushing long weeds aside as she went. At the back of the cottage, brambles had grown between the house and the hedge and Nell had to pick her way through the tangle.

Midway along, she sensed movement again, right by her. Nell looked at the ground. A pair of shoe-clad feet and skinny legs protruded from beneath the wall. Either the wall had fallen from the sky, à la *Wizard of Oz,* and crushed some poor unfortunate Cornish dwarf, or she had found the small person who'd been trespassing in her cottage.

Nell grabbed hold of the skinny ankle. The legs froze. "Come on, then," she said. "Out with you."

Another moment of stillness, then the legs began scrambling backwards. The boy they were attached to looked to be about ten, though Nell had never been particularly good at guessing the ages of children. He was a scrap of a lad with sandy brown hair and knobbly knees. Bruises up and down his bony shins.

"I presume you're the young monkey who's been making free with my cottage?"

The boy blinked dark brown eyes at Nell before looking to the ground at her feet.

"What's your name, then? Out with it."

"Christian."

So soft she almost hadn't heard.

"Christian who?"

"Christian Blake. Only I wasn't doing any harm. My dad works over at the big estate, and sometimes I just like to come and visit the walled—*your* walled garden."

Nell glanced at the bramble-covered wall. "So that's a garden behind there, is it? I had wondered." She looked back at the boy. "And tell me, Christian, does your mother know where you are?"

The boy's shoulders slumped. "I haven't got a mother."

Nell's eyebrows raised.

"She went away to hospital in the summer, and then . . ."

The heat of Nell's ill temper cooled on a sigh. "I see. Well. And what are you, nine? Ten?"

"Nearly eleven." Healthy indignation sent his hands into his pockets, his elbows out to the side.

"Of course, I see that now. I have a granddaughter about your age."

"Does she like gardens, too?"

Nell blinked at him. "I'm not sure."

Christian tilted his head to the side, frowned at her answer.

"That is, I imagine she does." Nell found herself skirting apology. Chastised herself. She needn't feel contrite just because she didn't know Lesley's daughter's mind. "I don't see her often."

"Does she live a long way from you?"

"Not really, no."

"Then why don't you see her much?"

Nell eyed the boy, trying to decide whether his impertinence was charming or not. "Sometimes that's just the way things are."

By the look on the boy's face, this explanation sounded as weak to him as it did to her. But there were some things that didn't need explanation, especially to strange little boys trespassing on one's property.

Nell reminded herself that the little scamp was newly motherless. There were none immune to poor judgment when their certainties had been pulled from under them, Nell knew that as well as anyone. Life could be so bloody cruel. Why should this boy grow up motherless? Why should some poor woman go to an early grave, leaving her lad to make his way in the world without her? Looking at the boy's skinny limbs, Nell felt something inside her tighten. Her voice was gruff but kind: "What is it you said you were doing in my garden anyway?"

"I wasn't doing any harm, honest. I just like to sit inside."

"And this is how you get in? Under the bricks?"

He nodded.

Nell eyed the hole. "I don't think I'll fit beneath there. Where's the gate?"

"There isn't one. At least, not on this wall."

Nell frowned. "I have a garden with no entrance?"

He nodded again. "There used to be one, you can see from inside where it was patched up."

"Why would anyone patch up the entrance?"

The boy shrugged and Nell made an addition to her mental list of necessary improvements. "Perhaps you can tell me what I'm missing, then," she said. "Seeing as I'm not going to be able to take a look myself. What it is that brings you all the way up here?"

"It's my favorite place in the whole world." Christian blinked his earnest brown eyes. "I like to sit inside and talk to my mum. She loved gardens, she loved your walled garden specially. She's the one who showed me how to get inside. We were going to try and fix it up. Then she got sick."

Nell pressed her lips together. "I'm going home to Australia in a couple of days but I'll be back in a month or two. I wonder whether you might not keep an eye on my garden for me, Christian?"

He nodded gravely. "I can do that."

"I'll be glad to know I've left it in capable hands."

Christian stood tall. "And when you come back, I'll help you fix it all up. Like my dad does over at the hotel."

Nell smiled. "I might well hold you to that. I don't accept help from just anyone, but I have a feeling that in this case you're the right man for the job."

FORTY-TWO

ROSE gathered the shawl around her shoulders and crossed her arms against a chill that wouldn't be warmed away. When she'd decided to seek sun in the garden, Eliza had been the last person she'd expected to see. As Rose had sat making notes in her scrapbook, looking up occasionally to see Ivory fluttering and swooping around the flower beds, there'd been no indication that the day's peace was to be so horridly shattered. Some peculiar sense had made her glance towards the maze gates, and there had been the sight that chilled Rose's blood. How had Eliza known that she would find Rose and Ivory alone in the garden? Had she been watching, waiting for just such a time when she might catch Rose off guard? And why now? Why after three years had she materialized today? Like a nightmare specter crossing the lawn, wretched parcel in her hand.

Rose glanced sideways. There it sat, masquerading as a harmless thing. But it wasn't. Rose knew that. She didn't need to look beneath the brown-paper wrapping to know what lurked within, an object representing a place, a time, a union Rose wanted so much to forget.

She gathered her skirts and smoothed them against her thigh, trying to create some distance between herself and it.

A flock of starlings took flight and Rose looked towards the kidney-shaped lawn. Mamma was coming towards her, the new hound, Helmsley, stalking close to her dark skirts. A wash of relief left Rose light-headed. Mamma was an anchor back to the present, to a safe world where everything was as it should be.

As Adeline drew near, Rose could contain her anxiety no longer. "Oh, Mamma," she said quickly. "She was here, Eliza was here."

"I saw it all from the window. What did she say? Did the child hear anything she should not?"

Rose ran the encounter back through her mind, but worry had conspired with fear to wrinkle the edges of her memory and she could no longer tease loose the precise words that had been spoken. She shook her head miserably. "I don't know."

Adeline glanced at the parcel, then lifted it from the bench cautiously, as if it were hot to the touch.

"Don't open it, Mamma, please. I cannot bear to see inside." Rose's voice was almost a whisper.

"Is it . . . ? "

"I'm quite sure it is." Rose pressed cold fingers against her cheek. "She said it was for Ivory." Rose looked at her mother and a fresh wave of panic surged beneath her skin. "Why would she bring it, Mamma? Why?"

Adeline's lips tightened.

"What did she mean by it?"

"I believe the time has come when you must put some distance between yourself and your cousin." Adeline sat beside Rose and lay the parcel across her lap.

"Distance, Mamma?" Rose's cheeks cooled, her voice dropped to a terrified whisper. "You don't think she might . . . might come again?"

"She has shown today that she has no respect for the rules that were agreed upon."

"But, Mamma, surely you don't think—"

"I think only that I wish for your continued well-being." As Rose's daughter fluttered beneath the dappled light, Adeline leaned close, so close that Rose felt a smooth upper lip against her ear. "We must remember, my darling," she whispered, "that a secret is never safe when it is known by others."

Rose nodded slightly. Mamma was right, of course. It had been folly to think all might continue indefinitely.

Adeline stood and rolled her wrist, motioning Helmsley to heel. "Thomas is about to serve luncheon. Don't be long. You needn't compound the day's upleasantness by catching a chill." She returned the parcel to the seat and lowered her voice. "And have Nathaniel dispose of that."

RACING FOOTSTEPS every which way overhead and Adeline winced. It mattered not how many times she delivered the well-worn diatribe on young ladies and fitting behavior, the child would not be taught. It was to be expected, of course: no matter the pretty wrapping in which Rose clad her, the girl was common-born, there was no escaping that. Cheeks that glowed too pink, laughter that echoed along the halls, curls that escaped her ribbons, she was as unlike Rose as was possible.

And yet Rose adored the girl. Thus had Adeline accepted her, schooled herself to smile at the child, meet her impertinent gaze, tolerate her noise. What wouldn't Adeline do for Rose? What hadn't she already done? But Adeline understood, too, that it was her duty to maintain a stern and ready hand, for the child would need firm guidance if she were to escape the pitfalls of her birth.

The circle of those who knew the truth was small and so must it remain: to allow otherwise was to invite the hideous specter of scandal. It was imperative, therefore, that Mary and Eliza be properly managed.

Adeline had worried at first that Rose might not understand, that the innocent girl might imagine all could continue as before. But on that count she had been pleasantly surprised. The moment Ivory was placed in Rose's arms, a change had come over her: she was seized by a fierce maternal desire to protect her child. Rose had agreed with Adeline that certainly Mary and Eliza must stay away: sufficient distance to preclude a daily presence, yet close enough to remain within the sphere of Adeline's influence. Only in that way could it be ensured that neither divulged what they knew about the child at Blackhurst Manor. Adeline had assisted Mary in the purchase of a little house in Polperro and Eliza had been permitted tenure at the cottage. Although a part of Adeline lamented the permanent proximity of Eliza, it was the lesser of two evils, and Rose's happiness was paramount.

Dear Rose. She'd looked so pale, sitting alone on the garden seat. Had barely touched her luncheon afterwards, merely moved it about the plate, this way and that. She was resting now, warding off the return of a migraine that had haunted her all week.

Adeline opened the fist which had clenched itself in her lap and flexed her fingers thoughtfully. She had made the conditions perfectly clear when everything was arranged: neither girl was to set foot again on the Blackhurst estate. The stipulation was simple, and to date each of them had complied. The wings of security had closed over the secret and life at Blackhurst had adopted a peaceful rhythm.

What, then, was Eliza thinking, breaking her word now?

IN THE end, Nathaniel waited until Rose was in bed, resting because of her nerves, and Adeline was out visiting. That way, he reasoned, neither need ever learn the method by which he ensured Eliza's continued absence. Ever since he'd heard what had happened, Nathaniel had been mulling over how best to set things right. To see his wife in such a state was a chilling reminder that, despite the distance they had traveled, the blessed reversal after Ivory was born, the other Rose, worry-worn, tense, erratic, was never far beneath the surface. He had known instantly that he must speak with Eliza. Find a way to make her understand that she could never come again.

Some time had passed since his last venture through and he'd forgotten how dark it was within the bramble walls, how briefly the sun's rays were permitted entry. He went carefully, trying to remember which turns to make. A far cry from the time, four years ago, when he had torn hotly through the maze in pursuit of his sketches. He'd arrived at the cottage, blood pulsing, shoulders heaving from the unusual exertion, and had demanded the sketches' return. They were his, he'd said, they were important to him, he needed them. And then, when he'd run out of things to say, he'd stood, catching his breath, waiting for Eliza to respond. He wasn't sure what he'd expected—a confession, an apology, a handover of the sketches, all of these things, perhaps—but she had given none. Rather, she'd surprised him. After a moment spent regarding him in the way one might a minor curiosity, she'd blinked those pale, changeable eyes that he itched to draw, and asked whether he would care to contribute illustrations for a book of fairy tales—

A noise and the memory fled. Nathaniel's heart stepped up its beat. He turned and glanced through the dim space behind him. A lone robin blinked at him before flying away.

Why was he so jumpy? He had the frayed nerves of a guilty man, a ridiculous state as there was nothing inappropriate in his actions. He intended only to speak with Eliza, request that she resist breaching the maze gates. And his mission, after all, was for Rose's sake; it was his wife's health and well-being that were uppermost in his mind.

He went faster, reassuring himself that he was manufacturing danger where there was none. His mission might be secret but it was not illicit. There was a difference.

He had agreed to illustrate the book. How could he resist, and why should he have? To sketch was his dearest wish and to illustrate her fairy tales allowed him to slip inside a world that didn't recognize the particular regrets in his own life. It had been a lifeline, a secret pursuit that made the long days of portraiture tolerable. At meetings with wealthy, titled dullards, when Adeline pressed him forward yet again and he was required to smile and perform convivially like a trained hound, he had nursed to himself the secret knowledge that he was also bringing to life the magical world of Eliza's tales.

He'd never had a finished copy of his own. Publication had been delayed for one reason or another, and by the time the book was published it was clear to him how unwelcome such would be at Blackhurst. Once, in the early days of the project, he'd committed the grave error of mentioning the book to Rose. He had thought she might be glad, might appreciate the union of her husband and her dearest cousin, but he had been mistaken. Her expression was one he would never forget: shock and anger, mixed together with bereavement. He had betrayed her, she said, he didn't love her, he wanted to leave her. Nathaniel had been at a loss as to how to understand. He had done what he always did on such occasions, reassured Rose and asked whether he might sketch her portrait for his collection. And he kept the project to himself from that day forward. But he didn't give it up. He couldn't.

After Ivory was born and Rose was restored, the trailing threads of his life had plaited slowly back together. Strange, the power of a tiny baby to bring life to a dead place, to lift the black pall that had covered everything—Rose, their marriage, Nathaniel's own soul. It hadn't been instant, of course. To begin with where the child was concerned, Nathaniel had trodden cautiously, taken his lead from Rose, mindful always of the possibility that the baby's origins might prove insurmountable. Only when he saw that she loved the girl as a daughter, never a cuckoo, did he allow the walls of his own heart to weaken. He permitted the baby's divine innocence to permeate his tired and wounded spirit, and he embraced the completion of his little family, the strength it gained as its membership grew from two to three.

And by and by he forgot about the book and the joy its illustrations had given him. He devoted himself to toeing the Mountrachet family line—ignored Eliza's existence and, when Adeline asked him to alter John Singer Sargent's portrait thus, bore willingly, if not happily, the dishonor at having tampered with the great man's work. It seemed to Nathaniel that by then he'd crossed so many lines of principle once presumed inviolable, one more wouldn't hurt . . .

Nathaniel reached the clearing at the center of the maze and a pair of peacocks appraised him briefly before continuing on their way. He went carefully to avoid the metal ring that threatened to trip a man up, then entered the narrow straight that began the way towards the hidden garden.

Nathaniel froze. Branches breaking, light footfalls. Heavier than those belonging to the peacocks.

He stopped, turned quickly. There—a flash of white. There *was* someone following him.

"Who is it?" His voice was raspier than he'd expected. He forced some steel into it. "I insist that you come out from hiding."

A moment's pause, then his pursuer was revealed.

"Ivory!" Relief was followed quickly by consternation. "What are you doing here? You know you're not permitted beyond the maze gates."

"Please, Papa," said the little girl. "Take me with you. Davies says there's a garden at maze end where all the world's rainbows begin."

Nathaniel couldn't help but admire the image. "Does he, now?"

Ivory nodded with the sort of childlike earnestness that captivated Nathaniel. He consulted his pocket watch. Adeline would be back within the hour, eager to check his progress on Lord Haymarket's commission. There wasn't time to take Ivory home and then return, and who knew when the opportunity would present itself again. He scratched his ear and sighed. "Come, then, little one."

She followed closely, humming a tune that Nathaniel recognized as "Oranges and Lemons." Lord knew from whom she'd learned it. Not from Rose, who had a terrible memory for lyrics and melody; nor Adeline, for whom music had little meaning. One of the servants, no doubt. For want of a proper governess, his daughter was passing much of her time with the Blackhurst staff. Who could guess what other questionable skills she was acquiring as a consequence?

"Papa?"

"Yes."

"I made another picture in my mind."

"Oh?" Nathaniel pushed a thorny bramble aside so that Ivory could pass.

"It was the ship with Captain Ahab on it. And the whale swimming just by."

"What color was the sail?"

"White, of course."

"And the whale?"

"Grey like a storm cloud."

"And what did your ship smell like?"

"Salty water and Davies's dirty boots."

Amused, Nathaniel raised his eyebrows. "I imagine it did." It was one of their favorite games, played often on the afternoons Ivory had taken to spending in his studio. It had surprised Nathaniel to discover that he so enjoyed the child's company. She made him see things differently, more simply, in a way that brought new life to his portraits. Her frequent questions as to what he was doing and why he was doing it required him to explain things he had long ago forgotten to appreciate: that one must draw what one sees, not what one imagines is there; that every image is comprised merely of lines and shapes; that color should both reveal and conceal.

"Why are we going through the maze, Papa?"

"There is someone on the other side whom I must see."

Ivory digested this. "Is it a person, Papa?"

"Of course it's a person. Do you think your papa might be meeting with a beast?"

They turned a corner, then another in quick succession, and Nathaniel was put in mind of a marble slipping through the twists and turns of the run Ivory had constructed in the nursery. Following the bends and straights with little control over its own destiny. A silly notion, of course, for what were his actions today if not those of a man taking charge of his own fate?

They made a final turn and arrived at the door to the hidden garden. Nathaniel stopped, knelt down and cupped his daughter's bony shoulders gently in his hands. "Now, Ivory," he said carefully, "I have brought you through the maze today."

"Yes, Papa."

"But you must never come again, and certainly not alone." Nathaniel pressed his lips together. "And I believe it would be best if . . . if this trip of ours today . . ."

"Don't worry, Papa. I won't tell Mamma."

Within the pit of Nathaniel's stomach, relief mixed with the uncomfortable sensation of having colluded with his child against his wife.

"Nor Grandmamma, either, Papa."

Nathaniel nodded, smiled weakly. "It's best that way."

"A secret."

"Yes, a secret."

Nathaniel pushed open the door to the hidden garden and ushered Ivory through. He had half expected to see Eliza, sitting like the Queen of the Fairies on the tuft of grass beneath the apple tree, but the garden was still and silent. The only movement came from a robin— the same one?—who cocked his head and watched almost proprietorially as Nathaniel made his way along the zigzag path.

"Oh, Papa," said Ivory, staring in wonder at the garden. She gazed upwards, taking in the creepers that snaked their way back and forth, from the top of one wall to the top of the other. "It's a *magical* garden."

How odd that a child should perceive such a thing. Nathaniel wondered what it was about Eliza's garden that made one feel such splendor could not have come naturally. That some bargain had been struck with spirits on the other side of the veil to procure such wild abundance.

He guided Ivory through the southern door and down the path that hugged the side of the cottage. Despite the hour, it was cool and dark in the front garden, courtesy of the stone wall that Adeline had

had built. Nathaniel laid a hand between Ivory's shoulder blades, her fairy wings. "Now, listen," he said. "Papa is going inside but you must wait here in the garden."

"Yes, Papa."

He hesitated. "Don't go wandering now."

"Oh no, Papa." Said so innocently, as if to wander where she shouldn't was the furthest thing from her mind.

With a nod, Nathaniel went to the door. He knocked and waited for Eliza to come, straightened the cuff of his sleeve.

The door opened and there she was. As if he'd last seen her yesterday. As if the four years hadn't passed between.

WHILE NATHANIEL sat on a chair by the table, Eliza stood on the other side, fingers resting lightly on its rim. She was looking at him in that singular way she had. Empty of the usual social nicety that would have suggested she was pleased to see him. Was it vanity that had made him think she might be pleased to see him? Something within the cottage light conspired to turn her hair brighter red than usual. Flints of sunlight played within its tangles, made it look as if it really had been spun from fairies' gold. Nathaniel chided himself—he was allowing his knowledge of her stories to permeate his vision of the woman herself. He knew better than that.

A strangeness sat between them. There was much to be said yet nothing he could think to say. It was the first time he'd seen her since the arrangements had been made. He cleared his throat, reached out as if to take her hand. Couldn't seem to help himself. She lifted her fingers suddenly and turned her attention to the range.

Nathaniel leaned back against his chair. He wondered how to begin, what words to wrap his message in. "You know why I have come," he said finally.

Without turning. "Of course."

He watched her fingers, such narrow fingers, as she put the kettle on the stove. "You know, then, what I have to say."

"Yes."

From outside, riding lightly on the breeze that swept through the window, came a voice, the sweetest voice: "Oranges and lemons, say the bells of St. Clement's . . ."

Eliza's back stiffened so that Nathaniel could see the small knots at her nape. Like a child's spine. She turned sharply. "The girl is here?"

Nathaniel was perversely pleased by the expression on Eliza's face, that of an animal on the unexpected brink of capture. He longed to put it on paper, the widened eyes, paled cheeks, tightened mouth. Knew he would attempt to do so as soon as he returned to his studio.

"You brought the child here?"

"She followed me. I didn't realize until it was too late."

The sick look left Eliza's face, transmuted into a weak smile. "She has stealth."

"Some would say mischief."

Eliza sat lightly on the chair. "It pleases me to think the girl likes games."

"I don't know that her mother is so pleased by Ivory's adventurous streak."

Her smile was impossible to read.

"And certainly her grandmamma is not."

The smile broadened. Nathaniel met it briefly, then looked away. He sighed her name—"Eliza"—and shook his head. Started what he had come to say: "The other day—"

"I was glad, the other day, to see that the child is well." She spoke quickly, anxious, it seemed, to prevent his line of conversation.

"Of course she is well, she wants for nothing."

"The appearance of plenty can be deceptive. It doesn't always mean a person is well. Ask your wife."

"That's needlessly cruel."

A sharp nod. Simple agreement, not a shred of regret. Nathaniel found himself wondering whether perhaps she had no morality, but he knew that wasn't so. She gazed unblinkingly at him. "You have come about my gift."

Nathaniel lowered his voice. "It was foolish of you to bring it. You know how Rose feels."

"I do. Only I thought, what harm could the delivery of such an item cause?"

"You know what sort of harm, and I know you, as a friend to Rose, would not wish to cause her anguish. As a friend to me . . ." He felt suddenly foolish, looked towards the ground, the floorboards, as if for support. "I must beg you not to come again, Eliza. Rose suffered dreadfully after your visit. She doesn't like to be reminded."

"Memory is a cruel mistress with whom we all must learn to dance."

Before Nathaniel could sculpt a reply, Eliza turned her attention back to the range. "Would you like tea?"

"No," he said, feeling somewhat bested, though he wasn't sure how. "I must get back."

"Rose doesn't know you're here."

"I must get back." He returned his hat to his head and started for the kitchen door.

"Did you see it? It turned out well, I think."

Nathaniel paused but did not turn. "Good-bye, Eliza. I will not see you again." He thrust his arms into his coat and pushed aside the niggling, unnameable doubts.

He was almost at the door when he heard Eliza in the hall behind him. "Wait," she said, some of her composure shed. "Allow me a closer look at the girl, at Rose's daughter."

Nathaniel pressed his fingers against the cool of the metal door-knob. Clenched his back teeth together as he pondered her request.

"It will be my last."

How could he refuse such a simple appeal? "A look. Then I must take her back, take her home."

Together they went through the front door into the garden. Ivory was sitting by the edge of the small pond, bare toes curled over the bank so that they kissed the water, singing to herself as she pushed a leaf along the surface.

As the child looked up, Nathaniel placed his hand gently on Eliza's arm and pushed her forward.

THE WIND had picked up and Linus had to lean against his cane to avoid losing his footing. Down in the cove, the usually mild sea had been agitated so that small waves with white tips rushed towards the shore. The sun was hiding behind a blanket of clouds—a far cry from the perfect summer's days he had once spent in the cove with his *poupée*.

The little wooden boat had been Georgiana's, a gift from Father, but she had been glad to share it with him. Hadn't thought for a moment that his weak leg made him any less of a man, never mind what Father said. On afternoons when the air was warm and sweet, they had paddled out together to the center of the cove. Sat, while waves lapped gently against the base of the boat, neither of them caring for anything but the other. Or so Linus had thought.

When she'd left, she'd taken with her the frail sense of solidarity that he had nursed. The sense that, though Father and Mother judged him a foolish boy with neither worth nor function, he had something to offer. Without Georgiana he was useless again, purposeless. Thus had he determined she must be returned.

Linus had hired a man, Henry Mansell, a dark and shadowy character whose name was whispered in the inns of Cornwall and passed on to Linus by the valet of a local earl. It was said he knew how to take care of matters.

Linus told Mansell of Georgiana and the harm done to him by

the fellow who stole her; told him also that the man worked on the ships in and out of London.

The next Linus knew, the sailor was dead. An accident, Mansell said, face registering no emotion, a most unfortunate accident.

It was a strange sensation that animated Linus that afternoon. A man's life had been extinguished at his will. He was powerful, able to inflict his inclination on others; it made him want to sing.

He'd given Mansell a generous payment, then the man had taken his leave, headed off in search of Georgiana. Linus had been filled with hope, for surely there were no limits to what Mansell could achieve. His *poupée* would be home presently, grateful for her rescue. Things would be as they had been before . . .

The black rock looked angry today. Linus felt his heart lurch as he remembered his Georgiana sitting on its top. He reached into his pocket and pulled out the photograph, smoothed it gently with his thumb.

"*Poupée.*" Half thought, half whisper. No matter how Mansell had hunted, he'd never found her. He'd scoured the Continent, followed leads across London, all to no avail. Linus had heard nothing until late in 1900, when word had come that a child had been found in London. A child with red hair and her mother's eyes.

Linus's gaze lifted from the sea, swept sideways to the top of the cliff that bound the left-hand side of the cove. From where he stood he could just make out the corner of the new stone wall.

How he had rejoiced at news of the child. He'd been too late to recover his Georgiana, but through this girl she would be returned.

But things had not played out as he'd expected. Eliza had resisted him, had never understood that he had sent for her, brought her here so that she might know she belonged to him.

And now her presence tormented him, locked away in that accursed cottage. So close, and yet . . . Four years, it had been. Four years since she had set foot on this side of the maze. Why was she so cruel? Why did she deny him over and over again?

A sudden gust of wind and Linus felt his hat lift at the sides. He reached, from instinct, to stop it and, as he did, his grip loosened on his photograph.

On the current of the hilltop breeze, while Linus stood helplessly, his *poupée* was blown from his reach. Down and up, fluttering on the wind, shining white beneath the glare of the clouds, hovering, teasing him, before being swept further away. Landing finally on the water and being carried out to sea.

Away from Linus, slipping through his fingers once more.

EVER SINCE Eliza's visit, Rose had been worrying. Tying her mind in knots as she sought a path through this dilemma. When Eliza had made her appearance through the maze gates, Rose had suffered the peculiar shock of a person who comes suddenly to understand that they are in danger. Worse, that they have been in danger for some time without realizing it. She'd felt a sudden onset of light-headedness and panic. Relief that so far nothing had happened, and dread certainty that such luck could not hold. For all Rose had weighed up the options, there was only one thing she knew for sure: Mamma was right, they needed to put a distance between themselves and Eliza.

Rose pulled the thread gently through her needlepoint and schooled her voice into a tone of perfect nonchalance: "I have been thinking again of the visit from the Authoress."

Nathaniel looked up from the letter he was penning. Chased quickly the concern from his gaze. "As I said before, my dear, think no more upon it. It won't happen again."

"You can't be sure of that, for who among us predicted this most recent visit?"

Sterner now. "She will not come again."

"How do you know?"

Nathaniel's cheeks flushed. The change was only slight, but Rose noticed. "Nate? What is it?"

"I have spoken with her."

Rose's heart tapped faster. "You saw her?"

"I had to. For you, dearest. You were so upset by her visit, I did what was needed to ensure it won't happen again."

"But I didn't mean for you to see her." This was worse than Rose had imagined. A surge of heat beneath her skin and she was filled with an even stronger certainty that they must get away. All of them. That Eliza must be extricated forever from their lives. Rose slowed her breath, schooled her face to relax. It wouldn't do to have Nathaniel think she was unwell, was making decisions without reason. "Speaking with her is not enough, Nate. Not anymore."

"What else can be done? Surely you don't suggest we lock her in the cottage?" He'd been trying to make her laugh but she didn't flinch.

"I've been thinking about New York."

Nathaniel's brows raised.

"We have spoken before of spending time across the Atlantic. I think we should bring forward our plans."

"Leave England?"

Rose nodded, slightly but certainly.

"But I have commissions. We spoke of engaging a governess for Ivory."

"Yes, yes," Rose said impatiently. "But it is no longer *safe*."

Nathaniel said nothing in return but he didn't need to, his expression spoke volumes. The little ice chip inside Rose hardened. He would come around to her way of thinking, he always did. Especially when he feared that she teetered atop the slide to despair. It was regrettable, using Nathaniel's devotion against him, but Rose had little other choice. Motherhood and family life were all Rose had dreamed of; she didn't intend to lose them now. When Ivory was born, placed in Rose's arms, it was as if they had all been granted a fresh start. She and Nathaniel were happy again, they never spoke of the time before. It didn't exist any longer. Not so long as Eliza stayed away.

"I have the engagement in Carlisle," said Nathaniel. "I've already started." In his voice, Rose perceived the cracks that she would widen until his resistance crumbled.

"And of course you must be able to complete it," she said. "We will bring forward the Carlisle engagement, sail directly after we return. I have three tickets for the *Carmania*."

"You've booked already." A statement rather than a question.

Rose softened her voice. "It is best, Nate. You must see that. It's the only way we will ever be safe. And think what such a trip will do for your career. Why, the *New York Times* might even report it. A triumphant homecoming for one of the city's most accomplished sons."

PRESSED BENEATH Grandmamma's favorite sprung chair, Ivory whispered the words to herself. "New York." Ivory knew where York was. Once, when they were traveling north to Scotland, she and Mamma and Papa had stopped for a time in York, at the house of one of Grandmamma's friends. A very old lady with wiry spectacles and eyes that looked always to be weeping. But Mamma wasn't speaking of York, Ivory had heard her clearly. *New* York, she'd said, they must go soon to *New* York. And Ivory knew where that city was. It was far across the sea, the place in which Papa had been born, about which he had told her stories full of skyscrapers and music and motorcars. A city where everything gleamed.

A clump of dog hairs tickled Ivory's nose and she fought to hold in a sneeze. It was one of her most impressive skills, the ability to halt sneezes in their track, and part of what made her such an excellent hider. Ivory so enjoyed hiding that sometimes she did so for no other reason than to please herself. Alone in a room she would conceal herself for the pure pleasure of knowing that even the room itself had forgotten she was there.

Today, though, Ivory had hidden with purpose. Grandpapa had been in odd spirits. Usually he could be counted upon to keep himself to himself, but lately he'd appeared wherever Ivory was, calling her his own. Always with his little brown camera, trying to take photos of her with that broken dolly of his. Ivory didn't like the broken dolly with her horrid blinking eyes. So although Mamma said she should do as Grandpapa asked, that it was a great honor to have one's photograph taken, Ivory preferred to hide.

Thoughts of the dolly made her skin prickle, so she tried to think of something else. Something that made her happy, like the adventure she'd been on with Papa, through the maze. Ivory had been outside playing when she'd seen Papa emerge from the side door of the house. He'd walked quickly and at first she had thought he might be taking a carriage to paint somebody's portrait. Only he didn't have any of his equipment with him, nor was he dressed in quite the same way he usually was when he had an important meeting. Ivory had watched him stride across the lawn, drawing closer to the maze gate, and then she'd known exactly what he was doing, he wasn't good at pretending.

Ivory hadn't thought twice. She'd hurried after Papa, followed him through the maze gates and into the dark, narrow tunnels. For Ivory knew that the lady with the red hair, the one who had brought the parcel for her, lived on the other side.

And now, after her visit with Papa, she knew who the lady was. Her name was the Authoress, and though Papa said she was a person, Ivory knew better. She'd suspected it the day the Authoress had come through the maze, but after looking into her eyes in the cottage garden, Ivory had known for certain.

The Authoress was magical. Witch or fairy, she wasn't sure, but Ivory knew the Authoress wasn't a person like any other she'd seen before.

FORTY-THREE

CLIFF COTTAGE, 2005

OUTSIDE, the wind worried the treetops and the ocean breathed heavily in the cove. Moonlight streamed through the windowpane, casting four silvery squares across the wooden floor, and the warm tomato smell of soup and toast had impregnated the walls, the floor, the very air. Cassandra, Christian and Ruby sat around the table in the kitchen, the range glowing on one side, a kerosene heater on the other. Candles were lined along the table and at various points about the room, but there were still spaces in the dark, lonely corners where candlelight failed to reach.

"I still don't understand," said Ruby. "How do you know Rose was infertile from that journal article?"

Christian spooned a mouthful of soup. "The X-ray exposure. There's no way her eggs would have survived."

"Wouldn't she have known, though? I mean, surely there'd have been a sign that something was wrong."

"Like what?"

"Well, did she still . . . you know . . . get her periods?"

Christian shrugged his shoulders. "I guess so. The function of her reproductive system would have been unaffected. She still would have released an egg each month. It's just the eggs themselves that would have been damaged."

"So damaged she couldn't conceive?"

"Or if she did, there'd have been so much wrong with the baby that she would most likely have miscarried. Or given birth to a child with massive deformities."

Cassandra pushed the last of her soup aside. "That's terrible. Why did he do it?"

"He probably just wanted to be among the first to make use of the shiny new technology, enjoy the glory of publication. There was certainly no medical reason to take an X-ray, the kid had only swallowed a thimble."

"Who hasn't?" said Ruby, wiping a crust of bread around her already smeared-clean bowl.

"But why a one-hour exposure? Surely that wasn't necessary?"

"Of course it wasn't," said Christian. "But people didn't know that then. Those sorts of exposure times were common."

"I suppose they figured if you got a good image in fifteen minutes, you'd get an even better one in an hour," said Ruby.

"And it was before they knew the dangers. X-rays were only discovered in 1895, so Dr. Matthews was being pretty cutting edge using them. People actually thought they were good for you in the beginning, that they could cure cancer and skin lesions and other disorders. The burns were obvious enough, but it was years before the full extent of the negative effects was realized."

"That's what Rose's marks were," said Cassandra. "Burn scars."

Christian nodded. "Along with frying her ovaries, the X-ray exposure would certainly have burned her skin."

A gust of wind set thin branches to tracing noisy patterns on the windowpanes and the candlelight flickered as a cool ribbon of air slipped beneath the baseboard. Ruby placed her bowl inside Cassandra's, swiped a napkin across her mouth. "So if Rose was infertile, who was Nell's mother?"

"I know the answer to that," said Cassandra.

"You do?"

She nodded. "It's all there in the scrapbooks. In fact, I reckon that's what Clara wants to tell me."

"Who's Clara?" said Christian.

Ruby inhaled. "You think Nell was Mary's baby."

"Who's Mary?" Christian looked between them.

"Eliza's friend," said Cassandra. "Clara's mum. A domestic at Blackhurst who was dismissed in early 1909 when Rose discovered she was pregnant."

"Rose dismissed her?"

Cassandra nodded. "In the scrapbook she writes that she can't bear to think that someone so undeserving should have a child when she has been continually denied."

Ruby swallowed a slurp of wine. "But why would Mary have given her child to Rose?"

"I doubt she just *gave* her the child."

"You think Rose bought the baby?"

"It's possible, right? People have done worse to secure a child."

"Do you think Eliza knew?" said Ruby.

"Worse than that," said Cassandra. "I think she helped. I think that's why she went away."

"Guilt?"

"Exactly. She helped Rose use her position of power to wrangle a child from someone who needed money. Eliza can't have been comfortable with that. She and Mary were close, Rose says so."

"You're presuming that Mary wanted the child," said Ruby. "Didn't want to give her up."

"I'm presuming the decision to give up a baby is never clean. Mary may have needed money, a baby may have been inconvenient, she may even have thought her child was going to a better home, but I still reckon it must've been devastating."

Ruby lifted her eyebrows. "And Eliza helped her."

"Then she went away. That's what makes me think the baby wasn't given up happily. I think Eliza went away because she couldn't bear to stay and watch Rose with Mary's baby. I think that when it came to separating mother and child it was traumatic and it played on Eliza's conscience."

Ruby nodded slowly. "That would explain why Rose refused to see much of Eliza after Ivory was born, why the two of them drifted apart. Rose must've known how Eliza felt and worried that she'd do something to upset her newfound happiness."

"Like take Ivory back," said Christian.

"Which she did in the end."

"Yes," said Ruby, "which she did in the end." She raised her eyebrows at Cassandra. "So when do you see Clara?"

"She invited me to visit tomorrow, eleven o'clock."

"Bugger. I'm leaving around nine. Bloody work. I would've loved to come, I could've given you a lift."

"I'll take you." This was Christian. He'd been playing with the knobs on the heater, turning the flame up, and the smell of kerosene was strong.

Cassandra avoided Ruby's grin. "Really? Are you sure?"

He smiled as he met her gaze, held it for a moment before looking away. "You know me. Always happy to help."

Cassandra smiled in reply, turned her attention to the table surface as her cheeks warmed. Something about Christian made her feel thirteen again. And it was such a youthful, nostalgic feeling—displacement to a time and place when life was yet to happen to her—that she longed to cling to it. To push aside the guilty sense that by enjoying Christian's company she was somehow being disloyal to Nick and Leo.

"So why do you think Eliza waited until 1913?" Christian looked from Ruby to Cassandra. "To take Nell back, I mean. Why not do it earlier?"

Cassandra ran her hand lightly along the top of the table. Watched the candlelight dapple across her skin. "I think she did it because Rose and Nathaniel died in the train crash. My guess is that despite her mixed feelings she was willing to stand back while Rose was made happy."

"But once Rose was dead . . ."

"Exactly." Her eyes met his. Something in the seriousness of his expression brought a shiver to her spine. "Once Rose was dead, she could no longer bear for Ivory to remain at Blackhurst. I think she took the little girl and intended to give her back to Mary."

"Then why didn't she? Why did she put her on the boat to Australia?"

Cassandra exhaled and the nearby candle's flame wavered. "I haven't quite worked that bit out."

Neither had she worked out how much, if anything, William Martin had known when he met Nell in 1975. Mary was his sister, so wouldn't he have known if she'd been pregnant? If she'd given birth to a baby she didn't then raise? And surely if he'd known she was pregnant, had known the part Eliza played in the unofficial adoption, he'd have said as much to Nell? After all, if Mary was Nell's mother, then William was her uncle. Cassandra couldn't imagine that he'd have remained silent if a long-lost niece turned up on his doorstep.

Yet there was no mention in Nell's notebook of any such recognition from William. Cassandra had pored over the pages, looking for hints she might have missed. William had neither said nor done anything to suggest that Nell was family to him.

It was possible, of course, that William hadn't realized Mary was pregnant. Cassandra had heard of such occurrences, in magazines and on American talk shows, girls who concealed their pregnancies the full nine months. And it made sense that Mary would have done so. In order for the exchange to work, Rose would have insisted on discretion. She couldn't have had the small village aware that her baby wasn't her own.

But was it really likely that a girl could fall pregnant, get engaged to her boyfriend, lose her job, give the baby away, resume her life and no one know anything about it? There was something Cassandra was missing, there must be.

"It's kind of like Eliza's fairy tale, isn't it?"

Cassandra looked up at Christian. "What is?"

"The whole thing: Rose, Eliza, Mary, the baby. Doesn't it remind you of 'The Golden Egg'?"

Cassandra shook her head. The name was not familiar.

"It's in *Magical Tales for Girls and Boys*."

"Not in my copy. We must have different editions."

"There was only one edition. That's why they're so rare."

Cassandra lifted her shoulders. "I've never seen it."

Ruby flapped her hand. "Enough, who gives two hoots how many editions there were? Tell us about the story, Christian. What makes you think it's about Mary and the baby?"

"It's an odd one, actually, 'The Golden Egg'; I always felt that. Different from the other fairy tales, sadder and with a shakier moral frame. It's about a wicked queen who coerces a young maiden into giving up a magical golden egg to heal the ailing princess of the land. The maiden resists at first, because it's her life's work to guard the egg—her birthright, I think, is how she describes it—but the queen wears her down and in the end she consents because she's convinced that if she doesn't, the princess will suffer eternal sorrow and the kingdom will be cursed to an endless winter. There's a character who plays the go-between in the transaction, the handmaiden. She works for the princess and then the queen, but when it comes down to it she tries to convince the maiden not to part with the egg. It's as if she realizes that the egg is a part of the maiden, that without it the maiden will have no purpose, no reason to live. Which is exactly what happens, she hands over the egg and it ruins her life."

"You think the handmaiden was Eliza?" said Cassandra.

"It fits, doesn't it?"

Ruby leaned her chin on her fist. "Let me get this straight. You're saying the egg was the child? Nell?"

"Yes."

"And Eliza wrote the story as a way to assuage her guilt?"

Christian shook his head. "Not guilt. The story doesn't feel guilty. It's more like sadness. For herself and for Mary. And for Rose, in a way. The characters in the story are all doing what they think is right, it's just that it can't have a happy ending for all of them."

Cassandra bit her lip thoughtfully. "You really think a children's fairy tale might be autobiographical?"

"Not autobiographical, exactly, not in a literal sense, unless she had some pretty wacky experiences." He raised his eyebrows at the thought. "I just reckon Eliza probably processed bits of her own life by turning them into fiction. Isn't that what writers do?"

"I don't know. Do they?"

"I'll bring 'The Golden Egg' with me tomorrow," said Christian. "You can judge for yourself." The warm ochre candlelight accented his cheekbones, made his skin glow. He smiled shyly. "Her fairy tales are the only voice Eliza has anymore. Who knows what else she's trying to tell us?"

AFTER CHRISTIAN left to make his way back to the village, Ruby and Cassandra laid their sleeping bags out on the foam mattress he'd brought for them. They'd decided to stay downstairs so they could take advantage of the still-warm range, and had pushed the table aside to make room. Wind from the sea blew gently through cracks beneath the doors, up between the gaps in the floorboards. The house had a smell of damp soil, more so than Cassandra had noticed in the daytime.

"This is the part where we tell each other ghost stories," whispered Ruby, rolling over heavily to face Cassandra. She grinned, face shadowy in the flickering light. "What fun. Have I told you how lucky you are to have a haunted cottage on the edge of a cliff?"

"Once or twice."

Kate Morton

She gave a cheeky smile. "What about how lucky you are to have a 'friend' like Christian, who's handsome, clever and kind?"

Cassandra concentrated on the zip of her sleeping bag, drew it up with a precision and attention to detail far outweighing the task.

"A 'friend' who obviously thinks the sun shines out of you."

"Oh, Ruby," Cassandra shook her head, "he does not. He just likes helping in the garden."

Ruby raised her eyebrows, amused. "Of course, he likes the garden. That's why he's given up the better part of a fortnight to work for nothing."

"It's true!"

"Of course it is."

Cassandra bit back a smile and adopted a slightly indignant tone. "Whether you believe it or not, the hidden garden is very important to Christian. He used to play in it as a kid."

"And that intense passion for the garden must explain why he's taking you to Polperro tomorrow."

"He's just being nice. He's a nice person. It's nothing to do with me, with how he feels about me. He certainly doesn't 'like' me."

Ruby nodded sagely. "You're right, of course. I mean, what's to like?"

Cassandra glanced sideways, smiled despite herself. "So," she said, biting her bottom lip, "you think he's handsome?"

Ruby grinned. "Sweet dreams, Cassandra."

"Good night, Ruby."

Cassandra blew out the candle, but a full moon meant that the room wasn't completely dark. A silvery film spilled across every surface, smooth and dull like wax gone cool. She lay in the half-light running the pieces of the puzzle through her mind: Eliza, Mary, Rose, then every so often, out of place, Christian, meeting her gaze before looking away.

Within a couple of minutes, Ruby was snoring softly. Cassandra smiled to herself. She might have guessed Ruby was an easy sleeper. She closed her own eyes and each lid gained weight.

As the sea swirled at the base of the cliff, and the trees overhead whispered in the midnight wind, Cassandra, too, drifted into sleep . . .

. . . She was in the garden, the hidden garden, sitting beneath the apple tree on the softest grass. The day was very warm and a bee droned around the apple blossoms, hovering near before floating away on the breeze.

She was thirsty, longed for a drink of water, but none was nearby. She reached out her hand, tried to push herself to standing, but couldn't. Her stomach was huge and swollen, the skin tight and itchy beneath her dress.

She was pregnant.

As soon as she realized, the sensation became familiar. She could feel her heart pumping heavily, the warmth of her skin, then the baby started to kick . . .

"Cass."

. . . kicked so hard, enough force that her stomach lurched on one side, she laid her hand on her bump, tried to catch the little foot . . .

"Cass."

Her eyes opened. Moonlight on the walls. The ticking of the range.

Ruby was propped up on one arm, tapping her shoulder. "Are you all right? You were groaning."

"I'm fine." Cassandra sat up suddenly. Felt her stomach. "Oh, my God. I had the strangest dream. I was pregnant, very pregnant. My stomach was huge and tight, and everything was so vivid." She rubbed her eyes. "I was in the walled garden and the baby started to kick."

"It's all that talk earlier, of Mary's baby, and Rose, and golden eggs, all getting mixed up together."

"Not to mention the wine." Cassandra yawned. "But it was so

real, it felt exactly like the real thing. I was so uncomfortable, and hot, and when the baby kicked it was so painful."

"You paint a lovely picture of pregnancy," said Ruby. "You're making me glad I never tried it."

Cassandra smiled. "It's not much fun in the final months, but it's worth it in the end. That moment when you finally hold a tiny new life in your arms."

Nick had cried in the delivery room, but Cassandra hadn't. She'd been too present, too much a part of the powerful moment, to react in such a way. To cry would have necessitated a second level of feeling, an ability to step outside events and view them within a larger context. Cassandra's experience had been too immediate for that. She'd felt fired from within by a sort of dizzy jubilation. As if she could hear better, see better, than she ever had before. Could hear her own pulse pumping, the lights humming above, her new baby's breaths.

"Actually, I *was* pregnant once," said Ruby. "But only for about five minutes."

"Oh, Ruby." Cassandra was awash with sympathy. "You lost the baby?"

"In a manner of speaking. I was young, it was a mistake, he and I agreed it was stupid to go through with it. I figured there was plenty of time later for all that." She lifted her shoulders, then smoothed her sleeping bag across her legs. "Only problem was, by the time I was ready I no longer had the necessary ingredients at my disposal."

Cassandra leaned her head to the side.

"Sperm, m'dear. I don't know whether I spent my entire thirties with PMS, but for whatever reason the greater population of menfolk and I failed to see eye to eye. By the time I met a bloke I could live with, the baby ship had sailed. We tried for a while but"—she shrugged—"well, you can't fight nature."

"I'm sorry, Ruby."

"Don't be. I'm doing all right. I have a job I love, good friends."

She winked. "And come on, you've seen my flat. I'm onto a winner there. No room to swing a cat, but hey—I haven't got a cat to swing."

Cassandra smiled.

"You make a life out of what you have, not what you're missing." Ruby lay down again and snuggled into her sleeping bag. She pulled it up around her shoulders. "Nightie-night."

Cassandra continued to sit for a while, watching shadows dance along the walls as she thought about what Ruby had said. About the life that she, Cassandra, had built out of the things, the people, she was missing. Was that what Nell had done, too? Forsaken the life and the family she'd been given, to focus instead on the one she'd been without? Cassandra lay down and closed her eyes. Let the nighttime sounds drown out her disquieting thoughts. The sea breathing, waves crashing against the great black rock, treetops shushing in the wind . . .

The cottage was a lonely place, isolated by day but even more so once darkness fell. The road didn't extend all the way up the cliff, the entrance to the hidden garden had been closed off and beyond it lay a maze whose route was difficult to follow. It was the sort of place one might live in and never see another soul.

A sudden thought and Cassandra gasped. Sat upright. "Ruby," she said, then louder, "Ruby."

"Asleep," came the slurred response.

"But I just figured it out."

"Still asleep."

"I know why they built the wall, why Eliza went away. That's why I had the dream—my unconscious figured it out and was trying to let me know."

A sigh. Ruby rolled over and propped herself on a bent arm. "You win, I'm awake. Just."

"This is where Mary stayed when she was pregnant with Ivory, with Nell. Here, in the cottage. That's why William didn't know she was pregnant." Cassandra leaned closer to Ruby. "That's why Eliza went away: Mary was here instead. They kept her hidden in the cottage, built the wall so that no one would accidentally catch sight of her."

Ruby rubbed her eyes and sat up.

"They turned this cottage into a cage until the baby was born and Rose was made a mother."

FORTY-FOUR

THE afternoon before she was due to leave Tregenna, Nell went a last time to Cliff Cottage. She took the white suitcase with her, filled with the documents and research she'd collected during her visit. She wanted to look over her notes and the cottage seemed as good a place as any in which to do so. At least that's what she'd told herself when she'd decided to make her way up the steep cliff road. It wasn't true, of course, not completely. For although she had wanted to look over the notes, that wasn't why she'd come to the cottage. She'd come simply because she couldn't stay away.

She unlocked the door and pushed it open. Winter was approaching and the cottage was cool: stale air sat thick and heavy in the hallway. Nell took the suitcase upstairs to the bedroom. It pleased her to look out over the silver sea, and on her last visit she'd spied a little bentwood chair in the corner of the room that would serve her purposes very well. The cane had unraveled from the back but that was no impediment. Nell positioned the chair by the window, sat tentatively and opened the white suitcase.

She leafed through the papers inside: Robyn's notes on the Mountrachet family, the contact details of the detective she'd hired to look into Eliza's whereabouts, searches and correspondence from the local lawyers about her purchase of Cliff Cottage. Nell found the letter relating to the property boundaries and flipped it over to study the surveyor's map. She could see quite clearly now the area young Christian had told her was a garden. She wondered who on earth had bricked up the gate, and why.

As she pondered, the paper slipped from Nell's hand and fluttered to the ground. She reached down to pick it up and something caught her eye. Damp weather had buckled the baseboard, pulled it loose from the wall. A piece of paper was wedged behind. Nell caught the corner between her fingers and retrieved it.

A small piece of card, spotted with foxing, on which a woman's face had been drawn, framed by an arch of brambles. Nell recognized her from the portrait she'd seen in the gallery in London. It was Eliza Makepeace, but there was something different about this sketch. Unlike the Nathaniel Walker portrait in London that made her look untouchable, this one was somehow more intimate. Something in the eyes suggested that this artist had been better acquainted with Eliza than had Nathaniel. Bold lines, certain curves, and the expression: something in her eyes both compelled Nell and confronted her.

Nell smoothed over the top of the card. To think it had been lying there in wait for so long. She pulled the book of fairy tales from the suitcase. She hadn't been precisely sure why she'd brought it with her to the cottage, only that there seemed a pleasant symmetry in bringing the stories home, back to the very place in which Eliza Makepeace had written them. Undoubtedly silly, embarrassingly sentimental, but there you are. Now Nell was glad she had. She opened the cover and slipped the sketch inside. That would keep it safe.

She leaned back against the chair and ran her fingers over the book's cover, the smooth leather and raised center panel with its illustration of a maiden and a fawn. It was a beautiful book, as beautiful as any that had passed through Nell's antiques shop. And it was so well preserved, decades spent in Hugh's care had done it no harm.

Though it was earlier times she sought to recall, Nell found her mind returning over and again to Hugh. In particular, the nights he'd read her bedtime stories from the fairy-tale book. Lil had been concerned, worried they might be too scary for a little girl, but Hugh had understood. In the evenings, after dinner, when Lil was clearing the day away, he would collapse back into his wicker chair and Nell would curl up in his lap. The pleasant weight of his arms wrapped around her to grasp the edges of the book, the faint smell of tobacco on his shirt, the rough whiskers on his warm cheek catching her hair.

Nell sighed steadily. Hugh had done well by her, he and Lil both. All the same, she blanked them out and willed her mind back further. For there was a time before Hugh, a time before the boat trip to Maryborough, the time of Blackhurst and the cottage and the Authoress.

There—a white cane garden chair, sun, butterflies. Nell closed her eyes and clutched the memory's tail, let it drag her into a warm summer's day, a garden where shade spilled cool across a sprawling lawn. Air filled with the scent of sunbaked flowers . . .

THE LITTLE girl was pretending to be a butterfly. A woven wreath of flowers encircled her head and she was holding her arms out to the sides, running in circles, fluttering and swooping while the sunlight warmed her wings. She felt so grand as the sun turned the white cotton of her dress to silver.

"Ivory."

At first the little girl did not hear, for butterflies do not speak the languages of men. They sing in sweetest tone with words so beautiful grown-up ears cannot hear them. Only children notice when they call.

"Ivory, come quickly."

There was a sternness to Mamma's voice now, so the little girl swooped and fluttered in the direction of the white garden chair.

"Come, come," said Mamma, reaching out her arms, beckoning with the pale tips of her fingers.

With a warm happiness spreading beneath her skin, the little girl climbed up. Mamma wrapped her arms around the little girl's waist and pressed cool lips against the skin beneath her ear.

"I'm a butterfly," the little girl said, "this chair is my cocoon—"

"Shhh. Quiet, now." Mamma's face was still pressed close and the little girl realized she was looking at something beyond. The little girl turned to see what it was that held Mamma's attention so.

A lady was coming towards them. The little girl squinted into the sun to make some sense of this mirage. For this lady was different from the others who came to visit Mamma and Grandmamma, the ones who stayed for tea and games of bridge. This lady looked somehow like a girl stretched to grown-up height. She wore a dress of white cotton and her red hair was only loosely tied in place.

The little girl looked about for the carriage that must have brought the lady up the drive, but there was none. It seemed that she had materialized from thin air, as if by magic.

Then the little girl realized. She caught her breath, filled with wonder. The lady was not walking from the direction of the entrance, she had come from inside the maze.

The little girl was forbidden to enter the maze. It was one of the first and sternest rules; both Mamma and Grandmamma were always reminding her that the way was dark and filled with untold dangers. So serious was the decree that even Papa, who could usually be relied upon, dared not disobey.

The lady was still hurrying directly towards them, half walking, half skipping. She had something with her, a brown-paper parcel, under her arm.

Mamma's own arms tightened around the little girl's middle so that pleasure slipped towards discomfort.

The lady stopped before them.

"Hello, Rose."

The little girl knew this was Mamma's name and yet Mamma said nothing in return.

"I know I'm not supposed to come." A silvery voice, like a spider's thread, which the little girl would have liked to hold between her fingers.

"Then why have you?"

The lady held out her parcel, but Mamma did not take it. Her grip tightened again. "I want nothing from you."

"I don't bring it for you." The lady put the parcel on the seat. "It is for your little girl."

THE PARCEL had contained the book of fairy tales, Nell remembered that now. There had been a discussion later, between her mother and father: she had insisted on the book's banishment, and he had eventually agreed. Only he hadn't thrown it away. He had put it in his studio, next to the battered copy of *Moby-Dick*. And he had read it to Nell, when she sat with him, when her mother was ill and unaware.

Thrilled by the memory, Nell stroked the front cover again. The book had been a gift from Eliza. She opened it carefully to the place where the ribbon bookmark had lain for sixty years. It was deep plum, only slightly frayed where the weave had begun to unravel, and it marked the beginning of a story called "The Crone's Eyes." Nell began to read about the young princess who didn't know she was a princess, who journeyed across the sea to the land of lost things to bring back the crone's missing sight. It was distantly familiar, as a favored tale from childhood ought to be. Nell placed the bookmark in its new spot and closed the book, laid it back on the windowsill.

She frowned and leaned closer. There was still a gap in the spine where the ribbon had been.

Nell opened the book again; the pages fell automatically once more to "The Crone's Eyes." She ran her finger down the inside of the spine—

There were pages missing. Not many, only five or six, barely noticeable, but missing all the same.

The excision was neat. No rough edges, tight up against the binding. Done with a penknife, perhaps?

Nell checked the page numbers. They jumped from fifty-four to sixty-one.

The gap fell perfectly between two stories . . .

The Golden Egg

by Eliza Makepeace

A long time ago, when seeking was finding, there lived a young maiden in a tiny cottage on the edge of a large and prosperous kingdom. The maiden had few means and her cottage was hidden so deeply within the dark woods as to be obscured from common view. There had been those, long ago, who knew of the little cottage with its stone fireplace, but such folk had long since passed and Mother Time had drawn a veil of forget around the cottage. Aside from the birds who came to sing on her windowsill, and the woodland animals who came in search of her warm hearth, the maiden was alone. Yet was she never lonely or unhappy, for the maiden of the cottage was too busy to pine for company she'd never had.

Deep within the heart of the cottage, behind a special door with a shiny lock, there was a very precious object. A Golden Egg whose glow was said to be so brilliant, so beautiful, that those whose eyes lit upon it were rendered instantly blind. The Golden Egg was so old that no one could properly remember its age, and for countless generations the maiden's family had been charged with its protection.

The maiden did not question this responsibility, for she knew it to be her destiny. The egg must be kept safe and well and hidden. Most importantly, the egg's existence must be kept secret. Many years before, when the kingdom was new, great wars had erupted over the Golden Egg, for legend told that it had magical powers and could grant its possessor his heart's desire.

So it was the maiden kept her vigil. By day she sat at her little spinning wheel in the cottage window, singing happily with the birds who gathered to watch her work. By night she offered shelter to her animal friends and slept in the warmth of the cottage, heated from within by the glow of the Golden Egg. And she remembered always that there was naught more important than protecting one's birthright.

Meanwhile, far away across the land, in the kingdom's grand castle, there lived a young Princess who was good and fair but very unhappy. Her health was poor and no matter that her mother, the Queen, had scoured the land for magic or medicine, nothing could be found to make the Princess well. There were those who whispered that when she was but a babe a wicked apothecary had cursed her to eternal ill health, but no one dared utter such sentiment aloud. For the Queen was a cruel ruler whose wrath her subjects wisely feared.

The Queen's daughter, however, was the apple of her mother's eye. Each morning the Queen paid a visit to her bedside, but alas, each morning the Princess was the same: pale, weak and weary. "It is all I wish, Mother," she would whisper, "the strength to walk through the castle gardens, to dance at the castle balls, to swim in the castle waters. To be well is my heart's desire."

The Queen had a magic looking glass from which she gleaned the comings and goings of the kingdom, and day after day she asked, "Mirror of mine, favored friend, show me the healer who will bring this horror's end."

But each day the mirror gave the same answer: "There is no one, my Queen, in all the land, who can make her well by his healing hand."

Now one day it happened that the Queen was so upset by her daughter's condition that she forgot to ask the looking glass her usual question. Instead she began to sob, crying, "Mirror of mine, that I so admire, show me how to grant my daughter's heart's desire."

The mirror was silent for a moment, but within its glassy center an image began to form, a tiny cottage in the middle of a deep, dark wood, smoke pluming from a little stone chimney. Inside the window sat a young maiden, spinning at a wheel and singing with the birds on the sill.

"What is this you show me?" gasped the Queen. "Is this young woman a healer?"

The mirror's voice was low and somber: "In the dark woods on the kingdom's edge lies a cottage. Inside is a Golden Egg with the power to grant its holders their heart's desire. The maiden you see is the guardian of the Golden Egg."

"How will I get the egg from her?" said the Queen.

"She does what she does for the kingdom's good," said the mirror, "and will not easily consent."

"Then what must I do?"

But the magic looking glass had no more answers, and the image of the cottage faded so that only glass remained. The Queen lifted her chin and stared down her long nose, holding her own gaze until a slight smile formed on her lips.

Early the next morning, the Queen summoned the Princess's closest handmaiden. A girl who had lived in the kingdom all her life, and who the Queen knew could be counted on to perform whatever task was necessary in order to ensure the Princess's health and happiness. The Queen instructed the handmaiden to retrieve the Golden Egg.

The handmaiden set off across the kingdom in the direction of the dark woods. For three days and nights she walked east and, as dusk was falling on the third night, she came to the edge of the woods. She stepped over fallen branches and cleared a path through foliage, until finally, standing in a clearing before her, was a tiny cottage with sweetly scented smoke pluming from its chimney.

The handmaiden knocked on the door and waited. When it opened, a young maiden stood on the other side and, although she was surprised to see a visitor on her doorstep, a generous smile spread across her face. She stepped aside and welcomed the handmaiden across the threshold. "You are tired," said the maiden. "You have journeyed far. Come and warm yourself by my hearth."

The handmaiden followed the maiden inside and sat on a cushion by the fire. The maiden of the cottage brought a bowl of warm broth and sat quietly weaving while her guest ate. The fire crackled in the grate and the warmth in the room made the handmaiden very drowsy. Her desire to slumber was so strong that she would have forgotten her mission had the maiden of the cottage not said, "You are very welcome here, stranger, but you must forgive me for asking whether there is a purpose to your visit."

"I have been sent by the Queen of the land," said the handmaiden. "She seeks your assistance in healing her daughter's ill health."

The birds of the forest sometimes sang of goings-on within the kingdom, thus had the maiden heard tell of the fair and kind Princess who lived inside the castle walls. "I will do what I can," said the maiden, "though I cannot think why the Queen has sent for me, as I know not how to heal."

"The Queen has sent me to seek something that you harbor," said the handmaiden. "An object with the power to grant its bearer her heart's desire."

The maiden understood then that it was the Golden Egg of which the handmaiden spoke. She shook her head sadly. "I would do anything to help the Princess, except that which you ask. Protecting the Golden Egg is my birthright, and there is naught more important than that. You may stay here tonight and shelter from the cold and lonely woods, but tomorrow you must return to the kingdom and tell the Queen that I cannot relinquish the Golden Egg."

Next day, the handmaiden set off for the castle. She journeyed for three days and nights until finally she arrived at the castle walls, where the Queen was waiting for her.

"Where is the Golden Egg?" said the Queen, looking at the handmaiden's empty hands.

"I have failed in my mission," said the handmaiden. "For alas, the maiden of the cottage would not be parted from her birthright."

The Queen drew herself to her full height and her face turned red.

"You must return," she said, pointing a long-taloned finger at the hand-maiden, "and tell the maiden it is her duty to serve her kingdom. If she fails, she will be turned to stone and left to stand in the kingdom court-yard for all eternity."

So the handmaiden headed east once more, journeyed for three days and nights until she found herself again at the door to the hidden cottage. She knocked and was greeted happily by the maiden, who wel-comed her inside and fetched her a bowl of broth. The maiden sat weav-ing while the handmaiden ate her supper, until finally she said, "You are very welcome here, stranger, but you must forgive me for asking whether there is a purpose to your visit."

"I have been sent once more by the Queen of the land," said the handmaiden. "She seeks your assistance in healing her daughter's ill health. Your duty is to serve your kingdom. If you refuse, the Queen says you will be turned to stone and made to stand in the kingdom courtyard for all eternity."

The maiden smiled sadly. "Protecting the Golden Egg is my birth-right," she said. "I cannot relinquish it to you."

"Do you wish to be turned to stone?"

"I do not," said the maiden, "and neither shall I be. For I serve my kingdom when I watch over the Golden Egg."

And the handmaiden did not argue, for she saw that what the maiden of the cottage said was true. Next day, the handmaiden set off for the castle and, when she arrived, the Queen was once again waiting for her at the castle walls.

"Where is the Golden Egg?" said the Queen, looking at the hand-maiden's empty hands.

"Again have I failed in my mission," said the handmaiden. "For alas, the maiden of the cottage would not be parted from her birth-right."

"Did you not tell the maiden that it was her duty to serve the kingdom?"

"I did, Your Majesty," said the handmaiden, "and she said that by guarding the Golden Egg she was serving the kingdom."

The Queen glowered and her face turned grey. Clouds gathered in the sky and the ravens of the kingdom flew for cover.

The Queen remembered then the mirror's words—"she does what she does for the kingdom's good"—and her lips curled into a grin. "You must return once more," she said to the handmaiden, "and this time you will tell the maiden that if she fails to relinquish the Golden Egg she will be responsible for the Princess's eternal sorrow, which will cast the kingdom into an endless winter of grief."

So the handmaiden headed east for a third time, journeying for three days and nights, until she found herself once more at the door to the hidden cottage. She knocked and was greeted happily by the maiden, who welcomed her inside and fetched her a bowl of broth. The maiden sat weaving while the handmaiden ate her supper, until finally she said, "You are very welcome here, stranger, but you must forgive me for asking whether there is a purpose to your visit."

"I have been sent once more by the Queen of the land," said the handmaiden. "She seeks your assistance in healing her daughter's ill health. Your duty is to serve your kingdom; if you fail to relinquish the egg, the Queen says you will be responsible for the Princess's eternal sorrow and the kingdom will be cast into an endless winter of grief."

The maiden of the cottage sat still and silent for a long time. Then she nodded slowly. "To spare the Princess and to spare the kingdom, I will relinquish the Golden Egg."

The handmaiden shivered as the dark woods grew quiet and an ill wind slipped beneath the door to worry the hearth fire. "But there is nothing more important than protecting your birthright," she said. "It is your duty to the kingdom."

The maiden smiled. "But what use is such duty if my actions sink the kingdom into an endless winter? An endless winter will freeze the land—there will be no birds or animals or crops. It is because of my duty that I now relinquish the Golden Egg."

The handmaiden looked sadly at the maiden. "But there is naught more important than protecting your birthright. The egg is a part of you, yours to protect."

But the maiden had already taken a large golden key from around her neck and was fitting it in the lock of the special door. As she turned it, there was a groan from deep within the floor of the cottage, a settling of the hearthstones, a sigh from the ceiling rafters. Light faded in the cottage as a glow appeared from inside the secret room. The maiden disappeared then appeared once more, holding in her hands a shrouded object, so precious that the air around it seemed to hum.

The maiden walked the handmaiden out of the cottage and, when the two reached the edge of the clearing, she handed over her birthright. When she turned back towards her cottage, she saw that it was darker. Light had disappeared, unable suddenly to penetrate the thick surrounding woods. Inside, the rooms grew cold, no longer warmed from within by the glow of the Golden Egg.

Over time, the animals stopped coming and the birds flew away, and the maiden found that she had no purpose. She forgot how to spin, her voice faded to a whisper and, finally, she felt her limbs grow stiff and heavy, immobile. Until one day she realized that a layer of dust had coated the cottage and her own frozen form. She allowed her eyes to close and felt herself falling through the cold and the silence.

Some seasons later, the Princess of the kingdom was riding with her handmaiden on the edge of the dark woods. Though once she had been very ill, the Princess had recovered miraculously and was now married to a fine prince. She lived a full and happy life: walked and danced and sang, and enjoyed all the vast riches of health. They had a dear baby girl who was much loved and ate pure honey and drank the dew from rose petals and had beautiful butterflies for playthings.

As the Princess and her handmaiden rode by the dark woods on this day the Princess felt an odd compulsion to enter the woods themselves. She ignored the handmaiden's protestations and steered her horse across the border and into the cold, dark forest. All was silent in the woods, neither bird nor beast nor breeze stirred the still, cool air. The horses' hooves made the only sound.

By and by, they came across a clearing in which a tiny cottage had been devoured by foliage. "Why, what a dear little house," said the Princess. "I wonder who lives here."

The handmaiden turned her face away, shivering against the strange chill of the clearing. "No one, my Princess. Not anymore. The kingdom thrives, but there is no life in the dark woods."

FORTY-FIVE

ELIZA knew she would miss this coastline, this sea, when she left. Though she would come to know another, it would be different. Other birds and other plants, waves whispering their stories in foreign tongues. Yet it was time. She'd waited long enough and with little cause. What was done was done and no matter her present feeling, the remorse that crept up on her in the dark, held sleep at bay while she tossed and turned and cursed her part in the deception, she had little choice but to move forward.

Eliza went the final way down the narrow stone steps to the pier. One fisherman was still loading up for the day's work, stacking woven baskets and rolls of line into his boat. As she drew closer, the lean, muscular limbs and sun-brushed features came into focus, and Eliza realized it was William, Mary's brother. Youngest in a long line of Cornish fishermen, he'd distinguished himself among a host of the brave and the foolhardy so that tales of his feats had spread like sea grass along the coast.

He and Eliza had once enjoyed a friendship, and he had kept her in thrall with his wild stories of life on the sea, but a cool distance had grown between them over the years. Ever since Will had witnessed that which he should not, had challenged Eliza and insisted she explain the inexplicable. It had been a long time since they'd spoken and Eliza had missed his company. Knowledge that she would soon be leaving Tregenna filled her with determination to put the past behind her, and with a steady exhalation she made her approach. "You're late this morning, Will."

He looked up, straightened his cap. A blush spread across his weather-hardened cheeks and he answered stiffly, "And you're early."

"I'm getting a head start on the day." Eliza was by the boat now. Water lapped gently against its side and the air was thick with brine. "Any word from Mary?"

"Not since last week. She's still happy there in Polperro, quite the butcher's wife she is, too."

Eliza smiled. It was a genuine pleasure to hear that Mary was well. After all she had been through, she deserved nothing less. "That *is* good news, Will. I must write her a letter this afternoon."

William frowned a little. His gaze fell to his boots as he stubbed the rock wall of the pier.

"What is it?" said Eliza. "Have I said something odd?"

William shooed away a pair of greedy gulls, swooping for his bait.

"Will?"

He glanced sideways at Eliza. "Nothing odd, Miss Eliza, only—I must say, while I'm glad to see you well, I'm a little surprised."

"Why is that?"

"We were all sorry to hear the news." He lifted his chin and scratched the whiskers that lined his sharp jaw. "About Mr. and Mrs. Walker, about them . . . leaving us."

"New York, yes. They leave next month." Nathaniel had been the one to tell Eliza. He'd come to see her in the cottage again, Ivory in tow once more. It was a rainy afternoon and thus the child had been brought inside to wait. She'd gone upstairs to Eliza's room, which was just as well. When Nathaniel told Eliza of their plans, his and Rose's, to start afresh on the other side of the Atlantic, she had been angry. She'd felt abandoned, used. Even more so than she had before. At the thought of Rose and Nathaniel in New York, the cottage had suddenly seemed like the most desolate place in the world; Eliza's life, the most desolate a person could lead.

Soon after Nathaniel had left, Eliza had remembered Mother's advice, that she was to rescue herself, and she had decided the time had come to set her own plans in motion. She'd booked passage on a ship that would take her on her own adventure, far from Blackhurst and the life she'd led in the cottage. She'd written, too, to Mrs. Swindell, said that she was coming to London in the next month and wondered whether she might pay a visit. She hadn't mentioned Mother's brooch—God willing, it was still stowed safely in the clay pot inside the disused chimney—but she intended to get it back.

And with Mother's legacy she would begin a new life, all her own.

William cleared his throat.

"What is it, Will? You look as if you've seen a ghost."

"Nothing like that, Miss Eliza. It's just . . ." His blue eyes scanned her own. The sun was full and heavy on the horizon now and he was forced to squint. "Is it possible you don't know?"

"Don't know what?" She shrugged lightly.

"Of Mr. and Mrs. Walker . . . The train from Carlisle."

Eliza nodded. "They've been in Carlisle these past days. Due back tomorrow."

William's lips settled in a somber line. "They're still due back tomorrow, Miss Eliza, only not in the way you think." He exhaled and shook his head. "Word's all over the village, in the newspapers. To think nobody told you. I'd have come myself, only . . ." He took her hands, an unexpected gesture, and one which set her heart to racing as all unexpected shows of closeness were wont to do. "There was an accident, Miss Eliza. One train hit into another. Some of the passengers—Mr. and Mrs. Walker . . ." He sighed, met her gaze. "I'm afraid they were both killed, Miss Eliza. Up at a place called Ais Gill."

He continued, but Eliza wasn't listening. Inside her head a loud red light had spread out over everything, so that all sensation, all noise, all thoughts were blocked. She closed her eyes and was falling, blind-folded, down a deep shaft without end.

It was all Adeline could do to keep breathing. Grief so thick it black-ened her lungs. The news had come by telephone late Tuesday night. Linus had been locked in the darkroom, so Daisy had been sent to summon Lady Mountrachet to the receiver. A policeman on the other end, voice crackly with the miles of air that separated Cornwall from Cumberland, had delivered the crushing blow.

Adeline had fainted. At least, she presumed that must be what had happened, for her next memory was of waking in her bed, a heavy weight upon her chest. A split second of confusion and then she'd re-membered; the horror had been born afresh.

It was as well there was a funeral to arrange, procedures to be fol-lowed, or else Adeline might not have resurfaced. For never mind that her heart had been hollowed out, leaving but a dry and worthless husk, there were certain things expected of her. As the grieving mother she could not be seen to shirk her responsibilities. She owed it to Rose, to her dearest one.

"Daisy." Her voice was raw. "Fetch some writing paper. I need to prepare a list."

As Daisy hurried from the dim room, Adeline began her list men-tally. The Churchills should be invited, of course, Lord and Lady Hux-ley. The Astors, the Heusers . . . Nathaniel's people she would inform later. Lord knew, Adeline hadn't the strength to incorporate their type at Rose's funeral.

Neither would the child be permitted to attend: such a solemn occasion was no place for one of her nature. Would that she had been on the train with her parents, that the beginnings of a cold had not kept her home in bed. For what was Adeline to do with the girl? The last thing she needed was a constant reminder that Rose was gone.

She stared out of the window towards the cove. The line of trees, the sea beyond. Stretching forever and forever and forever.

Adeline refused to let her eyes shift left. The cottage was hidden from view, but knowing it was there was enough. Its horrid pull exerted itself, brought a chill to her blood.

One thing was certain. Eliza would not be told, not until after the funeral. There was no way Adeline could bear to see that girl alive and well when Rose was not.

THREE DAYS later, while Adeline and Linus and the servants gathered at the cemetery on the far side of the estate, Eliza took a last walk around the cottage. She had already sent a case ahead to the port, so there was little for her to carry. Just a small traveling bag with her notebook and some personal items. The train left Tregenna at midday and Davies, who was collecting a shipment of new plants from the London train, had offered to drive her to the station. He was the only one she'd told that she was going.

Eliza checked her small pocket watch. There was time for one last visit to the hidden garden. She had saved the garden until last, purposely limited the time she would have available to spend there, for fear if she granted longer she would be unable ever to extricate herself.

But so would it be. So must it be.

Eliza went around the path and made her way towards the entrance. Where once the southern door had stood, now was only an open wound, a hole in the ground and a stack of huge sandstone blocks awaiting use.

It had happened during the week. Eliza had been weeding when she'd been surprised by a pair of burly workmen making their way through from the front of the cottage. Her first thought was that they were lost, then she realized the absurdity of such a notion. People didn't stumble upon the cottage accidentally.

"Lady Mountrachet sent us," the taller of the men had said.

Eliza stood, wiping her hands on her skirt. She said nothing as she waited for him to continue.

"She says this door wants removing."

"Does it, now," said Eliza. "Funny, it's never said as much to me."

The smaller man sniggered, the tall man looked sheepish.

"And why is the door being removed?" said Eliza. "Is there another replacing it?"

"We're to brick up the hole," said the taller man. "Lady Mountrachet says there won't be access needed from the cottage no more. We're to dig a hole and lay new foundations."

Of course. Eliza should have expected there would be repercussions after her journey through the maze a fortnight before. When all was done and decided four years ago, the rules had been clearly set out. Mary had been given funds to start afresh in Polperro and Eliza had been forbidden from crossing beyond the hidden garden and into the maze. Yet finally she had been unable to resist.

It was just as well Eliza would be at the cottage no longer. Without access to her garden she didn't think she could bear life at Blackhurst. Certainly not now that Rose was gone.

She stepped her way over the rubble where the door had once stood, around the edge of the hole, and crossed into the hidden garden. The scent of jasmine was still strong, and the apple tree was fruiting. The creepers had made their way right across the top of the garden and plaited themselves together to form a leafy canopy.

Davies would look in, she knew that, but it wouldn't be the same. He had sufficient duties to keep him busy, and the garden took so much of her time and love. "What will become of you?" said Eliza softly.

She looked at the apple tree and a sharp pain lodged within her chest, as if some part of her heart had been removed. She remembered the day she had planted the tree with Rose. So much hope they'd had then, so much faith that all would turn out well. Eliza couldn't bear even to contemplate that Rose was no longer in the world.

Something caught Eliza's eye then. A piece of fabric protruding from beneath the foliage of the apple tree. Had she left a handkerchief here last time she came? She knelt down and peered through the leaves.

There was a little girl, Rose's little girl, fast asleep on the soft grass.

As if by the lifting of some enchantment, the child stirred. Blinked open her eyes until her wide gaze fixed on Eliza.

She didn't jump or startle or behave in any way that might have been expected from a child caught unawares by an adult not well known to her. She smiled, comfortably. Then yawned. Then crawled out from underneath the branch.

"Hello," she said, standing before Eliza.

Eliza stared at her, surprised and pleased by the girl's utter disregard for the stifling dictates of manners. "What are you doing here?"

"Reading."

Eliza's brows lifted, the girl was not yet four. "You can read?"

Brief hesitation, then a nod.

"Show me."

The little girl dropped to her hands and knees and scurried beneath the apple tree branch. Withdrew her own copy of Eliza's fairy tales. The copy Eliza had taken through the maze. She opened the book and launched into a perfect rendition of "The Crone's Eyes," tracing her finger earnestly along the text.

Eliza concealed a smile as she noticed the fingertip and the voice were not in step. Remembered her own childhood ability to memorize favorite stories. "And why are you here?" she said.

The girl paused in her reading. "Everybody else has gone away. I saw them from the window, shiny black carriages crawling down the driveway like a line of busy ants. And I didn't want to be alone in the house. So I came here. I like it here, best of all. In *your* garden." Her gaze flickered towards the ground. She knew that she had crossed a line.

"Do you know who I am?" Eliza said.

"You're the Authoress."

Eliza smiled slightly.

The little girl grew bolder: tilted her head to one side, so that her long plait spilled over her shoulder. "Why are you sad?"

"Because I am saying good-bye."

"To what?"

"To my garden. To my old life." There was an intensity to the little girl's gaze that Eliza found bewitching. "I am going on an adventure. Do you like adventures?"

The little girl nodded. "I'm going on an adventure soon, too, with Mamma and Papa. We're going to New York on a giant ship, bigger even than Captain Ahab's."

"New York?" Eliza faltered. Was it possible the little girl didn't know that her parents were dead?

"We're going across the sea and Grandmamma and Grandpapa won't be coming with us. Nor the horrid broken dolly."

Was that the point from which there was no return? As Eliza met the earnest eyes of a little girl who didn't know that her parents were dead, who faced a life with Aunt Adeline and Uncle Linus as guardians?

Later, when Eliza looked back at this moment, it would seem that no decision had been made by her, rather that the decision had already been made for her. By some strange process of alchemy, Eliza had known instantly and certainly that the girl could not be left alone at Blackhurst.

She held out her hand, observed her own palm extended towards the girl, as if it knew precisely what it did. She pressed her lips together and found her voice. "I have heard about your adventure. In fact, I have been sent to collect you." The words came easily now. As if they were part of a plan made long ago, as if they were truth. "I am going to take you some of the way."

The little girl blinked.

"It's all right," Eliza said. "Come. Take my hand. We're going to go a special way, a secret way that no one knows but us."

"Will my mamma be there when we get to the place we're going?"

"Yes," said Eliza, without flinching. "Your mamma will be there."

The little girl considered this. Nodded her head approvingly. Sharp little chin with a dimple in its center. "I must bring my book."

ADELINE FELT the edges of her mind unfurl. It had been midafternoon before the alarm was raised. Daisy—stupid girl—had come knocking at Adeline's boudoir door, hedging her words, shifting sheepishly from one foot to the other, wondering whether perhaps the mistress had seen Miss Ivory.

Her granddaughter was a known wanderer, so Adeline's first instinct had been irritation. Just like the wicked girl to choose her timing thus. Today of all days, having buried her darling Rose, consigned her child to the earth, now to have to mount a search. It was all Adeline could do not to shriek and curse.

The servants had been enlisted, sent throughout the house to check the usual nooks, but all to no avail. When an hour had been fruitlessly exhausted, Adeline had been forced to contemplate the possibility that Ivory had gone further afield. Adeline, and Rose, too, had warned the child against the cove and other areas of the estate, but obedience had not come easily for Ivory as it had for Rose. There was a wilfulness about her, a deplorable trait that Rose had indulged by eschewing punishment. But Adeline was not so lenient, and when the girl was found she would be made to see the error of her ways; she would not offend so brazenly again.

"Excuse me, ma'am."

Adeline swung around, the folds of her skirt hissing against one another. It was Daisy, returned finally from the cove.

"Well? Where is she?" said Adeline.

"I couldn't see her, ma'am."

"You checked all over? The black rock, the hills?"

"Oh no, ma'am. I didn't go near the black rock."

"Why ever not?"

"It's so big and slippery and . . ." The girl's silly face turned bright as a ripe peach. "They say it's haunted, is the great rock."

Adeline's hand itched to slap the girl black and blue. If she had just done as instructed in the first place, and ensured the child remained in bed! No doubt she'd been off somewhere, talking to the new footman in the kitchen . . . But it would not do to punish Daisy. Not yet. It might seem as if Adeline's priorities were out of step.

Instead, she turned away, swept her skirts behind her and repaired to the window. Looked out across the darkening lawn. It was all so overwhelming. Ordinarily Adeline found herself adept at the art of social performance, but today the part of the concerned grandmother was proving her undoing. If only someone would just find the girl, dead or alive, injured or well, and bring her back. Then Adeline could close a door on the episode and continue unabated in her grieving for Rose.

But it seemed that such a simple solution was not to be. Dusk would be upon them in the matter of an hour and still no sign of the child. And Adeline's pursuit could not be ended until every option had been exhausted. The servants were watching, her reactions were no doubt being reported and dissected in the servants' hall, so must she continue the hunt. Daisy was near useless and the other staff not much better. She needed Davies. Where was that brute of a man?

"It's his afternoon off, ma'am," said Daisy, when asked.

Of course it was. The servants were always underfoot yet never to be found.

"I imagine he's at home, or visiting in the village, my lady. I think he said something about fetching some deliveries off the train."

There was only one other person who knew the estate like Davies.

"Fetch Miss Eliza, then," said Adeline, mouth souring as she spoke the name. "And bring her to me at once."

ELIZA LOOKED across at the sleeping child. Long lashes dusted smooth cheeks, pink lips sat plump and pouted, little fists bunched on her lap. How trusting children were, to find sleep at such a time. The trust, the vulnerability, made a part of Eliza want to weep.

What had she been thinking? What was she doing here, on a train, heading towards London with Rose's child?

Nothing, she had thought nothing at all, and that's why she had done it. For to think was to dip the paint-loaded brush of doubt into the clear water of certainty. She had known the child could not be left alone at Blackhurst in the hands of Uncle Linus and Aunt Adeline, thus had she acted. She had failed Sammy, but she wouldn't fail again.

What to do with Ivory now was another question, for surely Eliza couldn't keep her. The child deserved more than that. She should have a father and mother, siblings, a happy home filled with love that would grant her memories for a lifetime.

And yet Eliza couldn't see what choice she had. The child must be kept far from Cornwall; the risk otherwise was too great that she'd be discovered and taken straight back to Blackhurst.

No, until Eliza thought of some better alternative, the girl must stay with her. At least for now. There were five days until the ship departed for Australia, for Maryborough, where Mary's brother lived, and her Aunt Eleanor. Mary had given her an address and, when she got there, Eliza intended to contact the Martin family. She would send word to Mary, of course; let her know what she had done.

Eliza already had her ticket, booked under a false name. Superstitious, but when the time had come to make the reservation she had been possessed, suddenly, by an overwhelming sensation that a clean break, a new start, required a new name. She didn't want to leave an imprint of herself at the booking office, a path between this world and that. So she had used a pseudonym. A stroke of luck, as it turned out.

For they would come looking. Eliza knew too much about the origins of Rose's child for Aunt Adeline to let her slip so easily away. She must be prepared to hide. She would find an inn near the port, somewhere that would rent a room to a poor widow and her child, on their way to join family in the New World. Was it possible, she wondered, to purchase a ticket for the child at such short notice? Or would she find a way to board the girl without drawing attention to her?

Eliza looked across at the scrap of a child slumbering in the corner of the train carriage. So vulnerable. She reached out slowly and stroked her cheek. Withdrew as the girl flinched, wrinkled her little nose and nestled her head further into the carriage corner. Ridiculous though it was, Eliza could see some of Rose in the child, in Ivory; Rose as a girl, when Eliza had first known her.

The child would ask after her mother and father, and Eliza would tell her one day. Though which words she would find to explain she wasn't sure. She noticed that the fairy story that might have done so for her was no longer in the little girl's collection. Someone had removed it. Nathaniel, Eliza suspected. Both Rose and Aunt Adeline would have destroyed the whole book; only Nathaniel would pluck out the one story in which he was implicated, yet preserve the rest.

She would wait to contact the Swindells until the very last, for though Eliza couldn't see how they might pose a threat, she knew better than to be too trusting. If an opportunity to profit was glimpsed, the Swindells would seize upon it. Eliza had considered at one point abandoning the visit, wondered whether perhaps the risk outweighed the reward, but she had decided to take the chance. She would need the gems from the brooch in order to pay her way in the New World, and the plaited part was precious. It was her family, her past, her link to her self.

As ADELINE waited for Daisy's return, time dragged slow and heavy like a petulant child at her skirt. It was Eliza's fault that Rose was dead. Her unsanctioned visit through the maze had precipitated the plans for New York, and thus brought forward the trip to Carlisle. Had Eliza stayed on the other side of the estate as she had promised, Rose would never have been on that train.

The door opened and Adeline drew breath. Finally, the servant was back, leaves in her hair, mud on her skirt, and yet she was alone.

"Where is she?" Adeline said. Was she searching already? Had Daisy used her own head for once and sent Eliza straight to the cove?

"I don't know, ma'am."

"You don't know?"

"When I got to the cottage it were all locked up. I looked through the windows but there was no sign."

"You should have waited a while. Perhaps she was in the village and would have returned soon."

The girl was shaking her insolent head. "I don't think so, ma'am. Only the fire were raked clean and the shelves were empty." Daisy blinked in that bovine way of hers. "I think she's gone, too, ma'am."

Then Adeline understood. And knowledge heated quickly into rage, and rage seared beneath her skin, filling her head with sharp red shots of pain.

"Are you all right, my lady? Should you sit down?"

No, Adeline didn't need to sit down. Quite the contrary. She needed to see for herself. Witness the girl's ingratitude.

"Take me through the maze, Daisy."

"I don't know my way through, ma'am. No one does. None excepting Davies. I went round the road way, up the cliff track."

"Then fetch Newton and the carriage."

"But it'll be getting dark soon, ma'am."

Adeline narrowed her eyes and lifted her shoulders. Enunciated clearly: "Fetch Newton now and bring me a lantern."

THE COTTAGE was neat but not empty. The kitchen area was still hung with various cooking instruments but the table was wiped clear. The coat hook by the door was bare. Adeline suffered a wave of illness and felt her lungs contract. It was that girl's lingering presence, thick and oppressive. She took the lantern and started up the narrow stairs. There were two rooms, the larger spartan but clean, containing the bed from the attic, an old quilt pulled tight across its surface. The other housed a desk and chair and a shelf full of books. The objects on the desk had been arranged into stacks. Adeline pressed her fingers against the wooden top and leaned forward a little to see outside.

The last color of the day had broken over the sea, and the distant water rose and fell, gold and purple.

Rose is gone.

The thought came fast and jagged.

Here, alone, finally unobserved, Adeline could briefly stop pretending. She closed her eyes and the knots in her shoulders dropped.

She longed to curl up on the floor, wooden boards smooth and cool and real beneath her cheek, and never have to rise again. To sleep for a hundred years. To have no one looking to her for an example. To be able to breathe—

"Lady Mountrachet?" Newton's voice drifted up the stairs. " 'Tis growing dark, my lady. The horses will have difficulty getting down if we don't leave soon."

Adeline drew a sharp breath. Shoulders were wrenched back into position. "A minute."

She opened her eyes and pressed a hand against her forehead. Rose was gone and Adeline would never recover, but there was further risk now. Though a part of Adeline longed to let Eliza and the girl disappear out of her life forever, things were more complicated than that. With Eliza and Ivory missing, surely together, Adeline faced the risk that people might learn the truth. That Eliza might speak of what they'd done. And that must not be allowed to happen. For Rose's sake, for her memory, and for the Mountrachet family's good name, Eliza must be found, returned and silenced.

Adeline's gaze swept once more across the desktop and lit upon the edge of a piece of paper emerging from beneath a stack of books. A word she recognized though at first could not place. She plucked the paper from where it was lodged. It was a list of sorts, made by Eliza: things to be done before she left. At the bottom of the list was printed *Swindell*. A name, Adeline thought, though she wasn't sure how she knew.

Her heart beat faster as she folded the piece of paper and tucked it in her pocket. Adeline had found her link. The girl couldn't expect to slip from notice. She would be found, and the child, Rose's child, brought back where she belonged.

And Adeline knew just whose help to enlist to make it so.

FORTY-SIX

CLARA'S cottage was small and white, and clung to the edge of a rock sheer, a short walk uphill from a pub called the Buccaneer.

"Want to do the honors?" asked Christian when they arrived.

Cassandra nodded, but she didn't knock. She had been beset, suddenly, by a wave of nervous excitement. Her grandmother's long-lost sister was on the other side of the door. In just a few moments, the riddle that had plagued Nell for most of her life would be solved. Cassandra glanced at Christian and thought again how pleased she was that he had come with her.

After Ruby had left for London that morning, Cassandra had waited for him on the front steps of the hotel, clutching her copy of Eliza's fairy tales. He'd brought his, too, and they'd discovered that there was indeed a story missing from Cassandra's book. The gap in the binding was so narrow, the cut so neat, that Cassandra hadn't noticed it before. Even the missing page numbers hadn't drawn her attention. The figures were so swirly and elaborate, it would have taken a degree in penmanship to discern the difference between 54 and 61.

On the drive to Polperro, Cassandra had read "The Golden Egg" aloud. As she did so, she'd become more and more convinced that Christian was right, that the story was an allegory for Rose's acquisition of her daughter. A fact which made her more certain than ever of what it was that Clara wished to tell her.

Poor Mary, forced to give up her first child, then keep it a secret.

No wonder she'd unburdened herself to her daughter in her final days. A lost child followed a mother all her life.

Leo would be almost twelve now.

"Are you okay?" Christian was watching her, a frown of concern narrowing his eyes.

"Yeah," said Cassandra, folding away her memories. "I'm okay." And, as she smiled at him, it didn't feel so much a lie as usual.

SHE LIFTED her hand and was about to rap on the knocker when the door flew open. Standing in the low and narrow frame was a plump old woman whose apron, tied around her middle, gave the impression of a body formed by two balls of dough. "I seen you standing there," she said grinning, finger curled to point at them, "and I says to myself, 'They must be my young guests.' Now come on in, the two of you, and I'll make us all a nice cup of tea."

Christian sat beside Cassandra on the floral sofa and they juggled patchwork cushions between them to make room. He looked so hopelessly oversized among such dainty adornments that Cassandra had to fight the urge to laugh.

A yellow teapot occupied pride of place on the sea chest in the living room, shrouded in a knitted cozy shaped like a hen. It looked remarkably like Clara, Cassandra thought: small alert eyes, a plump body, sharp little mouth.

Clara fetched a third cup and strained leaf tea into each. "My own special blend," she said. "Three parts Breakfast, one part Earl Grey." She peered over her half-glasses, "*English* Breakfast, that is." When the milk was added she eased herself into the armchair by the fire. " 'Bout time I gave my poor old feet a rest. Been on them all day, organizing the stalls for the harbor festival."

"Thanks for seeing me," said Cassandra. "This is my friend Christian."

Christian reached across the sea chest to shake Clara's hand and she blushed.

"Pleasure to meet you, I'm sure." She took a sip of tea, then nodded towards Cassandra. "The museum lady, Ruby, told me about your grandma," she said. "The one what didn't know who her parents were."

"Nell," said Cassandra. "That was her name. My great-grandfather Hugh found her when she was a little girl, sitting on top of a white suitcase on the Maryborough wharf. He was portmaster and a ship—"

"Maryborough, you say?"

Cassandra nodded.

"Now that's a coincidence, that is. I've got family in a place called Maryborough. In the Queen's land."

"Queensland." Cassandra leaned forward. "Which family?"

"My mum's brother moved there when he was a young fellow. Raised his children, my cousins." She cackled. "Mum used to say they'd settled there for her name's sake."

Cassandra glanced at Christian. Was that why Eliza had put Nell on that particular ship? Was she returning her to Mary's family, to Nell's own true family? Rather than take the child to Polperro and risk having local people recognize her as Ivory Mountrachet, had she opted for Mary's faraway brother? Cassandra suspected that Clara held the answer, all she needed was nudging in the right direction.

"Your mother, Mary, used to work at Blackhurst Manor, didn't she?"

Clara swallowed a large gulp of tea. "Worked there until she was given her marching orders, 1909 that was. She'd been there since she was but a girl, near on ten years. Let go for being in the family way." Clara lowered her voice to a whisper. "Wasn't married, you see, and in those days, that wasn't the done thing. But she wasn't a bad girl, my mum. She was straight as a pound of candles. She and my dad were married in the end, right and proper. Would've done so before, only he was struck down with the pneumonia. Nearly didn't make it to his own wedding. That's when they moved here to Polperro, they came into a little bit of money and started the butchery."

She picked up a small rectangular book from beside the tea tray. The cover was decorated with wrapping paper and fabric and buttons, and when Clara opened it Cassandra realized it was a photo album. Clara turned to a page that had been marked with a ribbon and handed it across the sea chest. "That there's my mum."

Cassandra looked at the young woman with wild curls and wilder curves, trying to see Nell in her features. There was perhaps something of Nell about the mouth, a smile that played on her lips when she least intended. Then again, that was the nature of photos: the longer Cassandra looked, the more she seemed to see something of Aunt Phylly about the nose and eyes!

She handed the album to Christian and smiled at Clara. "She was very pretty, wasn't she?"

"Oh yes," said Clara with a saucy wink. "Quite the looker was my mum. Too pretty for service."

"Did she enjoy her time at Blackhurst, do you know? Was she sorry to leave?"

"She was glad to leave the house, but sad to leave her mistress."

This was new. "She and Rose were close?"

Clara shook her head. "I don't know about no Rose. It was Eliza she used to talk about. Miss Eliza this, Miss Eliza that."

"But Eliza wasn't the mistress of Blackhurst Manor."

"Well, not officially, no, but she was always the apple of my mum's eye. She used to say Miss Eliza was the only spark of life in a dead place."

"Why did she think it a dead place?"

"Those that lived there were like the dead, my mum said. All gloomy for one reason or another. All wanting things they shouldn't or couldn't have."

Cassandra pondered on this insight into life at Blackhurst Manor. It wasn't the impression she'd formed from reading Rose's scrapbooks, though certainly Rose, with her focus on new dresses and the adventures of her cousin Eliza, provided only one voice in a house that must've echoed with others. That was the nature of history, of course: notional, partial, unknowable, a record made by the victors.

"Her bosses, the lord and lady, were each as nasty as the other, according to my mum. They got theirs in the end, though, didn't they."

Cassandra frowned. "Who did?"

"Him 'n' her. Lord and Lady Mountrachet. She died a month or two after her daughter—poisoning of the blood, it was." Clara shook her head and lowered her voice conspiratorially, almost gleefully. "Very nasty. My mum heard tell from the servants that she was a fright in her last days. Face all contorted so that she looked to be grinning like a ghoul, escaping from her sickbed to lurch along the hallways with a great ring of keys in hand, locking all the doors and raving about some secret that no one must know. Mad as a hatter she was in the end, and him not much better."

"Lord Mountrachet got blood poisoning, too?"

"Oh no, no, not him. Lost his fortune making trips to foreign places." She lowered her voice. "*Voodoo* places. They say he brought back souvenirs that'd make your hair stand on end. Went quite queer by all accounts. The staff left, all but one kitchen maid and a gardener who'd been there all his life. According to my mum, when the old boy finally died there was none there to find him for days." Clara smiled so that her eyes concertinaed shut. "Eliza got away, though, didn't she, and that's the thing. Traveled across the sea, my mum said. She was always so glad about that."

"Not to Australia, though," said Cassandra.

"I don't know where, truth be told," said Clara. "I only know what my mum told me: that Eliza got herself away from the horrid house in time. Went away like she'd always planned and never came back." She held aloft a finger. "That's where those sketches came from, the ones the museum lady was so taken with. They were hers, Eliza's. They were among her things."

It was on the tip of Cassandra's tongue to ask whether Mary had taken them from Eliza, when she caught herself. Realized that it might be construed as bad manners to suggest this woman's dearly departed mother had thieved valuable artwork from her employer. "Which things?"

"The boxes my mum bought."

Now Cassandra really was confused. "She bought some boxes from Eliza?"

"Not *from* Eliza. *Of* Eliza's. After she was gone."

"Who did she buy them from?"

"It was a big sale. I remember it myself. My mum took me when I was a girl. It was 1935 and I was fifteen years old. After the old lord finally died, a distant family member from up Scotland way decided to sell the estate, hoping to raise some money during the depression, I don't doubt. Anyhow, my mum read about it in the newspaper and saw that they were planning on selling some of the smaller items, too. I think it gave her pleasure to think she might own a little piece of the place where she'd been treated so poor. She took me along because she said it'd do me good to see where she'd started out. Make me thankful that I wasn't in service, encourage me to try harder at school so that I might have more than she did. Can't say it worked, but it certainly did shock me. First time I'd seen anything like it. I'd no idea there were some that lived like that. You don't see much that's grand around these parts." She gave a nod to signal her approval of this state of affairs, then paused and gazed towards the ceiling. "Now, where was I?"

"You were telling us about the boxes," prompted Christian. "The ones your mother bought from Blackhurst."

She lifted a quivering finger. "That's right, from the manor up Tregenna way. You should've seen the look on her face when she saw them. Sitting on a table with other odds and ends—lamps, paperweights, books and the like. Didn't look much to me, but Mum knew right away they were Eliza's. She took my hand, first time in my life, I reckon, and it was almost like she couldn't get enough air. I actually started to worry, thought I should get her to a chair, but she wouldn't hear of it. She seized upon those boxes. It was like she was frightened to walk away in case someone else should buy them. Didn't seem likely to me—as I already said, they didn't look like much—but beauty's in the eye of the beholder, isn't it?"

"And the Nathaniel Walker sketches were in the box?" said Cassandra. "In with Eliza's things?"

Clara nodded. "It's strange, now I recollect it. Mum was so happy to buy them, but when we got home she had my dad carry them upstairs for her, put them in the attic, and that was the last I heard of them. Not that I thought much of it then. I was fifteen. Probably had my eye on a local lad and couldn't care less about some old boxes my mum had bought. Until she moved in here with me, that is, and I noticed that the boxes came with her. Now, that was funny, and really showed what they meant to her, because she didn't bring much. And it was when we were here together that she finally told me what they were, why they were so important."

Cassandra remembered Ruby's account of the room upstairs, still full of Mary's personal items. What other precious clues might be there now, buried in boxes, never to be seen? She swallowed. "Did you ever look inside?"

Clara took a sip of tea, surely cold by now, and fiddled with the cup's handle. "I must admit I did."

Cassandra's heart was thumping; she shifted forward. "And?"

"Books, mainly, a lamp, like I said." She paused, and a crimson flush cherried her cheeks.

"Was there something else?" Gently, oh so gently.

Clara moved the toe of her slipper across the carpet. She watched its progress before looking up. "I found a letter in there, too, right near the top. Addressed to my mum, it was, written by a publisher in London. Gave me the shock of my life. I'd never thought of Mum as a writer." Clara cackled. "And she wasn't, of course."

"What was the letter, then?" said Christian. "Why had the publisher written to your mum?"

Clara blinked. "Well now, it seems my mum must've sent off one of Eliza's stories. From what I could tell from the letter, she must've found it in the box, among Eliza's things, and figured it deserved reading. Turns out Eliza'd written it just before she left on her adventure. Nice story, it was, full of hope and happy endings."

Cassandra thought of the photocopied article in Nell's notebook. " 'The Cuckoo's Flight,' " she said.

"That's the one," said Clara, as pleased as if she'd written the story herself. "You've read it, then?"

"I've read *of* it, but I haven't seen the story itself. It was published years after the rest."

"That'd be right. It was 1936, according to the letter sent. My mum would've been real pleased with herself about that letter. She would've felt she'd done something for Eliza. She missed her after she was gone and that's a fact."

Cassandra nodded, she could almost taste the solution to Nell's mystery. "They had a bond, didn't they?"

"That they did."

"What do you think it was that tied them together like that?" She bit her lip, paced herself.

Clara knotted her gnarled fingers in her lap and lowered her voice. "The two of them were party to something that no one else knew about."

Something inside Cassandra released. Her voice was faint. "What was it? What did your mum tell you?"

"It was in my mum's last days. She kept saying something awful had been done and those what had done it thought they'd got away with it. She said it over and over."

"And what do you think she meant?"

"At first I didn't think much of it at all. She was often saying strange things towards the end. Insulting our dear old friends. She really wasn't herself anymore. But she went on and on. 'It's all in the story,' she kept saying. 'They took it from the young girl and made her go without.' I didn't know what she was talking about, what story she was on about. And in the end it didn't matter, she told me straight." Clara drew breath, shook her head sadly at Cassandra. "Rose Mountrachet wasn't the mother of that little girl, of your grandmother."

Cassandra sighed with relief. Finally, the truth. "I know," she said, taking Clara's hands. "Nell was Mary's baby, the pregnancy that got her fired."

Clara's expression was difficult to read. She looked between Christian and Cassandra, eyes twitching at the corners, blinked confusedly then started to laugh.

"What?" said Cassandra, with some alarm. "What's so funny? Are you all right?"

"My mum was pregnant, that's right enough, but she never had a baby. Not then. She lost it around twelve weeks."

"What?"

"That's what I'm trying to tell you. Nell wasn't Mum's baby, she was Eliza's."

"Eliza was pregnant." Cassandra unwrapped her scarf and put it on top of her bag on the floor of the car.

"Eliza was pregnant." Christian tapped his gloved hands on the steering wheel.

The car heating was turned on and the radiator whirred and ticked as they left Polperro behind them. The fog had come in while they were visiting Clara, and all the way along the coast road muffled boat lights bobbed on the ghostly tide.

Cassandra stared blankly ahead, her brain as foggy as the world outside the windscreen. "Eliza was pregnant. She was Nell's mother.

That's why Eliza took her." Perhaps if she said it enough times, it would make more sense.

"That seems to be about it."

She leaned her head to one side and rubbed her neck. "But I don't understand. It all added up before, when it was Mary. Now that it's Eliza . . . I can't see how Rose ended up with Ivory. Why did Eliza let her keep her? And how did no one ever find out?"

"Except Mary."

"Except Mary."

"I suppose they kept it quiet."

"Eliza's family?"

He nodded. "She was single, young, their ward so their responsibility, and then she fell pregnant. It wouldn't have looked good."

"Who was the father?"

Christian shrugged. "Some local guy? Did she have a boyfriend?"

"I don't know. She was friends with Mary's brother William; it says so in Nell's notebook. They were close until they had some kind of argument. Maybe it was him."

"Who knows? I suppose it doesn't really matter." He glanced at her. "I mean, it does, of course, to Nell and to you, but for the sake of this argument, all that matters is that she was pregnant and Rose wasn't."

"So they convinced Eliza to give her baby to Rose."

"It would have been easier for everyone."

"That's debatable."

"I mean socially. Then Rose died—"

"And Eliza took her child back. That makes sense." Cassandra watched the fog billowing among the long grass at the roadside. "But why didn't she go on the ship to Australia with Nell? Why would a woman take back her child, then send her on a long and treacherous journey to a foreign land, alone?" Cassandra sighed heavily. "It's like the closer we get, the more tangled the web becomes."

"Maybe she did go with her. Maybe something happened to her en route, illness of some kind. Clara seemed certain that she went."

"But Nell remembered Eliza putting her on the boat and telling her to wait, leaving and then not coming back. It was one of the only things she *was* sure about." Cassandra chewed her thumbnail. "How bloody frustrating. I thought we'd be getting answers today, not more questions."

"One thing's for sure: 'The Golden Egg' wasn't about Mary; Eliza wrote it about herself. She was the maiden in the cottage."

"Poor Eliza," said Cassandra, as the gloomy world drifted by outside. "The maiden's life after she gives away the egg is so . . ."

"Desolate."

"Yes." Cassandra shivered. She understood loss that took away a person's very purpose, left her paler, lighter, emptier. "No wonder she took Nell back when she had the chance." What wouldn't Cassandra have done for a second chance?

"Which brings us full circle: if she'd just reclaimed her daughter, why didn't Eliza go with her on the boat?"

Cassandra shook her head. "I don't know. It makes no sense."

They drove past the sign welcoming them to Tregenna and Christian turned off the main road. "You know what I reckon?"

"What's that?" said Cassandra.

"We should get some late lunch at the pub, talk it over some more. See if we can't figure it out. I'm sure beer will help us."

Cassandra smiled. "Yeah, I usually find beer just the thing to make my mind nimble. All right if we stop by the hotel so I can get my jacket?"

Christian took the high road through the woods and turned in to the entrance to the Blackhurst Hotel. Fog lurked still and moist in the gullies of the driveway and he went carefully.

"Back in a sec," said Cassandra, slamming the car door behind her. She ran up the stairs and into the foyer. "Hi, Sam," she called, waving at the receptionist.

"Hiya, Cass. There's someone here to see you."

Cassandra stopped midflight.

"Robyn Jameson's been waiting in the lounge for the past half-hour or so."

Cassandra glanced back outside. Christian's attention was absorbed in tuning his car radio. He wouldn't mind waiting an extra minute. Cassandra couldn't think what Robyn might have to tell her but she didn't imagine it would take much time.

"Well, hello," said Robyn, when she noticed Cassandra's approach. "A little birdie tells me you've spent the morning chatting with my second cousin Clara."

The network of country gossip was pretty impressive. "I have indeed."

"I trust you had a lovely time."

"I did, thanks. I hope you haven't been waiting too long."

"Not at all. I have something for you. I suppose I could have left it at the desk, but I thought it might require a little explanation."

Cassandra raised her eyebrows as Robyn continued.

"I went to visit my dad at the weekend, up at the retirement home. He likes to hear all about the comings and goings in the old village—he was postmaster once, you know—and I happened to mention that you were here, restoring the cottage that your grandma left you, up there on the cliff. Funniest look came across Dad's face. He may be old, but he's sharp as a tack, just like his own dad before him. He took my arm and told me there was a letter needed to be returned to you."

"To me?"

"To your grandma, more properly, but seeing as she's no longer with us, to you."

"What sort of letter?"

"When your grandma left Tregenna, she went to see my dad. Told him she'd be returning to take up residence at Cliff Cottage and he was to hold any mail for her. She was very clear about it, he said, so when a

505

letter arrived he did as she asked and kept it at the post office. Every few months or so he took the letter up the hill, but the old cottage was always deserted. The brambles grew, the dust settled, and the place looked less and less inhabited. Eventually he stopped going. His knees were giving him trouble and he figured your grandma would come and see him when she got back. Ordinarily he'd have returned it to the sender, but your grandma had been very definite, so he tucked the letter away and kept it all that time.

"He told me I was to go down to the cellar, where his things are stored, and pull out the box of lost letters. That in among them I'd find one addressed to Nell Andrews, Tregenna Inn, received November 1975. And he was right. It was there waiting."

She reached into her handbag and withdrew a small grey envelope, gave it to Cassandra. The paper was cheap, so thin it was almost transparent. It was addressed in old-fashioned writing, rather messy, first to a hotel in London, then redirected to the Tregenna Inn. Cassandra flipped the envelope.

There, in the same hand, was written: *Sender—Miss Harriet Swindell, 37 Battersea Church Road, London SW11.*

Cassandra remembered Nell's notebook entry. Harriet Swindell was the woman she had visited in London, the old woman who had been born and grown up in the same house as Eliza. Why had she written to Nell?

Fingers trembling, Cassandra opened the envelope. The thin paper tore softly. She unfolded the letter and began to read.

3rd November 1975

Dear Mrs. Andrews,

Well, I don't mind saying that ever since you made your visit, asking about the fairy-tale lady, I've been hard-pressed to think of much else. You'll find it yourself when you get to my age—the past turns into something of an old friend. The sort who arrives uninvited and refuses to leave!

I do remember her, you see, I remember her well, only you caught me unawares with your visit, turning up on the doorstep right as it was on teatime. I weren't sure whether I felt like talking over the old days with a stranger. My niece Nancy tells me that I ought, though, that it all happened so long ago it hardly matters now, so I've decided to write to you as you asked. For Eliza Makepeace did return to visit with my ma. Only the once, mind you, but I recall it well enough. I were sixteen at the time, and that's how I know it must of been 1913.

I remember thinking there was something strange about her from the first. She might of had the clean clothes of a lady, but there was something about her that didn't quite fit. More rightly, there was something about her that *did* fit with us at 35 Battersea Church Road. Something that set her apart from the other fancy ladies what might be seen in the streets back then. She came through the door and into the shop, a bit agitated it seemed to me, as if she was in a hurry and didn't want to be seen. Suspicious like. She nodded at my ma as if they was known, one to the other, and Ma, for her part, gave her a smile, a sight the likes of which I never seen too often. Whoever this lady was, I thought to myself, my ma must have known she could make a quid off her acquaintance.

Her voice, when she spoke, was clear and musical—that was the first sign to me that I might of met her before. It was familiar somehow. That voice was the sort what children like to listen to, what speaks of fairies and sprites and leaves no doubt in the mind as to their truth.

She thanked my ma for seeing her and said she was leaving England and wouldn't be back for some years. I remember she were awful keen to go upstairs and visit the room she used to live in, horrid little room at the top of the house. Cold, it was, with a fireplace what never worked, and dark, not a window to be spoke of. But she said it was for old times' sake.

It so happened that Ma didn't have a tenant at the time—nasty dispute about rent owing—so she were glad enough to let the lady make a visit. Ma told her to go upstairs and take her time, even put the kettle on to boil. As unlike my ma as you could find.

Ma watched as she climbed those stairs, then she beckoned me quick. Get upstairs after her, Ma said, and make sure she don't come down too soon. I was used to Ma's instructions, and her punishments if I refused, so I did what she said and followed the lady upstairs.

By the time I got to the landing, she'd pulled the door to the room closed behind her. I could of just sat where I was and made sure she didn't decide to return downstairs too fast, but I were curious. I couldn't for the life of me figure out why she'd of closed the door. Like I said, there was no windows in that room and the door was the only way to let light in.

There were a hole in the bottom of that door, eaten by rats, so I lay down on my stomach, flat as can be, and I watched her. I watched her as she stood in the middle of the room, turning around to take it all in, and I watched as she went to the old, broken fireplace. Sat herself down on the ledge, she did, and reached her arm up inside, then sat like that for what seemed an age. Finally, she withdrew her arm, and in her hand was a small clay pot. I must of made a sound then—I was that surprised—for she looked up, eyes wide. I held my breath and after a time she returned her attention to the pot, held it to her ear and gave it a little shake. I could tell by her face she were pleased with what she heard. Then she tucked it inside a special pocket what were sewn into her dress somehow and started towards the door.

I hurried down then and told my ma that she were coming. I was surprised to see that Tom, my brother, was standing at the door, heaving great sighs as if he'd run some distance, but I didn't have time to ask where he'd been. Ma was watching the stairs, so I did the same. Down the lady started, thanking my ma for letting her visit and saying that she couldn't stay for tea, as time was pressing.

Then she reached the bottom and I saw there was a man standing in the shadows at the side of the stairs. A man with funny little spectacles—the type that don't have arms, just a little bridging piece what pinches the nose. He was holding a sponge in his hand, and when she got to the bottom step he clamped it under her nose and she collapsed. Instant like, crumpled into his arms. I must of hollered out then, because I earned a slap across the face from my ma.

The man ignored me and dragged the lady to the door. With Pa's help he lifted her into the carriage, then he nodded at my ma, handed her an envelope from his breast pocket and away they went.

I got a clip around the ears later, when I told my ma all what I'd seen. Why didn't you tell me, you stupid girl? said my ma. It could of been valuable. We might of had it for our troubles. It wouldn't of done to remind her that the man with the black horses had already paid her handsome for the lady. As far as my ma were concerned, there was never enough money to be had.

I never saw the lady again and I don't know what became of her after she left us. There were always things happening on our bend of the river, things that didn't bear remembering.

I don't know that this letter will help you with your research, but Nancy said it was as well to talk to you as not. So that is what I've done. I hope you find what it is you're looking for.

Yours,

Miss Harriet Swindell

FORTY-SEVEN

THE "Fairyland" luster vase had always been her favorite. Nell had found it at a trash-and-treasure stall decades before. Any antiques dealer worth her salt would have known its worth, but the "Fairyland" luster vase was different. It wasn't the material value, though that was high enough, but what it represented: the first time Nell had struck gold in unlikely surroundings. And like a gold miner who keeps his first nugget, whatever its value, Nell had been unwilling to part with the vase.

She kept it wrapped in a towel, stowed safely in the dark corner at the very top of her linen cupboard, and every so often she would pull it out and unwrap it, just to take a peek. Its beauty, the deep green leaves painted on the side, the gold threads running through the design, the art nouveau fairies hidden among the foliage, had the power to cool her skin.

Nonetheless Nell was resolute: she had reached a point where she could live without her vase. Could live without all her precious things. She'd made a choice and that was that. She wrapped the vase in another layer of newspaper and placed it gently in the box with the others. Up to the shop on Monday and priced to sell. And if she had twinges or regrets, she just had to focus on the end result: having sufficient funds to start afresh in Tregenna.

She was itching to return. Her mystery grew ever more perplexing. She had heard, finally, from the detective, Ned Morrish. He'd conducted his investigation and sent her a report. Nell had been in the shop when it arrived; a new customer, Ben something-or-other, had brought the letter in with him when he came. When Nell saw the foreign stamps, the handwriting on the front, neat and flat at the bottom, as if written along a ruler's edge, she'd felt a flush beneath her skin. It was all she could do not to tear it open with her teeth then and there. She'd retained her composure, though, made her excuses when it seemed polite and taken the letter into the little back kitchenette.

The report was brief, had only taken Nell a couple of minutes to read, and its contents left her more confused than ever. According to Mr. Morrish's investigations, Eliza Makepeace had gone nowhere in 1909 or 1910. She had been at the cottage the whole time. He'd included various documents to support this assertion—an interview conducted with someone who claimed to have worked at Blackhurst, various correspondence she'd had with a publisher in London, all sent and received via Cliff Cottage—but Nell hadn't read those, not until later. She'd been too surprised by the news that Eliza hadn't gone away. That she'd been there all along, in the cottage the entire time. William had been so certain. She'd slipped from public sight, he said, for twelve months or so. When she returned she'd been different, some spark had been missing. Nell couldn't understand how William's memories could be made to tally with Mr. Morrish's discovery. As soon as she got back to Cornwall she would speak with William again. See whether he had any ideas.

Nell wiped the back of her hand across her forehead. A stinker of a day, but that was Brisbane in January. The skies might be glistening blue like a dome of fine, flawless glass, but there'd be a storm later tonight, there was no doubting that. Nell had lived long enough to know when angry clouds were thickening in the wings.

Down in the street, Nell heard a car slow. She didn't recognize it as one of her neighbors' vehicles: too loud for Howard's Mini, too high-pitched for the Hogans' big Ford. There was a dreadful din as the car mounted the curb too sharply. Nell shook her head, glad she'd never learned to drive, never had need of a car. They seemed to bring out the worst in people.

Whiskers sat upright and arched her back. Now, the cats Nell *would* miss. She'd have happily taken them with her, but feeding other people's cats was one thing, abducting them quite another.

"Hey there, nosy," said Nell, tickling the cat beneath her chin. "Don't you go worrying about that noisy old car."

Whiskers miaowed and leaped from the table, glanced at Nell.

"What? You think there's someone here to see us? Can't think who, m'dear. We're not exactly social central, in case the fact escaped your notice."

The cat slunk across the floor and out of the back door. Nell dropped the pile of newspaper. "Oh, all right, madam," she said, "you win. I'll have a gander." She scratched Whiskers's back as they went along the narrow concrete path. "Think you're clever, don't you, bending me to your will—"

Nell stopped at the back corner of the house. The car, a station wagon, had indeed pulled up outside her place. Coming up the cement path was a woman wearing large bronze sunglasses and tiny shorts. Lagging behind was a skinny child with slumped shoulders.

They stood, all three, regarding one another for a time.

Finally Nell found her voice, if not the words she wished to speak. "I thought you agreed to call first in future."

"Good to see you, too, Mum," Lesley said, and then she rolled her eyes the way she had as a fifteen-year-old. It had been an infuriating habit then, as was it now.

Nell felt the old grievances resurfacing. She'd been a poor mother to Lesley, she knew that, but it was too late now to make amends. What was done was done and Lesley had turned out all right. Had turned out, at any rate. "I'm in the middle of sorting boxes for auction," said Nell, swallowing the lump in her throat. This wasn't the time to mention the move to England. "I've things everywhere, there's no room to sit."

"We'll manage." Lesley flicked her fingers in the girl's direction. "Your granddaughter's thirsty, it's bloody hot out here."

Nell looked at the girl, her granddaughter. Long limbs, knobbly knees, head bowed to avoid notice. There was no doubt about it, some children were sent into the world with more than their fair share of difficulties.

Of all things, her mind tossed up an image then of Christian, the little boy she'd discovered in her Cornish garden. The motherless boy with the earnest brown eyes. Does your granddaughter like gardens, he'd asked, and she, Nell, had not known how to answer.

"All right, then," she said, "you'd better come inside."

Forty-eight

Horses' hooves thundered against the cold, dry earth, charging west towards Blackhurst, but Eliza didn't hear them. Mr. Mansell's sponge had done its work and she was lost in a fog of chloroform, her body slumped in the dark corner of the carriage . . .

Rose's voice, soft and broken: "There is something I need, something only you can do. My body fails me as it has always done, but yours, Cousin, is strong. I need you to have a child for me, Nathaniel's child."

And Eliza, who had waited so long, who wanted so desperately to be needed, who had always known herself a half in search of a double, didn't have to think. "Of course," she'd said. "Of course I'll help you, Rose."

He came every night for a week. Aunt Adeline, with Dr. Matthews's counsel, calculated the dates and Nathaniel did as he was bidden. Made his way through the maze, around the side of the cottage and up to Eliza's front door.

On the first night, Eliza waited inside, pacing the kitchen floor, wondering whether he would arrive, whether she should have prepared something. Wondering how people behaved at such a time. She had agreed to Rose's request without hesitation, and in the weeks that followed had thought little about what the commitment would involve. She had been too full of gratitude that Rose finally needed her. It was only as the day drew nearer that she began to contemplate the hypothetical becoming actual.

And yet, there was nothing she would not do for Rose. She told herself over and over that her actions would cement their bond forever, no matter how hideous the unknown act might be. It became a mantra of sorts, an incantation. She and Rose would be tied like never before. Rose would love her more than she ever had, would not dispense with her so easily again. It was all for Rose.

When the knock came that first night, Eliza repeated the mantra, opened the door and let Nathaniel inside.

He stood for a time in the hallway, larger than she remembered, darker, until Eliza indicated the coat hook. He removed his outer layer, then he smiled at her, almost gratefully. It was then that she realized he was as disquieted as she.

He followed her to the kitchen, gravitated towards the security, the solidity, of the table, leaned on the back of a chair.

Eliza stood on the other side, wiped clean hands against her skirts, wondered what to say, how to proceed. It was best, surely, to do what was necessary and be done with it. There was no point in drawing out the discomfort. She opened her mouth to say as much but Nathaniel was already speaking—

"—thought you might like to see. I've been working on them all month."

She noticed then that he carried with him a leather satchel.

He laid it on the table and slid a stack of papers from within. Sketches, Eliza realized.

"I started with 'The Fairy Hunt.'" He thrust a sheet of paper before Eliza, and when she took it from him, she saw that his hands were quivering.

Eliza's gaze fell to the illustration: black strokes, crosshatched shadows. A pale, thin woman reclined on a low bed in a cold, dark turret. The woman's face had been spun from lean, long lines. She was beautiful, magical, elusive, just as Eliza's fairy tale described her. And yet it was something else in Nathaniel's rendering of the hunted fairy's face that struck Eliza. The woman in the picture looked like Mother. Not literally, it was something more and less than the curve of her lips, the cool almond eyes, *the high cheekbones. In some indescribable way, by some form of magic, Nathaniel had captured Georgiana in his depiction of the fairy's lifeless limbs, her weariness, the uncharacteristic resignation in her features. Strangest of all, it was the first time Eliza had realized that in her story of the hunted fairy she had been describing her own mother.*

She glanced up at him, scanned the dark eyes that had looked somehow inside her soul. As he held her gaze, the firelight was suddenly warmer between them.

CIRCUMSTANCE HEIGHTENED *everything. Their voices were too loud, their movements too sudden, the air too cool. The act was not hideous as she had feared, nor was it ordinary. And there was something unexpected in its performance which she couldn't help but savor. A closeness, an intimacy of which she had been deprived for so long. She felt part of a pair.*

She wasn't, of course, and it was a betrayal of Rose even to entertain such a notion, however briefly, and yet . . . His fingertips on her back, her side, her thigh. The warmth where their bare bodies met. His breath on her neck . . .

She opened her eyes at one point and watched his face, the expressions and stories arranging themselves on his features. And when his own eyes opened, his gaze locked with hers, she sensed herself suddenly, unexpectedly, as a physical being. Anchored, solid, real.

And then it was over and they moved apart, the bond of physical connectedness evaporated. They dressed and she walked him downstairs. Stood beside him by the front door, making conversation about the recent high tide, the likelihood of bad weather in the coming weeks. Polite chatter, as if he had no more than stopped by to borrow a book.

Eventually his hand reached out to unlatch the door and heavy silence sagged between them. The weight of what they had done. He pulled open the door, pushed it closed again. Turned back to face her. "Thank you," he said.

She nodded.

"Rose wants . . . Her need is . . ."

She nodded again, and he smiled slightly. Opened the door and disappeared into the night.

As the *week wore on, the unusual became usual and they settled into a routine. Nathaniel would arrive with his most recent sketches, and together they would discuss the stories, the illustrations. He brought his pencils, too, made alterations as they spoke. Often, when the sketches were complete, their conversation moved to other topics.*

They spoke, too, as they lay together in Eliza's narrow bed. Nathaniel told stories of the family Eliza had believed dead, the hardship of his youth, his father on the wharf and his mother's hands, chapped from laundry. And Eliza found herself telling him things of which she had never spoken, secret things from before: about Mother, and the father she'd never known, her dreams of following him across the high seas. Such was the strange and unexpected intimacy of their connection, she even spoke of Sammy.

Thus the week passed, and on the final night Nathaniel arrived earlier. He seemed reluctant to do what they must. They sat on opposite sides of the table as they had the first night, but no words were exchanged. Then suddenly, without warning, Nathaniel reached out and lifted a strand of her long hair, red turned to gold by the glow of candlelight. His face as he looked at the threads between his fingers was focused. Dark hair fell to shadow his cheek and his black eyes widened with unspoken thoughts. Eliza suffered a sudden warm tightness in her chest.

"I don't want it to end," he said finally, softly. "It's foolish, I know, but I feel—"

He paused as Eliza lifted her finger and pressed it to his lips. Silenced him.

Her own heart hammered beneath her dress and she prayed he could not tell. He must not be allowed to finish his sentence—dearly though some disloyal part of her longed it—for words have power; Eliza knew that better than most. Already they had allowed themselves to feel too much, and there was no room in their arrangement for feeling.

She shook her head lightly and finally he nodded. Refused to look at her for a time, said no more. And as he set about sketching in silence, Eliza suppressed the burning urge to tell him she had changed her mind.

When he left that night and Eliza went inside, the cottage walls seemed unusually silent and lifeless. She found a piece of card on the table where Nathaniel had been sitting, turned it over and saw her own face. A sketch. And for once she didn't mind having been captured on paper.

ELIZA KNEW *they had succeeded even before the first month passed. An inexplicable sense of having company, even when she knew herself to be alone. Then her bleeding stayed away and she knew for certain. Mary, who had lost her own baby, had been reinstated at Blackhurst on a provisional basis and instructed to liaise between the house and the cottage. When Eliza told her, yes, that she believed a small life clung within her body, Mary sighed and shook her head, then took the message back to Aunt Adeline.*

A wall was built around the cottage so that when Eliza's belly began to swell, no one would see. Word spread that she had gone away and the world closed over the cottage. The simplest falsehoods are the strongest, and this one performed perfectly. Eliza's desire to travel was well known. It wasn't a stretch for people to believe that she had left without a word, would be back when time suited. Mary was sent nightly with provisions, and Dr. Matthews, Aunt Adeline's physician, attended every two weeks, under night's black veil, to ensure the pregnancy's health.

During the months of confinement, Eliza saw few other people and yet she never felt alone. She sang to her swelling stomach, whispered stories, had strange and vibrant dreams. The cottage seemed to shrink around her like a warm old coat.

And the garden, a place where her heart had always sung, was more beautiful than ever. The flowers smelled sweeter, looked brighter, grew faster. One day, when she was sitting beneath the apple tree, and the warm, sunny air moved heavily around her, she fell into a deep sleep. While she softly slumbered, a story came to her, as vividly as if some passing stranger had knelt by her ear and whispered their tale. A tale about a young woman who overcame her fears and traveled a great distance in order to uncover the truth for an ageing loved one.

Eliza woke suddenly, gripped with certainty that the dream was important, that it must be turned to fairy tale. Unlike most dream inspirations, the tale required little manipulation. The child, the baby inside her, was central to the story, too. Eliza couldn't explain how she knew, but she had the oddest certainty that the baby was connected in some way to the tale, had helped her to receive the story so vividly, so completely.

Eliza wrote the fairy tale that afternoon, named it "The Crone's Eyes," and throughout the following weeks found herself wondering often about the sad old woman whose truth had been stolen from her. Though she had not seen Nathaniel since the night of their final meeting, Eliza knew he was still working on the illustrations for her book, and she longed to see those that her new tale inspired. One dark night, when Mary brought her supplies, Eliza asked after him, kept her tone even as she asked whether perhaps Mary might let him know that he may visit her sometime soon. Mary only shook her head.

"Mrs. Walker won't have it," she said, lowering her voice, though they were alone in the cottage. "I heard her crying to the mistress about it, and the mistress was saying it wasn't right for him to be going through the maze, going to see you. Not anymore, not after what has happened." She glanced at Eliza's swelling stomach. "Things might become confused, she said."

"But that's ridiculous," said Eliza. "What was done was done for Rose. Both Nathaniel and I love her, we did as she requested to provide her that for which she longs more than anything else."

Mary, who had made quite clear her own opinions about what Eliza had done, what she intended to do after the child was born, remained silent.

Eliza sighed, frustrated. *"I wish only to speak with him about the illustrations for the fairy tales."*

"That's another thing Mrs. Walker isn't too happy about," said Mary. *"She doesn't like him drawing for your stories."*

"Why ever would she mind?"

"Jealous, she is, green as old Davies's thumb. Can't bear to think of him spending his time and energy thinking about your stories."

Eliza stopped waiting for Nathaniel after that. She sent her handwritten version of *"The Crone's Eyes"* back to Blackhurst with Mary, who agreed—against her better judgment, she said—to deliver it. A gift arrived by courier some days later, a statue for her garden, a little boy with an angel's face. Eliza knew, even without reading the accompanying letter, that Nathaniel had sent it with Sammy in mind. In the letter he had also apologized for not visiting, made inquiries after her health, then moved quickly on to how much he loved the new story, how its magic had overtaken his thoughts, that ideas for the illustrations overwhelmed him so that he could bear to think of nothing else.

Rose herself came once a month, but Eliza grew to receive such visits cautiously. Things always started well, Rose would smile broadly when she saw Eliza, inquire after her health and leap at the opportunity to feel the baby moving beneath her skin. But at some point in the visit, with neither warning nor provocation, Rose would recoil inexplicably, knot her hands and refuse to touch Eliza's stomach anymore, refuse even to meet her eye. Her fingers would pluck instead at her own dress, padded to suggest a pregnancy.

After the sixth month, Rose stopped coming altogether. Eliza waited in vain on the allotted day, confused, wondering whether she had mistaken the date somehow. But there it was in her diary.

Her first fear was that Rose had taken ill, for surely nothing less would keep her from visiting. When Mary next arrived with her basket of supplies, Eliza pounced.

Mary lay down the basket and set the kettle on the hot plate. Didn't answer for a time.

"Mary?" said Eliza, arching her back to shift the baby, who was pressing against her side. "You mustn't try to protect me. If Rose is unwell—"

"It's nothing like that, Miss Eliza," Mary turned from the range. "Only Mrs. Walker finds it too distressing to visit."

"Distressing?"

Mary didn't meet Eliza's eyes. "It makes her feel a failure, even more than before. She unable to fall and you looking ripe as a peach. After her visits she returns home and is unwell for days. Won't see Mr. Walker, snaps at the mistress, picks at her food."

"Then I look forward to the child's arrival. When I deliver the baby, when Rose is a mother, then she will forget such feelings."

And like that, they were back in familiar waters: Mary shaking her head and Eliza defending her decision. "It isn't right, Miss Eliza. A mother can't just give up her child."

"It's not my child, Mary. It belongs to Rose."

"You might feel differently when the time comes."

"I won't."

"You don't know—"

"I won't feel differently, because I can't. I've given my word. If I were to change my mind, Rose would never bear it."

Mary raised her eyebrows.

Eliza forced further determination into her voice. "I will hand over the child, and Rose will be happy again. We will be happy together, just as we used to be long ago. Can't you see, Mary? This child I carry will return my Rose to me."

Mary smiled sadly. "Perhaps you're right, Miss Eliza," she said, though she didn't sound as if she believed it.

THEN, AFTER months in which time seemed to pause, the end arrived. Two weeks earlier than expected. Pain, blinding pain, the body like a piece of machinery creaking to life to do that for which it had been created. Mary, *who had recognized the signs of impending birth, made sure she was there to help. Her ma had delivered babies all her life, and Mary knew how it was done.*

The birth went smoothly, and the child was the most beautiful Eliza had ever seen, a little girl with tiny ears pressed neatly against her head and fine pale fingers that startled periodically at the sensation of air passing between them.

Though Mary had been ordered to report to Blackhurst immediately on any sign of the baby's imminent arrival, she remained silent in the days after. Spoke only to Eliza, urging her to reconsider her part in the dreadful pact. For it wasn't right, Mary whispered over and again, that a woman be asked to forsake her own child.

For three days and nights, Eliza and the baby were alone together. How strange it was to meet the little person who had lived and grown inside her body. To stroke the tiny hands and feet that she'd grabbed at as they pushed against her stomach from inside. To watch the little lips, pursed as if about to speak. An expression of infinite wisdom, as if, in those first days of life, the small person retained the knowledge of a lifetime just passed.

Then, in the middle of the third night, Mary arrived at the cottage, stood in the doorway and made the dreaded announcement. A visit from Dr. Matthews had been arranged for the following night. Mary lowered her voice and clasped Eliza's hands: if there was any part of her that thought to keep the baby, she must go now. She must take the child and run.

But although the suggestion of escape knotted itself to Eliza's heart, tugged sharply and willed her to action, she hurriedly untied it. She ignored the sharp ache in her chest, and reassured Mary, as she had before, that she knew her own mind. She looked down at her child one last time, stared and stared at the perfect little face, tried to comprehend that she had made it, that she had done this wonderful thing, until finally the throbbing in her head, her heart, her soul, was unbearable. And then somehow, as if watching herself from afar, she did as she had promised: handed the tiny girl over and allowed her to be taken. Closed the door after Mary, and returned, alone, to the silent, lifeless cottage. And as dawn came to the wintry garden, and the walls of the cottage receded again, Eliza realized that she had never known the black ache of loneliness before.

THOUGH SHE despised Linus's man Mansell, had cursed his name when he'd brought Eliza into their lives, Adeline couldn't dispute that the man knew how to find people. Four days had passed since his dispatch to London, and this afternoon, as she'd pretended to embroider in the morning room, Adeline had been summoned to the telephone.

Mansell, at the other end of the line, was mercifully discreet. One never knew who might be listening on another extension. "I telephone, Lady Mountrachet, to let you know that some of the goods you require have now been collected."

Adeline's breath caught in her throat. So soon? Anticipation, hope, nerves set her fingertips to tingling. "And may I inquire, is it the larger item or the smaller that you have in your possession?"

"The larger."

Adeline's eyelids fell closed. She flattened the relief, the joy, from her voice. "And when will you make delivery?"

"We leave London immediately. I will arrive at Blackhurst tomorrow evening."

Thus had Adeline waited. Thus was she waiting still. Pacing the Turkish rug, smoothing her skirts, snapping at the servants, as all the while she plotted Eliza's dispense.

ELIZA HAD agreed never to go near the house and she didn't. But she watched. And she found that even when she had saved sufficient funds to book passage on a ship, travel to distant lands, something stopped her. It was as if, with the birth of the baby, the anchor Eliza had been seeking all her life had lodged into the earth of Blackhurst.

The child's pull was magnetic, and so she stayed. But she kept her promise to Rose and avoided the house. Found other places to hide from which to observe. Just as she had as a girl, lying on the shelf in Mrs. Swindell's tiny upstairs room. Watching as the world moved around her and she remained motionless, outside the action.

For with the loss of the child, Eliza found that she had fallen through the center of her old life, her old self. She had forsaken her birthright and, in the process, forfeited the purpose in her life. She wrote rarely, only one fairy tale that she deemed worthy of inclusion in the collection. A story about a young woman who lived alone in a dark wood, who made the wrong decision for the right reason and destroyed herself in the process.

Pale months formed long years, then one summer's morning in 1913 the book of fairy tales arrived from the publisher. Eliza took it inside immediately, tore the packaging to reveal the leather-bound treasure within. She sat in the rocking chair, opened the book and lifted it close to her face. It smelled of fresh ink and binding glue, just like a real book. And there, inside, were her stories, her dear creations. She turned the thick, fresh pages, tale by tale, until she came to "The Crone's Eyes." She read it through and as she progressed she remembered the strange, vivid dream in the garden, the all-pervasive sense that the child inside her was important to the story.

And Eliza knew suddenly that the child, her child, must possess a copy of the tale, that the two were connected somehow. So she wrapped the book in brown paper, awaited her opportunity, then did what she had promised not to: breached the gate at the end of the maze and approached the house.

DUST MOTES, hundreds of them, danced in a sliver of sunlight that had appeared between two barrels. The little girl smiled and the Authoress, the cliff, the maze, Mamma, left her thoughts. She held out a finger, tried to catch a speck upon it. Laughed at the way the motes came so close before skirting away.

The noises beyond her hiding spot were changing. The little girl could hear the hubbub of movement, voices laced with excitement. She leaned into the veil of light and pressed her face against the cool wood of the barrels. With one eye she looked upon the decks.

Legs and shoes and petticoat hems. The tails of colored paper streamers flicking this way and that. Wily gulls hunting the decks for crumbs.

A lurch, and the huge boat groaned, long and low from deep within its belly. Vibrations passed through the deck boards and into the little girl's fingertips. A moment of suspension and she found herself holding her breath, palms flat beside her, then the boat heaved, pushed itself away from the dock. The horn bellowed and there was a wave of cheering, cries of "Bon voyage!" They were on their way.

THEY ARRIVED in London by night. Darkness sagged thick and heavy in the folds of the street as they made their way from the train station towards the river. The little girl was tired—Eliza had had to wake her when they reached their destination—but she didn't complain. She held Eliza's hand and followed close to her clipping heels.

That night the two shared a supper of broth and bread in their room. They were both tired from the travel and little was spoken, each merely eyed the other, somewhat curiously, over her spoon. The little girl asked once after her mother and father, but Eliza said only that they would be met at the other end of the voyage. It was an untruth, but it was necessary: time would be required to decide how best to break the news of Rose's and Nathaniel's deaths.

After supper, Ivory fell quickly to sleep on the room's only bed and Eliza sat in the window seat. She watched alternately the dark street, jostling with busy wayfarers, and the sleeping child, stirring lightly beneath the sheet. As time passed Eliza edged nearer the child, observed the small face at ever closer range, until finally she knelt gently beside the bed, so close that she could feel the girl's breath in her hair, could count the tiny freckles on the sleeping face. And what a perfect face it was, how glorious the ivory skin and rosebud lips. It was the same face, Eliza realized, the same wise expression, she had gazed upon in the first days of the child's life. The same face that she had seen so often since in her nightly dreams.

She was gripped then by an urge, a need—a love, she supposed it was—so ferocious, that each grain of her self was infused with certainty. It was as if her own body recognized this child to whom she had given life as readily as she recognized her own hand, her own face in a mirror, her own voice in the dark. As carefully as she could, Eliza lay upon the bed and curled her own body to accommodate the sleeping girl. Just as she had done in another time, another room, against the warm body of her brother Sammy.

Finally, Eliza was home.

On the day the ship was due to leave, Eliza and the girl went early in search of supplies. Eliza purchased a few items of clothing, a hairbrush and a suitcase in which to house them. At the bottom of the case she tucked an envelope containing some banknotes and a piece of paper advising of Mary's address in Polperro—it was as well to be safe as sorry. The suitcase was just the right size for a child to carry and Ivory was thrilled. She clutched it tightly as Eliza led her along the crowded dock.

Movement and noise were everywhere: whistling locomotives, billowing steam, cranes lifting baby carriages, bicycles and phonographs on board. Ivory laughed when they passed a procession of bleating goats and sheep being herded into the ship's hold. She was dressed in the prettier of the two dresses Eliza had bought for her, and looked quite the part of the wealthy little girl come to see her aunt off on a long sea voyage. When they reached the gangway, Eliza handed her boarding card to the officer.

"Welcome aboard, madam," he said, nodding so that his uniform cap bobbed.

Eliza nodded in return. "It's a pleasure to have passage booked on your splendid ship," she said. "My niece has been beside herself with ex-

citement for her aunt. Look, she's even brought her own little pretend case."

"You like big boats, do you, miss?" The officer peered down at the little girl.

Ivory nodded and smiled sweetly, but she said nothing. Just as Eliza had instructed.

"Officer," said Eliza, "my brother and sister-in-law are waiting further along the dock." She waved into the growing crowd. "I don't suppose you'd mind if I take my little niece on board for a minute to show her my cabin?"

The officer glanced at the line of passengers now snaked along the dock.

"We shan't be long," said Eliza. "Only it would mean so very much to the child."

"I'd say it should be all right," he said. "Just be sure and bring her back." He winked at Ivory. "I've a feeling her parents would miss her if she left home without them."

Eliza took Ivory's hand and headed up the gangway.

There were people everywhere, busy voices, splashing water. The ship's orchestra played a jaunty tune on deck, while chambermaids scurried in all directions, postboys delivered telegrams and self-important bellboys carried chocolates and gifts for the departing passengers.

But Eliza didn't follow the chief steward inside the ship; instead she led Ivory along the deck, stopping only when they reached a set of wooden barrels. Eliza ushered the girl behind them, and crouched so that her skirts draped across the decking. The little girl was distracted, she had never seen such activity, and was moving her head about, this way and that.

"You must wait here," said Eliza. "It isn't safe to move. I'll be back soon." She hesitated, glanced skywards. Gulls were skimming overhead, black eyes watchful. "Wait for me, do you hear?"

The little girl nodded.

"You know how to hide?"

"Of course."

"It's a game we're playing." As Eliza said the words, Sammy appeared inside her mind and her skin cooled.

"I like games."

Eliza pushed the image aside. This little girl wasn't Sammy. They weren't playing the Ripper. Everything would be well. "I'll come back for you."

"Where are you going?"

"There's someone I have to see. Something I have to collect before the ship leaves."

"What is it?"

"My past," she said. "My future." She smiled briefly. "My family."

As the carriage hurtled towards Blackhurst, Eliza's fog began to lift. Awareness seeped slowly: a rocking motion, the muddy thud of hooves, a musty smell.

She cracked open her eyes, blinked. Black shadows dissolved into patches of dusty light. A swooning sensation as her vision focused.

There was someone with her, a man sitting opposite. His head was tilted against the leather seat and a slight snore flecked his steady inhalations. He had a bushy moustache and a pair of armless spectacles perched on the bridge of his nose.

Eliza drew breath. She was twelve years old, being dragged from all she knew towards the unknown future. Locked in a carriage with Mother's Bad Man. Mansell.

And yet . . . it didn't feel quite right. There was something she was forgetting, a dark humming cloud on the edge of her mind. Something important, something she had to do.

She gasped. Where was Sammy? He should be with her, he was hers to protect—

Horses' hooves, thudding on the ground outside. The sound

made her frightened, ill, though she knew not why. The dark cloud began to swirl. It was coming closer.

Eliza's gaze dropped to her skirt, her hands folded on her lap. Her hands, and yet surely not hers at all.

Bright light broke through a hole in the cloud: she wasn't twelve at all, she was a grown woman—

But what had happened? Where was she? Why was she with Mansell?

A cottage on a cliff, a garden, the sea . . .

Her breaths were louder now, sharp in her throat.

A woman, a man, a baby . . .

Free-floating panic plucked at her skin.

More light . . . the cloud was fading, coming apart . . .

Words, snatches of meaning: Maryborough . . . a ship . . . a child, not Sammy, a little girl . . .

Eliza's throat was raw. A hole opened up inside her, filled quickly with black fear.

The little girl was hers.

Clarity, so bright it burned: her daughter was alone on a departing ship.

Panic infused her every pore. Her pulse hammered in her temples. She needed to get away, get back.

Eliza glanced sideways at the door.

The carriage traveled quickly but she didn't care. The ship left dock today and the little girl was on it. The child, her child, all alone.

Chest aching, head thumping, Eliza reached out.

Mansell stirred. His bleary eyes opened, focused quickly on Eliza's arm, the handle beneath her fingers.

A cruel smile began to form on his lips.

She gripped the lever: he lunged to stop her, but Eliza was faster. Her need was greater, after all.

And she was falling, the cage door had opened and she fell, fell, fell towards the cold dark earth. Time folded over on itself: all moments were one, past was present was future. Eliza didn't close her eyes, she watched the earth coming closer, the smell of mud, grass, hope—

—and she was flying, wings outstretched across the surface of the ground, and higher now, on the current of the breeze, her face cool, her mind clear. And Eliza knew where she was going. Flying towards her daughter, towards Ivory. The person she had spent a lifetime seeking, her other half. She was whole at last, heading towards home.

FORTY-NINE

FINALLY, she was in the garden again. Between the bad weather, Ruby's arrival and the visit to Clara's house, it had been days since Cassandra had been able to slip beneath the wall. She'd been subject to an odd restlessness that had only now dissipated. It was strange, she thought, easing a glove onto her right hand: she'd never considered herself much of a gardener, but this place was different. She felt compelled to return, to plunge her hands into the earth and bring the garden back to life. Cassandra paused as she straightened the fingers of the other glove, noticed again the band of white skin around her finger, second from the left.

She ran her thumb over the strip of skin. It was very smooth, more elastic than that on either side, as if it had been soaking in warm water. That white band was the youngest part of her, fifteen years younger than the rest. Hidden from the moment Nick had slipped the ring onto her finger, it was the only part that hadn't changed, aged, moved on. Until now.

"Cold enough for you?" Christian, who had just appeared from beneath the wall, thrust his hands deep into the pockets of his jeans.

Cassandra pushed the glove on and smiled at him. "I didn't think it got cold in Cornwall. All the brochures I read talked about a temperate climate."

"Temperate compared to Yorkshire." He returned a lopsided smile. "It's a taste of the winter ahead. At least you won't have to suffer that."

Silence drew out between them. As Christian turned to inspect the hole he'd been digging the week before, Cassandra pretended to be engrossed in her weeding fork. Her return to Australia was a subject they'd avoided discussing. Over the last few days, whenever conversation threatened to skirt the topic, one of them had been quick to set it on a new course.

"I was thinking some more," said Christian, "about that letter from Harriet Swindell."

"Yeah?" Cassandra pushed aside unsettling thoughts of past and future.

"Whatever it was in the clay pot, the one Eliza pulled out of the chimney, it must've been important. Nell was already on the boat, so Eliza took a huge risk going back for it."

They had covered this yesterday. In a warm booth at the pub, with the fire crackling in the corner, they'd gone over and over the details as they knew them. Seeking a conclusion they both sensed was staring them in the face.

"I guess she didn't count on the man being there to abduct her, whoever he was." Cassandra plunged her fork into the flower bed. "I wish Harriet had given us his name."

"He must've been someone sent by Rose's family."

"You reckon?"

"Who else would have been so desperate to get them back?"

"Get Eliza back."

"Huh?"

Cassandra glanced over her shoulder at him. "They didn't get Nell back. Only Eliza."

Christian paused in his digging. "Yeah, that's odd. I guess she didn't tell them where Nell was."

That was the part that didn't make sense to Cassandra. She'd lain awake half the night running the threads through her mind, coming always to the same conclusion. Eliza might not have wanted Nell to remain at Blackhurst, but surely when she learned that the ship had sailed without her she'd have been desperate to stop it. She was Nell's mother, she'd loved her enough to take her in the first place. Wouldn't she have done everything she could to alert people to the fact that Nell was on a ship alone? She wouldn't just have said nothing and left a treasured daughter to travel by herself to Australia. Cassandra's fork hit a particularly stubborn root. "I don't think she could tell them."

"How do you mean?"

"Only that if she could have, she would have. Wouldn't she?"

Christian nodded slowly, raised his eyebrows as the implications of this theory sank in. He heaved his shovel into the hole.

The root was thick. Cassandra pulled the other weeds aside and traced it a little higher. She smiled to herself. Though it was worse for wear, devoid, for the most part, of leaves, she recognized this plant; she'd seen similar specimens in Nell's garden back in Brisbane. It was a wiry old rosebush, had likely been here for decades. The stem was as thick as her forearm, covered in angry thorns. But it was still alive and with some tending would live to flower again.

"Oh, my God."

Cassandra looked up from her rose. Christian was crouched down, leaning into the pit. "What? What is it?" she said.

"I've found something." The tone of his voice was odd, difficult to read.

Electricity fired hot beneath Cassandra's skin. "Something scary or something exciting?"

"Exciting, I think."

Cassandra went to kneel by him and peered into the hole. She followed the direction he was pointing.

Deep down amid the moist soil, something had emerged from the muddy base. Something small, brown and smooth.

Christian reached down and eased the object free, withdrew a clay pot, the sort once used to store mustard and other preserves. He wiped the mud from its sides and passed it to Cassandra. "I think your garden just gave up its secret."

The clay was cool on her fingers, the pot surprisingly heavy. Cassandra's heart thumped in her chest.

"She must have buried it here," said Christian. "After the man abducted her in London, he must have brought her back to Blackhurst."

But why would Eliza have buried the clay pot after taking such a risk to reclaim it? Why would she risk losing it again? And if she had time to bury the pot, why hadn't she made contact with the ship? Retrieved little Ivory?

The realization was sudden. Something that had been there all along became clear. Cassandra inhaled sharply.

"What?"

"I don't think she buried the pot," Cassandra whispered.

"What do you mean? Who did?"

"No one. I mean, I think the pot was buried *with* her." And for over ninety years she had lain here, waiting for someone to find her. For Cassandra to find her and unravel her secret.

Christian stared into the hole, eyes wide. He nodded slowly. "That would explain why she didn't go back for Ivory, for Nell."

"She couldn't. She was here all along."

"But who buried her? The man who abducted her? Her aunt or uncle?"

Cassandra shook her head. "I don't know. One thing's for sure, though, whoever it was didn't intend anyone to know about it. There's no gravestone, nothing at all to mark the spot. They wanted Eliza to disappear, the truth about her death to remain hidden forever. Forgotten, just like her garden."

FIFTY

ADELINE turned from the fireplace, inhaled suddenly so that her waist gathered tightly. "What do you mean, things didn't go to plan?"

Night had fallen and the surrounding woods were converging upon the house. Shadows hung in the corners of the room, candlelight teasing their cold edges.

Mr. Mansell straightened his pince-nez. "There was a fall. She threw herself from the carriage. The horses lost control."

"A physician," said Linus. "We must telephone a physician."

"A physician will be of no assistance." Mansell's steady voice. "She is already dead."

Adeline gasped. "What?"

"Dead," he said again. "The woman, your niece, is dead."

Adeline closed her eyes and her knees buckled. The world was spinning; she was weightless, painless, free. How was it that such burden, such weight, could lift away so swiftly? That one fell swoop could rid her of the old and constant foe, Georgiana's legacy?

Adeline cared not. Her prayers had been answered, the world had righted itself. The girl was dead. Gone. That was all that mattered. For the first time since Rose's death she could breathe. Warm tendrils of gladness infused her every vein. "Where?" she heard herself say. "Where is she?"

"In the carriage—"

"You brought her here?"

"The girl . . ." Linus's voice drifted from the armchair in which he was enfolded. His breath was quick and light. "Where is the little girl with the flame-red hair?"

"The woman uttered a few words before she fell. She was groggy and the words soft, but she spoke about a boat, a ship. She was agitated, concerned to get back in time for its departure."

"Go," said Adeline sharply. "Wait by the carriage. I shall make arrangements, then call for you."

Mansell nodded swiftly and left, taking the room's little warmth with him.

"What of the child?" Linus bleated.

Adeline ignored him, her mind busy racing towards solutions. Naturally, none of the servants could know. So far as they were concerned, Eliza had left Blackhurst when she learned that Rose and Nathaniel were relocating to New York. It was a blessing that the girl had spoken often of her desire to travel.

"What of the child?" said Linus again. His fingers quivered about his collar. "Mansell must find her, find the ship. We must have her back. The little girl must be found."

Adeline swallowed a lump of thick distaste as she ran her gaze over his crumpled form. "Why?" she said, skin turning cold. "Why must she be found? What is she to either of us?" Her voice was low as she leaned close. "Don't you see? We have been freed."

"She is our granddaughter."

"But she is not of us."

"She is of me."

Adeline ignored the pale utterance. There was no need to comment upon such sentimentality. Not now that they were finally safe. She turned on her heel and paced the rug. "We will tell people that the child was found on the estate, only to be stricken with scarlet fever. It will not be questioned; they already believe her ill in bed. We will instruct the servants that I alone shall tend her, that Rose would have wished it that way. Then after a time, when every appearance of a proper struggle against the illness has been made, we will hold a funeral service."

And while Ivory was receiving the burial befitting a beloved granddaughter, Adeline would ensure that Eliza was disposed of quickly and invisibly. She would not be buried in the family cemetery, that much was certain. The blessed soil that surrounded Rose would not be so polluted. She must be buried where no one would ever find her. Where no one would ever think to look.

THE FOLLOWING morning, Adeline had Davies show her through the maze. Ghastly, damp place. The smell of musty undergrowth that never saw the sun pressed in on Adeline from all sides. Her black mourning skirts swished along the raked ground, fallen leaves catching like burrs in the hem. She resembled a great black bird, her feathers gathered around her to ward off the chill winter of Rose's death.

When they finally arrived at the hidden garden, Adeline brushed Davies aside and swept along the narrow path. Clusters of tiny birds took flight when she passed, twittering madly as they fled their hidden branches. She went as quickly as was properly permitted, anxious to be free of this bewitched place and the heady, fecund fragrance that made her head swoon.

At the far end of the garden Adeline stopped.

A sharp smile thinned her lips. It was just as she had hoped.

A cool shiver and she turned suddenly on her heels. "I have seen enough," she said. "My granddaughter is gravely ill and I must return to the house."

Davies held her gaze a fraction of a second too long and a shiver of trepidation slipped down her spine. Adeline quashed it. What could he possibly know of the deception she planned? "Take me back now."

As she followed his large, lumbering form through the maze, Adeline kept her distance. She had one hand in the pocket of her dress, fingertips emerging at regular intervals to drop tiny white pebbles from Ivory's collection, the little jar in the nursery.

THE AFTERNOON dragged, the night-stretched hours passed and finally it was midnight. Adeline rose from her bed, pulled on her dress and laced up her boots. Tiptoed along the hall, down the stairs and out into the night.

The moon was full and she went quickly across the open lawn, keeping to the shadowy cool patches by the trees and bushes. The maze gate was closed, but Adeline soon had the clasp undone. She slipped inside and smiled to herself when she saw the first little stone, glistening like silver.

From pebble to pebble she went, until finally she reached the second gate, entrance to the hidden garden.

The garden hummed within its tall stone walls. Moonlight turned the leaves to silver and whispering breezes made them jangle lightly, like pieces of fine metal. A quivering harp string.

Adeline had the odd sense that she was being watched by a silent observer. She gazed about the moon-whitened landscape, drew breath when she noticed a pair of wide eyes in the fork of a nearby tree. An instant and her mind filled in the blanks, the feathers of the owl, his round body and head, sharp beak.

And yet she felt little better. There was something strange in the bird's stare. A worldliness. Those eyes, watching, judging.

She looked away, refused to grant a mere bird the power to unsettle her.

Noise then, coming from the direction of the cottage. Adeline crouched by the garden seat and watched as two night-draped figures came into view. Mansell she expected, but who was it he brought with him?

The figures walked slowly, something large strung between them. They laid it down on the other side of the wall, then one of the men stepped across the hole and into the hidden garden.

A sizzle as Mansell struck a match, then a flash of warm light: an orange heart haloed by blue. He held it to the lantern wick and turned the dial so the light expanded.

Adeline stood tall and made her approach.

"Good evening, Lady Mountrachet," said Mansell.

She pointed at the second man and spoke with a chill voice. "Who is this?"

"Slocombe," said Mansell. "My coachman."

"Why is he here?"

"The cliff is steep, the parcel heavy." He blinked at Adeline, the lantern flame reflected in the glass of his pince-nez. "He can be trusted not to speak." He swung the lantern sideways and the bottom of Slocombe's face came into view. The lower jaw, horribly disfigured, nodules and pocked skin where a mouth should be.

As they started digging, deepening the hole that the workmen had already made, Adeline's attention drifted to the dark shroud on the ground beneath the apple tree. Finally, the girl was to be relegated to the earth. She would disappear and be forgotten: it would be as if she'd never existed. And in time people would forget that she had.

Adeline closed her eyes, blocked out the noise of the wretched birds who had started to twitter eagerly, the leaves that were rustling urgently now. She listened instead for the blessed sound of loose earth falling on to the solid surface beneath. It would soon be over. The girl was gone and Adeline could breathe—

The air moved, cool on her face. Adeline's eyelids flew open.

A dark shape coming towards her, right by her head.

A bird? A bat?

Dark wings beating the night sky.

Adeline stepped back.

A sudden sting and her blood was cold. Hot. Cold again.

As the owl coasted away, over the wall, Adeline's palm began to throb.

She must have exclaimed, for Mansell paused his shoveling to swing the lantern near. In the dancing yellow light, Adeline saw that a long thorny rose tendril had wrested its way free from the flower bed to clutch at her. Its thick thorn was lodged in her palm.

With her free hand she plucked it from her skin. A bead of blood rose to the surface, a perfect, glistening droplet.

Adeline withdrew a handkerchief from her sleeve. She pressed it to the wound and watched as the red stain seeped through.

It was only a rose thorn. Never mind that her blood was ice beneath her skin, the wound would heal and all would be well.

But that rosebush would be the first item removed when Adeline ordered the garden razed.

What business had a rose now in the Blackhurst gardens?

FIFTY-ONE

As Cassandra stared into the deep hole, into Eliza's grave, she felt surrounded by a strange calm. It was as if with the discovery the garden had breathed a great sigh of relief: the birds were quieter, the leaves had stopped rustling, the curious restlessness had gone. The long-forgotten secret the garden had been forced to keep had now been told.

Christian's gentle voice, as if from somewhere distant: "Well, aren't you going to open it?"

The clay pot, heavy now in her hands. Cassandra ran her fingers along the old wax that sealed the rim. She glanced at Christian, who nodded encouragement, then she pressed and twisted, snapped the seal so that the lid could be prised open.

There were three items inside: a leather pouch, a swatch of red-gold hair and a brooch.

The leather pouch contained two old coins, a pale yellow color, stamped with the familiar jowly profile of Queen Victoria. The dates were 1897 and 1900.

The hair was tied with a piece of twine and coiled like a snail's shell to fit inside the pot. Years of containment had left it smooth and soft, very fine. Cassandra wondered whose it was, then remembered the entry in Rose's early notebook, written when Eliza first came to Blackhurst. A litany of complaint about the little girl whom Rose described as "little better than a savage." The little girl whose hair had been cut off as short and jagged as a boy's.

The brooch Cassandra turned to last. It was round and sat neatly in the palm of her hand. The border was ornate, decorated with gems, while the center contained a pattern, a little like tapestry. But it wasn't tapestry. Cassandra had worked long enough among antiques to know what this brooch was. She turned it over and ran her fingertip over the engraving on the back. *For Georgiana Mountrachet,* read the tiny print, *on the occasion of her sixteenth birthday. Past. Future. Family.*

This was it. The treasure for which Eliza had returned to the Swindells' house, whose price had been an encounter with a strange man. An encounter responsible for the separation of Eliza and Ivory, for all that had come afterwards, for Ivory becoming Nell.

"What is it?"

Cassandra looked at him. "A mourning brooch."

He frowned.

"The Victorians used to have them made from the hair of family members. This one belonged to Georgiana Mountrachet, Eliza's mother."

Christian nodded slowly. "Explains why it was so important to her. Why she went to retrieve it."

"And why she didn't make it back to the boat." Cassandra studied Eliza's precious items in her lap. "I just wish Nell had seen them. She always felt abandoned, never knew that Eliza was her mother, that she was loved. It was the one thing she longed to learn: who she was."

"But she did know who she was," Christian said. "She was Nell, whose granddaughter Cassandra loved her enough to cross the ocean to solve her mystery for her."

"She doesn't know that I came here."

"How do you know what she does and doesn't know? She might be watching you right now." He raised his brows. "Anyway, of course she knew you'd come. Why else would she have left you the cottage? And that note on the will, what did it say?"

How odd the note had seemed, how little she had understood

when Ben had first given it to her. *For Cassandra, who will understand why.*

"And? Do you?"

Of course she did. Nell, who had needed so desperately to con-
front her own past in order to move beyond it, had seen in Cassandra a
kindred spirit. A fellow victim of circumstance. "She knew I'd come."

Christian was nodding. "She knew you loved her enough to finish what she'd started. It's like in 'The Crone's Eyes,' when the fawn
tells the princess that the crone didn't need her sight, that she knew
who she was by the princess's love for her."

Cassandra's eyes stung. "That fawn was very wise."

"Not to mention handsome and brave."

She couldn't help smiling. "So now we know. Who Nell's mother
was. Why she was left alone on the boat. What happened to Eliza."
She also knew why the garden was so important to her, why she felt
her own roots connecting to its soil, deeper and deeper with each moment she spent within its walls. She was at home in the garden, for in
some way she couldn't explain Nell was here, too. As was Eliza. And
she, Cassandra, was the guardian of both their secrets.

Christian seemed to read her mind. "So," he said, "still planning
on selling it?"

Cassandra watched as the breeze tossed down a shower of yellow
leaves. "Actually, I thought I might stay around a bit longer."

"At the hotel?"

"No, here in the cottage."

"You won't be lonely?"

It was so unlike her, but in that moment Cassandra opened her
mouth and said exactly what she was feeling. Gave no pause for
second-guessing and worry. "I don't think I'll be alone. Not all the
time." She felt the hot-cold sensation of an impending blush and hurried on. "I want to finish what we've started."

He raised his eyebrows.

The blush found her. "Here. In the garden, I mean."

"I know what you mean." His gaze held hers. As Cassandra's heart began to hammer against her ribs, he let his shovel drop, reached out to cup her cheek. He leaned nearer and she closed her eyes. A sigh, heavy with years of weariness, escaped her. And then he was kissing her, and she was struck by his nearness, his solidity, his smell. It was of the garden and the earth and the sun.

When Cassandra opened her eyes, she realized she was crying. She wasn't sad, though, these were the tears of being found, of having come home after a long time away. She tightened her grip on the brooch. *Past. Future. Family.* Her own past was filled with memories, a lifetime of beautiful, precious, sad memories. For a decade she had moved among them, slept with them, walked with them. But something had changed, she had changed. She had come to Cornwall to uncover Nell's past, her family, and somehow she had found her own future. Here, in this beautiful garden that Eliza had made and Nell had reclaimed, Cassandra had found herself.

Christian smoothed her hair and looked at her face with a certainty that made her shiver. "I've been waiting for you," he said finally.

Cassandra took his hand in hers. She had been waiting for him, too.

EPILOGUE

COOL against her eyelids; tingles like tiny feet, those of ants, walking back and forth.

A voice, blessedly familiar. "I'll get a nurse—"

"No!" Nell reached out, still couldn't see, grasped for anything she could find. "Don't leave me!" Her face was wet, recycled air cold against it.

"It's all right, Grandma. I'm getting help. I'll be back soon. I promise."

Grandma. That's who she was, now she remembered. She'd had many names in her lifetime, so many she'd forgotten a few, but it wasn't until she acquired her last, Grandma, that she'd known who she really was.

A second chance, a blessing, a savior. Her granddaughter.

And now Cassandra was getting help.

Nell's eyes closed. She was on the ship again. Could feel the water beneath her, the deck swaying this way and that. Barrels, sunlight, dust. Laughter, faraway laughter.

It was fading. The lights were being turned down. Dimming, like the lights in the Plaza Theatre, before the feature presentation. Patrons shifting in their seats, whispering, waiting . . .

Black.

Silence.

And then she was somewhere else, somewhere cold and dark. Alone. Sharp things, branches, either side of her. A sense that walls were pushing in on both sides, tall and dark. The light was returning; not much, but sufficient that she could crane her neck and see the distant sky.

Her legs were moving. She was walking, hands out to the sides brushing against the leaves and branch ends.

A corner. She turned. More leafy walls. The smell of earth, rich and moist.

Suddenly, she knew. The word came to her, ancient and familiar. Maze. She was in a maze.

Awareness, instant and fully formed: at its end was a most glorious place. Somewhere she needed to be. Somewhere safe where she could rest.

She reached a fork.

Turned.

She knew the way. She remembered. She had been here before.

Faster now, she went faster. Need pushing in her chest, certainty. She must reach the end.

Light ahead. She was almost there.

Just a little further.

Then suddenly, out of the shadows and into the light came a figure. The Authoress, holding out her hand. Silvery voice. "I've been waiting for you."

The Authoress stepped aside and Nell saw that she had reached the gate.

The end of the maze.

"Where am I?"

"You're home."

With a deep breath, Nell followed the Authoress across the threshold and into the most beautiful garden she had ever seen.

Epilogue

And at last, the wicked Queen's spell was broken, and the young woman, whom circumstance and cruelty had trapped in the body of a bird, was released from her cage. The cage door opened and the cuckoo bird fell, fell, fell, until finally her stunted wings opened, and she found that she could fly. With the cool sea breeze of her homeland buffeting the undersides of her wings, she soared over the cliff edge and across the ocean. Towards a new land of hope, and freedom, and life. Towards her other half. Home.

—From "The Cuckoo's Flight" by Eliza Makepeace

ACKNOWLEDGMENTS

FOR helping to bring *The Forgotten Garden* into the world, I'd like to thank:

My Nana Connelly, whose story first inspired me; Selwa Anthony for her wisdom and care; Kim Wilkins, Julia Morton and Diane Morton, for reading early drafts; Kate Eady for hunting down pesky historical facts; Danny Kretschmer for providing photos on a deadline; and Julia's workmates for answering questions of vernacular. For research assistance—archaeological, entomological and medical—I'm grateful to Dr. Walter Wood, Dr. Natalie Franklin, Katharine Parkes and, especially, Dr. Sally Wilde; and, for help with specific details, many thanks to Nicole Ruckels, Elaine Wilkins and Joyce Morton.

I am fortunate to be published worldwide by extraordinary people and I'm thankful to everyone whose efforts have helped to turn my stories into books. For their sensitive and tireless editorial support on *The Forgotten Garden,* I'd like to make special mention of Catherine Milne, Clara Finlay and the wonderful Annette Barlow at Allen & Unwin, Australia; and Maria Rejt and Liz Cowen at Pan Macmillan UK. I'm much obliged to Julia Stiles and Lesley Levene for their fine attention to detail.

I would also like to pay tribute here to authors who write for children. To discover early that behind the black marks on white pages lurk worlds of incomparable terror, joy and excitement is one of life's great gifts. I am enormously grateful to those authors whose works fired my childhood imagination, and inspired in me a love of books and reading that has been a constant companion. *The Forgotten Garden* is, in part, an ode to them.

Finally, as always, I owe a huge debt of gratitude to my husband, Davin Patterson, and my two sons, Oliver and Louis, to whom this story belongs.

THE
FORGOTTEN
GARDEN

KATE MORTON

A Readers Club Guide

Suggested Discussion Points for *The Forgotten Garden*

1. On the night of Nell's twenty-first birthday, her father Hugh tells her a secret that shatters her sense of self. How important is a strong sense of identity to a person's life? Was Hugh right to tell her about her past? How might Nell's life have turned out differently had she not discovered the truth?

2. Did Hugh and Lil make the right decision when they kept Nell?

3. How might Nell's choice of occupation have been related to her fractured identity?

4. Is it possible to escape the past, or does one's history always find a way to revisit the present?

5. Eliza, Nell and Cassandra all lose their birth mothers when they are still children. How are their lives affected differently by this loss? How might their lives have evolved had they not had this experience?

6. Nell believes that she comes from a tradition of "bad mothers." Does this belief become a self-fulfilling prophesy? How does Nell's relationship with her granddaughter, Cassandra, allow her to revisit this perception of herself as a "bad mother"?

7. Is *The Forgotten Garden* a love story? If so, in what way/s?

8. Tragedy has been described as "the conflict between desire and possibility." Following this definition, is *The Forgotten Garden* a tragedy? If so, in what way/s?

9. In what ways do Eliza's fairy tales underline and develop other themes within the novel?

10. In what ways do the settings in *The Forgotten Garden* represent or reflect the characters' experiences?

For more on Kate Morton, visit simonandschuster.com or katemorton.com.